Vixen Phillips was born in Ballarat, Australia, in 1975. Mostly, she writes, programs computers, and plays guitar and keyboards, but in former lives she's also worked as an audio engineer, in & around various media production studios, as a graphic designer, and in computer sales.

Trapdoor is her first novel.

For more information, visit her on the web at

LYRICAL-TRANCE.ORG

FINALDAWN.NET

Also by Vixen Phillips:

NARCISSISM (e-book)

Coming in 2011:

THE AMORPHEUM KEY

TRAPDOOR

LOST VIOLET PRESS

Published by Lost Violet Press 2010
http://lostviolet.com
info@lostvioletpress.com.au

Visit the Trapdoor home page at
http://trapdoor.lostviolet.com

Copyright © Vixen Phillips 2003, 2010
All rights reserved.

Cover photography by Andrei Aristide & Raisa Kanareva, purchased/licensed with permission from Dreamstime.com
Cover design by Vixen Phillips/Lost Violet Press

No part of this publication may be reproduced, stored in a retrieval system, or transmitted, in any form or by any means, electronic, mechanical, photocopying, recording or otherwise, without the prior permission of Lost Violet Press.

This book is a work of fiction.

First published in Australia in 2003
by Vixen Phillips writing as September Dawn.

ISBN: 978-0-9805568-1-0
E-book ISBN: 978-0-9805568-0-3

TRAPDOOR

VIXEN PHILLIPS

LOST VIOLET PRESS
HTTP://LOSTVIOLET.COM

1 (RAVEN)

Of Winged Things

There's a moth trying to beat itself to death against the lightbulb on the ceiling.

And here I am, alone in the bathroom, holding a razor blade at the ready. Guess we all make do in lieu of a moon.

Beneath the mirror, a black feather—a gift, a worthless thing—waits and watches.

And I remember the screams, and the tears. And because I remember, I won't ever forgive myself for what I let her do to destroy me. I turn my back on my reflection, turn the razor over on my skin.

At least, tonight—after—I'll get to see him.

For now, I'm dreaming of wings.

I think I'm beginning to hate her...

Storm's about to break right on top of me when I throw myself against the green door of the Moondance hotel. So far as I can tell, maybe only twenty people ever thought of this place at the same moment in time. But here I am anyway, seeking sanctuary from the evening's bite. Like there's ever any refuge from the black howling winds.

Maybe I've always hated her.

Leaves skitter about my feet and stick to the ash-coloured carpet that reeks of stale beer and piss. Caught in the sudden light of the pool tables and the ceiling lamps and the bar and the cigarette machine like another confounded moth, I ignore the glares of several sets of eyes, all trained on me as if I stumbled onto the set of a cowboy film. Stand-off's broken quick enough though, once the door bangs shut, locking the night out and me in. Now that I'm accounted for—just another punter—they all turn back to their footy scores and recycled pick-up lines and pots of Vic Bitter, and leave me be. I shrug my black velvet jacket part-way off my shoulders, but the shirt underneath still chafes and clings to my skin, where not two hours ago I tried to play Icarus by carving out my own pair of wings. But there's never been any sun waiting for me. Only her words and the hatred that fuels them, to send me crashing back to earth.

"*God, you're such a fucking try-hard. Why do you always have to wear black? It's so morbid.*"

On my way through to the safer dark of the gig room, a long burst of feedback cuts across the six-string melancholy of some Stone Temple Pilots song. First thing I spy, over in the farthest corner, is good old cousin Monty, flailing about the mixing desk, arguing with a thick-set hirsute creature that all stereotypes point to as being the roadie, their conversation interrupted at random by the crackle of a mic input here, or more six kilohertz blips there. My hand sinks into my pocket, feeling for the ten dollars and bread crumbs in change that's gotta see me through the next few hours. Guess this won't be such a convenient time to hit him up for a drink. Well, that's just great.

"*When are you going to give up all this shit? There's no money in it. It's fine for your cousin, with his mail-order bride and his mansion up in Camberwell, but do you think this is any way to be some kind of role model, some kind of man? You're not a teenager anymore, Raven, or—fuck—don't tell me you think you've got* actual *talent?*"

A burst of laughter, and something moves in the shadows

at the far end of the bar: the familiar jingle of too many bracelets that accompanies a flirtatious toss of dirty blonde hair. I force myself to swallow, tuck my other hand into my other pocket, drive them both down deep as I lean against the counter. Wendy. Shit, she's here. *Why* is she here? She reckoned tonight she was off clubbing.

"*Don't expect me to wait up at home and look after your son while you get wasted and play pretend at being a rock star, all so a bunch of skanky bitches can fawn over you. This isn't the fifties.*"

I clear my throat just loud enough, then steel myself for what comes next. Straight away, her head whips round like a snake's. Behind her I catch a glimpse of some guy, half in suit and half in shadow, his arm sliding off her bare shoulders. Her diamond eyes dart over my face, before she turns away to murmur something in the suit's ear. I take this opportunity to fish a clove cigarette out of the pack in my coat pocket and light it up. She doesn't bother getting off her arse to join me till her new admirer's got the hint to move on out of the picture. No, seriously, take her. Any offer. Free to good home. Please. But he doesn't pay me any mind as he saunters off to the men's.

Hell, I don't care. Just go anywhere near my son and I'll kill you where you stand with my bare hands.

Pursing her lips, she slides down from her chair and slinks on over, all razor sharp stilettos and black sparkles, giant pupils telling the story of what she was up to before she changed her plans for the night. The shirt scratches at my skin again as I pull my collar up round my neck. We've all got our methods of self destruction, I guess.

"See you made it after all." I face the bar, noting out of habit the nearly-empty drink in her hand.

She smiles and sips at the pale liquid, twirling the short straw, playing at being a not-so-little girl sucking a lollipop.

I did love her, once. Least I think I did, the way you think you remember pain, but of course you don't, not really. These days I can only wonder: did she ever look at me like she *didn't* want to sink her claws deep into my chest and rip out organs and entrails to feast on?

"It's a Tuesday night. In May. In *Melbourne*." She sneers. "Might as well be a ghost town out there. So I thought I'd come by and keep you safe from all your groupies instead." With another laugh, she finishes off her drink and slides it across the counter, then leans into me. I fight the instinct to push her away. Boys are supposed to go out with girls—

"So where are they, Raven? All your fans, all your admirers?"

—give them children, get married. Two outta three ain't bad, isn't that what the song says?

"Still, I suppose it must be a relief, really. You'd have no idea what to do with a woman anymore, would you?" Her right hand crosses the counter, reaches down and gropes clumsily at my pants, and tugs hard at the limpness between my legs. It's no surprise to either of us when her taunting gets no reaction beyond a shudder. I sigh and let myself glance over at the door on my left. Not that I'm seeking an exit—

"I'm the only one that'd have you."

—cos there is no exit. But one in the cage is always lonely. I figured he'd be here already.

Change the subject. "Did you get Damien off to Noriko's okay?"

She rolls her eyes. "Yes. In the end. Wouldn't stop bawling till we got there. I hope you feel like the big man for that."

I grit my teeth. As though I'm the one who threw our three-year-old against a wall for wanting to come see Daddy's gig. I try not to dwell on the amount of money in my pocket versus how much I'd need to get so drunk I might be able to forget that scene. At least he'll be safe, for tonight.

"Another drink?" I hate myself for making the offer. *You're so fucking chivalrous, Raven.*

"Why don't you get it yourself?" she hisses, mindful to dig the nails in deep as she pushes herself away from me. Pulling up a sequinned spaghetti strap, she spins on her stilettos, and stomps off in the direction of the front bar.

"Fuck you." I spit the words in the direction of her long departed shadow, but tonight I'm surprised—and relieved—that she let me off so easily. We both know every question she throws in my face is only an alias for the real one, the big one, the one she really wants to ask.

Why don't you just leave?

Another burst of feedback, and the radio song cross-fades into Shirley Manson, so captivating with her post-goth homage to loss and waiting. I feel for the feather in my pocket, and I can breathe again.

A hovering bartender finds me, one of the regulars who knows me by poison if not by name. Scotch and coke's the usual good-to-go, but Jack Daniels does the rounds on this stormy Fitzroy Tuesday. Money's good for four more, once I've paid for this one. I slam the glass down empty before the coins even hit the till. No point pretending; when it's gone, it's gone.

Why *don't* I just leave? But there's only one reason, of course. A three-year-old reason. And the minute I leave, the minute I push it, she'll take him from me forever. *My son.* To her, he's nothing more than a ransom note, to me he's my angel, my saviour. Funny thing, perspectives.

I'm just about to raise my hand to call for another drink, when the door I've been watching on and off slams against the wall. Hard raindrops and an icy wind hit me in the face, forcing me to squint. Someone staggers up the steps, buffeted by the storm. "Shut the farking door!" a voice roars from the other bar, as a great gust tears through the building. And right as if it was granting a wish, a last puff of air shoves the silhouette in: this skinny boy all cloaked in black and silver and violet, shown up under the light.

I can't help smiling as the door bangs closed behind him and he dumps the great black coffin case loudly to the floor. You always did know how to make an entrance, Pegasus. Gets a few stares from the punters every time, that thing does. So it should, when it holds something precious. Twenty odd kilos of vintage 80s plastic and analogue circuitry, the Jupiter synth, and his only other reason for ever finding his way into and through a place like this.

"Hey," I say, hands in my pockets again as I shuffle on over.

"Hey yourself," he answers, voice soft and husky. He stoops to drape his damp wool coat over the keyboard's case, and in the moment before he straightens up, I get a glimpse of the little tattoo that bears his namesake, spreading its wings across his naked shoulder blade. Here under this light, the feathers look grey. Wrong colour for you, Peg.

I reach into my pocket, pull out the feather, and hand it over. It's gone a little limp since I took it from the bathroom, but even in this light, we can still make out its indigo gleam. He smiles as he takes it from me, tucks it into his lilac braid, and says, "It's very pretty. Is it one of yours?"

I look away, from him to the keyboard and back again. Then, sure enough, out come those five magic words: the ones we've rehearsed so well between us so many other times, guaranteed to break any awkward silence. He asks me, "Do you want a drink?"

I open my mouth to say yes, close it again. *Don't be a dick.* Watching him squeeze the last drops of rain from his hair, I find a convenient way to change the subject. "Please tell me you didn't get the tram here."

"Not tonight. Lenny dropped me off, after work."

"Oh."

He wanders to the bar. With a grunt, I pick up the case and coat and haul them over behind our stools. Seeing I've got company, the bartender adds another glass and fills this one with Midori and lemonade. As Pegasus pulls out a note to pay for both drinks, I assuage my guilt by sneaking a straw into his. It's kind of our running joke. He spots the straw right away, of course, and snatches at it, blow-piping drops of cold liquid onto my cheek. His lip twitches, but this time he's not smiling at me.

"I *can* handle my alcohol, you know."

I blink. Why so defensive all of a sudden? After more than four years with his sister, I've gotta remind myself to go in search of a reason. Doesn't take me long. *Idiot.* Last time we sat in a bar together, he spent most of the night till closing with his head submerged in a toilet. That one was my fault. *And all the ones before.* The longer I sit in a pub, the harder I find it to leave. Maybe that doesn't make me an alcoholic, but I almost always keep Pegasus along, partly so I can look after him, partly so he can look after me, or so the story goes. Knowing that last time I didn't keep my part of the bargain doesn't leave much of a sting for the poisoned coke.

I light up another cigarette. Hands are shaking. He's watching my every move, silver eyes that remind me too much of Damien, innocent and yet all-seeing. It's only in this way that I can bring myself to believe he's even remotely related to Wendy. And as for my son, he's got nothing of her inside him, not that I could ever see. But Pegasus… It's easier to imagine him as—

Jesus. I start to cough. In a reflex action, he puts out a hand, rubbing and patting me on the back and leaning right in, as though fearful I might choke. "Are you okay?"

Don't go there. Eyes watering, the best I can do is manage a nod.

"Maybe you should quit smoking." Amused, not judging.

"Maybe I'm just pissed." Could be true. Hands haven't stopped shaking. Strange thoughts and chain smoking; lack of inhibition and nicotine. Could be just the normal me.

"You? Already?" With a sad smile, he shakes his head. "Not

unless you've been holed up here for a week, my friend."

Friend. I dare a glance at his face, mostly at his lips, but I've got a different reason for why I can't look at his sister and I can't look at him. "I never ate today. Always kicks in harder on an empty stomach. You know that." My skin twitches as his hand runs down my spine.

"Is *she* here?"

I make a grumbling sound we can both interpret as a yes, and then he says, "She rang me at work, maybe half an hour before I left."

I throw back most of my drink, follow it with a long drag on the clove, try and figure out the way their conversation might've gone from the wariness in his voice. "Yeah?" Well, blood is thicker than water. But shit, Pegasus, I thought you were on my side.

"Yes." He finally remembers his own glass, and twirls it around on the coaster. For a while, the sight of the ice cubes floating about in nuclear green mesmerises us both, till at last he picks it up to take a swig. "You know she blames me for leading you astray. For encouraging you."

"Someone's gotta do it." Ain't that the truth. Far more than he'll ever realise, if I can help it.

"Maybe. Maybe not, if it means making so much trouble for you both." The touch of his arm on mine is so soft I almost miss it. "I don't want you to lose Damien," he murmurs close to my ear. There it is, like he's read my mind: *I am on your side, Raven.* At least, that's what I hear behind the words. Maybe I really am drunk, after all. I make an awkward show of noticing his hand, resting on mine. As though to distract us both, he stretches, kittenish, and begins to rub at my shoulders. I open my mouth, close it again, while he continues to knead the muscles around my neck. *Relax.* It's really kind of nice. Cruel, in its way. But nice.

"Hmm, you're tense."

You reckon? I bite back a laugh.

"Why don't we go backstage for a bit? Perhaps I can give you a massage, before the others find us."

Only problem there is it's starting to feel so good, the way his fingers go about undoing the knots in my shoulders, that I don't want to move. He works his way down now, down and down, and where his knuckles press hard along my spine, the wings I made myself break the skin in bursts of cold fire, unfolding in a gleaming mess of bloody feathers and sticky bones, no longer a mockery of what I meant for them to be. Pain's got a meaning here...

As my unwinged self, I finish off the drink, then push myself off the chair. I'm determined not to look at him till I can trust myself. "Sure."

Biting back a smile, he folds his arms across his chest. "Sure," he echoes with a laugh, and makes a move for the corner opposite the mixing desk. I turn to join him and almost trip over the keyboard case.

Love. The word catches me off guard, ricocheting around my head like a butterfly shut up in a jar. I hurry to deposit the coffin and his coat beside the drum riser, then follow him behind the black curtain backstage.

(PEGASUS) 2

Bleeding Hearts

Truth be told, I wasn't expecting a yes to my question.

Perhaps I can give you a massage.

Which is not so much of a question, come to think of it. It seems I'll do anything to distract myself from the pins and needles tapping my veins, and the seasick feeling in my tummy. Stage fright. Ridiculous, since this performance only involves a keyboard, not a piano, and it's our fifth gig already.

I follow Raven behind the black curtain. 'Backstage' they call it, but it's little more than an afterthought, a cell of rotten planks and bare bricks dressed up in posters of bands no one ever heard of, many of them acts that were born and died here. One of them ours: 'Cardinal Vanity'. It already looks faded. Only two sources of light in the room: the fierce orange glare of a bar heater on the floor, and a dull naked globe above our heads. In every other sense, we're drowning in shadows. *Living the rock'n'roll high life,* as Monty put it dryly. That heater's a new addition, though. There's one thing about bass playing lawyers from Darwin, they know how to nag about the cold.

Raven flops on the shabby corner sofa and pulls off his jacket—the black velvet one. "Change your mind already?"

Is he taunting me on purpose? Our eyes meet, and I make a beeline for the bottle of wine near his feet. It's supposed to be for after our set, but who waits so long? In Raven's case, leaving a bottle of alcohol lying around and then telling him he can't drink it is like leaving a steak with a German Shepherd, and expecting both to be hanging round the scene of the crime ten minutes later. Anyway, tonight I can't bear it when he looks at me.

I pour out two glasses, taking my time, my unsteady hands making his share more generous on purpose. Despite my snappy reproach at the bar, I know I can't handle my alcohol. I'm surprised he's talking to me, after last time. Last time again, when I made such a fool of myself.

"Poor baby," is what he always says. And every time, he holds my hair out of the path of the sickness that erupts from my gut and shreds my throat—so much vomit, surely soon there'll be blood, and then—

But I gave up on thinking I was going to die after the second occasion. Besides, to paraphrase Nick Cave, 'that really doesn't suit my style.'

Poor baby. Pegasus, the baby. Because I'm the youngest, everyone always thinks of me as 'the baby', someone who can't look after himself, someone who needs protecting. Sometimes I dare to believe that Raven's different. That he keeps me here, to look after him. To look after him when he might make a fool of himself by drinking too much and admitting to having any human emotions at all. That stupid, selfish hope is the only reason I allow him to do it, allow him to slowly kill himself, because it's the only time he needs me around. Selfish is too kind a word for it, whether or not it's as selfish as some...

"Let me help you out with one of those."

He's standing in front of me, reaching for a wine glass. Even under the shadow of that thick fringe, he's watching me, my face and every twitch; dark blue eyes that almost match the colour of his hair. Damien, his son—angel creature—has those same eyes, just devoid of adult disillusion. I'm careful not to grimace. 'Disillusion' seems a little too mild to apply to Raven, somehow.

His fingers brush mine. Just as I'm about to drop the glass, he plucks it out of my hand.

I blink, and it's already empty.

"Shall we?" He pokes a thumb at the sofa, and we both sit right on the edge, too close to face each other without it being awkward. I take a more reserved sip of my wine, but it's bitter and doesn't sit well. So I make do with folding my arms over my tummy and conjuring monstrous faces from the shadows on the floor. I've only just noticed our legs are touching, when he pushes himself off the sofa and hovers over me.

He's changed his mind. Why would he ever want you near him? And even if he did, you can't. You can't, because of your sister. Because of their son. And, because of the truth. Because you're nothing but a—

I blink again, clenching my hands so tightly into fists my nails start to carve those little half-moons in the skin. I'm trying my best to ignore the monsters that have gotten into my head, and at the same time not focus on his crotch, now inconveniently—and conveniently—around eye level. The telltale hotness is rising in my cheeks. At least there's not enough light to give away the fact that I'm blushing.

"Pegasus," he says softly, "you still want to...?"

He trails off into another awkward silence, but once I'm done gathering my thoughts, and locking them up in a steel tower where no one will ever suffer their poison, I get it together enough to nod. "Of course."

Taking this as a cue that everything's okay, he turns around and plonks himself down near my toes.

"Tell me when to stop." I wipe my hands on my black cords and wriggle my fingers.

"Don't worry, if you're really good, you'll be here all night." He finds my glass and does me the honour of finishing it for me, then leans into my waiting palms. I draw in a breath too quickly as I make contact with the nape of his neck. His flesh is so soft, so warm, I wasn't expecting—

What were *you expecting? Porcupine spikes?*

Holding my breath altogether, I begin kneading either side of the base of his skull, gently to begin with, shifting where I sit so that, should he happen to turn around, there'll be no evidence that I feel anything a mere friend might consider untoward.

Mere friend. I should consider myself lucky to have this much.

His head droops as I slide my palms down to his shoulder blades. I take my time with unknitting the tension that binds his muscles, then trace waves and spirals to the base of his spine, feeling the bones that poke close beneath the skin. So odd how this is the first time I've ever dared to touch him, like this.

Your first time, and your last.

No, stop. Don't say these things.

He breathes out in a soft moan, and a shiver passes across my belly, into my balls. I look at his neck, shags of blue-black brushing the collar. How would it be to see more than that one tantalising piece of flesh? Even on hot days, he never wears anything that reveals more than neck, face, and hands, and so I make do, like always, by imagining that this is more, that this is all I need. It's not like I haven't had plenty of practice in self-deception. That, and deceiving others. It paid for what I call my freedom. Freedom to torture myself twenty-four hours a day with thoughts of this beautiful boy, and what he could never feel for me.

Cautiously, my fingers hook themselves under the black shirt. I've given up all hope of being able to hold my breath now; my heart pounds against my ribs, the longing inside me strains for release. Can I be deceiving myself so well, or is this truly the first time I ever wanted this?

I begin to stroke the skin of his back. This, too, is soft and warm. Slowly I make my way up the spine again, taking as much of the shirt with me as I can without actually undressing him. He inhales sharply, and then I reach a spot where the soft skin is interrupted by something hard, prickly, and somehow wet. I frown, trying to lift enough of the shirt to see what it is, but before I can uncover it, he jerks to his feet. Now he glares down at me. Hatred twists his face.

"That's enough," he says.

Part of me wants to look away, but I can't. I don't understand. No, it's worse than that. This look of hate is something I do understand, because I've seen it before, just never directed at me.

It's the same way he looks at her.

I blink; my eyes have started to sting. Against all reason, I hate him, too. Yes, Raven, I really do. You bastard. You know exactly how I feel for you, and you set me up, didn't you? Go ahead: laugh, tease, despise. You think this is real pain? You flatter yourself, same as they all do.

But he's not laughing. I can't tell about the rest. "Wait here. I need a drink. Something that doesn't taste like cat's piss." And he's gone.

I put my hand up to my face to brush aside my tears, but never make it all the way. For what could be thirty seconds or thirty minutes I stare at my fingertips, while the light ticks on and off overhead.

They're stained red with blood. Raven's blood.

...something hard, prickly, and somehow wet.

Fresh scars. The reason why he pushed me away? Or just one of many reasons?

Trembling all over, I lean forward and lick the blood off my fingers. Destroying the evidence. It tastes sweet, and vaguely of alcohol, though of course that could be my own contribution. *Raven's blood.* Now I have something of Raven inside me.

By the time he returns with ye olde faithful scotch and

coke, I'm over fretting about his motives, and my almost ever-present hard-on has returned. Damn.

He takes a seat beside me on the sofa, not as close as before, nor as close as I'd like, but not too far either, considering. At least that terrible expression is gone, replaced by the more familiar air of sadness that usually veils him. I want steal another touch, but I had my chance and I blew it. So I stare at my fingertips, and the memory of the blood, as I watch him light another clove cigarette from the corner of my eye.

And we are silent.

Finally, he butts it out into a wine glass and turns towards me, though his gaze remains lowered. I want to speak, but no words come.

"Peg," he says, his voice cracking. A tortured twitch crosses his face. Then, "You weren't supposed to—"

Our eyes meet. Maybe, just maybe, I'm beginning to understand. I was never ever supposed to see the scars.

His self-inflicted scars?

He opens his mouth, but before either of us can say anything more the curtain spasms, and an excited cry of "Daddy!" echoes around the walls. I stand up, my head buzzing, as Damien clomps across the floorboards and launches himself into his father's lap. Raven becomes a completely different person in the presence of his son. I could never hope to make him so happy. At least my sister could give him this much.

"Hey, Pegasus!"

Two other figures emerge from behind the curtain, Monty and his girlfriend, Noriko. I can't help noticing her straight away. Perhaps a week ago, her hair was fluoro pink. Tonight it's a rather pleasing shade of grass-green.

"You like?" she asks, fluttering her henna-tattooed fingers against a geisha girl face, all made up for the stage. A smile and a nod is the best I can do, but it seems to be enough.

"So, lover boy, hope we weren't interrupting anything?" Monty waltzes over to lean against my shoulder, grinning conspiratorially. I slap his hand away, less of the playfulness than when I do it to Raven. Not that there's much of me left to out, but we all have a right to our secrets. Even when they're strangling us.

The curtain rips aside, and a shrill voice blasts across the room, "What the hell is *he* doing here?"

I don't need to look to know who it is. Raven instinctively clutches Damien tighter, and the little boy, sweetly oblivious to anything else, continues to play with his father's necklace, the silver Maltese cross on a black velvet choker, a birthday present from me. "*Bonsoir, ma soeur,*" I mutter under my breath.

"God, chill out Wendy," Noriko says, turning in the direction of the doorway and throwing out her hands in disbelief. "We came there, and *okaasan* was sneezing all over the place. She was afraid he'd get sick. Besides, he wanted to come. Hence—" she spreads her arms wide "—we're here."

My sister surges forward, her horror-shop painted doll face all pursed lips and narrowed eyes. "Maybe it's fine for gooks to have their brats crawling around in a shit-hole like this, but some of us have standards. Why don't you bugger off back to your own third-world country if you want to raise a pig."

"Whoa," says Monty, stepping away from me. "Not cool."

But Noriko holds up her hand to him, then forces out a smile for Wendy. "Actually, 'gook' is for Vietnamese. I'm Japanese. So if you want to be the good racist girl, you should say 'nip'. Anyway, last time I looked, Sydney wasn't a third-world country."

I have to stifle a smile. Noriko doesn't like Wendy one bit, though she does a good job of hiding it.

"Seriously, he'll be fine. I only need to be on stage for four songs. The rest of the time, I can look after him for you, easy."

Wendy grunts and rolls her eyes, then stomps over to the

sofa. After trying to stare Raven down without success, she gives up and grabs for the child instead, slapping at them both and yelling until Raven at last lets go. By this time, Damien's beginning to cry. I remember how it feels to be the one caught in the middle, and I hate her all the more for doing that to Raven's son.

"Yeah, right," she snaps. "Thanks for being so bloody useless, all of you. I'll take him home myself." Not even bothering to pick him up, she starts to drag him across the floor, towards the curtain. When Monty and Noriko take a step forward, she reels around and jabs a finger in Noriko's face. "I'm not having my son in a place like this. Don't you dare dictate to me what's right and what's not. *You're* not a mother, so you wouldn't know!"

I wince, seeing how these words dig in. Noriko adores children, but isn't able to have any of her own. Another of life's little ironies. As Raven once put it so eloquently, 'if God really does exist, my bet is he's one sadistic fucker.'

He's standing beside me now, close enough for me to feel him shaking. Damien looks up at us, sniffing in hope. "I want to stay with you, Daddy. Want to watch Daddy play music."

Raven kneels beside him, reaches for a tiny hand and grasps it in his own. He's just about to give it a kiss when Wendy wrenches the child away again. "Daddy doesn't play music. He plays with his cock. You're going home. *Now!*"

Raven's on his feet again in an instant, his hands hardened into fists, jaw set firm, and a sneer on his lips. "Don't talk that way in front of my son." Remembering the phone call, I want to grab for his hands as a warning, but that would be too obvious. After a moment he lowers his head, takes a big breath, and tries to calm himself. "Please, Wendy. There's hardly anyone out there. You and Noriko can keep an eye on him between you while I'm up there. Let him stay, for the first set at least. Hell, the first *song*. He really wants to."

So now he's begging her, and I hate her for this, too. Even Damien waits expectantly on her answer. But I know my sister. I know what she's going to say before she's even opened her big fat mouth.

"I said *get up*, you little shit. We're *leaving*."

Damien starts to wail. Noriko turns away, her face in one hand. Monty retires to the sofa and stares blankly at the wine bottle. Only Raven and I remain where we are, although I can feel him shaking worse than before.

She's still dragging Damien along, my sister—pushing him out in front of her until he falls over and scrapes his knee. Now he's screaming. Terrible screams. My coward self wants me to cover my ears, but in a show of its true form, all I can do is close my eyes. Of course it won't help. The memories find me through my self-imposed dark, guided by the blood-curdling yells. Until a loud slap startles me awake again.

I open my eyes. The screaming's stopped. Damien sits on the floor, crying and rubbing his bottom as though this was the last thing in the world he ever expected. Funny how it always comes as such a shock. Funny too how it hurts to fight the overwhelming urge to pick him up and comfort him, tell him everything will be all right and nothing will ever hurt him again. Exactly like I want to with his father. Even though it would only make the reality worse. Even though I know it's all a lie.

Raven's less of a coward than me. He rushes to his son, not allowing thought to cloud his instinct, but Wendy pounces and blocks him. "Are you happy? Look at what you did."

"Me?!?"

"Yes, you. If you were a real father to him, this would never be an issue. If you were at home with me instead of spending every waking hour in dives like this—"

Her yelling sets Damien off again, though at least it distracts Raven from what she just said. He tries to weave past her, but I know my sister. I can see it coming. But just this once,

I can stop it.

Before I even know what's happened, Noriko's face drifts into focus mere inches away from mine. I'm propped up on the floor against the sofa, and when she dabs at my face with a wet tissue, pain floods through my nose. She reaches for another tissue; turns out there's a pile of them heaped around us, all covered with blood. My left nostril stings, but I suppose they'd be making more of a fuss if anything was broken.

I risk a cautious glance around the rest of the room. Wendy and Damien are gone. Monty remains on the sofa, his palm rubbing my shoulder. And Raven leans against the wall in the farthest corner, ankle-deep in shredded posters. As I keep watching, he throws a half-hearted punch at one of the wooden boards. I hope he doesn't damage his hands, those beautiful hands that play his guitar so well. That don't quite protect his son, and have never touched me.

The red-rimmed eyes and blotchy cheeks are what make it real the most; I don't think I've ever seen more than a tear out of him. "Fucking bitch," he mutters, pulling at his hair, but all the fight's left him by the time he comes to sit beside us.

"What—" Argh. My voice sounds weird. My lips hurt, too. I lick them, try to block out the pain, start all over. "What just happened?"

He cocks his head at me, raising a brow. "Wendy. She knocked you out. She took my son. She left."

KO'd by a blonde in possession of the temperament of a Jerry Springer guest. That can only make a good impression, yes? "Well, my sister has always been efficient."

"You want to tell me why you decided to get in the way of me and her fist?"

I manage a laugh, lick at my lips again. Oh, there might be more than one answer to that question. Which do you want? "Because if she'd hit you, you would have hit her back," I say. "In front of your son. And they would have taken him from you. For always. You know how she is." At least it's not a lie. Just not the complete truth. I won't ever allow them to take away your son, because that would destroy you, and you are the only one I've ever—

A knock on the wall behind the curtain denies my confession, even to myself, and a gruff voice yells, "Sound check's on!" The roadie.

"Be there in two!" Monty calls, then stands, stretches tall, and takes Noriko's arm in his own. "Buy my *bijin* a drink?"

Laughing at his Japanese, she skips out alongside him.

"Can you do it?"

Raven stands above me, offering his hand. I nod, but need him to help me up. There's a moment when he doesn't let me go where I fall against him, smelling cloves, alcohol, and something else—pure Raven. One of his arms around my shoulder, the other squeezing my waist. Finally touching me.

But when I see the concern in his face—concern wasted for me—I give it up. "I can do it." Mustering all the masculinity I can, I push away from him, though I do stumble through the curtain on my way out of the room.

Behind me, I hear him sigh and mutter, "God knows how much longer I can." And wish that for once I hadn't been close enough to overhear.

3 (RAVEN)

Cracks in the Ice

I slam down the receiver of the public phone, hard enough to cause a loud crack. Whether it's plastic or bone, I can't tell; I don't care.

"What the fuck are you looking at?" I yell into the face of the nearest onlooker, a proverbial brick toilet maybe half my height again and twice my width. The pockmarked mess that barely passes for a face beneath steel wool hair contorts into a scowl. I just laugh. *Feeling lucky tonight, Raven?*

"Raven." A gentle voice echoes my name like a warning in my ear. No, I don't want to talk to you, Pegasus. Don't want to look at you, don't want to unleash this impotent rage upon you always and again.

I try and avoid those sad silver eyes filled with concerned pity. I don't need your pity, and I don't deserve your concern. "You're too late. I'm doomed anyway." That's what I want to say. Instead I find myself grabbing his wrist and tugging him towards the bar. If ever I had a sanctuary, this is it. Twenty dollars from the gig goes aside on a little something for my son, which means after I shout us a fifth drink, I'm back to scrabbling for change in my pockets.

I let him go to take possession of my JD and coke, while he tries to rub away the pain of my touch. "Poor baby." I'm aware of the mocking tone in my voice, not that I'm going to do anything about it. "You're not having a good night, are you?"

"I'm not a baby," he snaps, and snatches up the Midori and lemonade. After a moment's silence, he places the glass down on the counter. It's empty.

Guess I deserve that. He wouldn't see it as a term of endearment, of course. No different from last time, when he threw up, all for doing then what he's doing now—trying to keep up with me.

"Let's sit," I say, nodding towards a booth behind the pool tables. Most of the punters have cleared out now it's nearing last drinks. We finished up our set half an hour ago, but the anger hasn't stopped burning a hole through my brain, the embers newly stoked since she phoned in that abusive tirade.

I slide over, closest to the wall, taken by surprise when he moves right in beside me. I wish the couple of people who do linger around the bar would just bugger off. Maybe then he'd continue that massage, long enough for me to get up the guts to spell out my feelings for him, and finally put this charade to death.

"Was that her?" he asks.

I gaze into my drink. He's staring at my hands, and the scratches left by the bitch's claws. His nose is still puffy. At least the bleeding stopped before we went on. I can't believe she hit him. A blow meant for me, so why did he take it?

Because if she'd hit you, you would have hit her back. In front of your son. And they would have taken him from you. For always.

Well sure, that would be a reasonable explanation. But a voice that isn't Wendy's keeps nagging at the edges, insisting there's something more, another hidden reason. It gets louder, this voice, whenever I look into his eyes, when I felt his touch tonight, when I held him and he pushed away from me, just like I pushed away from him. Could it be—both of us using my son as an excuse to never get any closer?

I take a swig from my glass. How much more of this shit do I need to drink before I build up enough courage to tell him?

"Yeah. It was her. Demanded to know when I'd be coming home. Said Damien wouldn't go to bed cos I upset him so bad. Then she launched into the second-rate dad speech again." I bite down into a block of ice, hoping it cushions some of the hate.

"I guess this would be when you killed the phone, huh?" He tries to smile.

I laugh, all self-pity and self-derision. "No. That would've been when she told me what she did to get him to sleep." I glance in his direction, daring him to ask. For a moment he opens his mouth, then shakes his head, letting it pass. Guess he's got enough imagination to fill in the blanks. Enough experience, too, if what little I've put together of his childhood is true.

"Please don't get drunk tonight, Raven," he says at last, and reaches out, clasping my hand.

I stare at his pale, spidery fingers, nails painted to match my hair glittering in the light. Right now I feel as sober as I'm ever going to get, but I'm well-trained in the art of never betraying my feelings. "Too late for that." Meaning what, exactly? Too late for a warning, or too late to touch? He lowers his head, defeated by this statement. I squeeze his hand despite myself. Not too late to touch. It can't be. "Why do you care?" I ask.

He looks up again, pausing, evaluating the question. Seems most everything I say tonight ends up with two meanings. I'm a serpent with a forked tongue. One path leading to the truth I deny, fearing happiness, the other a lie that got me into all this trouble in the first place. He follows my lead, my rules, and chooses the second path.

"Don't give her more of an excuse than she already has. Finish up your drink, and go home."

"Oh, so now *you* don't want me around, either?" *What the hell are you doing, Raven?*

The way he looks at me, coupled with the words I couldn't stop myself from saying, spikes my heart. "It's never been about what I want."

Like I need another reminder that I'm too much of a coward to deal with any of this. What *do* you want, then? That's what I should be asking. "I'm sorry," I hear myself say, into my glass. *Finish up your drink, and go home.* Probably the best advice I could hope for.

Do you want...me?

A set of car keys materialises in front of my face, jingling like some bogan wind chime between both our heads. "Home time, kiddies!" Monty calls, his cheer well out of place. "Better come along before your coach turns into a pumpkin."

There must be enough combined angst in the look we shoot him to almost kill off that trademark grin. Almost, but not quite. Damn. But I agree to a ride anyway. *A small concession to your wishes, Pegasus.* I finish up and follow them out to the lane.

If I'd remembered that Monty's latest musical obsession involved Queen, I mightn't have bothered, Pegasus or no Pegasus. I sit beside him in the back seat, trying my best to call up the part of my childhood where I loved 'Bohemian Rhapsody' enough to sing along with it in true *Wayne's World* fashion, but that long-term memory loss that's supposedly associated with drinking as much as I do must be kicking in, cos I swear I can't do it.

Several times during the journey, I glance across at him, hoping to catch his eye, hoping he'll reach out for my hand again, so much so that I leave it unclenched on the seat between us, as close to his leg as I can without breaking the concrete subtlety that is Raven de Winter. But the whole time he just sits there, arms folded over his chest, staring out the window. Whenever I catch a glimpse of his reflection, he looks miserable. That'd be my fault, too. Again. *Always.*

We reach the top of my street, rather appropriately, as the late Mr. Mercury gets to crooning about how nothing really matters, and I roll out onto the patchwork asphalt, then poke my head back in to say my good-byes. Gosh, I'm feeling social tonight.

Truth is, the last place in the world I want to be is that house of hell only two picket fences away.

Pegasus still isn't looking at me, so I save a farewell especially for him. "Bye, Peg?"

Even Monty and Noriko look surprised when he ignores me. Monty raises a brow and Noriko waves sadly as they slowly reverse onto Punt Road.

"Nothing really matters...to me." The words ring in my mind as I watch the car till it disappears from view, leaving me like they always do, eventually, to face the nightmare alone.

His face is so beautiful. Perfection, frozen in sleep. I've never been into religion—something about the whole concept of faith I could never stomach—but tonight, looking down on something so precious, I find the term 'angel' again coming to mind. How two such worthless beings could produce such a lovely creature between them is completely beyond me.

You're all I've got in the world, Damien. The only thing I'm allowed to love. The only truth that can't be twisted into deceit, the only blessing I can't taint into a curse.

When a tear lands on the porcelain cheek, I get stiffly to my feet. I only hope he's dreaming, like all children are supposed to—a fantastic voyage of unbridled imagination, unbound by adult fears—and for this reason I won't wake him, even if all I want is to pick him up and hold him, hold him so tight that no one could ever come between us, that I could never—would never need to let him go.

"About bloody time you came home."

But the real world always creeps back in, casting a stain over everything. The twisted shadow on the wall is a far more accurate portrait of what lies within her soul than the figure standing in front of me. I push past her, forcing her to follow me out of the room. Whatever happens next, my son's got nothing more to do with it.

I close the door softly behind me. Only then do I let the same black poison stain spread to my heart.

She's hissing and spitting but I'm not listening, as she stalks me up the hall to our bedroom, that place I dread the most. Knowing she wants each night to be 'The One'; that I might actually have to let her swallow me up and confront the fact that my life is a lie. Not that I've been physically capable of doing that for too many months to count—at one stage she went as far as suggesting Viagra; I laughed so hard I spat in her face. Even my dick can't be suckered in that easy anymore. Pity how wisdom comes with so much hindsight.

Her spouting of the endless list of my failures drones on, as I walk towards the window, raise the blind, and find myself staring up at a full moon. A nice pagan explanation for my madness. My mind drifts back to Pegasus in the car, refusing to look at me, refusing to even say good-bye. How could I have fooled myself into thinking, even for a millisecond, that he could have feelings for me?

"It's never been about what I want."

Her voice—his words. The crossover of imagery, desire, and hatred makes me sick, the moon fading into a swirl as I spin away from the glass and shove her to the floor.

That was for Pegasus, for the one that I truly—

No, don't say that. If you say it, if you ever admit it to yourself, it becomes the truth, and then— And then, she'll see it, and she'll take it from you, like she's taken everything else.

I watch myself pull her up by the ends of her hair, covering her mouth since I can't stand to hear her squeal. Not one more word. I throw her against the wall. Not so nice when you're on the receiving end, is it, love?

Love? Is that what this is, this delicate fever, this gliding across the edge of a knife?

She thinks this is for her. Both of us, the deceived, the deceivers. Both of us living a lie, all for being so comfortable beneath everyone else's gaze, so 'socially acceptable'. Not tonight. No more. It takes a certain strength to lie, a certain faith, and all I feel is exhaustion.

The memory of the moon swirls in front of my mind's eye as I put a hand around her neck, keeping her flat against the wall. In one violent tug my other hand rips off her pyjama pants. I close my eyes as I unbutton my jeans, not seeing her, not feeling her, not feeling this incredible need— Not for her.

She's stopped squirming and struggling. Hoping this is finally it, she parts her legs and rubs against me, whimpering. Pathetic. I don't want to touch that—in my mind's eye her cunt's swollen in grotesqueness to some Gerald Scarfe caricature, all fangs and acidic drool. Swallowing the bile, I try and conjure up his beautiful face once again, his hands transforming the cuts into wings, and everything's okay.

As okay as it can be with the madness crashing in waves into my skull.

My fingers drift down, parting the flesh of her butt. One after another, I force two of them inside. Letting out a panicked screech, she struggles against me, mouthing something about, "Raven, I don't think you should—it hurts." No. No no no no. If I hear her moan, I'm going to lose it. Then there'll be no point to any of this. So I cup my hand around her mouth, so tight that nothing can escape. Then I ram into her arse, so forceful and desperate we both slam into the wall, and she's panting and grunting, biting my hand so hard I can feel her teeth break the skin, but it's too late for either of us now.

Pegasus. *Pegasus, Pegasus, Pegasus.* There is no her and no me. Only you. *Love.* I love you. I want to give myself to you. Please save me. Save me from her, from myself, from these terrible feelings that are only for you.

Have only ever been for you.

There it is.

This final stark confession is almost enough to make me cum. But I'm lost so deep, and I want us to be here, together, want to make him feel this, too. I want him to know...

"Pegasus..."

Beneath me, Wendy suddenly tenses. *Pegasus.* Did I—?

Yeah. I actually spoke the magic word out loud. Discovering an extra burst of strength from this ultimate rejection, she pushes me off, then whacks me across the face.

I fall onto the bed, my head spinning. Too numb to feel any pain, too relieved that I've announced the truth at last—if not to him, then at least to me—I gaze at the floor as a suitcase lands near my feet, and clothes fly into it.

Is she leaving me? If this was all I had to do...

No, these are my clothes. Of course. *Why don't you just leave?* Now she doesn't even need to ask.

When she sees me looking, she starts screaming at me, something about how sick I am, something else about me going to hell.

"I thought you wanted me to leave." *Don't think about touching her, don't think about what you did to her, don't close your eyes, just don't.* I wander across the hall to the bathroom, forcing myself not to run.

Half an hour later, after doing my best to scrub off her poison and what feels like half my skin, I pick up the single suitcase, grab my latest reading material off the night-stand on my side of the bed, and walk out of the room. Guess it's for good, this time. I linger outside Damien's door, but the numbness hasn't worn off enough yet to process that pain.

Something to look forward to tomorrow. Along with the hangovers I never get.

Wendy starts hitting and threatening me again. Afraid she might wake him, I let her hound me out of the house.

Two forty-two a.m., or so my watch says, when I take a seat on the park bench directly across from Peg's apartment. Another five hours before the first coach makes its run down the south-west coast. I'll be on it, of course. But till then, I can sit right here and look up at his window, wishing the same sweet dreams on him that I wished upon Damien, what already seems like hours before.

It's so cold, now the storm clouds have passed and the rain's gone. My breath leaves smoky trails in the air as I light up a clove, licking my lips and tasting the sweetness of the filter. I wonder if this is what Pegasus will taste, if we—

Yeah, well. No chance of that ever happening, I suppose. I'm a coward. Cowards run, so that's what I'm doing. Home to my mama. But it's no more a solution than staying put with Wendy. I just need a chance to—

To what? Think? Change my mind? Apologise?

None of the above. I feel bad for what I did to Wendy. Deep down I know such capacity to hurt is not an integral part of who I am. It's just—the moon, my feelings, my confession, retribution...

He didn't even want to say goodnight to me. What did I say, that was so wrong?

Several times during the course of the long morning, I give serious thought to ringing the buzzer and begging the price of admission to his loft. Only one thought stops me every time. What if I try to do to him what I just did to Wendy? What if I hurt him that way?

Is that really what I want?

No. On the edge of dawn, I finally feel sure of the answer, as I board the first tram to the city. Not that certainty helps. That's why I'm running, after all. It's what cowards do.

At Spencer Street, I glance over my ticket as I board the coach. Down near the back, sitting with my socked toes curled over a heating vent: this is the warmest I've been in over twelve hours. Two bus stops shy of the end of the line, followed by a half hour walk to work up the appetite. ETA, around one-thirty.

If old habits hold, I'll be just in time for lunch. It's been a while. Hope Ma's pleased to see me.

4 (PEGASUS)

Chasing Shadows

Ninety-eight...
Ninety-nine...
One hundred.

I place the brush on the dresser, and dart away from the mirror to avoid my own reflection.

Don't look. Don't think. Don't be.

The mantra for this evening. For always. And finally, inevitably: *Don't say his name.*

Raven...

Dammit.

I find myself at the window, numb fingers pressed to the glass, my reflection here all a blur. I may have had too much to drink tonight, in the hope of making myself sick. But even my tummy won't help me now.

A full moon floats adrift in the sky above. Its lonely light spreads shadows around the room, phantom selves sent to torment me. Sometime after two on a Saturday morning, and the world outside my window is dead. *Don't allow it to fool you. This is how it goes when your universe collapses in on itself. You've seen it before. Wasn't it just the same, nine years ago?*

No. I don't want to remember that now. Go away, go away. Raven, where are you?

Two hours, give or take, since Monty and Noriko appeared on the scene of a cheap and nasty bar at the wrong end of

Inkerman Street, and dragged me off to my cell. An hour and a half, thereabouts, since they told me, "Raven's gone, Pegasus." The only reason, "You saw how things were between him and Wendy."

Four days. Four nights since we touched, since I tried to tell him, but failed, same as always. After that, I couldn't bring myself to acknowledge either of us, couldn't bear to speak to him.

Bye, Pegasus?

Those words keep echoing through my head, terrorising me with their unforeseen finality. You bastard, why didn't you tell me you were *really* saying good-bye?

I take a seat on the edge of the bed, and pick up the photo of my mother. She never cried, so I won't either, but her smile doesn't hide the sadness, not once you know to look for it. This picture of her, and the dress she wore on that day, are among the only trinkets I managed to salvage after her death. I never feel as beautiful when I'm draped in her white lace and silk, but it feels right, in this moment, to be wearing it.

"Mama," I whimper, every bit the child she abandoned. Always, the child abandoned. Four days. Four years. Four years ago, Raven, when I first lost my heart, to you.

Monty and Noriko weren't the only ones I'd told about my feelings for him. That would be too simple. If they'd been the only ones, no doubt there'd be a 'they lived happily ever after' by now, but no. This was all my own stupid fault, for giving any surviving member of my family a chance. A chance to hurt me, all over again.

"I—I think I'm kind of...in love with him." The words stumbled out of my mouth, but once they did, I knew they were the truth. Poor baby Pegasus; yet another animal caught in the headlights of oncoming traffic.

Wendy's face lit up with a conspiratorial grin. She hadn't given up dancing yet, and her hair was longer than mine, framing her face in a curtain of gold. "Really? And what if *he* doesn't love *you*? What if he thinks that boys who like other boys are—?" She made a face, which in polite company maybe roughly translated to 'freaks'.

It seems laughable to admit that this had never come up in all my daydreams. The question caught me off-guard, led me down into a thick shadow of doubt. But I couldn't allow my sister to see. Or myself. "Ah, but what if he *does*?"

She snorted. "You want to be careful of getting too cocky, little brother. Even if you get beyond the gay, what about... what you do?"

My gasp only made her giggle. If he knew what I was, there was no way— Who was I kidding?

No. The voice at the back of my mind was far kinder to me in those days. *This is yours. You deserve to be happy, to be loved, just once. Why should Raven* not *be the one?*

He could be the one.

You know it.

"We'll see." My sister gave me a final shark-tooth grin, before she put out the light and went off to bed.

Two weeks later, we were at rehearsals. Noriko was doing her best Yoko Ono take on an early Kylie Minogue song, while I tried to program a drum loop for our latest track— one of our first originals—and Monty bounced around the warehouse wiggling his butt and ceremonially stripping off his tie, loafers and suit, since he'd just finished work and had drunk way too much coffee. Any old excuse. We long suspected he had some thing for 'the singing budgie'.

I remember him teasing me about my secret crush not thirty seconds before the door opened, and my heart froze inside my chest. In walked Wendy, that conspiratorial grin still on her face, hand in hand with Raven. As they stopped beside me, he said hello, but I barely caught a word of it. She was standing on tiptoe to plant a kiss on his neck. Then she turned to wink at me.

You fucking bitch. You knew he meant something to me, so you took him. Just like you always did when we were children.

We're children still.

Raven playfully pinched me on the cheek. "Hey, Earth to Pegasus? Anybody home?"

I slapped at his hand, hard enough to jar my wrist, and mumbling something along the lines of, "I think I'm going to be sick", raced into the bathroom with my tail between my legs. Not a heartbeat later, Noriko came after me, and held me in her arms as I shivered and wept. *Poor baby Pegasus.*

Here in the present, the land of the dead, and there's no one to hold me. No one to tell me everything will be okay. That's all right; I'm too old now for lies. I lost you four years ago, Raven. I should be over it already. Should be over you. But whatever disease took hold of me the moment I laid eyes on you refuses to let me go.

If only I'd told it to you, not her, things might have been different.

No, this is pure naivety. You know you're nothing but a whore. If Wendy didn't tell him, he would figure it out on his own. They can always tell. You don't deserve any chances. You never did. Why else would the only person who ever loved you leave you to this?

"Mama," I whisper again, falling face-first onto the pillow and biting down on it in an attempt to stop my choking sobs. I haven't cried, not like this, not since the funeral, nine years ago. I remember how they all surrounded me with their pity as I stood by the coffin, words of reverence and finality heavy in the air. I wouldn't have believed my beautiful mother was inside that wooden box. But the words of the priest made me believe it. And later that night, I learned that my one protector was truly gone, as my uncle made me pay the price for his kinder touches that day.

"Come here, baby boy. I've got something that'll take all your pain away..."

No, stop. Don't think of that.

But since when did I ever listen to myself?

The gates are open now, and visions flood my mind, memories of hands and tongues and dicks and what that man and too many others to count—what they did to me, while I pretended to be somewhere else, someone else; pretended this was all I deserved. Touching, tearing, beating...raping. Trying to force their way down deep into my soul and break me. I thought they never could, only because I always believed I didn't have a soul. But I knew different in the moment I met Raven. And in that moment, I learned another kind of pain, a pain so profound it left me terrified, paralysed, unable to confess even to myself that this was what I felt. And so, I doomed myself.

This same pain I feel now.

Four days, and you haven't even called.

Pathetic.

Exhausted, I pull myself up and rub at my eyes. Some part of me hopes he's coming back, that I have a chance. Better I fear the day the tears do stop, because then I'll have no more excuses. No more excuses to stay...

The telephone shrieks into life behind me, jolting me out of that not quite numb enough space between living and dying. I can't imagine who might be calling. At least not while I'm catching my breath. But then the crazy idea strikes, and I leap off the bed and snatch the receiver to my ear. "Raven?"

Straight away, I kick myself. *Fool.* Why did I have to drink so much?

"Settle, lover boy." It's a female voice. Instantly, my heart sinks beneath my toes. I imagine it falling through the floorboards and plummeting to its death in the apartment below. Wendy. Come to gloat again, to rub it in one last time?

"What do you want?" I almost hang up on her. Yes, that's what I really should do, because eventually I'm going to have to ask.

"I just rang to ask you a favour," she says, feigning innocence. Ugh. "I need you to look after Damien tomorrow."

"What?" Of all the possibilities, I never would have guessed. I smell a rat. "Why me? Why not Father? Or Noriko and Monty?"

"It's too short notice for Father. And I'm not leaving my kid with anyone in *his* family." She means Raven's family, of course. Seems like I managed to stop thinking about him for a full thirty seconds. "All my friends have shifts, and I can't afford a sitter. That leaves you. Don't give me any bullshit excuses, either. I know it's not like you've got a date or anything."

I start to mumble something about how low I am on the list of people she deems suitable to look after her child, but she's already giving instructions. "Pick him up at my place at eleven. Don't be late, okay? You screw this up and I'm coming after you with an axe."

I take in a breath. Raven's son. She's asking me to look after Raven's son. *Her son.* She can still rub it in, the bitch. She can still remind me that she stole my wish, whether he's there or not. That's what this is all about. Not to mention, she probably already has some other poor fool teed up. I know she wasn't always faithful. Why should she be? Another thing I could never bring myself to tell him.

"Hey!" Even through the distance of the telephone receiver, her voice burrows beneath my skin. "You got all that?"

"Sure, sure." Anything to distract my tongue from speaking the words. *But she's hanging up. You have to know, and if she won't tell you...*

If it's bad enough, she'll tell you, all right.

My voice breaks as I call out her name, hoarse from all the crying and drinking I've done tonight.

"What?" From the caution in her tone, she obviously knows what I'm going to say. Feeling put on the spot, I can't find the right way to phrase the question. But why be afraid, when there's nothing left to lose?

"Why did Raven leave?"

There it is. I can't do anything more. So she'll either tell me, or she'll hang up, or she'll advise me to go and get fucked. Most of our conversations go the way of the second or third option. But *if it's bad enough...*

"Wendy!" I spit her name into the silence at the other end of the line.

She makes me wait. And then she says, "You won, Pegasus." Her final words: "Don't be late."

She hangs up on me first, like always. I put the phone down and move over to the dresser, working up the courage to steal a glimpse of myself in the mirror... Not yet. I take off the dress, fold it up in white crepe paper, and stow it away in its white box in the wardrobe. Then I change into my pyjamas. All this while trying to get my mind around what she said.

You won, Pegasus.

All night, through waking and dreaming, these terrible three words echo inside me. It's far worse than I imagined. She was supposed to break my heart and spirit all over again, dammit, leave me with nothing to hope for. But no, she had to say it. And in a first between me and my sister, I don't doubt it's the truth.

You won, Pegasus.

What the fuck does that mean? What does it mean, now?

The alarm clock crashes in on my sleep at nine-thirty in the morning. I beat it into submission, then roll over on my back, straight into the path of the sun that streams in through the open curtains. Groaning, I cover my face with one hand. My tongue feels like I spent the night in intimate positions with a dozen furry kittens; meanwhile, inside my brain, it's as though every drop of moisture evaporated.

Water. Even as I think of it, something else begins pushing itself up from the recesses of my mind. Something I'm supposed to remember. Something else I don't want to remember. I stagger into the bathroom, find an empty glass, and turn on the tap. It takes three refills before any memories start to trickle in. I have to be at Wendy's at eleven. Shit. I have to pick up Damien. Raven's son. *Raven.* I have to find out where Raven is.

You won, Pegasus.

Then where do I pick up my prize, dammit?

I begin to laugh as I turn on the shower taps, scaring myself with the unfamiliar sound. *What is that supposed to be? You're... happy?* Me? Why is that?

Because now that it's finally morning, the shadows are beginning to fade, the shadows that have been covering my mind and my soul. Now that they're gone, I can almost start to see the way, and it's different from the one they'd convinced me was all I could have.

Raven. For the first time in five days, thinking of his face, his touch, his scent, brings me nothing but a smile. It's enough.

I arrive at Wendy's two minutes before eleven. It takes a minute extra to work up enough courage to cross the broken boards of the front step. I'm a stranger to this terrace house, never welcomed within. Besides, seeing my sister and Raven in action was a torture I'd never been willing to handle.

Now you don't have to handle it.

I hum snatches of 'Bizarre Love Triangle' under my breath as I knock on the metal screen. Soon I hear footsteps thumping towards me, the latch unbolted, and the door thrown wide. Wendy looks very pissed off and sounds very out of breath, so I smile at her as she leers at me. "You're late!"

I shrug, something inside me determined to play this as cool as the Cheshire Cat. "Whatever."

"Damien!" she hollers, not taking her eyes off me. I'm glad I'm wearing sunglasses; gives me an extra layer of protection from her glare. She won't invite me in, but that doesn't matter. Once I have Damien, there's no longer anything here that I want.

"Peggy-sis!" As soon as he sees me, he springs into my arms, before his mother has a chance to grab him.

"That was a big jump!" I say, while he plays horsey with my braid. Before I can say another word, Wendy shoves an overnight bag at me. A little toy rabbit sticks out the top, one of its ears poking me in the nose. I almost drop the backpack. *Mr. Rabbit.* My Mr. Rabbit, that she stole from me, all those years ago? What was that saying, about what goes around—?

"Wipe that stupid fucking grin off your face," she snaps. "Just make sure he's home before bedtime." She starts to turn away. Damien's bedtime is at seven-thirty. Public transport permitting, Raven was always at the hotel by eight.

Not this time you don't, Wendy. "Tomorrow morning."

She stops in her tracks. "What?"

"I said, I'll bring him back tomorrow morning."

"Oh, you will, will you? And why's that?"

As if he's able to read my mind, Damien calls out, "Daddy! Peggy-sis, I wanna see Daddy."

Shooting me a look that might have the power to kill if only I cared, she gets up in my face, her voice low. "You don't know where he is. Nobody does. If you don't have my son here by seven, I'm calling the cops."

"*You're* calling the cops?" I give her a patient smile. "Oh, I don't think so. After all, I do have three witnesses—none of whom like you very much—to an assault. You remember this, yes?"

Her eyes widen, but she's quick to smother her rage. "Fine! I could do with a night off from the little brat, anyway. Tomorrow morning. No later than ten, you got that?"

I shrug again, the cat who got the cream. "Fine."

"Fine!" she echoes, and slams the door in my face.

I walk very quickly, Damien on one hip, his backpack slung across my shoulder, until I find a tram stop bench to collapse on. He crawls off my lap and leans against me, playing with my hair more gently. As I put my head in my hands, I'm painfully aware of how my fingers are trembling. I can't believe what I just did. Or what I said. Can't believe I'm doing this when I have no idea where Raven is, when all I have as an assurance that he even cares is the word of my sister—my sister, of all people.

"What's wrong, Peggy-sis?" Damien asks in a sweet husky voice, wiping clumsily at my face. There are tears on my cheeks again. Serves me right for still believing.

He's watching me cautiously with Raven's eyes, and I can't help but smile at him. "Nothing. I'm okay." With a sniff, I wipe away the last of my tears, looking again at the little toy rabbit poking out of the bag. Dimly remembering the day that my mother gave it to me. Until now, all I could remember was the day Wendy took it. Something's changing. It has to be.

"We go see Daddy?"

I sigh, running my fingers through a strand of hair that pokes loose from my braid. "I want us to. But I'm not sure where Daddy is."

"Uncy Monty knows," he says, bouncing beside me. "Uncy Monty knows everything!"

I can't help laughing. It's probably true. And Monty doesn't work on a Saturday. "All right. Let's go find out."

As if even the gods of public transport are on our side, a

number 72 tram is already trundling up the road.

"Are you insane?" Monty yells at me, as I take a seat on the suede settee, and Damien makes a bee-line for the fairy ring of giant mushroom candles in a corner of their living room. "Don't touch those!"

Noriko flies in from the kitchen, sweeping the child protectively off the floor, shooting her partner a look as she does so. "You don't think he gets enough yelling at home?"

Monty holds up his hands in a peace offering. I take this opportunity to answer him. "Maybe. You've known me long enough to figure that one out."

With a sigh, he rakes his hands through his hair, making it stand on end.

"Tell me," I say again.

"I *did!*" he insists, stomping one foot. "I swear, I don't know where Raven is. You think I *wouldn't* tell you, if I actually—?"

"Montgomery," Noriko interrupts, and I glance up hopefully. When she uses his full name, that means business.

He shoots her a pleading look, so well-rehearsed that I almost feel sorry for him. But I've already spent too many nights alone, feeling sorry for myself. "I was *advised* not to let on."

"Stop being such a lawyer. You want me to tell him? Better yet, you should drive them."

"It's five hours away!"

Noriko puts Damien down. With a cooing noise, he promptly scuttles back to the candles. She folds her arms across her chest and sticks her nose in the air. "You take them there, or I don't talk to you again. And you know what else I don't do for you again?"

"Jesus, Nori."

I can't help but laugh. Reading between the lines, I'm guessing she just pulled out the big guns. Beyond this, I don't want to know. Instead I pick up Damien, and the bag, and smile and wave, all sweetness and light. "I'll wait in the car."

Moments later a very sulky Montgomery de Winter joins us, and the sounds of Queen fill our ears as the engine starts, and we're on our way, heading west out of the city, ever deeper into the spiral I still fear as my doom.

In just under five hours time, we turn off the Princes highway, onto a gravel road that winds its way down as far as the eye can see to a breathtaking expanse of unoccupied beach. I wake Damien and pull him onto my lap to take a better look. "Wow!" he breathes, with the awed enthusiasm only a three-year-old can muster. We're almost driving on sand when the car veers left onto a grassy track. A few hundred metres later, we come to a complete stop, outside an old two storey bluestone house. No other signs of humanity for miles and miles. My shaking returns.

"Well," says Monty, stretching. "This is it. Thought I might duck into that little pub on the highway and grab myself a counter meal. But I can come in, if you need me to."

I open my mouth, close it again. This is it, all right. The moment of truth. What if it isn't a truth I can handle? What if *he's* gone off to that little pub? What if Wendy lied, and there's someone else? What if he doesn't want me here at all?

"You don't have to," I manage to say, and open the car door.

Damien leaps out and darts about in circles. I grab the bag and crawl out stiffly. The wind is so cold here, driven by the waves that crash against the beach; it feels like they're coming up beneath my feet. From among a row of pines on a distant hill, a magpie warbles at the first signs of sunset. I shiver. Trust my courage to fail me now.

"See you tomorrow, then," Monty calls, shooting me a rueful smile as he revs the engine. "I'll pick you up around five. We've both got to be back by ten, remember, so no sleeping in."

Sleep. You're assuming I even make it past the gate, let alone the front door. "Sure." He sounds the horn once, before reversing up the track and cruising off up the gravel road.

"Damien!" I call. I won't give my legs a chance to run in the other direction, or my fickle mind a chance to change. Not that I know what I'd do, stuck out here all by myself. Go for a swim and keep going, I suppose. Or swan dive off the pier. Like mother, like son.

He comes running over, and I pick him up, grabbing him too tight as I walk through the gate to Raven's mother's house.

Raven's mother. I smile at the thought of Raven having a mother, someone he can turn to, for protection. I'm going to meet the woman who brought the tormentor of my soul into the world. What the hell am I going to say?

No time to think of that. Damien's already poking at the doorbell, and I hug him even tighter until he wiggles in my arms.

But nothing happens. Maybe no one will answer. I shake my head as the wooden door frame starts to blur. No, I can't lose it here. I have to look after Raven's little angel. He's not going to hurt me, not while I'm standing here holding this precious thing, this child whom I already love more than his own mother does.

Stop rambling. Stop thinking. Just be.

At last, the door opens wide. So does my mouth. I try to recite one of the speeches I spent all that time in the car preparing, but my mind's run empty. The woman who stands in front of me, apart from her age and the white hair that frames her pale face—well, there's no mistaking who she is. "Yes?" she asks, in a voice softened by years of illness.

Then, together, we both glance down at Damien. He looks up into the woman's face, into the eyes that are his father's and his own, and gurgles appreciatively. Tears stain her powdered cheeks as she whisks him out of my arms with a strength I didn't expect, holding him to her heart and sobbing, "Oh, my grandson, my darling little Damien." From somewhere in the distance, I hear more footsteps, fading out and in. My vision blurs again, only now no tricks of breathing or blinking will fix it. Since I don't have the responsibility of holding the child, my body's decided to let me go. At last...

"Pegasus!"

Just enough time to recognise Raven's voice. I think I catch a smile instead of a star, before darkness takes me.

5 (RAVEN)

Angel Visions

I'm looking down on the face of yet another dreaming angel...

I've been keeping a vigil by the bed, every so often running my fingers through his silky lilac hair. Five days. Doubt we've been apart so long since we met.

Absence makes the heart grow fonder.

"Pegasus." I rub my face against his limp hand. Now I don't need to be afraid of anyone overhearing my terrible secret, I feel kind of light-headed, almost champagne drunk. He must *know*. Why else would he be here? Why would he come so far to get to me, to bring me my son?

I guide his hands down to my lips—one kiss for each fingertip. Even in this deep sleep, weariness clings to him. I study the tear stains on his cheeks. Were you crying, for me? Did you miss me?

What if he doesn't wake up?

Ma said I should call a doctor. But I'm too selfish to do any such thing. If I can't have him in life, then at least, perhaps, in death—

Don't be an idiot. I scratch at my arms, deep enough to sting the skin, but I can't stay angry very long, not when he's here. I let his hand drop to the bed and turn my attention to his lips, which I trace very carefully with my thumb. This isn't the first time I've thought about kissing him. Would it be too late now?

I lean closer to his face. I could do it. Ma's outside, busy with Damien, becoming acquainted in the most practical sense with the grandchild Wendy never let her meet. I'm torn between being here and out there. But I missed you both, Pegasus, and I want you both.

No chance of being caught—

Unless he wakes up—

Which is what I wanted anyhow. This twisted logic, coupled with five days of despair and other more animalistic urges, talks me into it easy enough. I lean in even closer, try and ignore how my body trembles. I've never kissed a boy before.

His breath smells so sweet. I lick my lips; my mouth's gone dry in anticipation and desperation. Taking a deep breath, I prepare myself for the final moment—

And almost fall arse over teakettle off the bed as he opens his eyes and murmurs sleepily, "Raven, you're here."

Lucky for me, we've both got enough questions to distract us from what almost happened. For a while, Pegasus remains too disoriented to even realise where he is; as far as he can tell he's still at home, and everything's the same as it always was, before my secret got out. Wonder if he knows? I didn't tell Monty exactly why I left, and I doubt he'd be here if Wendy said anything.

"You passed out on Ma's doorstep." I watch his expression very carefully as I recount what happened. Briefly, he frowns, then lets out a heartfelt sigh.

"I'm sorry," he whispers. "I didn't mean..." Biting his lip, he stares down at his hands. Least I got to kiss his fingers before he woke up. "I—I haven't been taking very good care of myself lately." He looks into my face, and his expression hardens. "You didn't even call. I had no idea where you were, if you were okay, if you were ever coming back—"

I want to say, "Don't give up on me so easy. I've been waiting out this moment for four years."

Instead, I say, "I wanted to call, Peg. Every day. But, I just—"

"—forgot about it."

No. That isn't what I meant. I've never heard him use that spiteful tone, not on me. But before I can answer, he pushes me aside, and stands swaying above me. "I should leave."

I grab hold of his hand and yank at his arm. "No!"

A stunned silence settles in. It's hard to tell who's more surprised by my outburst, him or me. "Well," I add hastily, "how do you plan on getting home? Is Monty picking you up again?"

He nods. "Tomorrow morning."

"Looks like you're stuck here, then," I say. For tonight, at least.

He breaks out of my grip. "No, Raven! I'll only be in the way. You don't want me here, not really. Probably, your mother thinks I'm a freak." He laughs at himself. I recognise that self-derision only too well. "I brought you your son," he says at last, defeated. "Isn't that enough?"

"Do you want it to be enough?" I can't look at him anymore. This isn't how I wanted it to be.

"I already told you—" he starts to say. Yeah, I get how that one goes. *It's never been about what I want.*

"Son of a bitch." I get up and grab hold of him by the shoulders, then give him a good shake. Better this than a hug that gives away too much. "Have I been such an arsehole to you-always? I'm *asking* you what you want. Tell me, for Christ's sake, don't give me this...self-pitying shit."

I turn my back on him altogether, but there's nowhere to go short of leaving the room, which is the last thing I want, alongside this pointless argument. *Self-pitying, huh? Pot, meet kettle.* All other options exhausted, I sink down onto the bed again, my head in my hands. This is all your fault. You made me want to kiss you, my angel, my—

Eventually, I dare to glance up. He's still standing over me, crying in silence. But when he realises I've noticed, he turns aside. "What do you want me to say?" he asks.

Everything. Tell me what you feel. Tell me the story of your soul. Tell me you want me. "Tell me you'll stay," I whisper. As his shoulders start to shake, I get to my feet and spin him around, drawing him into a hug, tight against my chest. Now there's someone else I never want to let go of. "Stay. Please."

Slowly, the tears and shivers subside. I feel him grow calmer, stronger beneath my touch. So, this is it. I truly fucked up. Not like it's a first.

"Raven..."

As our eyes meet, my heart does a kind of somersault into my mouth. Then, he nods. Just once, but it's enough.

Not a minute after I get my reprieve, Damien zooms indoors. As if propelled by radar, he bounds up the stairs into the bedroom, screaming out, "Daddy!" and "Peggy-sis!" Now there are three people here to dote on him, all his Christmases have come at once.

Without hesitation, he grabs a sleeve each and drags us down into the dining room, where the aromas wafting in from the kitchen reveal that Ma's going to use this whole thing as an excuse to turn on the full dinner-time banquet. Sure enough, not a moment later, she emerges through the French doors, apron around her stomach, face flushed, newly dressed and styled in a tongue-in-cheek homage to the 50s house-mum. I can't help smiling. Stupid and childish, sure, but I actually missed her all these years.

"Well." She flutters her lashes, glancing between Pegasus and me. "You can introduce me to your friend. Raven?"

Taking her cue, I bow in mock ceremony. "Mrs. Nadja de Winter... Pegasus Belmont."

But he's not paying any attention. I hope he's not going to pass out again, but Ma follows his gaze across the hall to the grand piano taking centre-stage in the living room. "I used to play," she explains, wistfully, "before my arthritis." There's a pause. "Raven tells me you play, too. He says you're really very good."

Jesus, Ma.

"Would you care to play something for us, before dinner?"

I watch in fascination as he turns even whiter, and quickly shakes his head. "Oh, no. I'm only a keyboard player. I'm not so good."

Liar. He deliberately avoids my glare by faking a sudden interest in the drab aesthetics of the wallpaper. Sure I might be biased, but I know how good he is. And I've seen the way he stops whenever we get near a music store, transfixed by the mere sight of a grand piano. I know that's his dream. What game are you playing, Peggy? *It's never been about what I want.* Is that what you really believe?

Ma offers us a choice of coke, coffee, or juice. Damien opts for orange juice; I go with a coke. Been living on caffeine for four days straight, why break with tradition now? But Pegasus shows me up by asking if she needs a hand. She shoots me a look, dabbing at the corner of her mouth. "Well, aren't you the perfect gentleman?" Oh, here we go. "I see your mama brought you up well."

Halfway into my chair, I jerk upright again. "Would you like some help too, Ma?"

She winks at Pegasus. "Oh no, darling. We'll take care of everything." A glance at Damien. "Spend some time with your child. He's precious." And together they disappear into the kitchen.

Well, that was surreal. I blink, and help Damien into his

chair. He's already looking sleepy, all red cheeks, drooping eyelids, and a pouty lower lip. In an attempt to keep him awake, and to try and keep my mind off the old ghosts of our surroundings, I start reciting nursery rhymes, any old thing. I can't remember more than a few lines from each one, so there's something about blackbird pies and pretty maids and lost sheep and pea-green boats and moon-vaulting cows. He doesn't seem to mind, and it keeps my past embedded in the faded walls: Dad and Ma and what happened right here not long enough ago. Deep below the surface, being in this room with my son disturbs me, like nowadays I notice the difference, the wrongness, and all the similarities between this house and Wendy's.

I swear on my life, kittling, you deserve so much more. I'll give you a better life than this. I just haven't figured out how.

"I love you, Daddy." His head rests on the table, and he's smiling up at me. All that matters now is, *I've got a reason.*

And, *Don't you ever forget this.* "I love you too, angel."

Having survived the dinner table, I wander outside for a clove cigarette. It's dark, and the cold waters of the Southern Ocean shine silver on the horizon. Sounds of the sea, and sounds of cars on the distant highway, and the sound of my breath exhaling smoke and mist: this is all there is. It always did feel like looking out over the end of the world from here.

Pegasus appears in the doorway, holding a contented but still sleepy Damien. I can't do anything more than watch them from the corner of my right eye, these two exquisite, perfect creatures. I must be cheating someone, somewhere; I don't deserve a chance to love them.

"What's going on with you, Raven?" Peg asks at last.

Guess it had to come eventually. I shrug, forcing a laugh

like I don't care. "You want to know why I left."

There's another pause. Then, "No. I already know why you left."

My heart jolts in my chest. I turn my back against the railing; I can't face the lonely waves any longer. Too much. And for all this, I haven't come out of cryostasis. None of it's hit me, not yet. I've been dreading what happens when it does.

He inches forward, staring out at the sea. I know that look in his eyes, that longing. "I haven't been to the beach in nine years," he tells me.

I frown. "You live in St Kilda."

He dismisses me with a 'pfft' and a toss of his hair. "I mean the ocean. Wild, free, like this. Were you born here?"

"More or less." I shrug again. "Right about there, actually." I point at the window in front of me, through to the general direction of Ma's bedroom. "Or so they tell me. Ma reckons Dad was too wasted to get her to hospital."

"Your father was an alcoholic too, huh?"

I sniff. "Yeah, it's genetic, all right." But when I glance down at Damien, it's not self-derision I feel. God help me if I've passed my disease, my sickness, on to my son.

As though he's read my mind, Pegasus adds lightly, "That's okay. I heard somewhere that suicide's genetic too, and I'm still here."

I frown. This one's got me stumped. Who in your family—? Not his old man, I know that from bitter experience. Not his mama, who comes off as being so highly medicated it's doubtful she feels anything at all. Not Wendy either, and I'm not quite ashamed to admit I spend too much time wishing that were true. "I don't—"

His face disappears into a meld of lilac and blond hair. Then he says, "That woman you met. She's not my real mother, don't you know? She's nothing more than a shadow. Wendy calls her mother, but we never liked Wendy very much, not even when she was a little girl. I suppose I should have warned you." He shakes his head, a wry smile on his lips when he looks at me. "My mother was beautiful. She was fairytale, she was music, she was real. They did everything they could to destroy her. But she won, in the end. She walked into the ocean. And she never came back." His eyes drift back towards the sea, and he whispers tenderly, "Juliette", with that 'Zh' like French people say it. "Just like me." He smiles. "Your 'ma' seems nice. I'm glad I had the chance to meet her, even if it was against your will."

She walked into the ocean...just like me. "Do you want to be with your mama? Have I driven you to that?" No point bothering to think before I speak anymore. These are the only words that will come.

"It's going to rain." He squeezes my hand, and returns inside with my son. Not a moment later, a drop of water splashes on my wrist, and now the sky's breaking open, pelting down on the iron roof. I finish up my cigarette and follow him in.

Almost nine o'clock. Where the hell did all those hours go? Damien's bath is well past due, and I'm not so selfish I'll keep him up just to suit my wants and whims. So I take him into the bathroom, run the water, and help him undress. Only after we get through the layers of sweater and t-shirt and singlet, then pants and socks and Spiderman knickers, do I catch sight of the purple stain spread over the top of his left leg. Biggest bruise I've ever seen. *Jesus fucking Christ.* I reach out to turn off the tap, giving myself a chance to pull myself together.

"Day," I say at last, forcing out the words so they don't give too much away, "what's with the bruise on your leg?"

In answer, he hugs himself tight and stares down at the floor. My pulse keeps building, a distant drum getting nearer and louder.

"How'd you get it?"

He licks his lips. "Mama said don't tell."

I want to put out a hand to him, but I'm shaking so bad I don't dare. "Did Mama...*make* the bruise?"

"Mama's friend. Jonnyfen."

So who the hell is *Jonathan*? Maybe the suit at the bar, sliding all over her? That'll do, at least, as a face for dreaming up violent retaliations. Tarantino meets Oliver Stone for good measure, I reckon.

No. Not here, not yet. I take a deep breath, then lower him quickly but gently into the tub. "When? When did this happen?"

He stares at the wall, his back to me. "When you ran away."

When I ran away. Even my son knows I'm a coward. I start to wash him. Normally this sets off a dozen flights of fancy, but tonight he's got no play in him, no stories. Once he's dried, I put his t-shirt and knickers on, and pull him in close for a hug. At least he lets me. "This won't happen again. I promise."

I carry him into my old bedroom. Peg's already brought in his bag and made the bed look inviting. Mr. Rabbit's tucked in, and there's the book of the moment, *Where The Wild Things Are*. I lay him down, but as I sit beside him and reach for the book he darts a glance at Pegasus. "Peggy-sis, read me story! Please."

For a moment I'm upset, then delighted, then nervous. Wendy often got the same request, and refused every time. I glare at Pegasus, who sits up and hugs a spare pillow to his chest. "What? Me? Raven, I can't read him this book."

I shrug. "You know how to read, don't you?"

He frowns. "Yes, but—"

"Peggy-sis, read story!" a little voice insists. Please don't make him beg. Not like she does.

He puts out a hand and strokes Damien's cheek. Then, biting his lip, he opens the book to the first page. And I can breathe again.

After Damien and Ma are both in bed, Pegasus and I wander through the living room and out into the courtyard. My son's safe at last, and asleep. That and the buzzing in my head as the numbness wears off have settled it: now's as good a time as any to smoke this joint I've been carrying around ever since I left the city.

The rain's stopped. It's been too easy to forget how alive the sky is out here, so full of stars, those I remember and those I've forgotten. Before Melbourne claimed me, I used to spend hours lying beneath them every single night. Maybe when I was my son's age, maybe a bit older, I'd even dreamed of becoming an astronomer.

Now it's Pegasus who looks up at the sky in amazement, as I fish a lighter out of my pocket and flick it at one end of the joint. "So, when are you leaving?"

He raises a brow. "I knew you were trying to get rid of me. Five, or something."

"In the *morning*?"

He rolls his eyes as he nods; it's an ungodly hour to both of us. "Needs must when the devil drives."

I concede the point—it's certainly apt—and take another drag. "You did a pretty good job, tonight. With his bedtime story."

"Oh." He looks away, as though even in the dark he doesn't want me to know he's blushing. I burst out laughing, then he does, too. I really shouldn't have started this thing. Been so long since I smoked, it's already getting to me.

When the laughter dies out, his gaze drifts down to the

joint in my hand. "Do you want any?" I ask.

He darts another glance in my direction. "I—I don't really smoke."

Is he scared? Why? Still, far be it for me to force it on him. "Well," I hear myself saying, "you wouldn't need to smoke it yourself."

He twitches. "What do you mean?"

I shoot him an evil grin, and suck as much of the acrid smoke into my lungs as I can bear. Holding my breath, I lean carefully towards him, raising my eyebrows suggestively. For a second he pulls back, then lets me expel the smoke into his mouth. I feel my kneecaps turn to liquid as our lips brush together. Then he bursts into a fit of coughing, broken only by fragments of apology.

"It's okay," I whisper, though I don't feel as bad as I should while I stand here rubbing his back. "*I'm* sorry. I shouldn't have."

"It's not your fault." Choking out a final cough, he sinks onto the old sofa behind us. Once I finish off the joint, I'm left feeling so dizzy I'm more than ready to join him. *Love nests.* Isn't that what these are called?

I lose track of time while we sit, side by side, as I get to telling him all the constellation names my brain spits at me, improvising when nothing comes. Rather than boredom or polite indulgence, he seems impressed with how I know all this. How long's it been since I've felt so appreciated, by anyone other than my son?

I still can't bring myself to ask him why he came, but maybe it doesn't matter anymore.

Just before midnight, we go to bed. Separately.

Of course.

Sometime during the middle of the night I jerk awake, having fallen out of bed and onto the floor. *Damien.* I jump to my feet, fast enough to cause a head-spin from the pot that's still floating through my system. Sure enough, he lies sprawled sideways across the mattress, wrapped snugly in the doona, snoring softly. "Bed hog," I mumble. Anyway, it's a good opportunity to duck downstairs for a glass of water.

Halfway along the hall, I pass Pegasus's door. It's slightly ajar, but I resist the temptation to wander in. I'd probably only do something stupid. Like try and kiss him again. I grab hold of the railing, let it guide me down to the kitchen. My foot creaks on the second step, and a melody drifts up to meet me, something beautiful, like a memory from childhood...

The piano.

Starting to shake, I creep towards the living room, searching for clues to help me distinguish between reality, ghost, and reverie. Seated at the grand piano, nothing but the moonlight streaming in upon him, is Pegasus. His hair hangs loose and floats all the way down his naked back, glowing silver. If that wasn't enough, he's playing some classical piece, dark, stormy, melancholy, yearning. I've heard it before, I think. My angel...

I watch his hands and fingers glide effortlessly over the keys. Rapt in concentration, he doesn't notice my intrusion. If he makes any mistakes, I'm not good enough to pick them.

My dream...

My shaking intensifies to a violent shiver. I thought I could deny what I felt for you, all this time—no, worse, I did deny it. But no more. It still matters why you came for me, cos I'm in love with you, Peg, and I'm going to tell you, even if it kills me.

Tonight.

My heart stops beating altogether, as the song draws to a close, and he sits, panting, poised above the keys.

My hearts starts pounding in my chest, as he raises his head, and turns to look at me.

(PEGASUS) *6*

If I Should Die Before I Wake

I stop breathing as my eyes meet his. My lungs only fill with the poison of despair. I can't think in a straight line, not with him hovering under the archway, his expression unreadable in the dark. He's mad at me. That's what I hope for myself. I couldn't play anymore, anyway. My hands are shaking too badly, with a fear so intense it's crawling up from the pit of my tummy and trying to escape my mouth. I want to be sick, I'm so afraid.

Moving in slow motion, he takes a step forward, then another, and another, until he stands by the piano, gazing down upon me. Now reaching out, he takes hold of my hands, his thumbs encircling my wrists. A small sigh parts his lips, before he drops my hands in my lap and runs his fingers through my hair instead. The light shifts, to reveal his face...

I draw in a sharp breath. We were almost happy together, today. Me and him and Damien. Why did I have to be so stupid? Why did I have to go and spoil everything?

I hadn't been able to sleep at all tonight. Shortly after we went to bed, I heard a soft knock on the door, and froze, holding my breath like I'm holding it now. Don't make a sound and they won't know you're there. The logic of a child, alone and afraid in the dark. But who could it be? Raven?

"Pegasus, are you awake? May I come in?"

A female voice. His mother's. *Nadja*, I remembered from

when we were introduced, though this didn't make me any less afraid. Even if his relatives weren't anywhere near as sick and twisted as my own, it didn't mean they were powerless to hurt me.

I hesitated, for a moment. "I'm awake."

Slowly the door creaked open, and she padded in, coming to sit on the side of my bed, out of breath from her journey up the stairs. What do you want from me? I have nothing left to give.

"I won't stay," she assured me, as though sensing my fear in the dark. "I know you have to leave early in the morning." There was a pause. Then, "I just wanted to say thank you. You make him very happy. I haven't seen him lately, but I know he hasn't felt that way in a long time."

She struggled to rise from the mattress, and I felt suddenly ashamed, remembering my talk of suicide when I realised this woman probably didn't have the luxury of so much time left. "He's not good at—he doesn't talk about his feelings. Maybe only enough to make you worry." She laughed, and patted my hand. "But you know, I didn't raise him to be this way. His father—" But she stopped herself.

"You should tell him," were the words she left me with. "Tell him how I know you feel when I see the way you look at him. Life is too short. Goodnight, Pegasus."

Life is too short. The words echo in my mind. His hand cups my neck, and fingers so warm and tender disappear beneath my hair to make contact with my skin. *Your mother says I make you happy. But I have no power to do that. You're both wrong, if you think—*

He trails a fingertip across my cheek, and down to my lips and chin, before breaking contact. The expression in his eyes...it hasn't changed. Perhaps we're frozen in time. I wish we were. At least that way, I wouldn't have to deal with what I know will come next.

"Pegasus," he whispers hoarsely.

I squeeze my own eyes shut. *Don't say it, don't say it, don't say it.*

"Pegasus, I think—I think I'm—"

"No!" I leap off the piano stool and slap him across the face.

Another silence falls heavy on the room, before I realise what I've done. Hands over my mouth to prevent any further sound, I begin to back away. For a moment he just stands there, maybe more shocked than I am. But the moment he looks up, I turn and flee.

Underneath the archway, he grabs me by one wrist, pulling me against him so sharply I feel something snap inside my shoulder. Pain shoots down to my right elbow as he wraps an arm around my waist, the other round my throat, and his body presses closer from behind. This is it. He'll take what he wanted anyway. They always do. *I thought you were better than this, Raven.*

For a moment I hang limp as a rag doll in his grasp. Then something deeper, something feral, takes spark inside my soul. *I'm not* her. *You have no idea, and no right to do this to me.* I flail against him, wild enough to break free from one arm. That only allows him to spin me around so we're face to face again. All too quickly, the fire dies out. *Fine, do what you will. I don't care anymore. You can't keep me here forever, anyway. My mother's calling my name—can't you hear her? But you never did know my real name, did you. I never told you. There are lots of things I haven't told you.*

"Listen to me!" His voice reaches my ears through a choking sob. *Raven, are you crying?* Submissiveness fades to despair again. I've never seen him cry, except for that night Wendy took his son. "I just wanted to tell you," he says, letting go the arm that hurts, "I—I love you, Pegasus."

Something snaps inside my mind, like the muscle in my shoulder. From somewhere, I hear laughter. Horrible, hysterical laughter. Mocking both him and myself, such perfect fools.

"Peg?" He echoes my name, voice full of concern, his hand tilting my chin up. "Say something. Anything. Please."

He's already expecting rejection. He just needs your confirmation.

But I can't. Even though I know I'm unworthy. Even though I know I'm only a whore. Still, the ice comes creeping, across my flesh, seeping into my soul. "How can you say that? You don't know anything about me!"

I'm out of here, escaping. Where to?

I rip open the front door, and the chill night wind hits me full force. The answer comes at once, sent from the sea. *You know where to.*

Mother is calling. Go to her.

The wind moans in my ears. It's all I can hear, as my feet carry me further from the house. Moonlight guides my way through the blurry silver fields, on towards the beach. Halfway down a rocky embankment, I trip and tumble the rest of the way onto the sand. By the time I come to a stop, I'm only a few metres from the waves.

So cold. I'm hardly dressed for a winter's night at the seaside.

Not that it matters, of course. If I'm going to die like Mother, I might as well get this much right. They found her dressed in white lace and nothing more. As for me, I'm naked except for my white satin boxers. Both of us arrayed in such innocence in death, renouncing the filth and rape we'd borne through our lives.

I love you, Pegasus.

The wind dies down, and I can hear myself crying. No tears yet, but I'm wailing like Damien did the night Wendy took him. I don't want to leave you either, Raven. The realisation hits me as I stare out across the sea, into the inky blackness that seems to me to be the last great unknown. Was my mother this scared? Was she afraid to leave me behind? Did she have any idea what they'd do to me once she was gone?

Where are you, Raven? You say you love me, then why aren't you here to save me? Please, don't allow me to do this.

What's the point, in the end, of love? I struggle to my feet, wincing as I place too much pressure on my ankle. What's the point, when once he knew what I was, it would always come to this. Better now than later. After I become too attached, too deeply involved.

Too deeply involved. Oh, so that's it. Who the fuck do I think I'm kidding with this 'too deeply involved'?

I make my way towards the waves, limping to my death. How totally pathetic. How just like me.

On the edge of the shore, my foot sinks into the wet sand. I cry out in pain, falling onto my hands and knees. My hair trails in the waves.

I love you, Pegasus.

Stop it, stop it, stop it!

Even if you'd said something four years ago, I'd still be here. Even if I couldn't allow anyone else to touch me, not after we met, not after I knew. Despite how I hated myself for taking all the handouts I could get, the thought of *them* doing that to me once I'd looked into his eyes and realised I did have feelings and remembered I could be hurt was far, far worse.

And here I am, and I do hurt, more than I could have envisioned. But here is where it stops.

I ready myself and then stand up, like I don't feel any pain. Foamy water rushes over my toes as I take my first step into the waves. I thrust out my arms, close my eyes, open myself to the night's full force. Breathe in deep, clear my mind.

Once everything is gone, even his face, I throw my head back and look up at the stars. The sky returns my gaze, impassive, strong, and distant beyond imagination, making me dizzy. Both my mother when I was six years old and Raven tonight had told me, "We're made out of stars. When we die, perhaps that's where we'll return."

A beautiful sentiment. I have nothing better to stake my faith upon, since I don't believe in hell. What torture remains, outside this dimension? And physical pain is nothing. There are worse things you can do to a human being to break it, and I've passed through almost all of them. No more.

"This is the wrong ending," I whisper, and take my second step into the waves, followed more closely by a third.

So beautiful.

Like the sunset. That's what I'm seeing, beyond the night. A warm glow in the water above me, towards the sky, from which I'm falling, further down and down.

A blue glow spirals overhead, and invites me into its light. You were always better with words than me, Raven. You told me you loved me. I couldn't have said that.

Panic shivers through me as I remember. And Mother is nowhere to be found. I haven't gone far enough yet.

Do I want to go that far?

Is this what you want?

It's never been about what I want.

But now I'm asking you what you want.

You, Raven. I just want you.

"Pegasus!"

A ragged scream sounds in my ears, perhaps from a thousand miles away.

I'm wrenched from the blue glow, lifted from the arms—no, the womb—of my mother. Is this what it's like to be born? Or am I already dead?

I feel nothing but the need to get air into my lungs, the moment my head breaks the black waves. For so long, no oxygen enters—it's too late, breathe in, oh God, Raven, please—

A heartbeat pounds in my ears, and I fight and gasp for breath. Why am I here, above the water, beneath the sky, in the cold night air? Why am I alive?

I begin to choke, my chest hot and raw as I purge all the salt water from my system. Not this time, Mother. Not yet.

I'm moving along through the waves, both with them and against them, but all the while the shoreline draws closer and closer. Somebody holds me. Somebody who cares. I look down at the arm that encircles my body, and manage what I think is a smile. Then I look up into his face. *Somebody who cares. Who else would it be?*

I love you, Pegasus.

"Raven," I whisper, and fall against his body. At last the tears come to cleanse me.

Without his support, I'm too weak to stagger far across the sand before I drop to my hands and knees. Déjà vu. Only now I'm coming out, not going in.

He wraps me in a thick black coat, then pulls me into his arms. His teeth are chattering. As I lean against his chest, I can feel his body shivering from the cold and his own tears. "I'm sorry," he whispers at last, wiping at his face with a wet sleeve. "Oh, God, I'm so sorry. I—I misjudged you. I thought you wanted—"

He breaks off, helpless and confused. I *do* want you,

Raven.

"Come back to the house," he begs me. "We can just go to bed, pretend nothing happened. I mean, forget what I said to you, before— Can't we?"

Oh, Raven. Do you honestly think I tried to kill myself because I was so repulsed by those three words, coming from your mouth? I have to say something. But I can't say *that*, not yet.

He's helping me to stand.

Then say anything.

"I never thought you wanted me." I don't have the energy for more than a murmur, so I hope he can hear me.

Straight away he shoots me the most agonised look I've ever seen outside a mirror. He heard me, all right. "Tell me something," he demands, voice breaking against the tears.

I nod. Anything. Anything, except that most important thing.

"Tell me about the day we first met."

Huh? I shake my head, mystified by this question. How do I even start to tell you the truth, when I've become such an expert at hiding myself and my feelings from you?

But I have to try. He saved my life.

That means he owns you.

So what else is new?

I laugh, and set free the first words that come into my mind. I don't care whether they make any sense or not; God only knows none of it makes sense to me, and I've lived with this knowledge forever. "The first day I met you," I answer, "I decided to give up selling my body to everyone and anyone who thought they could destroy my soul, because you came along and did such a thing without even touching me."

I watch him swallow and nod awkwardly and stare down at the sand. Not the answer you were expecting, huh? Want to throw this little fish back out to sea now?

"It started with my uncle." Seems my confession's in motion, and I can't stop it. "I didn't want him to hurt me. I didn't want him to touch—" I rub at my eyes, resisting the urge to claw at the lids. The images are trickling back in, only I don't need any instant replay to tell this sorry story. "At least, mostly. It was worse when they tricked me into thinking I did. So much blood, at first. Father found out, of course, from the maid who washed the sheets. He asked me what happened, and truly, I told him." I laugh, but I've long forgotten how it felt to ever be so naive. "So he beat me. He told me I'd go to hell if this was a lie, and even more quickly if it was the truth. He accused me of leading 'decent men' to their temptation." My mother's religion was based around faith, my father's around fear and guilt. "While I lay there on the carpet of his study, he took off his belt and whipped me with it. I think before the end he was enjoying it. Later, my uncle came in and said that if I ever told again, he'd hurt me so bad I'd beg him for what he did to me next.

"I put up with it for a year or two, maybe, before I took off. But by then it was too easy to see what I was, so nothing changed, not really. I was nine years old when it started. I had nothing else." I'm trying to justify it to him, even after all this time. Even after Noriko, a professional counsellor, had spent months—years—drilling into my consciousness the assurances that none of it was my fault. We both thought I'd been starting to believe her. She'd be so disappointed to hear me talk this way.

I turn my back on him, ready to give him the chance to withdraw without guilt or the need for pity. "You see it too, don't you? I don't deserve your love. I'm just a whore. You're better off with Wendy. I'm sure she'll still have you." Sure, I'm overdoing it, but I just feel so fucking resentful now. I don't want any of this. Can you *really* see?

I want you. Only you.

"Buy her some flowers, some chocolates, take her out for

a romantic dinner at McDonalds. She'll come round. Look on the bright side. You can be with Damien anytime you want."

This last sentence is too much for him. Swearing violently, he rips me around to face him, and glares at me. Then he grabs me by the waist, hoists me over his shoulder, and carries me all the way to the house, caveman-style. I'm not sure yet who really won. But I guess I'll find out soon enough.

After hauling me up to my room, he sets me down in front of the heater, then wanders out without a word. I'm left to hug myself, as the warmth from the fan takes too long to seep into my chilled bones. Is he coming back, or abandoning me to my own misery?

When he returns he's wearing dry clothes, and carries a towel, a polar fleece top, and some track pants under one arm. Two cups of coffee balance precariously in his other hand. He dumps the clothes at my feet, then sits on the bed and slides the cups onto the bedside table. "Take those wet clothes off and get dry, for Christ's sake," he mutters, then moves away to open the window a crack. I watch as he pulls out a pack of his beloved clove cigarettes and lights one up. He doesn't want to watch me undress. I suppose I shouldn't blame him.

My heart feels leaden as I strip off the overcoat and boxers and rub myself quickly with the towel and squeeze the water out of my hair. I try not to think too much as I dress myself again. The top's a nice shade of purple; it almost matches my damp tresses. Warm, too. Now the only chill remains where heaters and towels won't reach.

I turn around. Our eyes meet right away; he's been watching me. From his pocket, he pulls out a comb and brandishes it in front of me. "Sit down. You look like a drowned rat." But his voice is kinder.

He kicks the wet clothes into the far corner, then sits behind me, and runs his hands through my hair before following it through with the comb. Soon I start to relax, despite myself.

"So beautiful," he whispers at last, allowing his fingers to brush my neck. A shiver that has nothing to do with cold runs along my spine. Then, "I want to tell you something. About—" He sighs and keeps up the grooming, though I can tell he's removed all the knots already. "About the day we met. I—I wanted—" He breaks off again, with a laugh. "I never thought you'd want me either. That's why I said yes to Wendy. That's why I didn't kiss you, when we were alone together, that first day when we met."

I put my hands up to my face, mainly with the intent to catch my heart as it makes a desperate leap for my throat.

"But I always loved you. And I still love you. You're not a whore, not to me. You're perfect."

I shuffle around to face him, take the comb from his hand, and drop it on the floor. We don't break eye contact for a long time. So many tears. Where do they all go?

Finally, he puts his arms around me and gently pulls me forward. Panic is never far away—now what does he want?

Fool. What do you think he wants? A kiss, of course.

A kiss. I've never actually kissed anyone before. Our mouths brush together, innocent enough at first, like when we shared the smoke. This time I focus hard to keep my body steady, my mind tame. Then his tongue licks at my lips, forces them apart, and finds its way inside my mouth. At first I flounder, making a complete mess of it, but once I relax and follow his lead, I find I'm able to kiss him back.

He guides me down onto the floor, lying protectively on top of me, his hands disappearing beneath the polar fleece to make contact with my skin. Oh, God. I'm certainly not cold anymore, judging by the familiar hardness between my legs, this time pressed against his belly. Nowhere to hide. You always did have a knack for getting this kind of reaction from me, Raven.

His kisses grow deeper and more desperate. I moan as his tongue spirals around my lips and penetrates my mouth with sharp little stabs, in a rhythm too much like the one I want to share with him. His fingers move up my tummy, my chest, to discover my nipples, which he promptly begins to squeeze and pull. Further down, I can feel the effect I'm having on him, too.

I giggle as his tongue tickles my neck, then gasp as his hand moves down to my crotch, running the length of my dick. He pulls down the track pants, just enough to reach inside and grab hold of me. Another little moan escapes my lips. I begin to move against him, trying to thrust up into his warm, soft palm.

For a moment he does nothing more than hold me there. But then he begins to stroke me, his breath heavy in my ear. *Oh, what am I doing, Raven? I've never wanted anyone before, let alone like this.* He raises himself up on one elbow, eyes glazing over, so pure in his need for me. *Could you make it all go away? Make me clean again. I feel cleansed when I watch you touch me.*

It hits me, how I want to say the words. I want to say them because they're true of course, but can I? Could I? "Raven." His name escapes my lips, beneath a wanton sigh.

"What?" Instantly, he freezes. "Do you want me to stop?"

In answer, I push his hand down towards my balls. "I—" *No, I can't.* The terrifying reality of it all is almost enough to bring my new-found attraction crashing around me.

He asked you if you wanted him to stop. That means if you'd said yes, he would have.

I love you, Raven. I rehearse the words in my mind, then sit up to aim a lick at his mouth, only to miss and swipe his nose instead.

With a laugh, he rubs at his nostrils, then swings me around to face in the opposite direction. Grabbing hold of my dick once more, he starts to move against me from behind, nibbling patterns from my ear down to my shoulder. He's distracting me. But I'm determined to say it. "Raven," I whisper again. "I—I think I—" Again I falter. Dammit.

"Hush." He leans into me, nuzzling my neck. "You don't need to say it yet. There's plenty of time." He laughs again. "Took me four years, after all."

A reprieve. I can feel his hardness pressed between the cheeks of my butt. Wanting to be inside me. Wanting to possess me. Thrusting against me in the rhythm I longed for, when we first began to kiss. Could I do that with him, even after they—?

"God, Pegasus, I really want to fuck you."

The words are a hot breath in my ear. Letting out a whimper, I pull away, hurrying to tuck myself into my pants. Once he realises, he grits his teeth and looks away. *I wish you were the same as all the rest. At least then I'd know what I was dealing with. And who I was expected to be.*

"Hey. Peggy...I'm sorry." I allow him to pull me out of my foetal pose, into his embrace. "I didn't mean now," he adds, once my shaking's subsided. "When you're ready. Only then."

"What if I'm never ready?" *You've seen all my other imperfections tonight, what's one more between friends?*

"Well, you'll just have to keep me in a steady supply of Kleenex, is all." He taps my nose gently. "I'm not like the others, babe."

My forced smile is fleeting. That wasn't what really bothered me. "And is that all we'd be doing?" I make myself look him right in the eye. "Fucking?"

He shrugs, ashamed, which in turn makes me ashamed—the fear that ran down my spine when he spoke those words almost made me come, right there in his hand. But I need to know.

"Let's go to bed." He switches off the heater and takes a tentative sip of his coffee, then makes a face. I look to my own cup. I'd forgotten all about it. Cold, without a doubt. Guess I was distracted. Like I'm being distracted now. Still, I can't be too antsy about it when he told me I didn't have to say the words. And he told me he loved me. I guess that will have to be enough.

It's more than I ever had, after all.

"What about Damien?" I ask, as he turns off the light and crawls into bed behind me, wrapping his arms around my waist and cuddling close.

"Oh, all the rooms have got intercoms connected to mine. Video too."

Wow. I can hardly imagine a mother so concerned for her son she'd effectively bug the entire household. "If only I'd known. I could have watched *you* undress."

He chuckles into my hair. "Well, I wasn't actually the first of my line. Which is why."

"What do you mean?"

"Raven One never made it." He sighs. "I think…maybe that's when it started, for Ma. Anyway, when she got pregnant with me, you might say she took a few extra precautions."

"Oh." But my mind's already reeling with fatalistic possibilities. You could have died. Or he, this first Raven, could have lived, and you might never have been born. Or—

"Go to sleep, Pegasus," he mutters, as though he read my thoughts.

I close my eyes, wriggling my body against his in an attempt to snuggle even more tightly together. I never thought I could feel so safe. Never thought I would.

I'm nearly asleep when he whispers so softly that I almost

don't hear him at all, "And when you're ready, we won't just be fucking. We'll be...making love."

I smile, and feather-float down and down, into a peaceful sea of dreams.

7 (RAVEN)

Beyond the Dawn

"Daddy!"

Damien lands on my stomach, knocking all the air out of me. Next thing I know, he's pulling at my hair, poking my eyes, and prodding my lips, experimenting with the magic combination required to wake me. I swat at his hands. No, not yet.

It's too late. I sit up in slow motion and reach for the switch on the bedside lamp. Too damn early as well; it's still dark out. At my side, Pegasus dreams on, most of his face obscured by the long mane of silken hair—dry by now. Even in sleep, his fingers grip the doona, and twitch. I glance at the alarm clock I might've forgotten to set. A quarter-to-five, and the memories of last night are coming back in waves. I saved your life, angel one, told you I loved you, showed you all I could to make you stay. And in fifteen minutes, give or take, you'll be nothing more than smoke and memory again.

"Breakfast!" Damien announces, as I try and make sense of the fragments rushing past my mind's eye. Visions of dragging him out of the water, refusing to believe I might already be too late, of his stories of what they did to him, before I could get there, get to him—

"Hush." I put a finger to my son's lips. "You'll wake him."

Of course I'm too selfish to wake him myself. I don't want you to go. And I don't want you to take him to her. Please don't leave me. Not after last night. Just cos I told you what

I felt, doesn't mean any of it's been magically resolved.

And is that all we'd be doing? Fucking?

What the hell do you think I meant when I said I love you?

Damien wiggles in my arms. He's reaching out towards Pegasus, for the threads of lilac that cover the pillows. "Pretty hair," he murmurs, stroking the long tresses, then leans down and plants a kiss on the top of Peg's head. In his sleep, Pegasus mumbles something in a sing-song voice and snuggles deeper into the pillow. I feel a smile cross my heart. If this is all I ever get, it could be enough.

When I'm old—or young—and dying of throat cancer or lung cancer or whatever other type of bloody cancer they warn you about on those ridiculous health labels on cigarette packs, at least I can remember a time when two boys and their son existed, together, doing whatever 'normal' families do. Definitely more than I've ever had.

"Come on, I'll fix you some cornflakes and bananas," I whisper in Damien's ear. We tiptoe from the room.

He's already on his second round when the doorbell rings. I'm standing at the sink, finishing the last of my coffee as I stack the dishwasher. My heart sinks to hear that sound. I've been hoping Monty won't come. Any excuse, really, ranging from flat tyres to last minute crises with Noriko to small, non-life-threatening accidents. I wash the last few grains out of my cup and leave it in the sink. Damn you all to hell.

"Should I get that?"

Ma's soft voice makes me jump. No. We're not home. Let's go hide behind the sofa, or upstairs in the bedroom, same as we did whenever Dad was due home from the pub.

"Sure," I say instead, though by the time I turn around she's gone. A moment later I hear cheery greetings passing between the three of them, Monty, Ma, and Damien. What are you sounding so chirpy about? He's only come to take you away from me. Would that make you happy? To go back to your mama, that bitch who's done her best to destroy us both?

Ugh. I rub at my hair. No, I'm not going to let myself even think that way. Bad enough that she fights with him around me—the lesser evil of all her sins, apparently. I won't stoop to her level. Me? I'm better than that. Which is why I'm just going to stand here and let you both leave, without uttering a single word.

"Hey there, sunshine." Monty lurches into the dining room as I march across to clean up the leftovers.

"Hello." I drop the bowl into the sink, with enough force to nearly break it. I want to smash something, but I can't, not here. Ma doesn't deserve that. It would resurrect too many ghosts from her own painful past, of what made her sick. What I really need right now is a drink.

If Monty notices my gloom, he ignores it. "Where's Peg?" I don't bother answering. "Not still asleep?" He sighs and takes off his glasses to polish them on his suit. One of his larger hints at frustration. "Better go wake sleeping beauty, I guess."

"I'll do it." Surprised by the possessive tone in my voice, I'm glad of a reason to shove past him and disappear up the stairs. But just as I reach the landing, the floor above us creaks, and Pegasus appears, looking down on us, looping his hair into a make-shift ponytail.

"Well, look what crawled out of bed," Monty drawls. "Are we ready, Cinderella?"

He giggles as Pegasus tells him, in no uncertain terms, to go and get fucked. "Oh, is that so? I'd be careful how you talk to me, young master Belmont. I do have certain secrets of yours under wraps, after all." I want to slap that grin off his face. What secrets? His mama? What his family did to him? What? What the hell do you know that I don't?

"All things die eventually," Pegasus murmurs, pushing his way between us. "Even secrets."

He moves past us into the kitchen, and Monty turns that grin on me. So that's what your secrets were about, huh? I turn my back on all of them. I've gotta get out of here, before the facade cracks and all the anger and frustration and confusion and despair and hopelessness seeps out like poison gas from a rock. "I should get Damien's stuff together," I mutter, but Ma appears, brandishing the backpack. There's Mr. Rabbit, poking out the top, and I envy him his stuffed oblivion.

"Oh, no need, darling. I took care of it already." Fuck. "And some of your things are over there, by the sofa. At least, what I thought you might want to take with you."

Take with me? Where am I going?

I glance up—now they're all gathered in the living room, watching me expectantly. I crush the little flower of hope that trembles to life inside my chest. "I'm not coming with you."

You could cut the air with a knife after that announcement. Ma lets out a sigh of familiar exasperation, and Damien starts mumbling, "Daddy, Daddy," under his breath.

"Oh, no you don't," Monty growls. "You're not doing this to me. The last time I walked out the door with him under my arm and left you behind, he screamed loud enough to wake the dead. I'm a goddamn defence attorney; I get enough people making me feel like I'm the devil without having a kid on my case." He glowers at Pegasus. "Dammit, I thought that was the whole reason you came here."

You at least knew why, then. I shove my hands deep in my pockets. Could really do with a cigarette as well, but I smoked my last one before we fell asleep, too few hours ago. Before we kissed and fell asleep.

Peg says nothing, just takes a seat beside the suitcase that

Ma got ready. I can't even pretend to ignore him when he's watching me like this. "I'm not coming with you," I say again, but the words don't carry half the conviction.

Monty lets out a noise of disgust. "You hear that? He's not coming. All righty then, might as well get this show on the road. Because this is going to be so much fun, I can tell." He makes a half-hearted grab for Damien, who clambers up onto Pegasus and immediately begins to howl. Just like you knew he would, you bastard.

Ma mutters something under her breath, and shuffles off down the hall. Pegasus glares at me, his arms wrapped protectively around my son. I keep looking from him to Damien, waiting for the little hole in the ground to open up and swallow me. Stop it, damn you. Sure, I said I loved you. But that doesn't mean—

Doesn't mean I'd stay with you?

That's so absurd, I almost laugh. *You're insane, Raven. And an arsehole. What's keeping you here? Get in the car, make them all happy, go ride off into the sunrise and live your life.*

But I can't. Going back there means I've gotta face the real world for what it is—a world where my son's own mama is responsible for his torture, a world where the one I love gets raped and abused, a world where my feelings are locked in a cage, where I don't dare to feel hope or joy.

And you're doing that here? Expressing your feelings? Daring to feel hope, daring to feel joy?

Sure I am. Look at where that got me, too. "Please," I whisper. "Pegasus…"

As though noticing the effect Pegasus is having, Damien swallows his tears and wiggles around. Now they both stare me out, not making a sound, both of them looking so sad and so betrayed, by me.

Everything I said last night must seem like a lie right now.

I struggle against giving in. But he already knows how

close I am to breaking. He's smiling at me.

"Well, shit," I mutter, trying to sound as casual as possible, "if it means that much to you all." I hoist up my suitcase, not bothering to check what Ma thought I might need. Material possessions never mattered all that much. And yet, there I was, willing to let the only ones who do matter walk out the door with barely a good-bye.

"Hallelujah!" Monty throws his palms in the air, then heads for the door. Damien bounces out after him, though he looks back once to make sure I'm coming. If I ever had half his intuition, I don't anymore.

"I'll help you, Raven," Pegasus says softly, and reaches out to take the backpack. We're standing too close together for me to resist a quick kiss on the lips. He smiles and lowers his head, blushing again. "Later," he whispers in my ear, "we'll have all the time in the world. I promise."

My turn to smile, though it takes my lips a moment to remember how it goes.

"At least there will be a later," he adds thoughtfully, then shoots a glance down the hall. "Will I wait for you in the car?"

I nod, just once. His fingertips brush mine on his way out. This time it's me who looks back to make sure he doesn't just disappear, somehow. I need to trust you, Peg, cos I've got no idea what I'm doing in any of this.

But I bet you did. I can't help grinning, as I shuffle off to her bedroom to say my good-byes to Ma. I only hope they won't need to last me through another five years.

The familiar sounds of *A Night At The Opera* bombard my eardrums as I open the front door driver's seat. Monty looks up, suspicious that I've changed my mind again, but all I want to change is the goddamn CD.

"Here." I toss one of the discs I salvaged into his lap. "You're outvoted. Freddy's off the air till further notice." Then I open the rear passenger door and squeeze in between Damien and Pegasus.

Monty examines the cover before he reverses out of the driveway. "Nick Cave. Great. Like the tone for the day wasn't already set in stone."

We turn onto the highway as the opening strum of 'Papa Won't Leave You Henry' floods the car. "So," says Pegasus, "how long have you been on the road now?"

"Oh, don't worry your pretty little head about me. I spent the night at a nice little joint in Portland. Have to take Nori there someday; she likes the ocean. And fish. Anyway, looks like I'm doing much better than you two. Can't imagine you got much sleep at all, with the way Raven snores."

"Shut up!" I snap. Damien giggles.

Pegasus changes the subject again. "So what case are you working on that drags you out on a Sunday?" I turn to look at him, surprised by his interest. Then again, he's tight enough with Monty to share secrets with him that he won't share with me.

Monty sighs, running a hand through his already slicked hair. "There was a man," he starts, as though he's telling a story. "You might have read about him in the papers a year or two back? Shot his wife and five kids with a rifle while they slept. Archie Springer, the Catholic charity dude?"

Pegasus doesn't remember this, but I do. For a minute or two, I might have contemplated the possibility of doing something similar to Wendy—though never to my own son. "So, how *do* you go about getting people to feel sorry for a psychopathic scumbag?" I ask.

"Well, there is his side of the story," Monty explains, then waits patiently.

"Which is?"

"It was supposed to be a murder-suicide, not just a murder.

He, er, ran out of bullets. One kid less and he woulda made it."

I shake my head, laughing despite myself. Pegasus only shrugs. "Guess that's what you get for being Catholic," he murmurs, then snuggles into my shoulder. Not a moment later, I lean in against him, and let my hand drift into his lap. In the rear-view mirror, Monty raises a brow suggestively. I flip him off, before closing my eyes. At my side, Damien's already snoring.

They can keep their 'normal' families. This is perfection.

The loud ding of a tram bell jerks me out of sleep. I wrinkle my nose at the smells of exhaust that seep in through the windows. Pegasus is awake already. As I straighten up, he brushes the hair out of my face. "Where are we?"

"Stuck in traffic," Monty grumbles, then returns to swearing under his breath. "Damn Neanderthals!" he yells, as a Toorak tractor surges in front of us, forcing him to slam on the brakes. Yeah, right. That would be why my frequent state of insobriety isn't the only reason I never bothered getting my license.

"Look, guys," he says, turning around as the lights up ahead change to red. "It's nearly ten already. I've still got to find parking, but we're right near Spencer Street. Would you mind?"

"Sure," says Pegasus, and I say, "No." When he finally notices me glaring at him, he only winks and says, "It's a Sunday morning. We'll have the whole train to ourselves."

Hearing the magic word, Damien rouses instantly, muttering, "Train, train..."

"You'll probably live to regret this," I say with a knowing smile, as we gather up our things and prepare to escape the car.

I will give him credit, though—the carriage is empty, apart from a gaggle of teenage girls up the front. I deliberately steer us to a seat down the other end.

Meanwhile, Damien's so over the moon he's gone speechless. Even waiting on the platform was a thrill; now he's actually on a train, he's got so much to say, he doesn't know where to begin. I laugh as he clambers onto my lap and makes a face against the window. Pegasus sits across from us, watching on with a strange little smile.

So we spend most of the journey with him pointing out every bit of scenery and observing all the passengers, only losing his tongue when a woman and her little girl get on. Pegasus giggles behind the safety of his sunglasses. "Who does that remind me of, hmm?"

But his smile morphs into a sneer a few stops later, as the girls from the front of the carriage suddenly converge on us and park their butts in the seats across the aisle. Subtle. All right, here we go. Money, cigarettes, or drugs? You're too late for any of the above, I'm afraid. But there's plenty of free angst. Want some?

"Hiii," says a blonde, her red greasy lips parting to a horsey grin. "What a gorgeous little boy. Is he yours?"

"Oh," I say, feeling guilty. Having a kid's kind of like walking a dog. People make conversation, not cos they're after anything in particular, just to admire. Especially women.

"What's his name?" another chimes in, green eyes smiling beneath burgundy pixie hair, plastic rose petals adorning her slender wrists and ankles. "How old is he?"

"Uh, Damien. He's almost four, aren't you, kittling?"

"What's *your* name?" asks a brunette, looking down her freckled snout at me.

I'm not used to this kind of attention, even if it is all on account of the boy. "Raven."

"Mmm." Seems she approves. "Now I know where the little one gets his good looks from."

This causes a new round of cackles and looks of scandalised admiration. Dammit. I look down at my son, down at my feet. Why can't they leave me alone?

Little miss rose pixie is asking if she can cuddle him. I can't think of any good reason why not, so long as she doesn't run off with him. But the minute she takes him in her arms, he begins to squirm. "He's just shy. It's okay, Day." I try and encourage them. Big mistake. He lets out a scream as she props him in her lap.

"Ooh." She pulls back, and her friends screw up their faces. As for Damien, he doesn't stop screaming or let me get near him till Pegasus lifts him off the girl. Straight away he snuggles down, perfectly content, and gazes out the window again.

Well, how about that?

Pegasus pushes his sunglasses onto his head, and shoots them all a look that makes even me a little afraid. "He's not shy. Not if you know how to do it right." Then he, too, returns his attention to the window.

Defeated, the girls traipse back to their end of the carriage, muttering, "Probably gay", and "Eww!" with as much subtlety as those in possession of a terminally low IQ can muster. The pixie miss casts me a regretful, apologetic look as she trails after them in silence. I feel compelled to offer her a wave. Thank God that's over.

I turn to Pegasus and Damien, but both of them are ignoring me pretty well. "Thanks, Peg," I tell him anyway, and reach for his hand. He jerks it out of my reach, then looks around, as though to make sure no one else is watching. Would me being affectionate with you in public bother you that much?

"What?" I demand.

"*'What's your name?'*" he repeats in a smarmy, slutty tone, mimicking the brunette. "*'Mmm. Now I know where he gets his good looks.'*" He fakes one of their laughs, then cuts it short, wiping the sneer from his mouth and turning away till his nose presses right against the glass.

For a moment I'm stunned into silence. You're jealous? Of *them*? "Silly," I mutter, dismissively. "They're just some girls."

"'Just some girls' who think nothing about sauntering up here and hitting on you, right in front of me. Thinking they can hold your son, ask you your name—" He frowns.

"That bothers you?" I'm trying very hard not to smile. Even if it is ridiculous.

"No, Raven." At least he's looking at me. "What bothers me is how much you got off on the whole thing, how you were like, '*Oh, look at what a fucking God's gift to women I am.*'"

All right, no, I wasn't stunned before, but now I am. Am I meant to be upset, apologetic, or what?

"You don't care who you're with," he continues in a low voice, "so long as they're better than no one, or better than Wendy. So long as they pretend the whole fucking universe revolves around you. This is the only way I ever stood a chance, yes? Well, if this is your price, fuck it, I'm not paying. You're not my—"

He forces himself to stop. But I can already guess where that was going. *You're not my uncle*, or *you're not my old man*, or *someone who did all those God-awful things to me*. Well, nice to know you think of your Raven so highly.

"So we're back where we started," is how he ends it instead.

I wait it out, giving myself a chance to compose my thoughts and emotions before I dare bring myself to speak. Anger fades through doubt into sadness. What if he's telling the truth? *You don't care who you're with.* Is that the sort of person I am? What sort of person am I?

"Are you finished?" I ask at last, wringing my hands together and cracking my knuckles.

He moves sideways, letting Damien slide onto his seat. "Whatever."

But the moment he starts to rise, I yank at his ponytail and use it to pull him close to me. "*Are...you...finished?*"

"Yes!" He spits the answer in my face.

"Good." I take hold of his neck instead and draw him even closer, into a kiss. Only the old anger drives me, to begin with. And then, my desperation takes control.

At last, we pull apart. He leans forward, panting, his forehead pressed against mine, two pulse points meeting. "You promised me all the time in the world," I remind him. "That's the only payment I'll hold you to. And I don't think I'm God's gift to women—unless God's a clown, that is—and I do care about you and I do want them all to know that you're mine and—" I close my eyes, take a breath, open them again. "And I do love you, Pegasus."

He finds his way up onto his seat, using Damien as some kind of emotional shield so I can't see his face. But I can see this is our stop. "Home sweet home."

I scoop up our luggage, using my free hand to steady Pegasus and my son as the train screeches to a halt. A quick glance around the carriage reveals several sets of judgemental eyes trained in our direction, all set in the same appalled expression, as if we just committed some atrocious act like sacrificing a goat and drinking its blood, or something. I lead both my loves quickly through the door. I'm not afraid of any of you.

Even after the train's long gone and we're out of the station, I haven't let go of his hand.

It's my decision to take Damien to Wendy's on my own, though the bitch either isn't out of bed yet or still isn't home when Pegasus calls. I'm really not looking forward to this. Which is truly the understatement of the century. I don't want her to take my child. I don't want to go back to that horrible house. I don't want her to tell me what happens next.

We never discussed it, so I've honestly got no idea what happens between me and Damien now that she and I— Now that Pegasus and I—

But all of my guesses leave me cold, enough to make me wish I'd let us both go last night, let him drag me down through the waves, like a Siren, a Rusalka.

I linger on the doorstep. I can't ring the bell. I can't do anything other than hold my son too close. I'm not going to cry, not in front of her.

"What's wrong, Daddy?" a little voice asks in my ear.

I take in a deep breath, then set him on the step and kneel beside him. I can't think what to say. I was never prepared for any of this, I was just—

I was just too damn selfish.

"Listen, Day," I begin, wiping at my nose. "Daddy's gotta tell you something. It's really important, and you might not understand, but you've gotta remember it, okay?"

"Daddy's got a secret!" he calls out. For a horrible moment, I'm paranoid he'll alert Wendy. I clamp my hand over his mouth.

"Yeah, all right, it's a secret, which means you don't go screaming it in the street for the world to hear, okay?" Or soulless demons like your mama.

I wait for him to nod before letting go his mouth. Straight away he whispers, in a conspiratorial tone, "Daddy loves Peggy-sis!"

I'm so blown away by this observation I almost fall over backwards. Might be better off leaning on my knees. "What— what makes you say that?"

He shrugs, looking away shyly. I've almost given up, when

he finally says, "Well, I love Peggy-sis. I love Peggy-sis more than Mama. Does that mean I'm bad?"

"No, kittling. You're an angel, and angels are never bad." I'm only a little ashamed of myself for seeing this as some kind of victory. *Do you hear that Wendy? Even your son hates you. I win.*

Lowering my head, I pull him close again. "And I love you, too. Forever and always. But, Daddy…might not get to see you much anymore. Not for a little bit." *Don't cry, don't you dare fucking cry.* For the first time, the true meaning of these words hits home.

My son puts his arms around me and snuggles into my neck. 'Angel' is right. *How will I ever do any of this without you?*

As if to answer my question, he lets go and says happily, "When I get big, I want Peggy-sis hair!"

I can't help a laugh, but it all drains away the minute the door opens. Wendy towers over us, leering at me with pure contempt.

I swore I'd never fight with her in front of my son, same as I promised him I wouldn't ask about Jonathan and the bruises. So, the minute she starts with the expletives and the accusations, I walk. How very fucking big of me.

Back to Monty's. Back to my old habits, clutching a bottle of scotch, a bottle of coke, and two cans of Midori and lemonade. I wait anxiously on the doorstep after ringing the bell, ears pricked for any signs of life. Hearing nothing, I ring the bell again, then knock: once, twice, three times. *Where are you, Pegasus? Did you change your mind so soon? Come to your senses?*

I pound on the door. Panic rises in my chest, constricts around my lungs. I fall against the stained glass panel, breathing in quick, shallow gasps, like I never stopped pretending I could keep it all at bay. Why the fuck did I come back here? Please, let me in.

One last time, I stab the buzzer. The door springs ajar, so that I fall through into the hallway. First I gather up the alcohol, then look at Pegasus, who stands above me with a bemused grin on his face, wearing only a red towel dressing gown covered in pictures of kittens and Kanji characters. "Sorry," he says, "I was in the bath. Asleep in the bath, actually."

I look to the floor. Little droplets are forming on the carpet. But it isn't raining out there.

Only here, in my mind. The storm's broken. Now it's washing me away, and there's nothing I can do. Nothing. He may hate her just as well, but she's always going to win cos she's his mama, and—and—

You won't be seeing him again until you're in hell.

—but I already am, goddammit.

It's only when Peg puts his arms around me that I realise how badly I've broken. He covers my forehead and neck with kisses, whispering some sort of sing-song melody till I go quiet and lie against him, listening to his heartbeat and the words. They're French.

"Are you okay?" he whispers at last.

"No." I'm not going to lie to him, I'm through lying to him. "What was your song?"

He flutters his lashes. "Oh, that. I don't remember what it's called. My mother used to sing it to me when I was small. Pretty catchy, huh?"

I let out a heartbroken sigh, and pull him up with me. Nose to nose, we stand together, holding each other's hands. I can't bear it anymore. I'm glad he put off what might've happened last night. Whenever I look at him, I'm so afraid to lose him too, I can't bear to think about what might happen if we actually—

"Yeah." I force out a smile and let him go to gather up the

supplies. "If you know how to do it right." My smile is a touch more genuine, as I lead him into the kitchen.

A few hours later, Monty and Noriko arrive home with food. We sit in silence, eating our Japanese take-outs—it's permanent take-outs here, I'm told; at least till the long-running dispute between the two of them as to whose turn it was to actually do the cooking and the washing-up's been resolved.

"How long has this been going on?" Pegasus feels obliged to ask.

There's a pregnant pause, before Monty looks up from his chopsticks and says calmly, "Two months, four days, six hours."

"Oh." Pegasus and I exchange a knowing look. Probably as good a time as any to go for the scotch. I bring the bottles and some glasses back to the table, juggling the can of Midori and lemonade under an elbow. Drinking may not solve anything—I know that from harsh experience—but at least it lets you fool yourself into thinking that it does.

After a few glasses of scotch, everyone's feeling more chatty, except for Monty, who'd rather brood over his impending case. Noriko tells us we're both welcome to stay the night, once they've drunk too much to drive Peg home, and this leads to a brief argument about who gets the sofa. He wins—guess he's got more experience being the humble guest than I do. Although, after spending the afternoon asleep in each other's arms, I don't feel too guilty.

We're in the kitchen together, he and I, having washed up and moved on to a tea-towel fight, when the doorbell rings. He drifts out towards the hall as I start to stack the glasses, pretending I don't care who it is.

"Ted!" we hear Monty exclaim, sounding pleasantly surprised. *See? Just a friend, paying a visit. Nothing for you to concern yourself with*. Then, "How's life at the old Barton and sons?"

Barton and sons. A law firm. How do I know that? Where do I know that name?

A law firm...the same one used by Wendy's parents.

The realisation hits just as Monty appears beside Pegasus in the doorway, not quite making eye contact. "Hey. Someone's here for you."

No doubt my chances of scoring a cameo in a George Romero flick would be pretty high as I trudge towards the front door. On my way past, Pegasus's hand brushes mine, but I shake off his touch.

A man with the jowls of a St. Bernard waits outside, dressed in a suit despite the late hour and the fact it's a Sunday. He's got a few years on Monty, and his thin lips and serial-killer cold eyes remind me of Peg's old man. "Raven de Winter?" he asks redundantly, plucking a stray rose petal off his jacket with distaste.

"Yes," I answer anyway, switching to auto-pilot. A strange sense of déjà vu, of being completely powerless, washes over me. Just like in high school, with the teachers, who thought they had me figured out based on the cut of my fringe and what bands I listened to.

He starts fishing through his briefcase, making it all look very official. "A few matters, so I'll try to keep it short. First—" he thrusts a document into my face "—your presence is required at the family court next Tuesday at eleven a.m. sharp. Second—" he hands me another page "—I have here a temporary restraining order, which decrees that you are not allowed to visit, make contact with any resident of, or come within five-hundred metres of the occupants or their residency at 112 Portugal Terrace, specifically those persons being Ms. Wendy Delaware or Damien de Winter. Do you understand?"

"Yes." No. No, I don't fucking understand. How can you

march round here and toss me this fucking worthless piece of paper that tells me I'm not allowed to see my son?

"Good." He beams, somewhere between butcher and politician. "Then I'll see you at eleven a.m. next Tuesday. Better bring a good lawyer, though I don't recommend Monty personally, you understand."

I've got no idea how long Peg's been standing behind me, but now I hear his voice, speaking the words that I can't say. "Just get the fuck out of our house." With that, he slams the door in the lawyer's face.

For a moment nothing, nothing at all. Then I let the papers fall from my hands. I figured I'd be angry, but I just feel—

What? I wish I could be angry, build myself up to a whirlwind of fire and ashes. Anything would be better than this slow black hole void. Pegasus grasps my shoulders, eyes wide, pleading with me to lose myself in them, in him, in his soul. Why would you offer me that, when you know it's not what you want yourself?

I can't feel, not anything. Not with those words buzzing around my brain, amplifying and multiplying upon themselves, till a million clones crowd my head, all babbling about family courts and times and addresses and restraining orders and cackling maniacally as they tell me what this really means, of course, is that I'll never be able to see my precious little angel ever again. Through the haze, Peg's lips are moving, but echoes of the evil laughter take the place of whatever he's trying to say.

I search the corners of my mind, desperate for some kind of sanctuary. Instead I stumble into an even darker recess—a red flash, and I'm wrenched back to a memory of the night we 'created' Damien, to when I could fool myself, although in truth Wendy was the one doing the fooling this time around. Forced to watch myself from the outside, being with her in that way I always despised, I see her transform as she starts to climax, putrefaction unfolding in fast-forward. Maggots bloom from her every pore, and drift out of her cunt instead of cum. Before I can blink, they're swarming across my dick, crawling up my torso, coming to eat their way through my ears and up my nostrils, into my brain—

Jesus. I've got no idea if I'm still breathing, or whether the scream that's reverberating through my mind managed to make it out of my mouth...whether I'm there or here.

But now I'm someplace different again. I recognise this place, where even the roses are white. I'm at the hospital. And, I know what day it is. September the sixth. Damien's birthday. Damien's very first birthday.

I find myself in the maternity ward, not entirely sure what new tricks my brain's got planned for me this time. On the surface, at least, everything about the memory plays out as normal. The nurse, a curvaceous black girl sporting a perfect smile, ushers me through into a private room. Only the best for Wendy and their grandchild. I step inside, but it's empty.

No, these are just first impressions, shallow of truth. I can't see the bed cos it's hidden by some kind of curtain that blends into the walls like smoke. I approach it as that last little voice of sanity begs me to stop—just turn, and run.

There is nowhere left to run. Another voice in my mind, a powerful voice. It overrides my terror, drawing me down into cosy paralysis. All I can do is watch, as my hand lifts up the curtain before me—

—and there on the bed sits my son, same as he looked the day he was born. It's been nearly four years, so I've almost forgotten such pure torment. It runs through my veins, pinpricks of sweetest agony, as I finally come to realise, in that tiny little blanket, that little creature, that little version of me—only so much more perfect—is the one thing that's going to save my life. That will give me a reason to keep living, after all others have become null and void. God's mocking me, all right.

In the dream, I turn to his mama, and find myself reaching out to stroke the long ice-blonde hair. No, wait—that's wrong. Wendy cut her hair once she started to get fat, and it was never that shade of blonde. The face that looks up at me glows with a pale angelic smile, and I recognise its voice as the one that drove off all my fears. "Raven," it says.

Pegasus…

The carpet reels beneath me. "Raven!" Now he's calling out my name.

Are we in the real world yet? I dash down the hall, and wrestle with the handle of the toilet door. Which layer of hell is this?

As it gives way, I fall in front of the bowl like it's an altar, so violently sick that it blocks out all other pain.

Therefore I never want it to stop.

8 (PEGASUS)

Blood Makes Noise...

I wish they would just stop.

I wish it would all just stop.

I lie on the sofa, staring at my reflection in the mirror of the blank TV. No light, no sound, no point.

They wouldn't allow me to see Raven, after he was sick. But I heard them talking, in the kitchen, once they thought I wasn't around to hear.

"Are you taking the case?" Noriko asked.

"I don't know, Nori," Monty replied, standing over the sink with his head down, arms folded beneath him. "It's hardly my area of speciality. Besides, even if I am free on Tuesday—"

"What? He needs you. You're *family*."

"Yeah? And what if I lose, huh? Could you imagine? He'd never forgive me. I couldn't deal with that. Fuck, I never asked for this kind of responsibility!" He seemed close to breaking, but I couldn't feel any pity for him. He was the one who'd told me not to see Raven. That it wasn't a good idea. He was the one who invited that son of a bitch in at the door, to tell Raven, to tell him—

"Yeah, it's not like you lawyers have a thing for dealing with responsibility, huh?" she said then, crossing her arms over her chest.

Monty rubbed at his hair, then straightened up. "There's

a colleague of mine—you met Judy. She's had more experience with these sort of things. I'll put her onto it."

"You don't think he's going to win, do you?"

They exchanged a glance, Monty open-mouthed but silent. Go on, say it, you bastard. Tell the truth.

"No," he said. And then they both turned to see me standing there, like two parents caught out playing Santa at Christmas. I ran off. Neither of them followed.

So here I sit, in the silence of my doom, broken only by her screams and his grunts and their moans coming from down the hall. They're fucking, like nothing happened. You don't care. Neither of you care. And you call yourself his family? You make me sick. I'm the only one who cares.

I'm the only one who cares, and yet here I am, just sitting here, staring off into space. To hell with this. I'm more than these fears.

I fight my way out of the doona and my numbness and follow the carpet down the hallway. With every step, the screaming and moaning and grunting and panting grows louder. I have no idea which room is Raven's. But at least I know which one to avoid.

The first door on the left, past the toilet where he was sick, is the first door I try. I knock gently to announce my entrance. Then I cautiously turn the handle. The door swings open, and I step inside.

My eyes don't even need to adjust to the light; white candles crowd the small space, burning constantly into the night, burning like they've always been here, as though, if their flames were ever to die, another more precious thing might die with them. Definitely not Raven's room.

I glance about the walls, feeling like an assassin who crept into a house, only to find the occupants already dead, massacred in their sleep. A cot sits in one corner, its edges draped with tiny crocheted clothes. A mobile hangs over it, plush figures singing a music-box lullaby, a sad and lonely sound.

As I sneak towards the dressing table, I spy a framed photo of Monty and Noriko, her belly round and big. And a letter, written in Japanese. I don't need to understand any of the words to figure out what's gone on here. Noriko's baby. So, she could get pregnant once. They lost a child, too.

They should know better, then. I leave the room, closing the door quietly behind me.

Past the laundry, beyond the bathroom, one last room, unaccounted for. Once again, I start to knock, when from inside I hear something. A soft hum.

"Raven, are you awake?" I ask the stupid question. "Can I come in?"

There's a long pause. Just when I'm about to either turn away and return to my gloom, or open the door and walk right on in anyway, there comes a "Sure...", so faint I wonder if I imagined it.

I step into the room. This time the harsh light stings my eyes. I squint at the bedside table, noticing the razor blade, covered with blood—and, too, the sheets—

And Raven.

"I—I couldn't sleep," I tell him. He's lying on the bed, semi-naked, hands folded behind his head, staring blankly at the ceiling. Every now and then he breaks in and out of that random humming again, each time finding a different tune. I want to hold him, I want to touch him, I want to—

But my feet seem to have grown roots down through the carpet. So instead I watch the red teardrops trail down his chest.

"Yeah, I knew there was a reason I left this place first chance I got." He chuckles without warmth as Monty and Noriko both give out a long final grunt-and-scream-and-sigh-and-moan, and everything returns to silence.

I take a seat beside him on the edge of the mattress, unable and unwilling to take my eyes off the blood. "Are they always this bad?"

"Usually. For about three weeks of the month." He grimaces. "And then, they're worse."

The implications of this timing make me cringe. "Eww."

He laughs. "I take it you're not into blood?"

"Not like that," I start to say, then look into his face. He's staring straight at me. I swallow; my mouth's begun to water. Ashamed of my shame, I feign a sudden interest in the Munch reprint hanging off the closet, and start to babble as fast as my mouth can save me. "Are you okay? They told me to let you—I wanted to see you—I didn't know what to do, I still don't, but I just wanted to make you—make everything—" At last my brain catches up with my tongue. I put a hand to my face. I must sound like an idiot. A stupid child. What am I trying to say?

"You cut yourself," I whisper at last, and my gaze wanders back to the slashes under his nipples. Around these new wounds, older scars poke through, and scabs the same as the one I touched, that night we first touched—

"Yeah, well." He tries to shrug it off. "I'll clean up the mess in the morning. I couldn't sleep either, okay." He glares at the ceiling again, then mutters, "I don't want to dream."

Anything I say tonight will come out wrong. I didn't come here to fight with you, Raven. I just want you to understand—

"Tell me why you do it," I say, my fringe trailing in the blood as I lean closer to his body. "Tell me what it makes you feel. I'm...curious."

Tell me you want me to do this to you.

No! The part of me that's always afraid cowers in a corner of my mind, as I lower my head completely and place my lips over his nipple. Gently, slowly, I begin to lick and suck at the broken skin. Soon, the sweetness of his blood washes over my tongue, down my throat.

This time, the response is immediate. With a shudder, he grabs at my hair and tries to pry me off, but this is before he realises he's enjoying it too much. His fingers grow limp, and he starts to breathe in short, ragged gasps—nothing as melodramatic as the fuss Noriko and Monty kicked up earlier.

I move down to his tummy, following my tongue, to discover another fresh cut, this one much deeper. He lets out a moan, and my mind trembles as lust flares beneath my skin. Why now? Why am I okay with this now? Because he has nothing left? Or because I'm so in control here, or at least feel that I am?

As if to confirm my thoughts, he whispers, "I'm not in control...of myself. Or anything. Don't want to be— Please—" He gasps again as I nibble at his belly, leaving ghosts of my teeth in the blood to mark out where I've been. "I need this to remember—oh, God—"

I strip off my own t-shirt and lie against him, press against him, naked against all the blood, feeling our hearts beat in sync. "I want to do it," I beg hoarsely.

After a moment, he nods and hands me the blade from the bedside table.

I trace my way down the centre of his torso with a fingertip, as though mapping out the imaginary cut, and pausing at the waistband of his track pants. I wonder... "Do you ever—?" I ask, trailing off as we look to where my hand rests, upon his crotch.

"I'm not that brave," he says, and we laugh, but it's a laugh without innocence, without happiness, without sanity or judgement. I draw the razor's edge carefully along the side of his throat. His eyes roll back, turning inwards to look upon pure ecstasy.

"Does this turn you on, Raven?" I ask, as I begin to suckle from his neck.

"You've got your hand on my dick, you tell me." But when our breathing grows too fast and too heavy, always keeping the perfect rhythm, he rolls over on top of me and straddles my torso, staring down into my face.

His eyes. His eyes tell me I'm fooling myself, that there's nothing more I can do. I'm playing with a wolf like a child plays with a puppy. Sooner or later, I'll get bitten. But no tears, not anymore. Because we're both too far gone to care. So is this what makes it okay?

"Does this turn *you* on, Pegasus?" he asks, spitting my question back in my face. Then, letting me go, he slides backwards onto the carpet. "We've both lost the plot, you know that?" Bending over, he scoops some clothes out of a suitcase, which lies open and partially disembowelled upon the floor, and tosses them into my lap. "Get dressed. We're going out."

I glance at the clock on the wall. Nearly two a.m. "Where?" I'm not sure whether to be disappointed or relieved at how he was the one to break it off this time.

"Just get dressed." He's already put on a long-sleeved black t-shirt, concealing the scars once and for all. Except for my own. *I've left my mark on you, Raven. To show the world you're mine.*

That I'm the reason you lost your son.

I look at the last item in my repertoire. The black velvet jacket. He's wearing the same long coat he wrapped around my body, the night I almost made it free.

Seeing me hesitate, he snarls and grabs my arm. "Come on. Not even you can stand between me and that bottle of scotch with my name on it."

At least you have something to turn to, then. Bitterness settles in the pit of my tummy as he pushes me out the door.

For more than half an hour, we drift through a suburban maze of lanes and alleys. By the time we stumble across the red painted warehouse, my heels are throbbing. A shabby sign lurches drunkenly over the doorway, announcing the word

JoJo's to the sleepy alley. As we linger outside the entrance, the ghosts of soulful guitar riffs echo behind the curtain.

"Here we be." Raven lets go my hand to light up a cigarette before leading me in. "Our very first date."

Somehow, indoors, it's even darker—the only lighting comes from the fridges by the bar, and the stage, where a feather-and-jewelled woman with dark skin perches under a spotlight, crooning and wailing alternately about her latest love gone wrong, while the cool cats in her shadow look suitably laid back as they jam effortlessly around her melodies. There could be more people here than the handful scattered around the stage and the bar, but it's too dimly lit to tell.

Raven guides me to sit at a table by the wall, and squeezes my hand. "I'll get us a drink." His warm breath against my earlobe sends a shiver down my spine. I lean back, try to relax, and keep an eye on his shadow as he lopes off towards the neon glow of the bar. He takes a seat next to a man wearing a big straw hat and a spotted fur coat, with a younger boy playing ruined-glamourous on his arm. I don't allow my thoughts to linger on this boy too long. Not so short a time ago, that could have been me. I can spot my own kind, even in the dark of a smoky club that probably isn't even open, legally speaking.

Now what are you up to? Money's changing hands between Raven and the faceless older man, before he takes our order from the skimpy barmaid. A moment later he slides back to our table, and finishes his drink in a couple of mouthfuls, all the while pretending to ignore me. But when I look away, from the corner of my eye I can see him glance at my glass. "Better start drinking, if you want to keep up with me."

My heart sinks. So this is how it's going to be. No protection, no remorse. You want me to be as sick as you were before. You don't want to be in control.

To hell with it, it's not like I care anyway. I scull the Midori and lemonade as fast as I can without gagging. It's a lie, of course. Feigning triumph, I thrust the empty glass under his nose. He merely smiles at me, in mockery of a proud parent, and goes to fetch us a refill.

It continues in this vein for the next few hours, before I give up. He's nowhere near as drunk as me, and probably never will be. I rest my arms on the table, lay my head upon them, and gaze up into his face. Is it pointless to wish? But I do. I wish things were different. I wish I could just hold you. I wish this would ever be enough.

He's stroking my hair, rubbing my neck, his sadness seeping into my skin down through his fingertips. On stage, the band finishes their last set and heads off to a round of scattered applause and whistles from the small but enthusiastic crowd. Please. I can't pass out here.

"What's the matter?" He drapes his arm around my shoulders, using his free hand to light up another cigarette. I've lost count of how many smokes he's had tonight. The scent of cloves irritates my nostrils, and I want to sneeze. Or vomit. "Not feeling sick, are you?"

Do you want me to say yes?

I peel myself off the table. Not my best idea. For a moment the world shudders violently around me. Violently, and violetly. Shades of purple. Like my hair.

"Sure doesn't look like you're having fun." His cruel undertone is easy to pick up on, even through my alcohol-induced haze. "You're s'posed to be happy. Out on the town for a night with your dreamboat."

"Stop it!" I slap him away, but can't focus on his face. "Stop punishing me," I say, in a quieter voice. *No tears, not anymore. Remember?* "I didn't ask for any of this, I didn't—"

Oh, but you did.

He frowns, his hand frozen in mid-air from where I pushed him off. "I'm not punishing you, Peggy," he says at last, then pulls me up towards him, towards his mouth, into a deep kiss filled with so much need I can barely fight the nausea.

He pushes me into the wall, pressing up against me so there's no second-guessing how turned on he's become.

"Tell me to stop," he begs, even as he claws a path under my pullover and over my ribcage and tummy. His tongue traces little spirals over my lips, across my tongue, and presses deeper towards my throat, as though he wants to swallow me whole. Then he wrenches my thighs apart and runs his hand up my legs, to scratch at my balls and feel me up from beneath the velvet jeans that are just a bit too big for me.

"Raven," I whimper, throwing my head back involuntarily, exposing my neck to his teeth. He grabs me by one wrist and forces my hand down between his own legs, so I can feel him, even harder than before. The only thing we have to fear is fear itself. The only fear is truth.

This is it, right here. What you can do to make him happy. What you can do to make everything all right, even if it all comes back to nothing. You don't have a choice. It's not like—with them—

Then why should I still not have a choice? I try to remember how it felt when I lapped at the blood from his tummy and felt so— No, not in control at all. Only afraid. Now and always.

He's moving against my hand, trying for the reaction that only flesh and skin can bring, unhindered by clothing.

We both seem to come to this realisation at the same moment, for he ogles me hungrily and says, "We should go...someplace else."

Home, perhaps?

I can't look into his eyes, so I nod dumbly, buying myself some extra time through the need to go to the men's. I don't think he wants me out of his sight, but I stagger off anyway and sway towards the dark green tiles of the hall, swallowing down the bile. Go on then, be sick, I dare you. Anything, so long as I don't have to go through with—

Anything to make him happy. I look into the mirror and burst into tears, letting my forehead fall against the glass.

Poor baby Pegasus.

I'm dousing my hands and face in the rusty sink when I first notice the orange smoke in the mirror. It wafts all around me to flood the room, but smells of nothing. Behind me, reflected in the glass, a figure separates from the fog and creeps into focus. It's the boy from the bar, all black lipstick and a hot pink t-shirt that barely covers his ribs. He closes in, his proximity burning my skin with how cold he is. "No salvation," he hisses in my ear. "You can't save me. You can't even save yourself. I am what you are. You are what I am. We are the same, always the same. Always."

I choke out a cry, and he dissolves.

"Pegasus, what are you doing?"

I spin around, a little too quickly. Raven leans against the doorway, glaring at me. My chest aches and my insides are churning on empty. There is no fog. So, which one of you is real?

I allow him to lead me away; the only realistic choice given the fact he's holding my wrist so tight my bones are ready to crumble. We make it all the way outside before he throws me against a fence, between a dumpster and someone's vintage 70s sandman van. Falling upon me, he savages my neck with nibbles and kisses; all the while keeping one hand busy with the belt that stops these pants from defying the laws of gravity.

"Raven, please—" A chance to beg, as he breaks off long enough to undo his own belt, followed by the button, and then the zip.

"Almost there," he tells me. As though I was encouraging him.

"—not here." I squeeze my eyes shut against the waves of confusion and pleasure and guilt that wash me away when he pulls down both the jeans and my underwear. Perhaps

I'm the one who isn't real.

But he knows the cruellest taunts to bring me back again. "Poor baby. Are you ashamed?"

"Cold!" A small sob escapes my mouth as his hand grips my dick. It's already hard, betraying me, like it always does.

With a smirk, he slides a hand down to my balls, then forces my legs apart once more. "Can't be too cold." As one of his fingers finds its way into the crack of my arse, we both let out a moan—one for pleasure, one for fear, but which is which? He drools into my mouth, eyes clouding over with desire.

You said you needed to cut yourself to remember—

With his other hand, he forces my arms up against the wall to pin me by the wrists. I must have been putting up a struggle.

Do you need this to forget?

Another finger finds its way inside. I dig my teeth into his shoulder blade, afraid to want this, afraid to tell him to stop.

Then a screech of laughter echoes down the alley, followed by a loud echoing boom. A primal sound, made to evoke the purest fear. My blood freezes to a halt.

Next come the cat-calls, and then the hate.

"Fucking poofters!"

"Bloody queers!"

"Should kill the fuckin' lotta ya!"

A bolt of terror gives me strength enough to push Raven off. He stumbles backwards, glaring at me in resentment and disbelief. Even as he tucks himself away again, I dare to imagine the yells and threats were just a fragment from another waking nightmare.

Until he turns his back on me and charges out into the centre of the alley. "How about you come here and say that to my face, you mother-fucking piece of shit!"

My pulse stops. I follow his gaze, all the way to where two

lumps of shadow moulded roughly in the shape of men stand under the streetlight where it intersects a lane. They look at least twice his size from here.

"Raven!" My pulse races as my fingers fumble with my own pants, desperate to get fully clothed again. "Don't be an idiot."

One of the lumps separates from the other and lurches towards us. Raven stands his ground, bristling and sneering, pissed off enough to take on the world, to hell with whether or not he wins.

"You say somethin', mate?" The thug stops about three feet shy of us, and folds its bare arms across a beer gut that pokes out beneath a striped football guernsey.

"You heard me," Raven growls. But even as he speaks, the thug catches sight of me and grins. Why do I fear Raven at all, when this face of humanity is the everyday alternative? A sickly grimace, missing a few teeth. With a piercing whistle, it calls up its reserve from out of the shadows. This other one scampers straight for me, lean like a mulleted ferret. Raven laughs coldly and saunters around to block their path, as though I'm become a pawn in some grotesque game of chess.

"Your boyfriend's about ter cry," ferret-man says in a high-pitched nasal whine. "'Sokay baby. I got something here that'll make it all better." It rubs at its crotch, giggling like a madman and writhing like a would-be rock star, waggling its tongue and pawing at itself clumsily. Once the dry wretches pass, my hands clench into fists. No. Not that. Kill me, beat me, anything but that. That belongs to Raven. It always did, you bastards.

I look to him again, the only guardian that stands between me and the old, familiar nightmares. I once managed to fool myself into thinking they were gone, but now I know I'll never be free of them. *You can't even save yourself.*

He takes another step backwards, as the two of them stalk

closer. Part of me wants to run, but here I am trapped in another dream, where every muscle shifts in slow motion. They're closing in on us: beer and sweat stings my nostrils, even as the blood drains from my head.

Raven, help me. Mother—

You know you're in trouble once you start calling on divine powers and ghosts. *No salvation.* Then if nothing matters no matter what I do—

I lunge at the one that's had its eye on me. This catches us both off-guard, and we tumble to the ground. It's a short-lived daydream: I haven't even caught my breath when it clambers on top of me, and grinds the side of my face into the asphalt. Now it's even yee-hawing while it humps my arse. How quaint.

I struggle to open my eyes. Through a little viewport beyond grit and pain, I watch the larger thug bounce off the opposite wall. On its way down, one of Raven's boots stomps the side of its face. Then a hand reels me back in, pumping my dick, rough, cold, and oily. "You like that, you little faggot?"

Does it really want an answer? I might even laugh, but a high-pitched scream cuts right over the top of me. Spitting out a mouthful of dirt, I spin around, just in time to see my tormentor slam into the van, and not get up. Now Raven's the one on top. He hoists it up by the hood, landing one… two…three punches into its cheek, then drops it back to the pavement. Next, five well-aimed kicks at the crotch. Finally, he crouches down and regurgitates those horrible words. "You like *that*, faggot?"

No response. I struggle to my feet and take a few curious cat steps closer. "Think we're done here, do you?" he continues on, not looking away from the figure on the ground. "Well, here's the story, morning glory. I'm not done with you. Not till your cock doesn't even raise a brow at the thought of Pamela Anderson and David Hasselhoff alone and naked in a hot tub." No response, no movement, except perhaps to breathe. Guess there's nothing like being confronted by a bigger psychopath than yourself to bring you back to earth.

Is it breathing? I can't tell. What if—? "Raven," I whisper, just as he's about to launch another kick at the lump of shadow.

Straight away, he freezes, and then, with a twitch of his neck, it's as though something resets inside his brain. He lowers his foot and sniffs with contempt. "You're not fucking worth it."

He raises his head, and turns to face me. I start to smile. At the very least, maybe we're free to leave.

But that desire, tinged with hate, still smoulders inside-out. "What do you think *you're* doing?" he demands, stalking over and making a grab for my belt. Intending to pick up where he left off, as though nothing happened—

"Dammit!" I couldn't fight off the ferret, which leaves me with no chance against him. He's not only stronger, he's all in my mind. "I don't want this! Please, just stop!"

He abandons work on my zip to snarl at me. "What, would you prefer *him*?"

Once again, I'm hurtling towards the shadow thing by the van, only this time propelled by Raven's grip. It's all I can do to stop myself falling right on top of the body. Instead I snatch at a side-view mirror, and collapse against the front tyre. Some part of me is always trying to escape. But there's nowhere to run. Inside my mind, only nightmares. Out there, insanity.

Why did you save me, if this was all you wanted?

I wish it would all just stop.

I'm shaking when he lifts me to my feet. Stop it. *Stop it.* "Stop it, stop it!"

Slowly, he raises a finger to my lips, putting an end to the words without and within. Then he says, "You're more afraid of me than you were of them."

No. *No?* I wanted—just, not here.

"I don't blame you." He glances from one body to another. Both lie groaning and squirming and bleeding on the ground nearby. Then, "I just want you…to want me."

I press my face against his, ashes to ashes, ice to ice. "I do." Even talking in a whisper is a struggle. "Just not here. Let's go home, okay?"

"Really?" He wants to believe, so badly. "You really want me? That would make you happy?"

"Of course." But I've already turned my back on him—on him and the curtain and the men and the lie and the fact that his hands are bleeding—as I lead him away from the club.

We both struggle to fit the key in the lock of Monty's door before finally tumbling inside. "Reckon I'll take this off now," he says, tugging the top he lent me over my head before I've had a chance to find my feet. Once I do, he starts on the jeans, but again I delay him.

"Let's go to the bedroom." Just give me more time. I need more time.

To my surprise, he consents, and we stagger down the hall, desperate to be quiet but failing as comically as possible. When we make it to his room, I fall upon the bed in a fit of giggles. He shrugs off his coat, takes a small lump of foil out of his pocket, and tosses it onto the bedside table, near the lamp and the razor blade, and I remember how I'm lying on sheets stained with his blood. Depending on how he decides to go about this, we could soon be even, I guess. That's a thought to sober me.

"Ahh, what would you like me to do?" So I'm giving him control, the one thing he said he didn't want. But then, he thinks that this is what I want, too.

"Get undressed," he says. "I want to watch you."

Okay, no problem. Ignoring the way my hands are shaking, which makes his request more difficult again, I pull off my shoes, followed by the jeans, the socks, and last of all my underwear. Now I stand naked and shivering in front of him.

He looks me over, gives me a smile of approval, then beckons to me. "Come here."

Nervously I approach, until we stand so close we're touching. He pulls me forward, and I fall against him, burying my head in his shoulder. In a flash, he jerks me up by my plait. I squeal in protest, but do my pleading in silence. I can feel how hard he is. Funny how fear proves such a powerful aphrodisiac.

He scoops me up in his arms, and carries me over to the bed, where he lays me down upon the mattress. With one hand, he unties my hair, and combs it out with his fingers. Then he reaches out, cautiously stroking my cheek, barely making contact with my skin. He's shivering too, as he gazes down at my body. But always he returns to the eyes, his expression so intense it burns into my soul.

He sits near me on the mattress, turning aside to remove his own clothes, all except a pair of black silk boxers. This is the first time I've ever seen him naked—almost naked. From the outermost edges of my mind, I dare to admire him. You did say those words to me. No one's ever said them before. Will you still say them, afterwards?

No, oh no.

I try to fool us both with an attempted grin. "So, what now?"

"Now I've gotta ask you something." He sounds serious enough that I can guess where he's going. AIDS? Hepatitis? Any other nasty little germs floating around down there?

"I'm...clean," I struggle to say, closing my eyes. "I never—they always—I've been tested, okay?" I spit it out eventually.

"No AIDS, no nothing. But if you don't believe me, that's your choice. Go invest in a condom."

When I open my eyes, his bruised hands cover his face. Then he lets go, and sighs. "That's...not what I was going to ask you."

I frown, unable to make sense of his expression. He leans over me, and rests his cheek against mine. I can't bear even this brief silence anymore. "What? What did you want to ask me?"

He smiles sadly. I look at his soft lips, so close to mine. Why won't you just kiss me already? Call me a fool, but what's so wrong with a little romance?

"Why are you doing this?" he says.

I almost swallow my own tongue. "What do you mean?"

"You know what I'm talking about."

He's seen through your disguise. I must really be losing my touch. I sit up; my mind, driven by instinct, plots a path to the door. But it seems so far away, and I'm so tired of running, anyhow. "I only wanted you to be happy." No. That's not it. "I wanted to make you happy."

"And you think letting me rape you would make me happy?" He seems so angry when he uses that word, that word that I hate. *What would you know about it?*

"It wouldn't be like that. You said we'd be—" I can't bring myself to say it. *Making love.* It seems I have a problem when it comes to even expressing the concept.

"Yeah, and it wouldn't be making love if you didn't want to do it," he counters. "That's the definition of rape, remember?" With another sigh, he rises off the mattress and starts pacing beside the bed. "What did I say I wanted, just before?"

I frown, trying to recall the context of the conversation. "That you wanted me," I come up with, my voice very small, like a child who knows they're in trouble but not why.

"That I wanted *you* to want me!" He storms back to the bed.

"Do you see the difference? Do you?"

"I don't see any difference." I gaze blankly at the wall. There's no need to see his reaction to that.

"Guess I really freaked you out tonight, huh?" he says, reaching for my hand. When I don't take his in mine, he grabs it anyway, squeezing it, holding on tight. "I know...I never did anything—" Now he's the one having difficulty with his words, but unlike me he trusts their importance and pushes on. "But I'd never hurt you. Please believe me. I'm not—" He breaks off with a laugh. "I think I may be going insane."

I don't understand. What do you want, then? Have I failed? "Do you want me to leave?" I venture cautiously.

"You're all I've got left," he whispers. Somehow he's in my lap, and I'm rocking him slowly to and fro, moving so my hair drapes across his skin, his scars, like a curtain. Feeling him break beneath me for the second time today, as I sit here in the shadows, thinking of ways to kill my sister.

"Not for much longer." I'll try to reassure him, even as my mind overflows with murder. It's all too easy to daydream about doing to Wendy what Raven did to those arseholes tonight. Only in my fantasy, there's no one to tell me to stop. Always Father's favourite, sweet little Wendy. That's why Father's lawyer comes knocking on our door. Bastard.

Too easy...

Breaking out of my violent trance, I notice he's staring at me again. "I'm going to roll a number," he announces, indicating the foil on the bedside table. "Do you want some?"

I shrug, not really thinking about the question. "Sure." Why not. He kisses me lightly on the lips, then unwraps the foil. While he works, the silence rings in my ears, and I train myself to relax, tracing imaginary patterns over his scars. Memories lurch past the boy at the club, to the conversation between Monty and Noriko in the kitchen. Now it's their doubts and fears that traipse the corridors of my brain.

"Raven?"

"Mmm?" he says, his tongue in the process of sealing the paper.

"We're not going to lose him, are we?"

Another question I regret, but it's already too late to take it back. A match flares, and he lights the joint and sucks the smoke into his lungs. He exhales a thick cloud before answering, "You just keep an eye on me. I'll worry about the rest of it."

I almost believe him. I'm nearly fooled. Just like he was nearly fooled, when he thought I wanted—

We know each other too well. It might be the one thing that saves us.

The next lot of smoke is reserved for me. Cautiously, I accept the shotgun toke. This time, I don't even cough.

Twenty minutes later, we're melting in the warm haze of embrace. Outside our door, over the birdsong, Monty and Noriko dash here and there, swearing and stressing for being late.

(RAVEN) *9*

The Sixth Degree of Separation

I'm lying on my back beneath the old, familiar ceiling of white and shadow, and I'm alone. Which should come as no surprise. The more I recall, about last night, the more I feel my tentative hold on sanity slip. The knuckles on both my hands are burning.

I sit up in bed, and my mind blurs in and out of focus. Of course I'm alone. What reason do I give him, to stay?

I dig my toes into the carpet as I get to my feet. An icy wind slices through the curtains and rakes its fingernails over my naked body. Down the hall, a tap drips. A clock on the wall tick-tick-ticks. I thought I heard an alarm go off earlier, but I'd simply rolled over and drifted back to sleep, incapable of facing any reality so soon. This reality.

For the house is entirely empty. Nobody here at all. Least of all myself.

I rub at my forehead and go on glancing around the room. The breeze at the open window gets into my chest, closing around my heart, and I let it. Everything gets easier, when I don't need to feel. What's the point in getting up?

But there's no sanctuary for me in this bed, not with a single strand of purple hair coiled across the pillow and my blood gone cold on the sheets. Did I hurt you, Peg? Is this what form my love for you takes? I don't understand anything, except *I want you till all the stars burn out*, but I don't even know what you feel.

Well, you do now. He couldn't have made it more obvious.

My knees start to tremble, so I sink to the mattress. For the first time, I've got absolutely no idea what comes next. There's always been somewhere else for me to run to—someone else—and now—

Tick. Tock (drip) Tick. Tock (drip.) Tick. Tock (drip).

A metronome to keep time with my madness, missing only the razor's beat. I seek for its cruel salvation on the bedside table, but the blade's gone, replaced by a sliver of white. A letter. For me.

Holding my breath, I reach out a tentative hand, then snatch it to my chest, fearing the paper might vanish the minute it realises I've become aware of its existence. I breathe in a sob and exhale his name, as I hold it up to what little light filters through the curtains. Might as well get it over with.

Yeah, that's his handwriting—delicate, like calligraphy. Even where some of the words are scratched out, this is a far too exquisite means to convey the final description of my doom.

My Raven,

By the time you read this, I'll be gone. I'm sorry I couldn't make you happy last night. Sorry I got you into all this…trouble. I wish you could forgive me, that I might forgive myself…and I thought…

If you still want…me…I'll be at work until seven. You could meet me there, perhaps? If you don't come, I'll understand.

But I'll wait for you. Forever and always.

The letter's signed with a single *x*. A kiss. A smile skitters across my lips, but I wipe it off before relief gets the chance to swell to hysterics. We're a pair of fools, me and you both.

I stare at the clock, registering what it says for the first time. Four-thirty, in the afternoon. A perfectly civil hour to be waking up. And that leaves me nearly three hours.

I glance once at the bloody sheets, then make my way into the bathroom. While the water from the shower quenches my scars and pounds my bruises, an image drifts into my mind, stealing my breath. Veiled in tears, he's lapping at my chest, my blood staining his tongue and lips. The razor blade flashes as he slides it down the arc of my throat, his touch so warm, the pain so exquisite. And he opens his mouth and says, *We're not going to lose him, are we?*

I turn off the water and hold myself close. Too many things to remember. Just once, I'd like to forget.

I get off the tram along Chapel Street. One hand grips the letter; the other's at my neck, reaching for the cross—his first gift to me. Back then, I mocked him for his faith. Now it's the last light in a vast, dark sea. What else could keep you next to me, Peggy? What else could make me want you to bind my soul with thorns, though I know all too well what power you hold, to destroy me, to take from me everything I define as my self, my life, my reason?

Only a few blocks to go, and I can already sense his presence, calming me, soothing me—just like that night I reached out to brush the ice-blond hair aside, and he held out my new-born son—

No. That was only nightmare, vision, dream. Another thing I don't understand, another thing that scares the hell out of me. Should I tell him about it, ask him what it means?

As if he's not scared enough of you already. I hardly need to go around advertising the true nature of my insanity.

I'm waiting for a car at the last intersection, when three figures turn the corner and head my way: man, woman, child. I take my foot off the road and step back, watching them get closer and closer, till the shop lights reveal their faces. An older man in a suit; yuppie, by the looks of it. Wendy. Damien...

She sees me first, and freezes mid-stride. With a flick of her hair, her features twist themselves into a mask of hate. Then

Damien screams out, "Daddy!", and the suit herds them into the nearest restaurant.

I draw in a deep breath, fingers twitching. So, Wendy. Now it's your turn to play happy families? And you think he wants that from you? Do you think he cares about Damien, thinks he's cute, wants to marry you and make a 'decent woman' of you? Are you thinking at all? Really, you almost had me fooled. I always thought I was the bigger idiot in our unfortunate relationship.

Whatever. In the end, it doesn't matter. I'm going to cross the road—*just act like nothing happened, show them nothing; you're a boy, a man, you can at least do that, can't you?*

Bang! A door slams, and footsteps pound the pavement straight for me. Next thing I know, I've dropped to my knees, and Damien's hugging me tight. His tears tickle my neck as I press my face into his hair. I never want to let go.

"Daddy," he sobs again, staring into my face. He looks so sad and so grown up. So much like me. "Mama says you don't want me. Mama says I'm bad so you don't love me anymore."

Don't know what I'm saying; anything that drifts into my mind will do. How much I do love him. How much his Peggy-sis loves him. How I'm going to take them both away from all of this real soon, somewhere— Somewhere we can be safe. And happy.

Somewhere she can't blame him for my mistakes.

"Come on now, don't let's be stupid." A lazy male voice—Wendy's companion. *Jonathan?* I glance up, shifting around to shield my son. But there's no sign of the queen bitch herself. Only her joker. "You know the situation. You wouldn't want to get in any trouble, would you? Not with the court case coming up. Remember?"

How much did she tell this ponce? But Damien's grip tightens around my neck. He's whimpering in my ear, and trembling. Why is he so fucking scared—of you?

I sneer at the piece of shit in a suit till he backs off, fishing in his pockets for...a gun, mace, a hand grenade?

A mobile phone. Of course. The ultimate in high-class wanker defence systems. "Put the kid down, or I call the cops, okay?"

I raise a brow. Oh yeah? You think you can hold me to ransom? You think I give a shit? Go ahead, call the fucking cops. The more the merrier. Tell 'em after I ram your head up your arse, I'll shout them all a round of fucking donuts.

But a little hand brushes against mine, a reminder to keep my mouth shut. It's true: he can hold me to ransom. I'm just a puppet, with too many cut strings.

Damien starts to wail as I put him down reluctantly. Prying off his fingers one by one feels as bad as if I'm breaking them. I sicken myself. You sicken me, Wendy. "Daddy! Don't you want me, Daddy?" he screams in my face, hugging himself till his whole body stiffens. I shove my hands deep in my pockets, otherwise—fuck it all to hell and back—I'm going to kill this bastard lapdog of hers. Then storm into that restaurant and make an entree out of her innards. Instead, I hate myself for looking away as the sleazebag snatches my son out of reach.

"You think you've got a chance?" I spit. "He's *my* son. He'll always be my son."

The suit just laughs, lugging my little angel under one arm as though he's a slab of beer, not a precious life. Not my entire fucking universe. "Hell, I don't give a shit about the rugrat. I only want to screw *her*."

With that, he tosses his scarf and retreats to where that bitch is holed up. Damien keeps his eyes fixed on me, till the door slams closed. I spin round and kick a garbage can out onto the street. Its guts spew across the road, straight at an oncoming car. The driver swerves out of the way, blaring his horn in a stream of protest. I pick up the stray lid and hurl it after him, stumbling into the gutter on my follow-through. All my energy drained, I put my head in my hands, laughing or crying I don't know which, except that no tears ever come.

It's five minutes to seven when I push open the door of Lenny's Instruments, ignoring the 'get a life, we're f***ing closed!!!' sign hanging in the window. As I step inside, I gape at the rows of guitars, but only out of habit. Soulless copies, most of them.

"Heya blackbird!" Lenny calls from the rear end of the shop, holding up a half-rolled joint. "You musta been able to smell me! Lock that door, will ya? Don't want no more strays like you blowing in."

I manage a nod, flick the latch, then wander towards him. He slaps me hard on the shoulder, then goes on sealing and lighting the joint. I make myself at home by shrugging my coat onto the floor and fixing a cup of coffee. "So," he says, past a cloud of smoke. "How's tricks?"

I stir two sugars into the tepid black liquid, forcing myself to concentrate on each little action. I'm not the only one. Blue eyes watch my every move from beneath scraggly burgundy tufts—despite the fact he seems to breathe marijuana, Lenny always looks so alert. No doubt pot's got the same effect on him as alcohol does on me. "Oh," I say, playing it down, "to quote Saint Nick, you could say I've been contemplating suicide."

"Well, so long as you remember how it *actually* goes." He sings the rest of the line in a low, soulful voice. Then, with a smile that could be knowing or pitying, he passes over the joint. "It doesn't suit your style, blackbird."

I shrug and suck back a deep toke, feeling the smoke burn down my lungs. Straight away, a not unpleasant haze drifts across my mind. Damn, he always knows how to get hold of the good stuff.

"Speaking of style," he adds, turning away as I try to pass on the joint, leaving me to take another drag instead, "check out what came in today." He turns back, cradling a guitar in his arms. But not just any guitar. A black and white Fender Telecaster, in mint condition. We trade—the joint for the guitar. I lift it out of his arms and do the customary check of the insignia on the head. No soulless copy here. "Original?"

"You betcha." Lenny grins. "Don't get any of that cheap Mexican crap in here." He pretends to look hurt as he adds, "You know me better than that, blackbird."

Sure I do. I pull up a milk crate and turn the guitar over, then place it in my lap. "How much?"

He gags on a mouthful of smoke. And when he's done coughing, he's still laughing. Yeah, thanks. "Much more than you could ever afford, my friend. Better for you to hope that kid of yours grows up and becomes a lawyer, or investment banker, or something. Then he can buy it for you." He giggles, spooning three sugars into his own coffee.

"No, then I really would kill myself, style or no." My left hand's already forming random chord patterns on the neck, testing the tension of the strings, admiring the smooth polish of the maple fretboard beneath my fingertips. "Am I at least allowed to play it?"

"What, you think I'm an arsehole?" He tosses me a lead, then plugs the other end into an amp that barricades the nearest door. After fishing through his pockets, he hands over a plectrum. Taking in a deep breath, all the better to savour the moment, I strum a chord: my favourite, E minor 7. The rich bass resonates through the floorboards, and vibrates up into my toes. I grin at Lenny, who nods approvingly. Just to piss him off, I rip out a few bars of 'Stairway to Heaven', stopping only to laugh when he charges forward, intent on reclaiming my temporary prize.

"Don't give me the fucking shits," he whines, settling down

into his corner. "You know how many fucking thirteen-year-olds I get in here, reeking of pubescence? You know what they say to me? *'Can you teach me to play that song?'* I hate that fucking song. Play that again and you're banned for the next six months. Consider yourself warned."

I hold up my hands in surrender. But he's stuck on his anti-Led Zeppelin fixation. "Twenty years of playing guitar, and all these little shits wanna learn is Stairway to fucking Heaven and Nirvana songs. Well I'm sure as shit Kurt Cobain never went to heaven, I can tell you that for free. Hendrix, or Velvet Underground, or Jeff Buckley? No, just goddamn Triple J try-hard classics. Makes me sick."

I sigh. "You done there, old-timer?" Thinking back to our guitar lessons, a bit of 'Purple Haze' should at least shut him up.

Well, I'm half right. Except for the fact that as I hit the second bar, he starts to bounce around the already cramped space, crooning the lyrics in what approaches a decent Elvis impersonation. I stop playing and glare at him.

"What?" he demands innocently, using my silence as an excuse to take the guitar off me. He idly strums a few chords before unplugging it and closing it up in its coffin.

"Hendrix'd be tossing in his grave right now, I reckon." I down the rest of my coffee, and dump the cup on the sink.

"Yeah? Well that shows how much you know." His shoulders stiffen. I must've hit a nerve. "Everyone knows the soul leaves the body when it dies. Unless you're an atheist, but those nihilist bastards are all fucked up. Energy never dies, just changes form. Remember? Or were you always too hung over in high school to pay attention to Physics 101?"

Ouch. I crack my knuckles and check my watch again. Don't want to be here. "When's Peg done?" I just want to take my angel home with me, lock the door, and throw away the key. Keep all these clowns out of our world, at least till we've designed some plan to get my son.

It's ten minutes after seven.

"Ah, any minute, I guess." Lenny shrugs, grinding the joint into the carpet with a shiny boot. The sparks have only just gone out when he quickly grabs hold of me, and draws the curtain across the doorway. A silhouette glides past us. Growling, "Wait here, don't move!" in my ear, he steps out into the showroom.

I frown, not in the mood for his little games. Even less so when I hear Pegasus ask, "Has Raven come yet, Lenny?"

"No, no, no," Lenny's quick to respond, and a flash of hatred bursts inside my forehead. "I'm just having a smoke out back. Care to join me?"

I miss the answer, but I know he won't be saying yes. Only *I* can get him to do that, arsehole. I'm on the verge of storming out of my hidey-hole when Lenny reappears and pushes me towards the dark side of the room, a finger pressed to his lips. I glare him down, till with an impatient sigh he beckons me over and tugs on my hair so we're both staring out across the shop through a gap in the curtain. Now Pegasus approaches the grand piano in the centre of the floor, takes up a seat in front of the keyboard, and stretches high. Then he slumps forward, and begins to play.

Wait. I know this song...

"The last time he caught me doing this," Lenny whispers in my ear, annoying me with his constant proximity, "he didn't speak to me for two whole weeks, let alone come out and play. He's a shy one, isn't he? Hiding his light under a bushel, you might say."

He grins, but I'm no longer paying attention to him. My eyes are all for Pegasus, and in my mind I'm caressing his black velvet shirt, unbuttoning the burgundy jeans, letting his silken hair flow freely over his shoulders, over my naked skin, pulling the shirt over his head, kissing his chest, his nipples, moving lower across his stomach, down to—

I just manage to stop myself choking on desire, painfully aware of my growing hard-on. If you could only want me half as bad as this.

Ignoring Lenny's hisses of protest, I step out behind the curtain and move towards the piano, a moth drawn to a flame. To hell with whether my wings get burned. I am not afraid.

As I come nearer he stops playing and turns around, hands folded contentedly in his lap. "Where did you materialise from?" he asks, a mysterious smile on his lips. I grab him by the wrists and pull him into a deep kiss. He doesn't fight me, doesn't even tense beneath my touch.

"The seventh layer of hell," I answer, hugging him as tight as I held my son, before—

Not here. I can't do any of this here.

"Let's go home." It doesn't take any more saying. He nods.

We wave goodnight to a bemused Lenny. I don my overcoat, and drape Peg's coat and scarf around his shoulders. Together, we step out to face the cruel night.

"So, what will I cook?" he asks, as we head towards his apartment, arm in arm.

This simple question throws me. "What?"

He slaps me, grinning playfully. "You like hot food, right? I think I have chillies, and capsicum, and rice—Hmm." He drifts off, distracted by the gaudy window display of the Retro Chique Boutique. I drag him right, down another street, then cut across the lane.

"You don't need to cook for me."

"Don't be silly." He frowns. "You didn't have to come and meet me, either."

He begins to speed up, so I pull him back into my arms.

"Yeah, I did," I whisper, drawing him into another kiss.

He makes a half-hearted attempt at breaking my hold. "If this is how you feel about things," he starts to say.

No, Pegasus. "I can't bear the thought of being without you." *This* is how I feel. I cover his lips and tongue with more little kisses, and lead him on towards home.

Home. Such a strange word. I don't have a home. You don't have a home, not really. But when I'm with you, I *feel* home.

We reach the apartment, and I let go his hand so he can fish through a pocket for his keys. Like two excited kids, we race one another up three flights of stairs and stumble onto the top landing, panting and laughing. I've never been inside his little loft before. As the door swings open, I kiss him more sombrely, wanting to mark the occasion. After tossing aside his coat and scarf, he shoves me inside, shuts the door, and snips the latch.

Turning around, he notices my grin. "I just didn't want you going anywhere."

"I haven't got anywhere else." Hastily, I add, "There's nowhere else I'd want to be."

He looks at me a moment longer, before a slow smile crosses his face and he waves in the direction of the bed. "Um...I kind of don't have anywhere to sit, so—"

My grin broadens. "Now that's just asking for trouble." I fall onto the mattress, about to make a start on removing my own coat, when together we notice the flashing red light, coming from a coffee table crowded with random appliances. This one's an answering machine. He frowns, but presses the switch to play the message. He's got nothing to hide from me.

"Uh, Peg?" I jump as a loud, familiar voice cuts through the tinny speakers. "It's Monty. I guess you're at work. Um, I don't suppose you've seen Raven? Probably off somewhere getting pissed." Pegasus shoots me a knowing look. I poke out my tongue. "If you do see him," Monty's voice continues, sounding more uncertain than usual, "could you tell him to swing round to my place ASAP? It's really important. Yeah, thanks. Oh, and don't forget the gig tomorrow!" The voice drops out with a crunch, replaced by the beep-beep-beep of the engaged signal.

Pegasus sighs and switches off the machine. "Sounds like dinner might have to wait."

Damn you, Monty. I run my hands through my hair. You don't want any chance of me being happy, is that it? "I'm not going."

Footsteps cross the floor, and he wraps me in his arms, his breath warm on my neck. I already know what he's going to say. "You have to, Raven. He said it's important. That probably means it has something to do with Damien."

My fists clench, involuntarily. "What more can they take? I told you, I'm not going. I don't want to go. I thought you wanted me to stay."

Pathetic. I should be used to these feelings already. Fear. Desire. Pain. Nothing new. Once upon a time, I would've called these feelings my friends. Till they turned around and stabbed me in the back, like all friends do eventually.

He taps me under the chin, and it works to get my attention. "Listen to me," he says. "This matters. I'm not going anywhere. I'll call ahead and tell him you're coming. We'll have something to eat when you get home. Okay?"

I just shrug, lowering my gaze, playing it silent, martyred, heroic.

He sighs, pulling away. Instantly I miss the warmth and comfort he offered. Don't you understand? I don't need to hear them say it. I don't need to hear them tell me again that they're taking him away from me. Please don't make me go.

"Besides," he says at last, "it might give you a chance to grab the rest of your stuff. You didn't bring anything with you, Raven."

I frown, quashing the feelings of hope brought on just by hearing him speak my name, let alone the two sentences that went before it. "What—what do you mean?"

He folds his arms around his chest. He's expecting to be hurt, same as me. But he's got no right to ask for that, not like I do. "Well, I thought you might like to stay. Here."

I reach out, catching him on one cheek before he can dodge me. "You don't have to," he says, his gaze dropping to his feet.

My hand finds the cross again, seeking out its reminder. "If you let me stay, then I'll go." Gotta love the stupid logic of that sentence.

"Really?"

There's only one way to answer his question. Sighing heavily, I get off the bed. "Yeah." I even manage a wink before I pull the door shut behind me.

"Damn you, Monty." This time the curse isn't so silent, as I again set foot into the night that doesn't want to let me go.

Upon my arrival at Monty's, I'm swept inside by Noriko and dragged before a woman called Judy Mirkle, a creature with all the personality, warmth and flair of my final year English teacher—and I hated *her* with a passion. "She'll be looking after you on Tuesday," Monty announces cheerfully.

So, I'm *supposed* to be impressed? I glare at him till he makes some weak excuse and dashes off into the kitchen with Noriko. You certainly know when to leave the betting arena, don't you, cousin?

I barely pay any attention to this Judy Mirkle, but like a good boy I answer all her questions, questions about my 'lifestyle', my situation, my relationship with Wendy, my income. No doubt she likes me about as much as I like her. No doubt she's already made up her mind about me from the way an extra line appears in her forehead for each extra note she's gotta take. And I know she doesn't think I've got a snowball's chance in hell of getting custody of my son.

The only thing she does to earn an ounce of my respect through the entire ordeal comes at the end of our meeting. Turning to me as she makes her way out the door, she says, "I think you should realise the odds are stacked against you here."

No shit, Sherlock.

"I mean," she stops to explain, as though it needed explaining, "in ninety-nine percent of cases, the mother always gets the child. No matter how good a parent the father is. Then you throw the word 'homosexual' into the mix and—well." She lets the thought slide. "Just a fact of life, I'm afraid. And our antiquated legal system."

"So why bother?"

"Ah, well." She laughs, patting down her hair. "It pays well? What more can I tell ya?" Shaking my hand once, she departs with a light-hearted, "See you next Tuesday."

Yeah, right. See you in hell, more like. Bitch.

I linger in the doorway, till Monty and Noriko reappear behind me, both of them looking hopeful. "Well?" Monty's the first to lose his patience. "How'd it go? What did you think? She's a really good lawyer."

"She's all right," I murmur, hoping my voice conveys the more truthful answer. No, none of this is fucking all right. You gave up too quick, and now you're palming me off on some cow who doesn't even know me, much less give two shits about what happens in court, so long as she gets paid.

"Raven, what is it?" Noriko moves in with open arms, all full of big-sisterly concern that makes me want to vomit.

I hold up a hand, keeping her at bay. "I'm going back to Pegasus," I say, trying to retain my calm. You both betrayed me, and now you don't get the honour of seeing me break.

"It's a little late for that, don't you think?" Monty says.

You'd like it to be, wouldn't you. "I'm going to get the rest of my stuff." I force my way past to the spare bedroom, and throw all my clothes into the suitcase. But I can't find that purple top I gave Peg to wear. He must've taken it home with him already.

I close the door behind me, and step into the hall. At the far end, Monty and Noriko haven't moved, like statues frozen in time. As I head for the exit, he reaches out and grabs me by my free arm. I stare past him, waiting till he lets go. In a weak voice, he says, "You're going to stay there?"

That's right. Try and stop me and it'll be the last thing you ever do. I'm ready to lash out if either of them try to touch me again. I just—I just don't care anymore.

"Where will you sleep?" he asks, before Noriko hastily elbows him in the stomach and makes a hissing face. He frowns at her in incomprehension, before understanding finally crosses his face. "Oh." They both look down at their toes.

I wrench open the door and stare up at the night sky. "Have a nice life." *Almost there.* I think of Pegasus, among the pale stars. Can you hear me? I'm coming home. I'm not leaving you again.

"Hey, don't forget the gig tomorrow!" Monty calls after me.

"Sure," I say, slamming the door, locking them out of my life.

Like I've even got the key.

Pegasus lets me in warily, though he manages a smile when I dump the suitcase and my coat on the floor. This time I'm the one who locks the door, before I turn and sweep him into an embrace. I carry him to the bed, sit him down on the edge of the mattress. Then I fall forward and bury my face in his neck, nipping at his throat.

"I don't know how," he tells me slowly, "but just now I knew you were coming. I was in the kitchen, and suddenly I felt...warm." He tries to laugh it off, but I remember my silent plea before I left Monty's. So, you did hear me.

Dropping the smile, he asks, "Do you want to talk?"

"Kept you from your dinner long enough, didn't I?"

Realising the answer's no, he nods and shuffles off into the kitchen. Not five minutes later, the most wonderful aromas waft under my nose to tease my stomach, make my mouth water. I find the remote for the corner-mounted TV, then slide off my boots. All the while, restless, I gaze around the room. Most of the walls are covered in psychedelic swirls in red and purple and black, matching the bedding. Probably Noriko's contribution to the decor. On the bedside table, a Chinese lantern and a picture frame sit side by side, and it's on this photo that I linger longest. From a distance, it's Pegasus, but up close the most beautiful woman I've ever seen undoes layers of skin and bone and spirit with no more than a defiant tilt of her head and the consumptive sadness that stains her proud silver-blue eyes. An elaborate ice-blonde braid sweeps away from elfin features and coils over her shoulder in a rope of liquid frost.

I always thought of me and Ma as pretty close replicas, till I see how much this woman resembles Pegasus, from the inside out. And Damien.

The mattress moves, snapping me out of my trance. He's kneeling behind me now, wrapping his arms around my chest. For a moment, we stare at the photo together, and then he draws back and sniffs.

"Mother," he whispers, by way of explanation, as if it weren't already obvious.

"Juliette." I hope I get the pronunciation right.

He squeezes my shoulder. "She's beautiful, yes?"

"*You're* beautiful." I return the frame to its rightful place, then pull him onto my lap. The conversation I had with Lenny earlier keeps nagging at the edge of my memory, an echo of something that's been bothering me ever since he tried to—

"Where do you think she is, now?"

After a long silence, he rises off the bed. Muttering, "I don't know," he retreats to the safety of the kitchen.

Liar. Random laughter erupts from the TV, and I switch it off in annoyance. No need for that. I came here to shut out the rest of the world; all its trivial emotions and short-lived genius. I intend to keep it this way—

For so long as I possibly can—

Till Tuesday, at least.

After dinner, I make for the window to partake of a ritual clove cigarette. The pot I scored last night can wait.

I push up the frame, let in the cold winter night, and blow my smoke back in its face. From behind, Peg wraps his arms around my waist. "Did you like it?" he asks, nuzzling into my shoulder blades.

"Yeah." It might even have been the best meal I've ever had, and I'm ashamed for being so distracted. "Thanks."

With a sigh, he wedges his body between me and the open window. "Will you tell me nothing?"

Maybe I don't want this cigarette, after all. I butt it out on the ledge, then poke it down into the pack. "I think we need a Plan B." I try and play it casual, but as I hold him in my arms, my lower lip starts to tremble. Too many shadows, haunting my head.

"Do you think—? Do you think…I'm a good dad, to Damien?"

"Of course," he murmurs without hesitation, gripping me

tighter. "Raven—"

"I'm nothing like my old man, you know." I gaze over the top of his head, out across the dark side of the city. "Apart from the drinking. Never told you why I had to leave home, did I? Ma—after he died, she got ill. They sent her to a mental institution." I shrug. "Anyhow...every night, when I was real little, Dad would get in, blind drunk, and beat the crap out of both of us. She never did anything, she never said anything, she just— She let him do it. To her. To me."

Let's see if you still want to get close to echoing those three little words by the time I'm done here. "But eventually, I learned to defend myself. So he couldn't pick on me anymore. He could only pick on her. Sometimes, if I was feeling resentful, if I remembered all the nights I spent alone, praying for Death—" I close my eyes. "Sometimes I let him get away with it. Just to teach her a lesson, for never once protecting me."

Something wet tickles my cheek, but I don't much care whether Pegasus sees me cry. My true nature is far more ugly. "I've never forgotten, not since they sent me to live with Monty. I don't protect my son from anything. And Monty's betrayed me. So now...what right do I have to feel anything? I'm no better than my old man." The realisation kicks me hard in the chest. For a moment I can't breathe.

Then he sighs, and kisses my eyelids. "Oh, Raven," he says.

We sit on the bed, and he pulls me against him, and I let my head fall into his lap. "I don't understand you," he whispers, stroking my hair, my cheeks, my lips, one long wisp of lilac trailing against my skin, tantalising me through my sorrow. "How can you think you're this horrible person? You have emotions, intelligence...beauty."

I laugh bitterly, but he's not giving up.

"Why else would I be here?"

I shrug. "You just never figured out how you'd be better

off with anyone but me. You don't realise what a horrible person I am, cos—"

"Because?"

All right, then. "Because you love me," I whisper, reaching up to touch his face.

He smiles down on me, angelic, serene, and presses a finger against my lips. At last he says, "I met so many horrid people, Raven. They killed my mother. They might have killed your mother, in their way. But not me, and not you. And you're not one of them. Trust me; I know. I'll never lie to you. Damien needs you. You deserve him. You deserve happiness."

A different confession. "You make me happy."

"I hated my mother, too, you know. Only once that I can remember, but I remember it was enough."

I sit up; our noses press together. His soft velvet shirt tempts my fingers. I fight the urge to pull it off him. "What happened? Tell me."

He sighs and draws back. "It was the day before she died. My father held me down on the living-room floor. He read something—I think it was meant to be out of the Bible. Then he cut off my hair, from where I'd asked her to braid it. I screamed for her to help me—until he brought out the belt, anyway—but she just stood there, crying. I didn't understand why he was punishing me. I only wanted to look like my mother; I had done nothing wrong." He frowns, eyelids fluttering to obscure a darker thought. "I didn't figure it out until later—much later—that none of this was to punish me. It was all for her." He smiles as I take up his fragile hands, kiss each and every finger in turn. "I think this was the only time I saw my mother cry. The next day…she—"

I hold him tight. Then, "I don't care what anyone says," he tells me. "We deserve this. We deserve a chance to be happy. Just once."

Is he crying, too? But that's okay. I can play this role, I can make it all better, I—I've got to. "Yeah." I try and return to our kissing, my fantasy from the music store, but he pushes me away and jumps off the bed.

"Why don't you roll a joint, or something."

Did I do something wrong? "Do you want to share?"

He shrugs. "I'm thinking maybe I shouldn't, and feeling like maybe I need to."

I don't know why, but I'm so relieved I actually smile as I retrieve the foil from my suitcase.

I even get him to smoke some for himself, though it makes him cough so violently that we revert to the traditional shotgun toke, and I don't try and encourage him again. Fifteen minutes later we switch off the light and fumble a way out of our clothes and into bed, both well and truly stoned. Pegasus squeals as my tongue teases his nipples, then moans with delight as I spiral down his belly. Breathing in his rose-scented skin, tasting him on my lips, I wish—

I wish I could go further. But I can't, not yet.

I free his hair from its binding, and lie over him. "So beautiful," I whisper in the moon dark. "I'll never let you cut it. And I'll kill anyone who tries to."

He murmurs something under his breath. I pick up just enough to know he's teasing me. "You can be whoever you want, with me. I'll always protect you," I answer. A vow, and another promise.

"I'll come up with a Plan B, my sweet," I hear him saying, but the words drag me too close to the surface, too close to pain, regret, consciousness. I don't want any of those things here with us tonight. Even if it means I've got to forget—

Damien—

Which I could never do. Trapped and helpless in too many ways, I let him roll me over, crawl on top of me, start kissing his way down my face—

"Peg?"

Down my neck—

"Mmm?"

Across my chest—

Out comes his tongue, leaving delicate trails of spit where my stomach dips away from my ribs. What was my question? "What do you reckon happens, when we die?"

He lingers a moment, tracing patterns through the saliva, then slowly works a now moist hand over the head of my dick. I clench my teeth, stifling a moan of beautiful agony. "Why should you ask me this?" he murmurs, closing his fingers around me. Together we gasp, as he squeezes too hard and pushes down towards my balls.

"Does it matter, the reason why?" I ask, once I've gathered my thoughts. "I just wondered...where you thought you'd be going the other night?"

There's a moment's silence. And then he whispers in my ear, "Close your eyes, and I'll show you."

I start to ask what he means, but a strange sensation drives every thought and memory from my mind. I cry out in the darkness, reach for his head, try to pull him off me, try to warn him how this is too much. But somehow, my hands just get lost in that beautiful silky mane. I breathe in violent sobs, my thoughts left to collapse in on themselves again.

His tongue licks greedily over my foreskin, my balls, my thighs, and then suddenly, impossibly, I'm inside his mouth, warm, and wet, and—*home?* I've begun moving against him, trying to work my way deeper into his mouth—

You should stop. Now. He'll hate you for this tomorrow. First you get him stoned, then you let him do this, and you're not stopping him—oh, God.

Somehow he's sucked me all the way in. My cock presses up against the lining of his throat in an identical rhythm to how he squeezed me with his hand—

Then he pulls back, just far enough that I'm overcome by a sudden wave of longing and loneliness. But he isn't planning on leaving me at all. One hand wraps around the base of my dick, and he's devouring me again, his hand moving against his mouth in the opposite rhythm. *Stop it, stop it, stop it.* Of course I don't mean a word of it, as the heat burns through my cheeks, my heart thumping. I think I'm going to—

"Stop...Pegasus," I whisper hoarsely, more desperate to drag him off. His only response is to swallow me up again, and bite down on me, hard. I surrender control, and go back to running my hands through his hair. Outside and inside I'm moaning—sobbing and shuddering and sweating and throbbing—and spilling into his mouth.

I lie sprawled on the bed, arms outstretched, fighting to catch my breath. He waits for my hard-on to die down completely before he lets go and falls against me. I wrap my arms around him, precious thing, hoping the wet heat on his cheeks is nothing more than perspiration, not tears. Half of me can't believe what happened.

Our heartbeats return to some speed approaching normal, and he wriggles up my body till his head rests next to mine on the pillow. "Sorry, obviously I was still a bit peckish," he jokes, but falters when I don't say anything. "Did—did you like that?" he feels compelled to ask.

I almost laugh in his face. What a question. And then, there's my secret. "No one ever did that for me before."

He giggles, then rolls onto his side and pulls me across with him like a blanket. I snuggle into his soft little butt. Only... What's the etiquette in this situation? Should I—? Am I supposed to—?

"Anyway, how did that answer my question?" I say instead, nuzzling into his neck.

"Perfectly, I thought." One more giggle, before he elaborates. "It doesn't matter, Raven. Death, I mean. It doesn't matter *where*. It only matters who *with*. Do you see the difference?"

I frown. "Sort of." Not really.

"Souls joined, no more barriers, no more cages between anything...spirals to true freedom. If you find your soul mate— At least, some people call them this. I think this is what they should mean."

"What do you call it?"

"Raven," he responds in a cheeky voice. Then, more seriously, "When we die, we unify, same as drops of water returned to the ocean. I always thought I should die alone—it was what I'd always been told, only...the other night, I began to realise..." He trails off. Is he asleep?

"What?" I insist.

"I'll never leave you."

"Angel." I touch my lips to his cheek, right before he escapes me, into the sanctuary of dreams.

10 (PEGASUS)

The Rapunzel Syndrome

What is this?

I'm lying on my back, watching the light bulb on the ceiling expand to become a ball of flame. Gold and amber and red—phoenix wings and phoenix tail—unfurl to encompass the entire room. Ashes drift down, cloaking my body in embers, and burst into musical notes as they touch my body: C-sharp minor, E-flat minor arpeggios. The plaster dissolves into a cloudy vortex. Red swirls to purple, and fades to blue.

A blue glow, spiralling overhead.

So why am I not afraid? I've felt this song, I recognise this place that all men fear. I've been here before, or nearly so—

Tranquility, found in the eye of the storm. It feels so right, as though this is the moment I've been waiting for, all of my life.

Waiting for death.

The blue glow descends, cloaking me in a warmth that burns brighter than flame and sinks deeper than flesh, until this is all I see, all I am. Blue pales to white, and I'm flying.

No. This isn't right. Where am I? Where are you taking me?

Home, a voice whispers inside me, and I cry out in surprise, the two sounds echoing around the emptiness that somehow isn't empty, building up into a melodic symphony of sorrow and regret. C-sharp minor, E-flat minor, arpeggios tinkling inside my head. That voice—

A voice I haven't heard for nine years.

Now, I am afraid. I want to run, want to hide, want to escape, but when the fog starts to clear, I'm floating above the room, somewhere inside the cloud-ceiling.

Below, on the bed, the symbol—the physical form that I and the others call Pegasus—dreams. He looks so peaceful in this sleep, so I turn from him, willing myself to face the light. Only this seems to be dissolving, too. The only thing left is for me to become this feeling of sky. Warmth flares as hands reach down to part the clouds, to pull me into embrace.

I thought you would never return to me.
Mother.
I don't understand. How is this happening?
Mortal thoughts. Human thoughts. You haven't yet learned to break the shell, mon ange.
No, not that. Something is wrong—
You brought only half of yourself to me.
I struggle to make sense of this. Groping blindly in the light with hands that have no form, for a presence that is formless. When meaning comes, it sends a sickening jolt through my gut. No. I can't have been wrong, Mama. You always said— you always said this is how it would be, when—
Raven, where are you?
Patience. The warmth spins threads of light around me, soothing fear and dulling agony. *Soon, he comes. Did you not realise? Long before you ever knew, then he made this choice. Long before he even knew himself.*

The warmth drains slowly, leaving only emptiness. She's moving away.

You must wait here. You will know what to do. When it is over, you will find me. Both of you.

No, Mama! Don't leave me. Not again.

Patience, she echoes, and a rainbow traces a memory of my body and hers, interwoven, before its colour disappears. *I shall wait for you, as I have waited, always.*

Mother!

But she's gone. And I'm still here.

I don't want to be here anymore. I don't want to be without you, Raven. How long must I wait? Is this my punishment? But I thought—I thought that was the point of being there. I thought, once I was here, then everything would be—

What a fool I've been, thinking I could cheat death. Trick it into offering me happiness. Why should things be different? Why should anything ever be different?

So, is this really death? Then my funeral—? I hope they didn't bury me in a box, underground, far from the sea. Did I die in my sleep? Whose hand cut the thread? Or was it simply that which we call Fate?

A cold mist settles in. Hugging myself offers no protection; the chill penetrates so deep. Of course. I have no physical presence here. I can't use it to hide from the cold or the pain. Maybe I was wrong. Maybe, after everything, this is hell.

Now on the horizon, flecks of ice come swarming along a spiral path, all headed towards a central point. Whiter than white, each little flake seems filled with such purpose, joining together to mould a cage like spun glass. Once this sculpture has taken shape, I understand, at last. With a secret smile, I begin my approach.

Raven stares out from behind the bars of the cage, watching me with confusion, but no pain. Inside, I'm already healing, becoming whole again. He crouches before me, naked except for the silver cross, and the thorns that bind his wrists and ankles. His turn to wait, but not for so long.

Where am I? he whispers, as I kneel before him, examining the lock on the cage. I unfurl my wings, allowing my love for him to flow around us both, an aura of white gold, my own phoenix thing.

Home. You're home, Raven. And I've come to set you free.

I peel open my eyelids and focus on the ceiling, ensuring it remains constant. The pulse in my ears, throbbing continuously, brings me only relief.

No blue glow, and no wings. No death, then. Not today.

A weight presses down on my bladder, and wrenches me into the physical world. I start to crawl out of bed, only to fall back and bang my head against the steel frame. What the—?

I glance over my shoulder, only to discover one wrist has been tied to the metal frame. Tightly, too; no matter how much I jerk my arm about, the scarf that binds me refuses to work itself free or break. "Fuck." I inspect the knot. I can barely make out the loop. Patience will be required to slip out of this one. Patience I don't have.

Crossing my legs underneath me, I begin wishing away the need to go to the bathroom. I'm not going to wet my pants, like a child. Or Father will come—

No, that isn't right either. I'm not there anymore. I'm no longer a child.

What did I do to you this time, Raven? What did I do, to make you want to punish me?

And now I remember. It's been hanging over our heads like a thundercloud, ever since that night I went down on him. Today. Today is Tuesday.

I was supposed to meet him…afterwards. Five o'clock; we'd arranged it, down the local hotel. Guess this is his subtle way of letting me know I'm not welcome.

A tear trickles down my cheek, as the pain in my bladder

grows to a sharp twinge. No, no, no, no, no! Another trickle runs hot down my thigh. I clench my eyes shut, straining against all my instincts not to allow any more to escape. I'm no longer a child. And you're not my father. You can't humiliate me like this.

Too late creeps closer and closer. I scan the room, desperate to find something—anything—within reach that might help. At last, on the bedside table, beside the photo of my mother, I glimpse one of Raven's lighters. I grab for it, flicking it several times, struggling with one hand to get it lit. Tears of frustration stream freely down my cheeks, but at least not down my leg.

Finally the spark catches, and the flame leaps up. I try to steady my shaking hand as I lower it towards the scarf. I'm terrified the tiny light might flicker out prematurely, but once it makes contact with the fabric, the flame takes off and zooms towards my flesh. I grab a pillow, beat at the fire until it dies out, then race into the bathroom. At last—

When I'm done, I lean against the mirror, staring a hole through my own reflection. *That was too easy. Too easy for you, Raven.*

I dash out of the bathroom, straight for the table by the door. The place where I always leave my keys. They're gone.

Just to be sure, I turn everything on it upside down, but they're nowhere to be found. I know where they are.

Feeling the laughter building in my throat, I cautiously approach the door, reach out, and turn the knob. It doesn't shift. The deadlock. So, I'm trapped, made Rapunzel in her tower, waiting for her handsome prince to come to the rescue.

Will you save me, Raven? Or will you just leave me to my fear and your doom?

The carpet sinks beneath my toes as I pace the floor beneath the window. Eight paces across, eight paces back… Eight paces across, eight paces back…

Only when the phone rings, shattering my numbness like nails on a chalkboard, do I stop to wonder how long I've been going. It keeps on ringing, even as I stare at it. Should I answer it? Perhaps it's Raven. But I already know it isn't.

Eventually it stops, and I sigh, relieved to return to my pacing, angry that its intrusion made me lose count—how many steps left to make it to the window? Dammit. I'm going to have to start all over, now.

I wander over to the door that will never open, steady myself with a deep breath, and prepare to take it from the top. But just as I place my first foot down, the phone rings again. With a growl of frustration, I race to the wall and almost rip the whole thing off as I yank the receiver to my ear. "What?!"

"Uh, hey sleepyhead, how's it hanging?"

Lenny. Shit. I glance at the clock. Ten forty-five. In fifteen minutes, Raven will be in court.

And fifteen minutes ago, I was supposed to be at work.

"Are you going to be late?" he presses, as I don't say anything.

"Um…" I search every corner of my mind for an excuse.

You could always tell him the truth.

"I think I'm coming down with something," I say, trying to make my voice sound weak. "I might have to give it a miss, today." I finish it off with a cough, for good measure.

On the other end of the line, he sighs. Tough luck for you, Lenny. And tough luck for me. I actually enjoy teaching, and a chance to play without feeling threatened. But neither of us have much choice here. "Are you bullshitting me, Peg?" he demands in an ugly voice. "After everything I've fucking done for you, are you bullshitting me?"

"No, Lenny." I glance at the window, just in time to catch

sight of a butterfly, flitting in and out of the wavering curtains. I should put down the phone at once and go to it. Butterflies have such short lives. All that time they spend, waiting, in transformation, cocooned. Emerging brilliant and beautiful only to die. If there's any such thing as karma and rebirth, I want to be a butterfly next time.

Maybe I already am. You and me both, Raven.

I don't realise I'm crying until Lenny's voice crawls into my ear, sounding more concerned. "Is something wrong?"

My answer hasn't changed. "No, Lenny. I just—I can't, okay?"

Like flicking a switch, things are as they were. "Fuck you, you little slut, you're going to do this to me ten minutes before a lesson? Do you know who your first student is, huh?"

I humour him. "Betty Mitchell, I believe."

"That's right, Betty-fucking-Mitchell. With her mother in tow. Have you seen that fucking bitch? She'll never let me forget this. I'm warning you, Pegasus, unless you get your arse in here now, you're in deep shit. Trust me when I tell you that."

"I do," I murmur. "But—" I smile at the door, which still refuses to open. "I can't. I told you, I don't feel well. I'm sorry I didn't call earlier, but—"

"Yeah, sure you're fucking sorry. Raven's moved in to mooch off you, hasn't he?"

The sudden change of topic catches me off-guard. "Yes."

He snickers. "I should have known. He always was a bad influence. He never got you as a kid, so now—"

I'm so not in the mood for this. I turn my back on the butterfly, unable to have these two conflicting states of being present in me at once. "What the fuck are you talking about, Lenny?"

"What, did you stay up late last night? Get a little drunk, a little high?" I have to stop myself from laughing—coming from Lenny, these moral accusations are a bit much. "You never did any of that for *me*. Then again, I always said that bastard was the devil, could get you to sign over your soul if you weren't looking in the right direction."

He already did. And I was looking, in the right direction, that is. Even so, Lenny's words make me uncomfortable. "I wasn't drunk. And you know I don't smoke." I've never been very good at lying, but this one flows right off my tongue.

"Yeah, bet that's what all the kiddies at school said, too."

I start to trace invisible patterns on the wall. Sure, I'd heard the rumours about Raven and what he did when we were together in that place. Selling pot, suicide attempts, and a psychotic temper. That was my love.

"So, how much is he paying you?"

I blink, and swallow silence.

"No, seriously, what's your going rate these days? Must've come down quite a bit, if he can cough up for it."

I bite back my tongue's most instinctive reply, and wait for my nerve-endings to stop tingling before I answer, "He doesn't need to pay me anything."

Laughter on the other end of the line, mocking, but insulted too. "Yeah? What a joke that is. Well, guess what, princess? Now *I* don't need to pay you anything, either."

"What?"

"You're fired." And just like that, he hangs up.

With a trembling hand, I replace the receiver in its cradle. Then rip the whole phone off the wall and hurl it against the door.

It lands in a hundred little pieces around my feet. I blink in surprise. Must have thrown it harder than I thought. Crouching down, I toy with a plastic shard, and inspect the broken receiver, still attached to the body of the phone by its cord, like a severed finger dangling from a single thread. You tried. But nobody escapes this door. You should have gone for the window instead.

The butterfly...

I creep towards the rippling curtains, spread them wide, then press my nose against the glass, seeking out any signs. But it's long gone.

Only as I crawl out from under my makeshift veil do I notice the amber wings, motionless on the floor. I tiptoe towards it, no longer bothering to count my steps.

The beautiful butterfly has fallen, doomed to a silent forever, here on my carpet.

So be it. I crawl back into bed, turning from the splendour that will be no more. Everything dies.

Perhaps even love.

It would be easy enough to fool myself into believing that was truth. But it's all a place I've been before. Just reassurances my mind sends when it thinks I need protecting. My mind doesn't know me very well, it seems.

I'm not looking at the photo of my mother. She's in my mind, though not as she was in the dream. Here in my head, she's only a still image—her hair, her face, her expression a perfect copy of the picture. If I hadn't salvaged it, I may have forgotten her altogether already.

But not today. There's a feeling about this day, too much a refrain of nine years ago. Then, as now, I'd been locked in my room, only I escaped by crawling out the window, out to the beach, to where I saw her walk beneath the waves. I didn't understand. Or perhaps I understood perfectly. I yearned to follow her. But Father caught me. Afterwards, once he knew for sure, he laughed at me.

So, you see, love doesn't die. It simply isn't, or it is. That's all I know. But I'm certain, when I'm not certain of anything else, that this is the truth. It must be. And today feels like that day because I know I'm about to lose—

I cover my face with a hand. Dangerous, these thoughts. If I'm not careful, they'll make me cry. Death is such a finality, yet no one ever says good-bye.

With a shaky sigh, I lift myself off the bed. Stepping over the butterfly, I wander over to turn on the stereo, pressing play on a tape that's been copied so many times there's more hiss than music. But my mind can fill in the gaps.

This was my good-bye, from my mother. For my ninth birthday, she wrote and recorded this song for me. She was always so much more refined in her technique, a better pianist than I'll ever be. I tiptoe into the bathroom and perch on the edge of the tub, my hands clasped against my heart, staring into the running water. Until this moment, I've never thought of it. If I went, that night, I never would have said good-bye to Raven. He would have thought it was all his fault.

The song always ends too soon. I turn off the taps, and move to switch off the tape. Then I crank up a New Order CD, before settling down into the bath. The water's hot, but soothing too, lulling me to sleep.

Next time, I'll at least say good-bye.

Because good-byes aren't forever. Only love is.

I wake to find myself shivering, the last rays of sunlight giving way to sunset. The window is open, and the water's freezing. Why am I here, all alone?

Love? What do I know of love, anyway?

My tummy growls as I clamber out of the tub and rub myself down with a towel. Beyond the bathroom, the first thing I notice is the butterfly, still dead upon the carpet. I pick it up gently and take it to the window, leaning out over the roof. All across the city, people are returning home from work to nothing in particular—ambitions and lives and relationships

I don't understand, and don't want to understand.

"Perhaps it's better this way," I whisper, letting the weightless husk fall from my palm, watching as it spirals off on the breeze, heading for the sky, until it floats out of sight. I gaze into the sad, pale sunset, before closing the window and turning my back on everything.

My tummy growls again. I suppose I should eat. I drift into the kitchen on automatic, grab a knife and a loaf of bread. I'm just reaching for a plate above the sink when I catch sight of a coloured fragment. Another photo.

Things are out of place here. I don't leave it like this. I leave these hidden, buried. I wasn't planning to take them out again until I could no longer remember your face. That's how it was, with my mother.

I flick through the photos. Most are in order, except for one sequence. Pictures of me and him, mostly from our high school years.

Dammit, why did you have to do this, Raven? Why not leave them be?

My gaze falls across the picture that should be second from the bottom—not third. Am I seeing it for the first time? Why did I never realise before? He looks at the me in this photo the same way he did the night he told me how he felt. A recorded confirmation, of truth.

Did you not realise? Long before you ever knew, then he made this choice. Long before he even knew himself.

Then I hear a scream, and the nearest plate hurtles towards the window, bounces off, and shatters in the sink. I throw myself at the glass instead, satisfied at last by the window's smash as it breaks against my fist.

I pull my arm out, and study the bloody tears and little pieces of glass glittering in the flesh. The pain hasn't reached me yet. I run to my bed, and the tears don't stop for the longest time, long after it's too dark to eat and I've lost the will to get up and turn on the light.

I crouch forward, squinting through the shadows, picking out glass fragments, making my arm bleed again. Are you ever coming home, Raven? I can't be here anymore, and yet I can't leave. Was this your wish? Or did you just forget all about me?

By now, the court case must be over. I look at the remains of the telephone in the corner.

He wouldn't have called you anyway. He never does.

Then does that mean—?

Don't. I can't afford to think about that. Because I already know what it means.

I laugh, and reach for the remainder of a joint he left on the bedside table. As though he knew I'd need to stop thinking, eventually. I manage the lighter with more success this time, forcing myself to keep in the smoke, and not to cough. Seems strange to be doing this when you're not here. Seems strange, that you're not here.

I attempt a few more drags, but the third puff fills my throat with fire and leaves me doubled over and choking on the floor. By the time I recover, the rest of it's burned out, leaving me to my darkness. At least now I don't have to think.

Feeling even more miserable, and sick as well, I crawl into bed, just as the throbbing waves hit. I focus on my breathing until everything passes, and I can zone out by staring at the ceiling again. Everything travels in circles. My mind won't stop. It won't allow me to stop caring for you.

When are you coming home?

Please don't leave me here.

I must have slept, because the minute I hear a door slam I jerk upright, awake in an instant. There's a shadow on the wall. Maybe it's nothing more. I look at the clock. Two a.m.

I roll off the bed and dash towards him, so grateful he's finally home I'm willing to ignore the stench of alcohol and sickness that poisons the rest of the room. But instead of the hug I hoped for, he shoves me face-first onto the mattress, knocking the air from my lungs as he falls on top of me, rubbing against my butt. Before I can even whisper his name, he pulls down my underwear, and bites and sucks at my balls.

Is this your love for me, then? Are you so surprised I'm always afraid?

I manage the strength to push him off, long enough to roll onto my back. Despite his drunkenness, he's able to keep a firm grip on my boxers, and now his tongue and teeth go to work on my dick instead.

He's too drunk to notice that, after about five minutes of this, I'm still not responding in the 'usual' way. "What'sa matter, Peggy?" he asks, slurring his words. "You don't love me no more?"

Why does he always ask? Doesn't he know? Or does he just need to hear me say it? "You locked me in here all day." As he tries to keep kissing me, I slap at him.

"I thought you'd leave me, angel," he murmurs, unable to focus on any one part of my face. "Thought you'd—" He lets go of me to wave a hand absently through the air. "Thought you'd fly away."

I'm not going to say it. "Dammit, it's my goddamn house!"

His eyes narrow into pinpricks of hate before he lashes out, striking me across the face so hard I fall onto the bed. Then I'm on my tummy again, the shock of my stinging cheek not enough to prepare me as three fingers force their way inside my arse, so cold and savage I cry out in pain.

He chuckles in my ear. "Does that hurt you, babe? Pain is so...exquisite, dontcha think? It's what makes us human. It's what makes us more alive than them."

You think we're in on this together? You think, by doing this to me against my will, we'll reach some higher spiritual plane? Oh, Raven. What have I done?

I hear myself sobbing long before the tears come. I'm surprised they still fall, after all this. I should be able to block it all out, like I did with the others, but—

Damn you, this is different. I didn't want it to be like this, I just wanted—

What? Love?

His thrusting grows fiercer, more urgent, inflicting a new kind of pain. "Raven, please, not when you're drunk!" But of course he isn't listening. I can hear him in the dark, fumbling with his belt. There is no more time left.

He has to extract himself eventually, to pull down his suit pants. The moment he lets go, I'm barrelling towards the door, every instinct screaming escape. My fingers reach the knob and slide down the frame as he tackles me to the carpet.

"Ah, so you'd prefer the floor?" He pins me with his knees, and finishes up with his pants. I try to claw him off, but he shifts into a position where any sudden movement on my part would leave me in a great deal more pain. Now his flesh presses against mine, and I don't know whether to feel relief or dread as he begins to laugh hysterically.

Once he calms down, the explanation comes. "How about that. I finally got you right where I want you and I can't even get it up." Giggling, he struggles to his feet, and helps me to mine. I meet his gaze with only a glare, snatching my hand away. But I'm surprised to see him blink back a tear before he turns his face from me. "Go to bed, Peg," he says, and buries his face in his hands. Not taking my eyes off him, I do what he tells me, pulling up my underwear and tugging down my t-shirt. When I run into the mattress, I let myself slump, and wrap myself in the doona like it's a cocoon.

He approaches me cautiously, and kneels at my feet. I shrink away from him as he reaches out a hand, guilty when he withdraws. Some part of me wants to let him in despite everything. And yet, I just—I just can't.

"I'm an arsehole," he whispers, with no sense of self-parody. "Anybody who knows me will tell you that."

I tremble, unsure where this speech could lead. Confused and alone in the dark. Like I have been all day. Like I have been always.

"I can promise I won't ever hit you again." He draws in a shaky breath, seeing the look of disbelief I can't hide cross my face. "And I won't ever hurt you—"

"That's what you always say."

"No. This time I *can* promise. I'll show you."

He staggers to the wardrobe, and almost pulls the suitcase down on top of himself. Next, he fishes the few items that belong to him from off the hooks, and stuffs each one inside. For some reason, I'm more afraid now than I was when he was hurting me. "What are you doing?" I ask.

He rubs at his nose, then starts to fiddle with the latches. "Keeping my promise. Just for once. Just to prove that I can, okay?" The suitcase locks, and he drags it to the door, but he doesn't come back to me.

I don't want him there, in that horrible place that he is. *The seventh layer of hell*, he said. Then mine must be the sixth. "Raven! Where are you going?"

The silence lasts so long I'm almost ready to ask him again, before he says very quietly, "Away. Somewhere I can't hurt anybody."

My heart stutters. Anybody? Not only me? What does that mean?

Slowly, an answer begins to take form, the only explanation that could be the truth, and yet I beg not to be the truth. "You lost, didn't you."

He lets out a single laugh, then falls silent. But even in the dark, I can see his shoulders shaking. He can't answer me.

He doesn't need to. He must hate me right now.

"Don't leave me," I tell him, surprised by the strength of my words.

He turns to glare at me, his face lit by the street lamps, a beautiful ghost. "Aren't you worried what will happen if I stay?"

"Yes. But I'm terrified of what will happen if you leave."

He shakes his head in disbelief, too drunk to come up with any logical arguments. "You're insane. And better off without me."

"No!"

"Why?" he yells, stalking towards me, and I hate myself for shrinking away again. "See? I can't get near you without you thinking I'm going to hurt you, or fuck you. I may be too drunk tonight, but I *will* hurt you, Pegasus. Same as I hurt my son."

A weight grows hard in my chest. Hurt your son? When? "You never—" Feeling my faith falter, I close my eyes, calling up images of him and Damien. That doesn't make sense. That wasn't you, it was her. I saw it. We all did. That bitch. That bitch I want to— "You never hurt him."

He laughs again. "Try telling that to his mama."

"She said this?"

He glances down at the floor. "Forget about it." Looking up again, he meets my gaze defiantly. "Forget about me."

"No." I grab for his hand, but he promptly jerks it out of my reach.

"Fuck! Am I that drunk? Am I having that much trouble making myself understood? I can't be here anymore."

"Then where will you go?"

"Why do you care?"

I look down at my fingers, quavering in my lap. "Because I know how it ends," I whisper, recalling my dream, and fall into his arms so he has no other choice but to accept me here now, to warm me and hold me and stay.

Eventually we draw apart. He tucks me into bed, then sits nearby, facing towards the window, but doesn't climb in next to me, nor remove any of his clothing. "Pegasus, I—I'm sorry."

"I could just hold you." Two broken creatures, you and I. If we can't fit the pieces together again, let's just make something new.

But again, he shakes his head. "How can you be so—?" He breaks off and changes tack. "How can you want to give me so much, when I'll only ask for ten times more in return?"

I can't do anything more than shrug. "Faith?"

He looks at me; even in the dark I can feel his gaze, piercing the depths of my soul. "You really believe that, don't you."

I nod mutely. He smiles sadly, but stops himself from reaching out to me again. "Maybe one day, I might too. But tonight it's beyond me, I think."

What does that mean? "Raven?"

"I'm so sorry," he repeats.

He faces me now, raising his hand in what appears to be a fist. In another heartbeat, a heavy dull ache pounds my forehead. A darkness I can't fight drags me down, into the sleep with no dreams. Rapunzel falls from her tower window, finally free.

(RAVEN) *11*

Sole Destruction

Faith...

This is your faith. This is where it leads you. This is what I am.

Alone...

I hold the silver cross up to my face, as a gust of wind outside the window lashes the curtains and scatters its blades of ice around the room. I just listen. I don't feel. I can't feel.

I feel too much.

I can't turn around, can't look at what I've done, can't face this eidolon thing you call faith.

I had to do this. I couldn't let you see. Couldn't let you care.

So why am I still here? This place, this time—I've been here before. As a child. A child whose old man put him to bed, not with fairy stories or teddy bears, but his breath and his fists reeking of booze.

This is what I've become. Same as him. That's what she said. It's what she told all of them. It doesn't matter whether they believe it or not. The problem is, I believe it.

I may not do it to my son, but I do it to you, Pegasus.

I put my head in my hands, pressing the cold silver against my eyelids. Powerless to protect myself from the chill within. Please, not tonight. Just leave me alone. Isn't this enough?

All I can do is hurt you, but that's not what I wished. I don't expect you to believe that. I don't expect you to believe me. I did this to you so you wouldn't have to see. I did this to you so I couldn't hurt you anymore.

What if he doesn't wake up? What if you hurt him too much?

No. I knew what I was doing, exactly what I was doing when— When I hit him.

I stare at a spot on the carpet, somewhere between the suitcase and the door. I know how to knock someone out without killing them. I trained myself to retain control, even when I'm drunk, cos of my dad. And now I'm using my hatred, my defences, against the only person left who—

Don't use that word. You've got no right to use that word. What do you know of love?

I move towards the suitcase. *Time to run away.*

Time to leave.

Instead I find myself in the kitchen, staring at the shards of broken glass littering the windowsill and the sink. I pick one up, to examine a spray of blood. Pegasus's blood. That cold wind now caresses my cheeks. Were you trying for a way out? Or were you just angry? Angry at me.

Who could blame you? I hold the glass against my wrist, making a tight fist out of habit, an age-old attempt at getting the veins to stand out from my opaque skin. I recall the sight of the phone, scattered over the floor in a hundred tiny pieces, another victim of his anger, anger only I deserve.

I'm making you the same as me. Poisoning everything you are.

My fingers let the glass shard slide back into the basin. Feeling sick, I sink to the floor, flattening myself against the cold, hard tiles. Nothing I can do. Nothing left for me to do. Leaving's easy. But then what?

Shadows dance across the ceiling, creeping up on me. I

wish—I wish I never hit you. I wish you were here, to put your arms around me, to whisper my name, to tell me it's all going to be okay, to tell me there's some way to save—

"Damien," I whisper, my pathetic sob loud and intrusive in this small, lonely space.

Nothing left to lose. So what do I do now? What am I supposed to do?

Step forward and introduce yourself to the rest of the human race.

I laugh at myself, and a new emptiness echoes in mad zigzags through my head.

I'd always associated courtrooms with men in wigs, and grand juries, and swearing oaths on the Bible. Not surprisingly, the real thing was nothing like I imagined.

The morning turned out sickly-sunny. I met up with Judy, who insisted we go for coffee, though I refused to indulge in her need for small talk. My mind was off elsewhere, practising my numbness. I already knew I was failing miserably.

Wendy and her lawyer, the same one who'd materialised at Monty's that night, turned up ten minutes late. I knew it was all over when I couldn't even bring myself to hate her as she swanned into the courtroom, face all done up like some macabre exhibit from Madame Tussauds. So there I sat, a wolf in a trap, forced to suck up all her lies. Watching Judy and the lawyer and the magistrate watching me and believing her, till in the end I started to believe her too. Don't think my hand strayed too far from the silver cross the entire time.

Pegasus. His name chanted in my mind as an incantation, to make those terrible words—that feeling—disappear. Please save me. Show them how this isn't the truth. They'll believe it, coming from you. Please.

But Peg wasn't there. He was never going to be there, all cos I'd been so afraid. She said I—

She said I was like my dad. She said I always came home drunk, and hurt them, and she told them I—

She said I did to Damien what her family did to Pegasus. "I can't prove it, of course, but the poor little thing's so terrified, it's all he can do to let me get near him. That bastard—" here she flashed those evil eyes at me. "You hear how they are, these *queers*. I just know he had...*sexual relations*...with my son."

Every scandalised face turned to gape at me, but her smug smile was all I could see as I launched myself across the table. I was crying, too far gone for stoicism or shame. "Why the fuck are you doing this to me? That's bullshit, all of it, and you—"

"Raven," Judy said, touching my arm, but I slapped her away. You believe her. You all fucking believe her. You think I'd honestly—?

"What the fuck are you doing? How can you say that? It's not the truth. It's never been the truth, I would never—"

I stopped short as Wendy snorted at me in disdain. I'd fallen for her act, same as the rest of them. Then Judy dragged me outside, tried to calm me. I couldn't stop shaking. I couldn't believe—

"I never did that," I whispered, over and over, my hands blurring beneath my tears.

"I know," Judy said quietly. "There is some bruising, but as to the rest of it, there's no conclusive medical proof. Calm down already."

No medical proof. They needed to check?

After that, I had to come up with some speech on why I should get to keep my son. What I could give him, in 500 words or less. And all I could come up with was something blurred along the lines of, *I love him...and he loves me. I've got nothing else. Ask him.* But he was too young to get any say in the matter. All three of us, powerless against her. Judy sat forward and reminded them all of the fact that I was 'the primary caregiver'. Only by then, it was much too late.

And so she won, so easily. They led my angel away, too late for good-byes as well. They even gave me papers to commemorate the event, which I promptly tore to shreds and scattered outside in the street. Judy tried to touch me again. I pushed her off, not as roughly as I wanted to. Then I started walking, letting my feet lead me where they would.

They led me to the one place I so didn't need to be. A pub.

By the time sunset bled across the sky, I'd lost count of how many drinks I'd had. I sat at the bar—an older haunt—staring out the window, alternately ignoring and despising everyone else. Somehow, I kept hoping Pegasus would sweep through the door at any moment, pull me into his arms, and take me someplace safe and warm. But whenever the door opened, some happy couple came breezing in instead, and each time I shivered as I remembered—again—that it could never be him. I'd locked him away, for his own protection.

No, that's not true. Not to protect him. To protect myself.

For the first time I could recall in recent history, I was drunk right on dark. I didn't even notice Lenny till he towered over the top of me, already halfway through a sentence. I blinked, barely registering his anger. No big deal. Anger was just another emotion, and emotions meant nothing anymore.

"What?" I said blankly.

"I said," he repeated in a louder voice, "your little whore lost his job today on your account. Hope you're fucking proud of yourself."

I frowned, struggling to think of who and what he was on about. When I did figure it out, the frown only intensified, bringing with it something I didn't want, dragging me out of my apathy and off to some place I wanted to be even less than here. I heard myself muttering a threat about using that word to refer to my angel, while another part of my mind wondered what I'd actually do about it, and yet another dreamed up a response.

"Oh, what, you think you're gonna be his first? He sure as shit ain't no virgin. I can vouch for that. He's a fucking whore, and he'd still be a whore if I hadn't given him a job that didn't involve blowing suits old enough to be his daddy and bending over to—"

It was as far as he got before what was left of my scotch and coke, and the glass, landed smack in the centre of his forehead. There was a loud smash. When he faced me again, blood streamed down his eyebrows and dripped down his cheeks. You...

You were one of them?

And then it all became so clear: how he spied on Peg at the store, how he acted around Pegasus, how Pegasus acted around him— But then, it must've been a long time ago. Did Peg remember him?

What if he did?

A few women standing nearby screamed as I threw myself at Lenny, sending him crashing to the ground, too angry to care how well-placed the punches I was laying into him were. I just wanted to hurt him. I just wanted to make him suffer, for what he'd done to my Pegasus. I just wanted to hear the bones of his skull fracture beneath my fists. "I'm going to kill you, you son of a diseased hag," I spat, blinded by a red cloud of hatred.

Then I was being dragged away, lifted and thrown out onto the pavement in the cold night air.

I remember springing straight back up, trying to plough through the two bouncers—a pair of Maori guys who were probably five times my size between them—anything to get in another shot at that bastard. This time, I was going to kill him.

Instead, I found myself unceremoniously dumped arse-first

on the pavement again. One of the bouncers laid a heavy hand on my shoulder, to prevent me going anywhere. "Calm down, Raven. Go home. Sleep it off."

"What would you fucking know about it?" I glared at him with as much venom as I could muster.

"I know that if you don't, someone's gonna call the cops," he replied, so calm and self-assured as he popped me right side up. Easy enough for them. They had something to live for.

"Go home, Raven," he said, pushing me in the other direction.

I'd staggered two blocks to the next pub, half-hoping Lenny would find his way over so I could at least finish the job. But after waiting a moment I got bored and ordered another scotch and coke, desperate to quash all the little voices in my head. Not like my dad. Like Ma. This is what drove her insane.

When will they realise I'm insane? Lock the door and throw away the key. Who do I need to call, to get them to do that to me?

Pegasus—Pegasus with...Lenny. I couldn't bear to think about it, and yet the more I tried not to, the more it kept poking into my conscious mind, teasing me, mocking me, tormenting me. Those past tortures never had a face before, and now that they did—

About half an hour before closing, the real truth of the matter finally struck home, as I threw up over the concrete stairwell, too late to make it to the men's. *Pegasus and Lenny.*

So, you could want him, you could let him...do that to you. But not me. You can't even say *I love you, Raven.* If he'd asked you, if he'd named the right price, would you have said it to *him*?

I downed one last drink, filling myself with a sense of nausea and a sense of destiny, before staggering home, my heart black with jealousy and sorrow and self-righteous disgust.

If you want him, you can want me too. Or you don't get a choice in the matter. Just like I never do.

Stupid. I'm nothing but a fool. What else could I be, to have thought—

To have thought he could want me, he could love me at all, let alone like that.

Once more, I find myself sitting on the edge of the bed, my shaking hands stroking his long silken hair. Why am I doing this? Why am I pushing away the only one who cares, the only one who cares enough to want to help me?

Because if I care, I can lose. I can still be hurt. She can still take it from me—

No. He said he had a plan B. That he would help me. That I've got to...trust him.

Why am I so afraid, when there's nothing left to lose? Why are these self-preservation instincts still around, when there's nothing left worth preserving?

"Damn you," I mutter to no one in particular, tracing an imaginary path down his tear-stained cheek. He asked me to stay. Even after I hurt him. He said—he said—

Because I know how it ends.

And he cried.

Damn you, wake up. Please don't leave me all alone. I'm so tired of being alone. Tell me how it ends. Tell me, somehow, that at least some of this pain is worth it.

He doesn't answer. He can't, of course.

I look away, helpless. Too many times, helpless. Is this how it's always going to be? I was meant to protect you. I promised— I said I loved you. But what I've shown you, that isn't love.

How could I have said those words? How could I have been

so stupid? I've got no idea how to show anyone love, no idea of its true meaning.

Only my dad ever told me he loved me; every night, after he got done hurting me and Ma. He swore the same thing to her, too. I try and laugh, but nothing comes. It's too close to the truth. This is the only love I've got, Peg. I can't stay. I can't bear to see the ways I hurt you, and yet—

I can't bear to leave.

Slowly, very cautiously, like he's some china doll, I pull his slender body close as I strip off his t-shirt, then lay him to rest on the mattress. Next I arrange his long hair in swirls around his face and shoulders. Last of all, I peel off his underwear. But don't worry, my angel. I don't want to do that to you. I'm not your uncle. I'm not Lenny. And I'm not like the rest of them. I just want you to think that I am.

I trail my hand down his arm, my fingers coming away slick with blood. He hurt himself tonight, with the window. Another sin I've committed against him.

I get off the bed and enter the bathroom, jumping at the sight of the reflection that stares at me from the mirror. *Don't look.* Hastily, I avert my eyes and start rummaging through the cabinet under the sink till I uncover some bandages in the dark. Then I make my way back to his inert form.

Kneeling on the floor beside him, I take hold of his wrist and start wrapping the bandage round his hand, working my way up to his elbow, where the cut trails off. At that end I tie a little bow. As I sit up, I steal a glimpse of his naked body. You're still too beautiful. In you, the power to remind me of my reason. In you the power to give me hope.

I bend forward for a single kiss, tasting sorrow and marijuana on his lips. *I'm making you the same as me.* I crawl onto the bed, nuzzling his cheeks, his neck, his chest, dotting his stomach with kisses, then burying my nose in the downy pubic hair that shines silver in this light. I kiss the tip of his penis once before returning to his face, just watching him sleep.

I could watch you forever, angel, if only you'd let me. *Forever.*

That's why I'm so afraid. This is why I'm being so terrible to you. *Because I know how it all ends.*

I kiss my own tears off his lips, and stroke his forehead gently. Please come back to me. I can't promise you anything. I can give you nothing. But I want you here with me, for eternity.

I sniff, running my arm under my nose, and get to my feet. On my way past again, I glance at the stereo. There's blood on the tape deck. Something compels me to touch my own fingertip to the little red imprint on the button marked 'play', before I turn back to look at him. Gotta keep doing that, to remind myself he's still here.

Still alive.

Now, for the last time, I crawl to him on all fours. I pick the cross off the mattress, and fasten it around my neck. Then I lie next to him, aware all the while of the hairs bristling on my arms. I've begun to feel again.

I'm taken by surprise when the soft music floats in. It's a piano piece, though the tape's so worn out that anyone else probably wouldn't catch the melody. But I do. I've heard this one before. It was the song Pegasus played to me, the night— the night I told him, how I felt. I thought I'd sentenced us both to our doom. Maybe I was right. But here, in this pain and this dreadful silence before the first refrain of dawn, I come to realise I've finally found a definition.

A definition of love.

I wrap my arms around him, and press my head to his heartbeat. Closing my eyes, I settle in to wait for him to wake once more and give me a reason—any reason. A reason to give me what I want. Not to hurt him, not to touch him in the way all those others did, not for hunger, or abuse.

A reason to make love.

To me.

※

Weak sunlight steals through the curtains, as birdsong and traffic outside and dull voices downstairs announce the onset of a new day. I lie here listening to the dull thud of his heart, as his body grows warm beneath me again. And now his fingertips touch the edges of my face. I stop breathing, too afraid to do anything.

When I dare to look, the first thing I see are those sad silver eyes, fixed on me. I sit bolt upright, waiting out the moment till I can trust myself to speak. Then, "Are you okay?"

The mattress pings, as he rises more slowly. I want to help him, but I don't dare touch. I've already done enough.

"My head's a little sore. But…I think I'm okay. What—?"

"I'll run you a bath." I roll off the bed, the sudden movement bringing waves of nausea flooding back. He wanted to ask me what happened. I can't tell him, not yet. Delaying the moment he pushes me out of his life.

I head for the bathroom, turn on the taps, and find some fragrant oils to squeeze into the water. Soon, rose-scented bubbles rise towards the ceiling. I'll tell him. Then there'll be no way he'll ever forgive me. Too many reminders that nothing lasts forever.

I turn off the taps, testing the water's temperature, before I return to the bed. Pegasus hasn't moved. He glances at me, twisting a lock of hair absentmindedly around one finger. Too ashamed to look into his face, I lift him in my arms, carry him across the floor, and lower him into the bath. Then I take up my seat on the edge of the claw-foot tub, deliberately facing away from him.

He lets out a heartfelt sigh. I start to scratch at one of the scars on my left wrist. "What—what did we do last night?" he asks me.

"You don't remember?" My voice is cold, challenging him to dredge up those horrible memories.

"I—I remember I was waiting. Waiting for you to come home. I was worried about you. I felt as though—" I can hear the uncertainty in his words. "I don't remember much after that. It—it hurts. What's going on, Raven? What have I done?"

I start to laugh; can't remember when I did this cos I was actually happy. "Not you," I say at last. "Me."

"What does that mean?"

I shrug and gaze off into the living room. "I locked you away cos I was scared you'd leave me. Then I came home drunk, and tried to fuck you. Then after all that, I knocked you out. I couldn't let you see me cry, not this time." I'm amazed at how nonchalant I sound. Does he hate me all the more for that?

When he doesn't say anything, I at last turn to face him. He's staring at his hands, most of his body and hair submerged in the bubbles, a little frown shadowing his face. Finally, he looks at me and says, "I woke up naked. Did you—while I was asleep—?"

I blink in surprise, then disgust, then shame. "I didn't rape you while you were asleep. I wouldn't. I...couldn't." My voice breaks. He won't believe me. Why should he? Nobody ever does. They didn't believe me when it came to my son, either. You're the only one who knows me, Pegasus, and this is the side of myself I've chosen to show you.

It's already over. So why am I still here?

"I—I betrayed your trust. I didn't want—" *No. No excuses. No begging forgiveness. Just leave. It's over. Go.*

"There's nothing left of this," I mutter, and get off the tub. "I can't stay here."

Behind me, I hear the sounds of splashing water, and he grabs hold of my arm, whipping me around to face him. His eyes burn little holes into me, two moons that give off heat with their intensity, and somehow, now, I'm afraid to look away.

"You can't leave me," he says, quiet but firm. "I've waited too long for this. For you."

I can't answer, but he wants more than that. He wants me to believe. "This is about Damien? I told you, we'll get him, somehow. We'll still be a family, I swear."

Our foreheads press together. "Not about Damien," I murmur. One of his hands clasps my own; the other pulls me close against him, back into the bathroom, to the sanctity of the water. "Not just about Damien," I correct myself, as he lowers himself into the tub again. "About you, Pegasus."

He smiles as I say his name. Why is he letting me do this? "I can't stay here. I'll—" *make you the same as me* "—destroy you."

He looks aside, considering this. "Not my destruction," he says at last. "My salvation."

I choke on a sob and his name, as he turns that gaze, bright and defiant and full of hope, loose upon me.

"Stay," he says simply, pulling me down into the water above him.

I want nothing more than to curl up inside him, forever protected by the light that burns within. That would be home. "Yes," I agree weakly, and he holds me tight against the flood of fear and relief that fills us both, drawing us even closer together.

I was a fool to think we could ever be apart.

12 (PEGASUS)

True Faith

The front bar of the Olive Branch is swarming with a freak show assortment of scenesters and bogans. I weave through the sweaty throngs of flannel shirts or turtlenecks and tight black jeans, to find Noriko tucked behind a corner table with two glasses of Midori and lemonade, one set aside for me. Ugh. So this would be our first Friday night gig.

As I take up a spot beside her, I catch sight of the clock above the bar. Strange that a hotel should have a clock. It reads five minutes to ten. Five minutes before we're meant to be on stage. Five minutes to summon the last dregs of inspiration from my threadbare soul. And Raven hasn't surfaced. I take a sip of my drink, and Noriko smiles at me, hopeful, sad, and knowing. It's too loud to hear myself think, let alone waste energy on small talk. This isn't the place I should be. I need to find him, before we go on.

I scull the rest of the glass, then turn from the table. But she grabs at my wrist and tugs me towards her, wide-eyed and worried. I can't bring myself to pity her. "What?" I mouth, wrenching myself out of her grip.

She shrinks down into her seat, and feigns a sudden interest in her straw. I think I hear her say, "Nothing."

"Good." I creep through the tail end of the crowd, and slip behind the curtain backstage.

Here in this quieter dark, I can breathe again. Once my eyes adjust to the low light, I spot Raven, leaning against the far wall, arms folded across his chest, staring off into space. The rhythmical twitch of his jaw is the only external clue to the madness that consumes him. Has been consuming him, ever since that night he tried to leave me. Ever since the day they took his son.

I'm all he has left, and I am not enough. If I was enough, I could save him. I would have saved him already.

But it's not over yet. This isn't how it ends. I know you're the truth. I know you don't want me to believe, but I can see beyond everything. I've touched you, tasted you, hurt you, been hurt by you, and now— And now, I know.

I cross the floor and put my arms around him, though there's no way to tell if he even notices. His entire body seems made of ice, hard and cold, too afraid to allow any warmth to escape his skin and flow through to me. He still believes himself capable of hurting me.

I'm not afraid. I snuggle into his shoulder, comforted by the scent of cloves that lingers about his skin. Feeling his muscles tauten before he says, "I don't think I can do this."

He's staring down at me, trying so hard to hide it, but I know the sorrow that smoulders within. As long as you feel this, I have hope. I feel it too. Don't you see?

I catch hold of his fingers, lift them to my face. He whimpers as I take each one into my mouth in turn, licking it, suckling it. His arms reach out to enfold me, absently stroking my hair, until a small cough from the other side of the room interrupts.

Monty lurks near the coffee table, holding a glass in either hand. "Er, thought you might want a drink," he says, not quite looking at either one of us. "Sound's playing up, seems we've got a ten minute reprieve."

I stand on tiptoe to nibble at Raven's ear. "There's a lot I can do in ten minutes…"

But the way he stiffens only fills me with shame. Of course. It took me far less time than this to drag your life down so low.

At last he turns that gaze on Monty—it's my turn to be granted a reprieve. "Fuck off," is all he says.

Monty only shrugs, then puts the glasses down on the table and raises one hand in a mock salute. "Yessir," he mutters, and disappears through the curtain, back to the maniac circus. Strange we should find such a place to express our souls. Just like the butterfly.

I force myself to move aside and fetch Raven his drink. He takes the glass—an automated response—though a hateful sneer pinches his lips as he stares into its depths. Now his body tenses, and I duck, and a loud smash reverberates behind me. He grabs hold of my left wrist and pulls me up, shoving me against the wall, glaring into my face. "You shouldn't encourage me," he whispers hoarsely. Then he leans forward and plants one tender kiss upon my forehead. When I dare to open my eyes, I'm all alone.

Don't encourage you.

I reach up and touch the spot where he kissed me, still warm beneath my fingertips.

But that's all I know how to do.

I leave my own glass untouched as I trail out after him, the eternal shadow.

It's closer to half an hour before we finally make it on stage. I have no real idea how I make it through our reduced set. My fingers find every note like they've been trained to, but there's nothing else behind the mechanical interpretation. No soul.

Towards the end of the last song, I gaze out across the floor. The audience seem apathetic, at best. Why do they bother with any of this? Why not shut themselves in with a six-pack of beer and TV screen?

Not all of them, though. Through the sea of bad hair dye, thick eyeliner, and face paint, I catch sight of two familiar faces. The hated, and the loved. Wendy's eyes meet mine mid-gasp, and Damien stares at me, misery emulating his father too perfectly, clutched tightly in her arms.

I have to focus extra hard on my playing not to miss a note. You bitch. What the hell do you think you're up to? You think you haven't done enough? Anxiously, I glance at the other side of the stage, but Raven's focused on his guitar, pretending he hasn't noticed.

Only I know the difference, as the seemingly endless song finally comes to a close, and he pushes past me to get out from under the spotlight. It's all I can do not to chase after him as I scamper down the stairs.

On the floor, over by the bar, it would seem Monty and Noriko have beaten me to it already. Raven's not there, of course, but I can hear them arguing with Wendy from where I stand. Hypocrites. Snarling, I storm towards all three of them, and knock Monty and Noriko aside before I come face to face with my sister. *Soeur.* I can't believe I ever called you by that name. That's never what you were. Mother never wanted you. You were a product of rape, what Father did to her. We both despised you. If Mother was here, she'd show you herself. But now, I am all there is.

I pry Damien loose from her grip, hiding my relief behind his thick mess of hair as he buries his face in my chest. "Peggy," he whimpers, clinging to me.

"Give him to me!" Wendy shrieks, making the mistake of reaching out, coming too close.

If I sent her to hell, that would still be too close. She deserves complete death, exile to some place where no one can ever remember her.

I catch hold of her wrist, twisting her arm back as far as it can go, until she squeals. She's wearing more make-up than usual, but not enough to hide a purple bruise that swells around her left eye. "He's not yours to give," I say.

"Please," she begs, going limp in my grasp. "Give him back, or I'll call the cops."

I laugh at this tired threat, and shove her away from me towards the bar. She stumbles over a couple of faux goths, who seem none too pleased at the intrusion. They can deal with it later. I'm not finished with her yet. "Go right ahead. Call whatever person you please. I'm sure they'd be intrigued to hear all about your reasons for coming here—or do you think a restraining order works one way only?"

"Goddammit, Pegasus, don't you get it? This isn't about you. I need to talk to *him*." Then she bursts into tears.

Aided by her show of weakness, I recover quickly, though I remember to loosen my grip on Damien. "You lost, remember?" I say. "You think you have this child, to use as a weapon whenever it suits you, but it's only a matter of time."

I take a step back, disgusted by her manipulative attempts at garnering sympathy. "Daddy," a little angel voice whispers in my ear.

"I know." Turning aside, I almost walk into Noriko and Monty, who stand behind me, their mouths hanging open. "You may continue," I tell them, carrying Damien away.

Just outside the curtain, I place him down gently, and ruffle his hair. After this, I can't stop myself from sweeping him into a loose embrace, murmuring the words, "I missed you, little angel," in his ear. But when he only trembles and says nothing, I pull back. In slow motion, he touches my face, my hair, my lips. He's too quiet. What's wrong?

A horrible sense of déjà vu overwhelms me. This is familiar—why?

Not his father's eyes. My own.

I cover my mouth, feeling sick. Wendy, what did you do?

Why are you really here? More revenge?

Nothing's worth that.

"Hey, listen," I say to Damien, very carefully taking hold of the tiny hands. "Daddy's behind this curtain. He doesn't know you're here, so he's very sad—" it's a lie, of sorts, but for now it will do "—so we're going to be really quiet when we go in and act like it's a surprise, okay? Okay?" He nods quickly, giving me a smile that's far too anxious and sad to belong to a three year old. I press a finger against my lips before we push aside the curtain.

Raven sits in the centre of the floor, knees up, his head resting on his arms, an unlit cigarette dangling from long graceful fingers. He doesn't look up as I creep forward and drop to my knees beside him. Damien squeezes and tugs on my hand; he won't have the patience for this game too long. *You see?* I stop myself from touching the beautiful blue-black hair that drapes across one wrist, hiding the scars he no longer cares to conceal. *You're the saviour of us both. You just don't realise it yet. Come out from the shadows. I can show you.* "I brought you a present."

Taking that as his cue, Damien burrows in beneath his father's arms, and now both of them are locked in embrace, some kind of beautiful, living sculpture. I begin to stand, resigned to leaving them be, but I'm being pulled into their hug too, with Raven's kisses on my neck as his son huddles in between. "You're an angel," he tells me. "How can you keep doing this?"

"Destroying your soul?"

"Not my destruction," he recites, mustering a small smile as he uses my own words against me. "My salvation."

I swallow hard and find strength enough to return the embrace. "This is just a preview. Soon, my love, it will always be this."

"Promise me," he demands, reminding me of his old self as he searches my face for a confirmation of truth.

"I've never lied to you," is all I say. "I never will."

Good enough. He returns his attention to Damien, rocking him side to side. I frown as I get up, trying not to stare at the odd shading on the child's leg, just below his cords: one to match the bruise on Wendy's face. I should leave. Now. I don't think I want to be around when Raven notices it.

As I know, inevitably, that he must.

How things have changed when I return to the bar. Monty and Noriko sit at a table with Wendy, more than willing to hear out her side of the story. I slink towards them, fixing her with a look that's fit to kill.

She edges away as I squeeze in right beside her. But after a while, as she rabbits on about all the terrible things her latest excuse for someone else to blame has done to her, and I haven't made any attempts to kill her, Monty and Noriko drift off into the thinning crowd. Yes, yes, we're all being very civil—if they can play charades, so can I, dammit. Anyway, I'm only pretending to listen, while I wait for something else to happen. It only takes a little while.

She's just spoken Raven's name when her expression morphs from self-absorption into pure fear. I follow her gaze towards the doorway, where a man in a suit loiters on the threshold, staring in our direction. It's so easy for me to tell. The bruising, the quiet terror... He is the one. He must be.

Now Raven appears from behind the curtain. He kisses Damien, passes him off to Noriko, and makes a bee-line for the new arrival. Halfway across the floor, Wendy flings herself off the stool and leaps into his path. She opens her mouth, and his hands clench into fists, but he forces himself to stay cold and calm. "I've got nothing to say to you here. Get the hell away from me."

After a moment of hesitation, she skulks back to my side. I nod in the direction of the doorway. "Is that a friend of yours? I think Raven's going to kill him."

As though hearing my prophecy, the man in the suit turns pale and backs out of the door. Raven lopes after him in hot pursuit.

"Please, you've got to stop him," Wendy sobs, as I slide off the stool. "I can't have them fighting over me."

I spare her a moment more of my time, and the coldest glare in my repertoire. "Why would I do that, even if I could? This isn't about you." Tucking my scarf into my coat, I push on the door and head out into the misty night.

"I said, are you Jonathan?" Raven's hoarse voice demands. Next comes a thud. I quicken my pace, turn the corner, round the back of the hotel. That's where I find them: two shadows—one hunched over on the cobblestones, moaning and panting as steam and blood pours out from his mouth, and the other wiping the sweat from under his nose. I steal in closer. This is just like that night, outside *JoJo's*. Raven sticks his hands deep into his pockets, fidgeting with a few coins and a lighter. I crouch down and stare into the man's face. Knocked around, bloodied, but breathing.

Even as I stand, Raven aims another kick between the man's legs. I grip his arm, keeping it steady. You're not going to kill him. He's not worth it.

I take one of his hands in my own. He struggles to focus on me as I examine his fists more closely. Blood. Your blood.

Oh, Raven. I want to take you home.

I lick off the mess and kiss his bruised knuckles. "I can't let him go back there," he murmurs, his voice trembling against my ear. "What the hell is she doing to him, Peg?"

I take a deep breath. "I'm taking you home," is all I say, meeting his sadness with the one thing I have left tonight: determination.

Defeated, he nods, and so I guide him away.

I lie awake, waiting for the dawn. Beside me, Raven slumbers on. Though we never speak of any attempts at intimacy, and barely communicate with words at all, it comforts me to hear his short, shallow breaths, feel the rise and fall of his chest, and know the way he falls asleep with his arm around me and wakes to find it still there. How he kisses me and brushes aside the teardrops, while I resurrect myself from apparitions that are part dream, part nightmare.

But this morning I won't sleep, though my latest vision is gone. I try to hold him; from within the depths of his slumber, he trembles and twitches against me. What visions haunt your dreams, my love?

Almost six a.m., and the world outside our window remains cloaked in darkness. Not long now, though. Saturday. The day for his first supervised visitation, with Damien.

The morning can start, in a moment. I want to make him breakfast, before we leave. I have to do something. I feel so useless. No—worse than this. I feel as though everything is my fault.

Around the walls, shades of grey begin to pale. I roll off the mattress and put on my robe. Raven moans, still half asleep, patting the spot where I lay beside him. "Mmm… come back to bed, Peggy."

He looks so snug, beneath the doona. I smile and move to sit near him. After laying a single kiss on his forehead, I begin plucking at stray locks of his hair, curling them around my fingers until he swats me away. "Have you forgotten what day it is?" I ask solemnly.

He opens his eyes, fully awake. One long sigh, and then he says, "There are things you don't forget, angel."

I jump as something by Regurgitator blasts out of the tinny speaker on the alarm clock. Taking this as my cue, I leave him to deal with the noise, and get up to fix our coffee.

We arrive a bit after eight. Raven says nothing for the entire journey, but as we shuffle off the tram, his hand grabs for mine, and so we walk the rest of the way. When we turn onto Monty's street, he pulls me up and says, "I don't think— Not like this."

I glance over my shoulder, looking to the familiar blue and grey house. "She's not here yet," I tell him. "I'll wait for you. Right there." I nod towards the bus shelter on the opposite side of the road. "Go on. Even like this, he'll know you haven't forgotten him. Besides, Noriko makes the best coffee, remember?"

I squeeze his hand once, and step aside. He gazes at me, so lost in sadness, until new resolve sets on his face. *There are things you don't forget, angel.* Nodding once, he lopes up the driveway and into the house.

With a sigh, I cross the road, and take up my place in the designated spot, huddling deep inside the purple fleecy top I've conveniently forgotten to hand over. It's another reminder. *Angel. You always call me by this name, Raven. Mon ange.* Only Mother ever called me that, before.

Only Mother told you she loved you, too.

I watch the house and both ends of the street for any signs of my sister, my nemesis. Sure enough, a taxi soon appears on the corner, idling down the street, before it draws to a sharp halt right outside Monty's. Damien springs out, darting away the moment Wendy tries to grab for his hand. Her shoulders slump as she watches him race inside. Then she turns and crosses the street, coming straight towards me.

I pull out a book from the depths of my top and flick open to a random page, pretending to be engrossed in the story as she takes a seat beside me. *Wuthering Heights.* It doesn't matter where I pick up the threads. I dreamed this one already, in early adolescence.

"So you're going to sit here all day, waiting for lover boy? Aren't you a good little doggie."

I knew it wouldn't take her long to get stuck in. I only blink to turn the page.

"Oh, and that guy he beat up in the alley? That was Jeff, not Jonathan. Jeff's much worse. You couldn't imagine. Then again, that's right, maybe you could."

My hands twitch. I turn the page again, even though it's not time. Does she *want* me to hurt her?

There's a long silence, and then she rubs her palms together, breathing on her fingers. "Fuck, it's cold out here. Look, do you want to go for a coffee, or what?" I'm about to turn another page, far more calmly, when she says, "Don't think I don't know I made a big mistake by throwing him out on your doorstep. But I'm going to get him back."

I slide the book closed and tuck my hands deep into the fleecy pockets. Staring straight ahead, I say, "You make it sound like you actually have a choice in any of this. You lost, remember?"

She's silent a moment. Then she shakes her head, pity on her face, pity for me. "You really believe that, don't you. You really believe he—what? Loves you? You believe in *love*? God, you're so fucking naive. Why do you think he came to me first? What does that tell you, huh?"

I smile without warmth. "That we were both whores, for a little while." I close my eyes, leaning against the pebble wall of the bus shelter. From dreams a memory resurfaces: her lifeless form in my hands, the pulse ebbing away beneath my fingertips, my grip loosening around her throat. "You're going to die, Wendy."

"Are you trying to threaten me?"

"No. I don't need to threaten you. It's simply the truth. *A* truth. You're going to die, before your time."

She cackles wildly, but the minute I brush my fingers against the bruise on her cheek, her laughter falters. Without getting up, she skittles across the seat to be further away from me.

"You thought they loved you," I murmur sadly. "My mother didn't love you. And neither does Raven. You always knew that, didn't you. It's why you always tried to take everything from me." I smile at her, as though absolving her of sin, even if I'm no priest. "I never played your games of deceit. I never needed to, no matter what you did. But you're not the truth, *ma soeur*. Some day soon, you'll be gone, and no one will remember you. Not even your son. Who will be to blame for that? Only you."

Her face scrunches up with rage. As she aims a slap at my face, I grab hold of her wrist, but this time place it back into her lap. Now she stares at me, wide-eyed, understanding nothing. "Are you insane?"

I laugh at the simplicity of her question. "If that makes it easier for you, then yes. I am insane."

She stands over me and spits at my feet. "He's mine," she insists, her spite recalling memories of our childhood. "And Damien's mine, too. They don't belong to you. They don't love you. You've got nothing. I'll take them from you, I'll take everything from you!"

I smile, waving a hand dismissively. "As I already told you, you're assuming you ever had a choice." A chill runs down my spine, even as I say, "Get over it. Life is too short. Especially yours."

With a snarl, she spins on her heel and stomps off down the street. I wait until she's out of sight before I fold my legs to my chest and lower my head, trying to hide myself much too late.

The angry blare of a car horn is the only signal that alerts me to Raven's approach—it's already sunset; all this time I've been somewhere else, fallen into a daze. He's crossing the road, coming towards me, head down, hands buried in his pockets.

He takes hold of my fingers, my skin a tell-tale blotchy purple and blue. "You waited here for me all day?"

"More or less." I shrug. "Where else would I go?"

His only response is to nod, mostly at the ground. Then, "I want to go home with you, but...I don't know where I'm supposed to be. I don't know what's going to happen anymore." He lifts my chin, so I can't hide the tears. "Pegasus?"

Don't you dare apologise. I don't think I could bear it.

I grab for his palm, and press it against my icy cheek. "I know what's going to happen. I'm going to save you, and Damien, too. You always said I was your angel. That's what angels do, is it not?"

He holds me tight. I twine my fingers through his, and lead us on through silence and darkness. Home to our one small corner of the earth, our only shelter in a world that seems intent on exiling us both.

I forgot to switch off the heater this morning but remembered to close the window, so the loft has quite the tropical feel when we crawl inside. Raven goes straight to work, making coffee and hunting through the fridge for something fast and edible. I fold up on the floor, kicking away my shoes, and peeling off my top layer of clothing. He emerges from the kitchen, first with two cups, then a bowl of noodles. I offer to warm it up, but he puts a firm hand on my shoulder. "Too hungry."

He passes me a fork, then sets the bowl down between us and helps himself. With a patient sigh, I join in. We finish off all the noodles even before our coffee cools off enough to drink. At last, he strips off his black woollen pullover and lays it beside the bowl. "You must get sick of my fashion sense," he says, with a small smile. Bemused, I shake my head, but he's already changing the subject. "Maybe I should run you a bath? Get the chill out of those bones." His gaze darts across me, then back to the pullover. Strange, he seems so shy tonight.

Some winged thing inside me does a fluttery leap.

"Perhaps," I agree, waiting until our eyes next meet before I lean forward and kiss him. Soon after, we're on the floor, me on top of him, pulling his t-shirt up over his ribcage, revealing the scars again. I lift it over his head, then start on the zip and the button of his cargo pants, and last of all his underwear and socks, just to complete the effect. My breath comes fast and heavy as I take in his naked form, lying beneath me, glowing in the moonlight. *Is this what I feel for you? This...love?*

This truth.

He gazes at me, searching my face, questioning, but not afraid. There's a sadness to my smile as he pulls out my hair tie. Then I take off my own t-shirt and gather him into my arms. Our pulses meld together, too jittery, too fast, as the warmth of the room presses in on us, a third heartbeat. I lean forward again to kiss his lips, my tongue exploring his mouth deeper and deeper, my hands stroking his chest, tweaking his hardened nipples, and brushing against his tummy.

The moment I place my palm over his new erection, he breaks the kiss. "No. You don't want this."

No? I slide down the length of his torso, and start to kiss a path along the soft skin of his thighs, teasing his balls with a few strands of my fringe, pushing him back to the floor with one hand. I nibble and lick my way up his dick, drooling over it, exhaling a warm breath, tormenting him sweetly. My intent is to move up to his belly and down again, but he grabs my shoulders and forces me level with his glare. My smile dies altogether, leaving only shadows to play with my heart. "What's the matter?"

"Guess."

I sit up, facing the heater instead. I take a sip of my coffee, though it's gone cold during my unexpected—and apparently undesired—display of passion. Am I not allowed to *want* to give myself to you now?

You're assuming you ever had a choice. Tears sting my eyes as those words return to haunt and mock me. Is this how it is? Do you want her still, after all she's done?

All I've done.

"You—you don't have to stay, you don't have to pretend, if I'm not the one to make you happy," I manage to choke out. My voice sounds so pathetic, so small.

He remains on the floor, silent. He's watching me, but I can't read his expression. I thought—I thought I'd begun to understand you, but this? What is this?

Faith. I wrap my arms around myself to contain my shivering.

Finally, he says, "I'm not faking it for you, Peg. It's—not that, okay?"

Sure. Whatever. "So—?" I press anyway, unable to help myself.

He shrugs. "You never— You never say it." When my only response is a twitch, he finds himself forced to elaborate. "You've never once told me you…love me."

My shivers spread to within as I glare at him, showing just enough pain to make him flinch. Good. "Just because I never say it doesn't mean it's not the truth. This is the whole basis of faith."

"I don't believe in faith." He raises himself up on his elbows. Is he ready to walk again?

No, not this time. Not this time when I've done nothing wrong. When you've done nothing wrong.

I pounce on him and pin him to the floor by his wrists. You will not run from me, not like this. You need to see the truth. "That's not the truth."

A shaky sigh escapes his lips, but he can't escape me. Drawing in a deep breath, I gather the last of my courage about me. "There's only one way to show you," I whisper, brushing the hair off his face. Strange that we should be so frightened now. But no more.

This stops. Tonight.

One last kiss before I tell him, "This is all I have, Raven.

"It's time."

13 (RAVEN)

Little Deaths/Garden of Eden

Silver eyes gaze down upon me. Into my soul. Beyond my soul.

Both of us, so naked in our truth that not even the moonlight can come between us now. *It's time.*

The breath escapes my lips with a shiver. Finally.

Finally, you…want me. Before this, I always doubted, always found a reason, but now— Now I don't even need to ask. This thing you speak of, faith? Is that what this is? Or is it this love?

Now it's here, whatever it is, I know I've felt it, always. The most exquisite pain, from the moment we met, intensifying above and beyond, to this present, this conclusion.

No. This beginning.

Understanding… And yet, I don't understand anything. But that's okay. *I know how it ends*, you said to me.

That's okay, too. I know how it begins…

He whispers my name, kisses my lips. Nothing else exists. *It's time.*

His hands pin my wrists to the floor, over my head. *Were you scared I'd leave you again, angel? Where would I go? This is all I've got. This is home.*

"Raven?"

I smile; just hearing my name lends a sense of completion, justification.

I am afraid. Very afraid. "Tell me you want me," I beg.

He blinks, startled, but it's clear in the way he looks at me that he knows it, too. And what if this knowing terrifies him as much as me? I hope not. Everything rests upon this moment. With no beginning, how could there ever be an ending?

I don't recognise what I see in him now; something new, and unfamiliar. No, not fear then. I've been both the cause and witness to that emotion. He hides it from me with another kiss before I've got it figured, then presses his weight against my wrists, sitting up to let me look at him. No more to hide. "I want you, Raven," he tells me, and a shiver travels down my spine.

"Then show me."

He opens his mouth, closes it again, cocking his head to one side. He starts to smile, but seeing how serious I am he lets it fade. "I—I don't understand," he whispers.

I close my eyes. If he rejects me now, I don't want to see it.

"Yes, you do," I answer, opening them again. If he accedes to my wishes, I don't want not to see. "Make love to me."

He lowers his head, but his hands still trap my wrists. Powerless...is this what I want?

"It will hurt you," he warns me.

Not powerless at all...this is what I want.

I can't say anything with him sitting above me like this, glowing silver without and within. So I close my eyes again, and lure the words to me. Words I've spoken to no one else, since never before was there this truth. This beginning. "Every time I look at you," I say, my throat constricting, "it hurts me. This is love. This is truth. You've never seen this? Tell me you see it now."

He sets my wrists free. Nothing left but silence, and the cold night's touch to remind me who I am, and why I stay. Pegasus, please.

His hair shimmers across my chest as he plants a slow and tender kiss on my lips.

It's time.

In the beginning, there was...

Hope.

"Don't be afraid," he tells me. "There's no meaning in fear, not here, not tonight. I won't hurt you. I can't hurt you." He's shaking as he kisses my face, my shoulders, and my neck, his tongue painting spirals over my chest. I can't help the moan that escapes my lips. I know where he's headed.

I smile. "Not like that."

He glances up and puts a finger to my lips. Then, with a "Shh," he returns his attention to my body, teeth grazing my nipples, taking each one in turn into his mouth, sucking hard, devouring me. And so, I want to be devoured. *Anything you want to give me. This isn't my beginning—it's yours.*

No. Ours.

He nibbles a path down my stomach, lingering a moment before licking at the foreskin of my cock, scattering little shivers of pain and pleasure all around me. "Pegasus," I whisper hoarsely, stroking his hair.

I'm inside his mouth, these sensations growing stronger, teeth and tongue driving me deeper into desperation, need, desire...love. It's all I can do to stop myself jerking up into his throat as he starts to suck me, one hand round the base of my dick, his fingers warm, his mouth so inviting.

I look down, the sweat already breaking across my body as he gazes up at me, that look on his face—I recognise it now. *I want you, Raven.* He pauses, letting me fall from his lips, his hand moving up to the head of my dick, then driving down. Pre-cum covers his fingers. He licks it off, washing his fingertips like a cat—oh, God.

"Do you want me?" He's searching my face for the slightest hesitation.

There is none. "Yes," I hiss urgently. Could he ever guess how much? I start to grind against his palm. All I need to see is his face. All I need to do is look. It's enough. It's more than enough.

He grins, leaning down to kiss my lips, then lowers himself once again, sucking me deep into his throat, taking me all the way in...

I moan, quivering, letting go to grab at my face instead. Pleasure spirals in, taking control, taking over...

You, when did you do this to me, possess my soul?

You know when. The moment you first looked, it was all over.

This is the beginning. This is all I can see.

I cry out against the silence of the night as his suckling grows more intense. Inside his mouth, I can feel his tongue working against me, teeth digging into my flesh. I don't care. I don't care.

I do care. I feel everything.

A hot flush blossoms outwards, lighting up my cheeks, as I climax inside his mouth, more than mere bodily fluids, more than a gift from something I've never been able to love. I bite down hard on my lip to trap the scream, tasting blood, my mind pulsing with white fire, his heart beating fast against my leg. I don't care if I die now. I don't care if you tell me this is all there is.

I lie panting on the floor, arms outstretched in a crucifixion pose. How apt.

He lets me fall from his mouth, not waiting for my hard-on to catch up and disappear, not like last time. Moving over me, encircling me with his warmth, he lowers himself to kiss me, and I taste myself spilling over our lips, smell myself on his breath. I let his tongue penetrate deeper, unable to move except to raise my arms and fold them around him. I understand your faith, your love...

He pulls away from the kiss, stroking the hair off my forehead. All of a sudden, I feel so exhausted and alone. This day—too much. Too much has happened.

But that's not what I feel at all. *Disappointment.* Not enough.

"You didn't enjoy that?" But his voice isn't so soft as to conceal the sweet mocking tone.

I smile, defeated. "What do you—?" I start to say, then let out a hiss of surprise as his finger presses against the entrance of my arse. As it forces its way inside, my whole body squeezes itself shut, my muscles clenching instinctively against the strange discomfort and unexpected intrusion. With more of him inside me, the pain grows stronger: those beautiful spidery fingers, his nails scratching hidden flesh. And this from someone who cuts himself open with a razor blade when he's bored...

I open my mouth to attempt a laugh, and find myself crying out instead. He silences me with a kiss, his eyes distant and sad. I blink the tears from my blurring vision, still squeezing softly against him as his fingers lie motionless inside me. He waits for my breathing to calm, wiping the sweat from my brow with his free hand before speaking softly in my ear. "You have to relax, or I have to stop. I told you, I won't hurt you. I can't."

I gaze into his face, helpless, trapped. Wanting to believe, only to find my body urgent to deny him. I've been holding my breath; now it escapes all at once in a horribly broken sob.

"Shh," he whispers gently, kissing me again. "This is your beginning. Our beginning. I've never done this before either. Please..."

Did he read my mind? More kisses, scattered across my face. "Relax," he murmurs, stroking my forehead, nuzzling my cheeks. "This is the dream...while softly you sleep...describing who I am, how I touch your soul." I breathe in deep, slowly letting my body unfold and unwind beneath him. "Until such time as we wake, this is all there is, all I want...I can't hurt you, I won't...just relax, fall and I'll catch you...we are one, and the same. This is the circle. This is forever."

I can feel him drifting away. I moan, not in pain, but loneliness.

It's time.

"I want you, Raven," is the last thing he whispers in my ear. Smiling, heavy lidded, I part my legs, letting him raise my knees, pull me forward, such strength in his gentleness, his hands warm on my stomach, lowering himself, continuing to whisper his words of love and reassurance in my ear, now in French—such a romantic language. *This is the dream. But I can't fall here.*

I take a breath, and a red-hot pain shoots straight into my brain from the base of my spine, searing my vision, blinding me. From somewhere distant, a hoarse scream, and I can't get enough air, gasping for breath as I tremble beneath him, clawing his shoulders and fighting against my body's need to escape...he won't let me go, I won't let me go. I want to tell him, how much it hurts, but I can't find the words, can't find anything beneath this—

My mind's turning me loose, like the first time I cut myself, when Noriko found me on the bathroom floor, thought I'd tried to kill myself... Maybe that first time, yeah, but afterwards, I grew to need it too much. Now and then, just the same.

Pegasus, please, you promised you wouldn't hurt me, you couldn't—

But he's not. That's all you.

I am...what?

Nothing. Nothing at all.

I open my eyes, with the distinct impression I've been somewhere else, somewhere far from here. Pain, a distant memory. No longer reality.

I focus on his sadness, till I know where I am, and can remember where I've been. "Am I hurting you?" I ask him.

He blinks in surprise at my question, and then in a shaky voice, he tells me slowly, "It's like pain, but much deeper."

I put my hands up to his face. He's inside me still, not daring to move. But I've absorbed all the hurt, and I'm no longer afraid. What was it he said? *This is the dream...This is the circle...This is forever.* "Love?" I suggest, in answer to his last statement.

He pulls away before I can kiss him, then nods. I take a breath and wrap my legs around his body, granting him deeper entry. My gift. To you. Anything you want. I belong to you. I always did.

He keeps a close watch on me as he begins to move, inside me. I wrap my arms around him too, letting my hands trail down to the soft flesh of his butt, pushing him in deeper, encouraging him, wanting him. This pain, it's different. Much deeper, just like love. Giving meaning to everything. Consent.

Possession.

"Yes..." As his thrusting grows more urgent, my mind again threatens to let go of me. But this time for a different reason. To feel such desire. To let him take control, so that I might forget.

My dick's already stiffening between us again. In an instant, the warmth evaporates my cold sweat. He drives himself harder, testing me, the limits of my need.

There are no limits. I spread my arms across the carpet once more, breathing hard and moaning soft words of want and love as the urgency fires between us. He's looking at me, heavy-lidded, the lust clear on his face. "Your eyes...," he whispers in wonder. "How truly they express your soul."

"You are my soul." I raise my hips off the floor, to let him have me completely. A growl of ecstasy sounds in my ear—at last, he's given in to this desire as well. He grabs hold of my waist, and I rescind my control, letting him push me down against him, impaling me, long hair falling across his face and chest, panting, skin slick with sweat and tears. Pegasus, my Pegasus. My love.

We're so close, so near to finality, the end of the beginning. I start to laugh, even as he shudders and falls against my chest, driving me hard to the floor. Wrapping his fingers around my cock, he squeezes and strokes and tugs, and I thrust against both his hand and his dick, our breath quickening, our hearts racing—I can feel it—I can feel everything...

As we start to climax, I'm swept off to a place of no remorse—somewhere between living and dying. Here, no beginnings nor endings, just meaning and sensation and pleasure beyond the flesh. I'm looking out through the bars of an icy cage, to see him kneeling before me, a smile on his face, one hand on a bar, melting the ice, the other reaching out to me. Does he know how it feels for me to be set free after so long? *I've never done this before, either.*

My lust, longing, and love echoes in his eyes as the ice cracks and the rest of the cage splinters around us. In a burst of flesh and blood, the wings erupt through the scars on my back and unfurl across the sky, white feathers on black. His wings. Purity. Freedom. Love.

He cries out, but not with pain. I've heard his pain; I've never heard this. Not with both of us here together, crying out with one mind, one voice.

See what you've done...you made me your angel.

He's sobbing into my neck. I wrap my arms around him,

clutch him tight, whisper reassurances in his ear. My heart's racing, my stomach wet. He's still inside me. I don't want him to be anywhere else. Not just yet. "Don't ever leave me," I tell him.

Straight away, there comes a muffled giggle. "I think it's too late to be worrying about such things."

"Then save me," I murmur. In my dream, both sets of wings are already disintegrating, dissolving back into clouds and sky, and everything's gone grey again.

"It's already begun," his voice reassures me. He's kissing my chest, our heartbeats slowing. I never want this moment to end.

Tonight was the beginning.

Tonight I saw your soul, Pegasus.

It's beautiful.

I open my eyes to the light of morning. Can't see anything beyond the white and the grey. Am I still in the dream? I don't remember going to bed, or sleeping, or waking. But here I am, lying on my stomach, with an angel leaning behind me and planting kisses on my neck. The world shifts into slow focus as I turn my head. Pegasus.

I push down on my elbows, forcing us both up. He's pressing against my thigh, already hard. Last night it hurt. And yet—Maybe now, I'll be able to take the pain into me, become one with it, same as the razor's kiss.

"Will I make you breakfast?" he whispers in my ear, faking casual, till I reach down between our legs and take hold of his dick.

"Not yet." I wriggle against him, helping to guide him, even as he laughs at me.

"Hungry for something else?"

"You..." *Mind, be still. Remember. Breathing in, and breathing out. Forget.* Even as I let him go, his palms are on my butt cheeks, spreading me open, letting a finger trail in. I remind myself to inhale.

This time, no torment; he's inside me, a silver spark of electricity crackling through my veins. I cling to the metal bed head, watching my knuckles turn white. Together, we blur in and out of conscious thought, moaning with desire, these sobs of need the only anchor to keep me from drifting away altogether. He grips my dick in one hand, the other on my hip, squeezing both in the perfect rhythm—*breathe in, breathe out*—before we climax. Together, and yet not, too soon for my wishes.

This is how I know for sure I'm no longer in the dream.

He whispers my name and returns to kissing me. My forearms and thighs are trembling, but the sheets beneath me are soaked in my own cum. Laughing sheepishly, I start to apologise.

He leans over me, gazing down to inspect the mess. "Well, there goes breakfast." One languid sigh, and then we both burst out giggling. With the sudden movement, he falls out of me. A strange little shiver crosses my skin like the touch of barbed wire. I struggle to sit up.

"You're bleeding again," he says from behind me.

Wings erupting through the scars on my back... Perhaps that part was real. "Where from?" I ask, nonchalant.

The answer takes me by surprise. "From me."

I roll over and sit up. Blood stains the tip of his dick. My blood. Just like the razor's kiss, all right.

He pulls me into a strong embrace, pressing his hands to either side of my face. "It's okay," he tells me. "I promise. We bleed for each other. This is my rose...for you, Raven."

I break his hold. Those words get into me, deeper than any wound that draws blood. Straight away, he jumps out of bed, dragging me with him, standing close. "Are you afraid?" he asks.

I can feel something trickling slowly down my leg, but I shake my head, defiant. I already made my wish.

"I'm not afraid either," he says, before his gaze drifts down to my feet. I think I might be leaving little spots on the carpet. "Strange," he murmurs, "I always thought I would be—or should be."

Turning aside, he gathers up a sweater and a pair of corduroy overalls, and shimmies into them. Then, with a grunt of effort, he rips the sheets off the bed and bundles them in his arms. He even winks at me before bouncing out the door.

I sneak a glimpse at the alarm clock. It's barely seven. How the hell can he be so awake, first thing in the morning? Especially after—

"I'm just going down to the laundry," he tells me. "You might run us a nice hot bath?" He and his smile and my mess vanish as the door slams behind him. All right, then. I stare at the mattress sulkily. It's not like I can just go back to bed anyhow.

Cursing softly, I totter into the bathroom and twist the hot water tap, swiping a hand towel to wipe off the worst of the mess. Traces of you and I, emotions, thoughts, and actions I once thought impossible. I think I'm starting to learn, with you, that nothing's impossible. What are you doing to me? Who told you you could love me, leave me feeling these things? I should be broken, dust and ashes at best. But I'm not.

I find myself a pair of black track pants in the other room, and flick on the heater as I go past. I'm just crawling under the curtains to shut the window when I hear voices in the distance, someone calling, "Daddy!", followed up with a cry of, "Mama!" Straight away, my thoughts are full of Damien; his face in my mind no more than a jigsaw-puzzle, a collage made up of my eyes and everything else blurs of Pegasus—or Juliette, that fey creature from the photo, mama I will never meet. I cover my face. Damien...my son. *My* son, goddammit.

Your son, too, Peg. You want him here with us, don't you? Just as badly as I do.

Yeah, that's what he said. Trust. *You know that word now as well as any razor—you gave it to him freely last night and this morning. He's taken nothing from you, and given you everything.*

I need to trust. There's nothing else.

The circle is almost complete.

Remembering the bath, I close the window, and return to check on the water.

I've just started the cold tap running when Pegasus gets in, lingering at the front door, a frown twitching at his eyebrows, playful no longer. So what did I do wrong, this time?

"What's the matter?" I ask instead, only daring to move nearer once he shuts the door behind him.

As if in answer, he takes a few steps forward and holds out an envelope. No stamp. Unmarked, except for my first name. In a cold voice, he says, "It's yours."

I take it from him reluctantly and examine the handwriting. My turn to frown. I recognise this illegible scrawl. No doubt we both do.

Wendy.

He pushes me aside and vanishes into the bathroom. Does he expect me to open it? If I don't, will it only make things worse? My fingers itch to tear the whole thing to shreds, set fire to the scraps. No stamp, and only a name. That means she delivered it all by herself, which means she was here, near our home—when? Last night? Last night, while he and I were—?

No. I don't want those thoughts or feelings. Let him be mad, if that's what he wants. I'm done with anger, and I've got bugger all to say to her. I'm not opening this letter. If he wants to read it, fine, he can be my guest. He's all I ever wanted, anyway. Him, and Damien.

My sigh gets unexpectedly louder as the water stops running. He appears in the doorway, arms folded across his chest. I hate her even more for how she's made him feel. He fears it—that I'm going back there, either one day in the distant future, or maybe soon. Doesn't he know? Even when I die, the hell I end up in will be nothing close to what I went through with her.

"What did it say?" he asks in a subdued tone, looking past me.

"Nothing." With a grimace, I place the obviously unopened envelope on top of the TV set. But when I turn around, he's standing right behind me. I pull him close, tenderly stroking his cheek.

Slowly, he returns the hug, nuzzling against my neck. "Are you sure?"

I nod, my expression darkening.

"Nothing at all..."

(PEGASUS) *14*

Red Letter, White Rose

Nearly sunset. Almost time.

I'm alone in the park, leaning over the little wooden bridge, gazing into the pond. One sunset above, and one below, and my reflection all trapped in the looking-glass water. And soon it will be spring, I can tell. I can smell it in the air, stirring up memories in my blood, this impending hour of birth and rebirth. But there is no true birth, no more originals. While the temporary wither and fade, only to be forgotten forever beneath the crushing wheel of time, the permanent are reborn, to suffer the same dreams, loves, and hells, again and again and again.

I crouch down, put my hand out to the water, though not to touch it. If I make contact, it may hear my thoughts, read my mind, deny my hopes and my attempts to deny its truths. But truths can be denied. There is always more than one truth. This defines choice, creates freedom, engenders hope.

Choice? Which truth do I choose? Yours, Raven? Or yours, Mother?

No. I stare at my palm, fingers outstretched, casting shadows across the liquid mirror. There is only one truth I can qualify.

My own.

Time changes nothing. But time, itself, can be changed, distorted, recreated, retold. Envisioned and recalled, in the exact same heartbeat.

I love you, Raven. I can't say the words, won't record them within the boundaries of time, or give them to you as the gifts you believe you deserve—and yet this, also, changes nothing. But my love will never change. It exists outside of time. This is my only hope. All I have to hope for. All I can offer you.

And less than you deserve.

Sighing, I stand up and reach into the pocket of my black cords, feeling for the seven coloured stones. Each carefully chosen for its unique purpose. Seven is a good number. A number for luck. A number for truth. Marking beginnings, and endings.

I take the first one, roll it around on my fingertips, and hold it up to the last of the light. A delicate pink, with flecks of grey at its centre. Heavy and cold, it rests in my hand, as I hold my arm out over the railing.

One, the first, for beginnings, my beginning, my... mother.

I part my fingers, allowing the stone to slide through. It sinks into the water, casting ripples across the surface. With no hesitation, I hold out the second: deep brown and tinged with wisps of red. Not as smooth as the others in my collection.

Two, for the pain I learned from those who could only poison love, or strangle it. Father. Uncle. Wendy.

This one lands with a loud splash as I hurl it into the water. For a moment it bobs up and down on the surface, before inevitably sinking like the first. The third stone is dark blue, nearly black, enough to remind me of the colour of his hair.

Three, for love, truth, and salvation. Raven. Damien...

Four, for the uncertain future. That which I may yet be powerless to change.

Five, for the certain future. Reunion with Mother, unification with Raven. Hope, purity, despair. Forever.

A tear falls down my cheek, joining the stone below. I can taste the death of winter on my tongue.

Six, for the words I don't say. For the things I fear and yearn for. The courage I will need, to one day unlock your cage of ice, free you within me, as it's begun already. The will that flows within the circle, to begin, and to end.

I gaze down at the final stone. Pure white, and the smoothest and roundest of them all. It's warm in my palm, as though absorbing my spirit, my thoughts, my intentions.

Seven, for finality. Death, destruction, revelation. Forgiveness. To not see, in those final days, my hands stained with blood, but light. Self love. Acceptance. Completion.

A breeze whips around me and stings my eyes. I stretch out my arms, spreading my wings under a seafoam sky. Only in a dream...

I lob the white stone across the water. The moment I hear that last splash, I turn my back on the bridge and the pond and climb back to the road. Too many things to face up there. Wendy's words. The letter... I haven't read it, though I can tell he wants me to. All because he won't. He thinks, by keeping himself from her, that her infatuation will die a natural death. But this is not the nature of my sister. This is not something that can be changed.

Except, I can change it. I will change it. This is the reason I came here, invoked my ritual, created the future. Everything exists inside me. I can no longer afford to think myself worthless. That's their legacy.

You taught me otherwise, Raven. I have to believe you. This is the nature of faith.

This is the truth that I choose.

The stars might be cold and distant, but they're closer than you are, here tonight.

We're lying out back in the overgrown garden, staring at the sky. His head rests on my shoulder, one of his arms drapes over my body, palm lying flat across my tummy. Not looking at the stars just now. He's looking at me. "Peggy?"

I close my eyes, wanting to deny that intimacy in his voice. Wishing he could hate me, wishing he'd feel nothing. And yet, not wishing for any such thing at all. I wished for otherwise today, standing on the edge of a new evening. Wishes and promises carefully planned, enacted; slowly fulfilled. That was the truth, right there, right then. This, here, is nothing meaningful or new. Only another shade of fear.

"How was Damien this time?" I ask cautiously.

He takes in a breath, his voice breaking as he starts to say, "I don't—" He rubs at his face, attempting to laugh away my question. "—Good."

I'm not fooled, but I pretend I am. "Did he mention me?"

"Didn't really talk. Not much, not to me."

He touches his lips to my cheek, melting the ice. I slowly open my eyes. "Then what did he say?"

Swearing under his breath, he sits up and glares at me. I look at him a moment, making a brief study of his passion and pain. Then I'm back to gazing at the stars. And after all, why not? They're made with the same essence, and burn with the same intensity. The same distant light, that reminds me of places I long to be.

"Please don't be so cold," he murmurs.

I hug myself, then sit up, too. "That's not how it is. It's only...a disguise, what happens, when we—" *When we what?* I can't go on.

When we come too close. When we know the truth. When we just want to be held, even as the walls of the world come crumbling down. When we're too scared to ask, even for that.

He's already drifting away; I can see it in his face. I put out a hand, lay it on his shoulder, and rub the base of his neck, like the night we first touched—

I'm so lost in memories of black velvet against my fingertips that it startles me when he speaks again. "What do you dream about?"

"Huh?" my mouth shoots back, before my mind actually registers the question.

He laughs softly, then grabs hold of my hand, squeezing my fingers together until it hurts. "You were screaming this morning, when I woke up. Screaming in your sleep." He lowers his head, ashamed, and releases his grip. "Do you still dream about what they did to you?" He sniffs. "Or about me, and what *I* do to you? You sounded hurt, and afraid. But I didn't know what you wanted me to do, what you needed me to do, so I—I made out I was asleep. And I left you, crying and alone, till the alarm went off and you hid your tears, and we pretended everything was fine."

I touch my fingertips to his. "It was only a dream," I whisper. "An answer I've been seeking. A future I can't avoid. Something done against my will. But not like in the past. Necessary deaths. The path to salvation. Yours, and my own."

"I don't understand," he says, sounding helpless in the dark.

"It doesn't matter. Understanding will come. Even if only in the final days."

I can see him turning that thought over in his mind, trying to unravel an interpretation to fit in with his darkest fears, his limited understanding of himself, the person he believes himself to be. "Are you going to leave me?"

I smile, tenderly kissing his forehead. "If I do, I'll always come back to you. Remember this."

"Is that how it ends?"

"We go home," is all I can bring myself to say. Slowly his arms go around me: a loose embrace, tightening to leave me feeling warm and protected, no longer so alone. I begin to forget the dream.

I'm somewhere else, nearly asleep, when he speaks again, so softly I almost miss it. "Peg, I think Damien— I think she might be hurting him. In ways that I can't see."

"Like me, the ways I was hurt?" I ask carefully.

He sniffs again, then nods quickly. "Yeah."

I reach for his wrist, holding him steady, pretending not to notice the tears. He turns from me, back to the sky, cold but no longer so distant. *We go home, Raven. Like stars in the night. Soon...*

She won't be able to hurt him anymore, by then.

"A shooting star," he murmurs.

I look up, following his gaze. Too late to catch a glimpse of anything. "So, did you make a wish?"

"Yes... Yes, I did."

I wait.

"I wished you'd read the letter."

My heart sinks deeper into my chest. I don't want to read her words. I don't need any confirmation. I don't even need any justification.

"It's not something— I did try. But I could never bring myself to do it. It would be like going back..."

No, Raven. That doesn't make it all right to ask such a thing of me.

I look at him, and the familiar sense of impending doom steals across my consciousness. *The three of us—you, me, Damien... We are all we have, in the entire universe. Too much for her to want to take. Too much for any of them to escape retribution.* "When will we leave for your son?" I ask.

A twinge of pain crosses his face. "I don't know. I can't seem to find a way through this dark, not anymore."

I run my fingers over his cheek, an invitation to kiss my hand. Time stands still within me, as I give him my vow.

"Then I will be your guiding light. A white rose, shining illumination and truth, on into the night. A rose that never dies."

He focuses on my hand, fallen into his lap. "There's something else... A wish I made, before tonight."

"Anything," I whisper, before I can stop myself. No doubt I'll regret it, soon enough.

"Something else you never told me." He looks at me, defiant and cruel. "Your real name."

I bite my lip and look away. Why ask me for this, of every possible thing? Why feel the need to remind me of more words, more things I can't bring myself to say? Snarling, I rip my hand from his and push myself to my feet, intending to storm off.

"Pegasus!" he calls from behind me, his surprise to my reaction the only reason I hesitate. Maybe it's not your fault, Raven. But that doesn't mean I'm going to tell you. Not when you asked for the name my father, my uncle, my sister all used on me to inflict their pain, transmit their disease, their—

"Hey," he says, more gently.

I stifle a sob, barely. You're not the only one in possession of things you want to forget. And these are the things I need to forget, so that one day I might have a chance to say those more cherished words. Please don't make me remember any more. For you to think of me like that, I couldn't bear—

"I will not read your letter," I say, and return inside, slamming the stairwell door behind me.

All night, I watch him from my chair by the window, lying alone in the garden, contemplating the universe. Sometime before dawn, with my eyelids heavy and my conscious mind sinking, I make the most reluctant promise.

I will read your letter.

You've done everything for me. It is only right, that I do the one thing you won't.

Raven, my love. Yes, love.

You don't deserve it. You've never been good to me. But I forgive you, for everything you did to me, even that horrible night. I would have given you what you wanted, until you said his name. His name. Never mine.

But it doesn't matter why you chose to be with him. You have to wake up to the truth. I deserve that much from you. I can't keep dealing with all the bad things in my life anymore. It's not fair. I shouldn't have to do this on my own.

All the men I've been with, trying to get you to notice me. They're not who I want. I'm so tired, and I'm afraid of them, Raven. Sometimes I let them hurt Damien, hoping it would hurt you too. I wish I could take back those things I said in court. But it's too late now anyway.

The one you beat up that night, do you know what he did? Do you care? I didn't help him, but I watched. I didn't stop him. I was too afraid to make him stop.

You see? Now you have to come home to me. This is where you belong. If you hadn't run off, none of this would have happened to your son.

If you ignore this letter, the truth will come out. That you never loved either of us. And I don't know how to tell our child, on top of everything else, that his father doesn't love him.

Yours forever and always,
Wendy.

I sit on the bed, trembling. Somehow holding onto that godawful letter, disgust and futility and sadness and murderous hate tearing up my mind like a razor blade whirlwind.

I want to be sick.

You couldn't read this, Raven. You couldn't face the truth. Her truth. Her lies. Her disgusting confession, her—

I can't control my shaking. I don't care to, come to that. I'm not sure I can even feel myself breathing; something hot and heavy presses down on my chest when I try to inhale.

I didn't help him, but I watched. I didn't stop him.

You bitch. You worthless, pitiless bitch. I will rip out your heart and spit on it; in the dream I didn't enjoy it, but now I will—I will—

A soft knock sounds at the door. Not a moment later the handle turns, and Raven steps into the room, rubbing the sleep from his eyes and the frost from his bones and muttering something about good morning.

He stops mid-mumble when I launch myself off the bed and charge across the carpet towards him. For a long time, I just glare at him, but that's no good. I need to get rid of some of this poison, before I self-destruct. I reach out a hand, and he starts to back away, right into the wall. I shove my fingers into the pockets of his cargo pants and rip out a cigarette lighter. His eyes focus on the letter mere seconds before I condemn it to the fires of hell.

In silence, we watch it burn. I stamp out the last embers with my socked feet, until I begin to remember things about myself other than this all-consuming contempt. Drained of what strength I had, I collapse forward into his arms. "Remind me of what it means. To have faith, the need for faith," I murmur. I don't imagine he can hear me.

As soon as I can stand again, he loosens his hold. "What did the letter say?" he asks.

Revulsion flickers through my body. She, unable to stop her son's tormentor; him, unwilling to read about it. What a perfect pair you two make. You *should* be with her. You should leave here; go. She wants you, I don't want you, I don't—

"Why didn't you read it?" I scream at him, pushing him off. "You couldn't read it, could you? Because that would mean you might have to care. And you don't care about *anything*.

Least of all your son!"

I want to die the instant the words leave my mouth. I'm no better than she is, after all.

I'm nobody. Please let me go.

The minute my body answers my prayer, I shove him aside, rip open the door, and escape down the stairs, tripping over my own feet in my haste to be nowhere.

Déjà vu, déjà vu...

The memory of his expression—not sorrow, not anger, just acceptance—follows me all the way down.

I stand at the bottom of the stairwell, staring down at my naked feet. So, now I'm up for braving the rainy St Kilda streets without any shoes. Stupid, stupid, stupid...

The least stupid of all the things I've done today.

My shaking hands fumble with the doorknob. But even as my fingers scrabble at the latch, the door's already opening inwards. A great shadow blocks my path. I stumble away from it, backwards, into the foyer.

Not now. Any time—preferably never—but not now.

I think that wish for my heart to stop beating has finally come true, as my father folds up his umbrella and steps in beside me, brushing at the rain on his tailored suit. A perfect copy of the one he wore to my mother's funeral.

I bet you think I've forgotten. But I will never forget.

"Hello, Jaime," he says, and beneath that cold smile all the hatred I ever felt freezes to an icy panic in my veins. I keep backing away from him, along the ground floor corridor. Of course the neighbours are watching; I can see them out of the corner of my eye. All three doors open wide enough to peek, not to help.

I don't want your help. I don't need your help. But he can't be here. He's never come here before.

Of all things, I didn't dream of this. I will myself to be dreaming now, that this time Raven won't pretend to be asleep when I wake screaming, that this time he'll hold me instead, unravelling time, whispering reassurances.

I can fool myself with many things. But my mind refuses to believe in this.

"What are you doing here...Father?" Even by speaking to this man, I'm giving him something he wants and craves. An opportunity to hurt me.

He grimaces, hanging his umbrella from the nearby coat stand, before turning to me, his hands folded above his thighs. "Oh, you needn't worry. It's a simple enough matter. Personally, I disagree and feel she could do better—so much better—but it seems your sister has decided to take this Raven character back into her home, and her life. I'm merely here to ensure that my princess gets what she wants. Minus your constant interference."

I can only gape at him. He smirks before continuing on. "You were always your mother's favourite. She loved you more than she ever loved me, until I finally succeeded in pulling you both apart, for good. Wendy is my daughter—*our* daughter—but you... You never belonged to me. You were merely the product of some...fling, some high-spirited, meaningless affair. And yet, for nine long years, you did your best to destroy my happiness. She refused to have you aborted. By the time I knew the truth, it was much too late.

"But I am an old man now, blessed with the benefit of hindsight and experience. True, you may have destroyed my happiness. But I will personally ensure you do not destroy that of my daughter, with your sinner's ways and your debauched... lifestyle choices."

I struggle to keep him in focus, as his words go ricocheting about my head. *You never belonged to me.*

I am not your son.

For all that you did to me, I never even belonged to you.

You think you *separated* Mother and I? You think you can waltz in here and take Raven from me, too? I laugh in his face. I feel like I'm running off an electric shock, but whatever I am, it's five steps beyond being afraid. "Blessed with experience, *Father*?" I spit the word at him, pleased when he flinches. "You speak of sin, only because you know nothing of love. But I know it. I know Raven *loves* me."

His face turns red, and my instincts scream at me to run. Instead, I lean against the stair rails, forcing myself to stand my ground. "There is no love in such an accursed union," he says between his teeth. "*'If a man lies with a male as he lies with a woman, both of them have committed an abomination. They shall surely be put to death. Their blood shall be upon them.'*"

Really, Father? We're reduced to quoting Leviticus? All right, if such is your wish. It takes two to play the game of damnation versus faith. I look him right in the eye, focusing all my mind and will. "*'He who speaks evil of a brother and judges his brother, speaks evil of the law and judges the law. But if you judge the law, you are not a doer of the law but a judge. There is one Lawgiver, who is able to save and to destroy. Who are you to judge another?'*" I take a breath, and proclaim proudly, "James 4:11." Via my mother.

I'm still smiling at him triumphantly, even as I watch his arm curve back, right before he strikes me...hard.

I crash to the floor. My vision folds in on itself in a violent wave of static, dragging me under. I fight to hold onto any one thought that might keep me on this side of reality.

You are not my father.

Out of breath, I struggle to raise my head. Pain stabs at my left temple. All around me, I can hear doors closing, one by one by one, latches and bolts and chains drawn and snipped. None of them will bear a willing witness to the truth. Am I the only one left?

His black leather shoes swim in and out of focus in front of my face. "How dare you," he growls. "You're still nothing but a whore."

I laugh, but no sound comes. It's probably the truth. I test out the phrase in my mind. *I am nothing but a whore.*

Oh, God, it hurts. I pull my hands away from my forehead. They're covered with blood. My blood.

They shall surely be put to death...

I'm merely here to ensure that my princess gets what she wants.

Now I understand. You're going to kill me for it. And why should it matter? I'm not your son. I'm nothing...nothing but a whore, just like you said. And yet—

At once, Raven's voice enters my mind, dulling the pain, filling me with the memory of the night he lay beneath me, gave me everything, his torment, his love, his soul...

Every time I look at you, it hurts me. This is love. This is the truth... of love. You've never seen this before?

Am I too late? Another memory flashes before my eyes, that of my mother holding me tight, protecting me while the man I called my father hit her again and again.

Yes, Raven, I have seen this before, but—

Understanding. That is what comes too late.

I look up at my father. The expression of detachment on his hard face only confirms my belief: he's going to kill me. This stranger, this shadow, this person who draws my blood and pain yet has no right to lay claim to either of them.

I have to escape. I have to make it back to Raven. I already left him with so much of my hurt. I have to return to my one true salvation. I will not die here. My life belongs only to one. You have no right to take it.

I fight against passing out as I roll across the floor and stumble to my feet. Once I can stand, I begin to run, although now it really is like a dream, and I flee across the carpet in slow motion, falling to my knees on the stairs before finally picking up speed. I can make it.

I must.

Raven, forgive me. Please. And I will still be your guiding light. A white rose, shining illumination and truth, on into the night. A rose that never dies.

All the way up the stairs, laughter follows me, ominous and threatening. As though I'm still a child on the run. Like nothing ever changes.

(RAVEN) *15*

Lost in the Darkness Before the Dawn

Remind me of what it means. To have faith, the need for faith...

Those words; an understanding he begged me to share with him. An understanding I don't have, apparently. You think I don't care, Pegasus? How the fuck could I not care?

I sink onto the bed, staring down at the carpet, waiting for numbness to consume me again. You're angry at me, just cos I made you read her words. Words I couldn't bear to see, an understanding I never wanted. And now, you've run away.

I should go after you—the thought of you wandering the streets all by yourself, so angry at me, so alone in the rain, breaks my heart. The heart you think I don't possess.

I bury my face in my arms. Fuck this. This isn't what I wished for; this isn't what I wanted. I was never supposed to stay.

"Damn you," I whisper. The rain pelts against the window. I can't let him leave me.

I'll always come back to you.

No, that's not the truth. You're not coming back, not after this. She said I hurt my son. Is that what she wrote in the letter, too? Did you decide to take her word for it?

It doesn't matter. My apathy, my inaction, is a bad enough sin. I know this, I know all of it, and yet still, here I am—why am I still here? Why don't I help you, why don't I help

Damien, why can't I help…? Myself.

I can't let you go. After this, there'll be no other reason, nothing to hope for, nothing to keep me here.

Please don't leave me. Please.

A soft knock sounds against the front door, and I'm dashing across the carpet, already reaching for the knob.

No. I withdraw my hand, checking myself, even as Peg's tiny voice echoes through the keyhole. "Please let me in."

So you can leave me again? Or was there something else you forgot to say to me? Some other imperfection you forgot to point out? I want to let him in, but I haven't forgotten all his accusations yet. So I put my ear to the keyhole instead. At first I can only hear him whimpering, broken, terrified. Then more footsteps coming from below, heavy and ominous, thumping up the stairs.

"Raven! Open the fucking door! *Please.*"

I turn the handle, just as a sharp thud reverberates against the wood. Taking a deep breath and plunging a knife into the coward in my heart, I wrench open the door.

Pegasus zooms straight past me, catapulted through the room. He slams into the mattress, and crumples to the floor in a fit of sobs, hands shuddering as they try to protect his head. Then something grips me round the throat and pins me against the wall.

"Hello, Raven."

That voice…

Wendy's daddy. The only man on this planet deaf, dumb, and blind enough to think of that bitch as his 'darling little princess'. The man who put Pegasus, and his mama, through all this hell. I don't even need to ask why he's here. Let me guess. You've come at the command of your *darling little princess*, to get me to rejoin the ranks of hell. Am I close?

"Fuck off." An impotent curse, since he's got hold of me so tight I can't do anything to save myself.

Dammit. I can't go back there. Don't make me go back there. I'd rather fucking die.

But of course he doesn't care, no more than she does. And you, Pegasus, what about you? You only came back to me cos of him, and he wants me to run off and play happy families, pretend nothing ever happened, love never existed, this pain—

And yet—

Damien. I squeeze my eyes shut and focus on a broken memory of my son, to block out the killing words in my ear. I'm not listening. I'm not—

But if I did go back... I could see him again. What does my happiness matter, when—? My son. I could be with my son. I could always fake it. I faked it before, all for him, all for that love beyond love—anything to stop all this shit from happening to him.

What else *can* I do, when everything's so fucking inevitable anyway?

Now Wendy's old man lets go his stranglehold and shoves me across the room, towards Pegasus. ...*My Pegasus...*

He lies trembling at my feet, huddled and staring into the void. In one fragile moment, whatever it is I supposedly want or don't want disperses into thin air. Right here: my only other love, the only one I ever trusted, the only one I ever gave myself to, so completely yet so incompletely as well. It's not over yet. How could it be, when it's barely begun?

"I want you to wait outside, Raven. There's a few words I need to say to...my *son*. In private."

That voice, the voice of a demon lurking over my shoulder. Pegasus looks right at me, both defiant and condemning. As I try and break his gaze, nausea settles heavy in my stomach. Here comes the point of no return—the moment of truth. Just like that poem about two paths in the wood.

I swallow, clench my fists, and turn around, putting myself between him and his dad. "You know I can't go back to her," I say. "I think you know why, too."

I see where Wendy gets so much of her poison from in the look her old man shoots me. He stiffens and licks his lips, then darts one hand into his jacket pocket. I squint, but I'm too slow to make out what he pulls out of it. "I'll pay for a taxi to escort you to my daughter's house once I've finished up here," he tells me, like I never said anything. "This won't take long."

I step forward, nerves and muscles pin-pricking all up and down my arms. "Do you think I could even stand the sight of your little princess now, knowing what she did to my son? Like daddy, like daughter. Is that how things work in your family tree?"

He smirks, poking at one of his cufflinks. "Tell me, *Pegasus*," he says, "do you dress up as your mama for *him*, too?"

Behind me Pegasus utters a single laugh; cold, mocking, but not the least bit surprised. Then his dad goes on talking.

"I prayed to the Lord every day, the moment I knew my daughter was carrying that seed inside her. Prayed for the strength to talk her into having the abortion. But she refused. And now, I don't see any of her in the boy. I see my wife, beautiful whore that she was, and worst of all, I see you. Don't ever mistake my intentions. I care nothing for you, Raven, and I care little for the child. This is all about Wendy. She's all that matters."

Something flashes in his palm; a sharp gleam of silver. Is he carrying a knife? "Dead or alive, is that it?" I ask, nodding at the blade.

He smiles at Pegasus, and with a flick of his wrist, he's twirling a carved hilt between his fingers. Some kind of dagger. "This?" he says, looking at it fondly. "Oh, this is not for you. As I said, I care nothing for you. This is justice. This is for whichever child you leave behind. I should have thought the choice was obvious. But perhaps not for a coward."

I can't tell who makes the first move. There's no clear transition between me trying to process the fact that he's going to kill either Pegasus or Damien, and me and him locked in one another's arms, grabbing throats and pushing against chests and twisting heads away from each other. Fuck, he's strong. Ex-military training; he's knocked me to the ground before my brain's even caught up. I struggle to breathe, and to see clearly, as he towers over Pegasus and aims a kick at the lilac hair. Ready for his foot on the second swing, I grab for his leg, throwing him off-balance, and clamber on top of his torso. Even so, I need to be quick. Pegasus sounds like he's choking, and his head's already bloody.

I put my hands around the neck of Wendy's old man, and squeeze as tight as I can. Everything turns red.

"Son of a bitch!"

I storm into the bathroom and slam my fist into the mirror, scattering shards of glass and echoes of my face all across the floor. Choking on bile, my body follows them down. So much for seven years of bad luck.

I laugh, even as the blood starts to dribble down my arm. I know the secret for real now. As human beings, this is all we are. Nothing more than flesh and blood, flesh that rots, blood that ebbs away. Amazing, in the end, how easy a pulse can be stilled...

But it's enough, that I remain. Enough that he'll never hurt my beautiful Pegasus again. I don't need to go back there, not ever. Damien...there's another way. Peg told me how, even if he's told me nothing. He can save you, even if I can't.

He's going to save me, too. He's got to. He's all we've got left, you and I. All we've got left in the entire world. I'm no good for anything good, except hope. And even then, I don't know if I'm strong enough. But I must be, or else—

Why am I still here?

When it came right down to it, I couldn't protect either of you. I was only protecting myself. My worthless self. This cage that I hate.

Beyond emptiness, I become aware of unsteady footsteps padding across the carpet, stepping gingerly around the puddle of glass and blood. Strong hands grab my shoulders and haul me to my feet, and Pegasus leads me over to the bed and collapses on it. I fall into his lap, and his arms go around me, holding on like he knows I'm fighting to contain everything. A bloody strand of lilac splatters against my cheek.

Out of the corner of one eye, I can just make out the inert form lying in a heap near the kitchen. I try and imagine the chest rising and falling, make-believe there's some sign of movement. I don't know why, when I got what I wanted. It really was all I could do, to protect you. To protect myself.

I could never leave you.

Please, tell me if I made a mistake, tell me if this is all wrong.

I grab hold of his hand as his grip loosens around my shoulders. My mouth's already open, and the words are coming out in sobs, but who can tell what I'm trying to say?

"Shh," he hisses, extracting one hand to brush my hair off my face. "It's going to be okay. We have to leave for Damien now. Yes?"

I've got no answer to give him. He bends forward, wincing from some wound that bastard inflicted, and plants a kiss on my cheek. I find myself nodding. It's as if, in some part of my subconscious, I've got all the answers I need.

He kisses me again, then sits up, groaning. "But I don't think...I can make it there yet. I don't—don't feel very well." Drawing in a shaky breath, he folds his arms across his stomach. "I think you might need to— I should go to the hospital. But after we have Damien, there won't be any more time. Paths close. And I won't allow them to take you from me. Either of you."

I lean in, inspecting him more closely. Blood stains a good quarter of his hair a dull brown, the main culprit a gash on his forehead. His eyes, glazed over but glistening with tears, flicker in and out of focus on the body in the corner. "Is he dead?" he asks calmly.

I shudder and bury my face in his chest. What if he knew I could kill someone? What if *I* knew?

"No," I lie, not looking up just yet. If he can't see my face, he won't be able to tell. I won't need to see that he already knows. I could never lie to you, Peg. "I...don't think so," I add, as a concession to this.

But I knew right where to hit that bastard, even as he fought me off. And I knew, the moment I heard the sickening crack of the Adam's apple, that it was all over.

"So much blood," he says. Now I do look up, following his gaze across the room to the prostrate figure and the dirty halo swelling around the broken head. "Better it staining the carpet than my soul."

I'm suddenly compelled to kiss the blood off his own forehead, and lick clean his cheeks and chin. God, I can't believe I let that bastard get so close—

Please let me in.

Can't believe I dicked around so long before letting you in—

You don't care about anything. Least of all your son!

Can't believe I let you leave at all, or think that of me, or—

"God, I'm sorry," I whisper, pulling his hair away from the blood, kissing around the wound, this simple gesture all I can do, wanting him to know my heart, know he's the only one who can guide us home. "I'm sorry, I'm sorry, I'm sorry..."

With the softest of sighs, he falls against me, letting me

hold him close. I listen to his quiet steady breathing, till it calms my pulse and brings my thoughts under control. So long as you're here, we're going to be okay. I can believe in this much, can't I?

I pull back, intending to draw him into another kiss. His eyes are closed, and his head lolls forward the moment it loses my support. Shit. I shake him rapidly, till he blinks at me sleepily. As if he never left me at all, he murmurs, "Raven... I can see all the way through, to the other side. I can see it will be—" That's as far as he gets, before passing out again.

Dammit. I try and repeat the trick with the shaking, but this time he's not waking up. That bastard hit him pretty hard. And I can hardly leave him here. Which means I've gotta find some way to get him to the hospital. Another place that I hate.

"Fuck!" I yell, to no one in particular. Laying him against the pillow, I storm across to the wardrobe and yank down my suitcase. I start by tossing together a heap of random clothes for both of us, when I notice a sliver of white lace hanging out of some crepe paper at the bottom of the closet. Kneeling down, I examine it more closely. Some kind of dress. His mother's, perhaps, or—

Tell me, Pegasus, *do you dress up as your mama for* him, *too?*

Ah, now I think I see. Another piece of the puzzle. Holding it carefully, I put it in with the other clothes. Then I collect the tape and the photograph off the bedside table, along with a small amount of pot wrapped tightly in foil hidden under the alarm clock. I tuck the foil between the picture and the frame, then deposit them all in the suitcase as well, stopping to trail a hand across his cheek. Now there's only one more thing that I want.

Stepping over the body that doesn't exist and doesn't mark the beginning of this particular nightmare with a giant spike, I enter the kitchen. I know all about the pile of forgotten portraits, taken soon after we first met and I suspected I loved him, but was too stupid to do anything about it. I fold them inside the purple fleecy top, before slamming closed the suitcase and setting both the combination and the lock. With a single heave, I drag it out to the top of the landing.

I return to the bed, gazing down on him. I hope he's only sleeping. "Please don't leave me," I beg again. Then, pulling my resolution about me like a shield, I sling him over my shoulder and carry him out of the loft, locking the door behind us.

So, that place isn't home anymore. Not somewhere we can return to. But it doesn't matter. So long as I'm with you, anywhere can be home.

I haul both the suitcase and a half-conscious Pegasus out of the taxi, fling the driver thirty dollars, and stagger over to the front door, banging on first it and then the window when it takes more than five seconds for anyone to answer. "Fuck you, hurry up!" My leg twitches as I scan the side of the house. At least Noriko's car is in the driveway. Someone's gotta be home.

Come on, you bastards. Quit letting me down. Just for once, that's all I fucking ask.

"Raven!" Noriko exclaims, as the door opens and her eyes grow wide to see us both in such a state. I push past her, dragging him along with me, and collapsing against the wall in the hallway, leaving her to lug the suitcase inside.

"I need you to do us a small favour," I tell her, more than a touch of cynicism lacing my voice. Hard to say if 'small' is the right word for it.

"God, what happened? Did you two get in a fight? You're bleeding all over my carpet."

"Fuck your carpet, Noriko!" But I feel guilty when she flinches at the volume in my voice and then glares at me, bug-eyed. "I need you to take Peg to the hospital."

"Tell me what happened."

I free one arm to grab her by the neck and pull her close to my face. "Do I need to translate it into fucking Japanese? Get in the car, start driving, and help me take care of this. Please."

I wait till she nods—albeit with great difficulty since I'm keeping her in a partial stranglehold—before I let her go and help him into the back seat. We leave the suitcase behind, in safe-keeping, for later.

Later, when my family is finally reunited.

All the way to the hospital, Noriko keeps the questions coming, even once it's obvious I'm not going to tell her anything. Maybe she's punishing me for my silence. Whatever.

I gaze down at Pegasus in my lap, and run my hand through his hair. If that's the worst I've gotta take in any of this, I'll consider myself a lucky man. Either way, I don't care. So long as they look after him, exactly like they're supposed to, and not like they did with my—

A little moan and he stirs beneath me, reaching blindly for my hand, gripping it tight and squeezing my fingers. "Pegasus," I whisper. The wound on his forehead's started bleeding again, but I can't get down low enough to kiss him.

"If I do," he mumbles, his voice so soft I need to lean in to catch the words, "I'll always come back to you." He kisses my fingertips, before his grip loosens and he fades into whatever limbo place he's trapped in.

I'll always come back to you. What...? It takes me a moment. *Please don't leave me.* Is that it? The last thing I said to him, before we fled the apartment. An echo of what he told me last night. Up the front, Noriko must've noticed, since she holds her tongue till we pull up near the hospital.

Once inside, the nurse who examines him wants to ask the same sorts of questions. "He's got concussion," I tell her, trying not to be too much of a smart-arse, more for his sake than anything.

"You reckon, Doctor Seuss?" She's got a good twenty years on mine, which means she won't be taking any shit from the likes of me.

I sigh. Fine. "His old man roughed him up. Both of us."

"You call the police?"

I just shrug, but hold her beady-eyed gaze and raised brow till she signals to an orderly, and they wheel my angel into some faceless white room, flooded with light, no black curtains, but where the sun never shines. Fuck.

Noriko pulls on my arm, dragging me back to reality. My mind's skirting dangerously close to the borders. What the hell was I thinking, bringing him here? I should've taken him, taken Damien as well, and gotten the fuck out while I could.

Gotta keep it together.

But what if they don't let him leave? What if they come for me, right now, right here? I'm a wanted man, after all. Maybe I'll even be on the news. Jesus fucking Christ.

Last time I was in a place like this, with someone I loved, they didn't let her leave either. Not for three long years. But I got out of it then, and I'll get out of this.

"You should get those cuts looked at, too," Noriko murmurs.

Knowing I'm being an arsehole, but unable to do anything about it, I slide off the seat and stalk down the corridor, lighting a cigarette the minute I get beyond the entrance. I suck in a long, unsteady drag and trip across to the far corner wall, past the chemist's shopfront, resting my skull against the grainy concrete. More white. More light. And no escape.

Another drag, as I try to distract my mind from interrogating me with its own set of twenty questions; number one on the list being, *How the fuck do we get out of this alive?*

Down the road, an ambulance pulls up, siren blaring. A stereotypical nuclear family gathers near the chemist's, arguing and swearing at each other so loud they even manage to drown out the siren. I stick the cigarette between my lips. Don't need to watch how this plays out. I'll just move along and find someplace else to fester among my morbid thoughts.

But as my gaze starts to wander, I notice the little girl creature, huddling bruised and shivering between the drunken couple and an older brother. Big blue eyes, miserable with a knowledge beyond her years, already resigned to her fate. I'm rooted to the spot, overwhelmed by a sudden need to pick her up and comfort her, even though I know such well-meaning intervention always makes it worse.

Is this how all parents end up? Is this how it really works, out here in the wastelands beyond the TV mythos? Peg's mama loved him, but she went ahead and left him, in the hands of his old man, and his uncle, and...people like Lenny. Ma...my dad. I shake my head. Wendy. What she does to Damien. What I let her do to him.

No more. I'm never going to be like you. I sneer at the mama, who's wrenching the little girl away, still engaged in a slanging match with what I can only assume is the dad. I'm ashamed at myself for feeling relieved that they're moving on, but there's only so many times you can stomach a man calling his little girl a slut and a cunt without wanting to dash what's left of his brains against the footpath. I take a deep breath, make a promise. My child will be happy, when he's with me—and Pegasus. No matter what happens, before the end.

I slide down the wall into a crouching position, fingering the silver cross. *You are the personification of any faith. I* hope wherever you are right now, you can hear me, somehow. Without you—

No. I can't think about that alternative. There isn't one. I stare at all the concrete. Old suburbia here, long devoid of any life. Is there anything left, beneath the rock and the asphalt, under the cracks in the pavement? Spreading out from my shoes and fingertips, ancient flowers and buds to break through the gaps, and vines arising to devour the buildings on all sides. And every one of these cars with their poison breath melt down into the road. It's a grey river now, while views of unending mountains grow solid out of the smog...

I finish off the clove and stamp it out, gazing up at the clouds. Several people make a point of gawking. *What the fuck do you think you're looking at? I'm allowed to dream.* This is the kind of place we want to be with Damien, isn't it, Peggy? This is where we're going, once you're all better. Somewhere far from this toxic city, and far from the ocean, where you can't be tempted to leave me. Somewhere high up, in the mountains. A place of trees and starlight. Somewhere they'll never find us.

Damien's never seen the snow...

My heart lifts. I know exactly where I'm taking them. Pegasus, how did you—?

It doesn't matter. You told me you know how it ends. And if this isn't it, then I trust you.

I roll up my sleeves, examining the pale flesh and the various marks running the length of my arms. Scars on my wrists, from when I first tried to kill myself, auditioning kitchen knives and scissors and razor blades, and stupidly hoping, if I couldn't find anything to do the job properly, that I'd have the patience to bleed to death anyhow. I don't mind so much anymore. I wasn't meant to go that day. And when I cut myself afterwards, it's only for hating this cage of skin. Yes. The cage and this concrete are one and the same, and my soul the nature I'd imagined, lurking beneath the surface, waiting to slough off the fleeting bindings of humanity. Is that what it's like when we die, Peg? Is this what you hope for, is this what you see?

I can't feel him in my mind anymore. A shiver crosses my soul. Maybe they've drugged him, or something worse. But the last thing I want is to go mad out here, so I return to tracing the scars and remembering how it feels, till the same burning sensation tingles beneath my fingertips. The razor's ghost.

A pair of sparkly green heels come tapping across the pavement and stop right beside me. Noriko crouches down, avoiding my face, her eyes red with stillborn tears. I open my mouth, hesitating. Pegasus? No, these tears are for me. I want to tell her not to feel anything, but that means talking to her, and I can't, not yet. Besides, she was the one who found me, originally. And this time, she caught me looking.

At last, she forces a smile and says, "I never thought I'd say this to you, Raven, but you look like you need a drink." She squeezes my hand and helps me to my feet, then guides me over the road, heading for an old-fashioned corner pub.

We're halfway across the tram lines when I feel a strange twinge. I pull up abruptly, turning to the hospital. No. I can't leave you behind. That's what I did to Ma, and they—

"Pegasus," I say. Right then, a bell dings loudly, and she hauls me out of the path of an oncoming tram, shoving me onto the pavement in front of the bottle shop.

"Jesus!" She jerks me around to face her, upset like I thought a real-life game of Frogger might be the latest, most fashionable way to die. No thanks. Raven-go-splat was never one of the many ways I envisioned for my death. I swore an oath, long ago, to take no one else down with me.

"Listen to me," she says, speaking every word slowly and clearly, to make sure I understand, even if I don't believe. "Pegasus will be fine. He only has to stay there overnight.

He's going to be okay."

But my mind stopped recording when it hit the previous sentence. "He's gotta stay there?" I eye the big concrete slab warily.

Straight away, she softens. She must remember too, what they did to Ma. I don't want this, as she puts her arms around me, drawing me into a hug, not letting me pull away, though I do try, for all of about five seconds. Shit. When did I get so weak?

As if in answer to my own question, I find myself confessing, "They can't take him from me, Noriko. He's all I've got left."

"No one's taking him away," she assures me, in her best 'I'm the shrink here and I know what I'm talking about' voice. I swallow, then nod, and let her nudge me closer to the pub. Looking in at the window, the bar seems fairly empty, apart from a smattering of the older crowd. Right about now is 'the serious drinker' hour. She lets go my hand to push open the door, but for some reason my feet refuse to follow.

Some reason. Plenty of them. The drunken couple back there. The misery of that little girl. Peg huddled on the floor. Lenny. My dad. Damien. In the end, this vicious circle can only stop with me. I can't keep doing this. Not if I'm going to help my loves.

I fold my arms across my chest, feeling ashamed and stupid as I stare at the footpath. But Noriko doesn't even ask. She just nods and takes my hand. "All right. Let's go home."

Home. I look over my shoulder one last time at the ominous building. You're in there, somewhere, Pegasus.

Nowhere is home, without you.

I lie on top of the covers in my old room at Monty and Noriko's, desperate not to think. Watching afternoon turn to twilight, twilight to evening, not speaking to either of them. Through the walls, I can hear them talking about me. Monty reckons this is just how I was after Ma got sent down. "He's afraid, to the point of paranoia." That's Noriko's diagnosis. "Beyond that, I don't have a clue what's going on in his head. That's what scares me."

But why should you feel any fear? You're outside the circle, all of you. Just let us go.

She keeps knocking on the door, asking about food; on the fifth occasion demanding I eat something. All the while, I pretend I can't hear, sinking into that safe house in my mind reserved only for me, when things get too much and I can't deal anymore. So I never ate. And I'm not thinking. I'm watching the shadows go round and round, and making all sorts of shapes out of their patterns on the ceiling. This madness is kind of comforting. So long as I'm not aware, I don't need to feel any pain. Alcohol doesn't give me that. It makes me think too much, feel too much. I don't need any of that, till the day—

Till tomorrow, when you come back to me, and we can finally leave.

But even locked down in the confines of my cage, the memories find me. Pegasus memories, little beginnings, and how it was that I knew. I'd been staring at my scars that day, as well. They were new then, though, virgin scabs. I think I was wondering why I'd tried to kill myself. Wondering what was left for me, as I held my wrists under the light filtering in through the bathroom window, examining the thin white lines where they'd already begun to heal. I wondered if someday the scars would fade altogether, and I'd simply grow up into one of those happy, vacuous adults, forgetting everything.

That was the moment I realised I didn't want to be like anyone else. That whatever I was, I was different, and the scars were a key to being me. Someone I couldn't love, cos I didn't know how. I wondered if anyone else ever would.

And then the door opened and Pegasus walked on in, taking hold of both my wrists, his touch so gentle it terrified me. "You too," was all he said. I tried to pull away, but he didn't let go, not straight away. I knew in that moment I'd met someone who...understood. I knew in that moment I loved him. Surface deep, like the scars, but love just the same.

"There's always a new dawn," he murmured, "if only you can survive the night. At least, that's what I believe." We were standing so close, and I was trying real hard not to lean towards his lips, not to let all those feelings overwhelm me.

"What if the dawn never comes?" I asked instead, seeking safety in more familiar pain.

He only shrugged. "That's not what you believe." No doubt whatsoever in his voice. That's how I knew he was telling the truth.

At last he dropped my wrists and walked out, leaving me feeling more alone than ever.

Just how you always leave me. Alone.

I close my eyes. Inside and out, only shadows. Slowly, I let myself slide into the vast black emptiness.

It's always darkest, before the dawn. But darkness doesn't last forever.

At least, that's what I believe.

16 (PEGASUS)

Non Omnia Moria (Not All of Me Will Die)

Such strange shadows, dancing for me, across a sky I've never seen...

I open my eyes, only here I'm staring up at a ceiling, not a sky. Raven? Where are you?

Where am I?

I blink, struggling to sit up in this refrigerated bed with its stiff white sheets, adrift in the centre of a crisp white room. I shake my head to clear the last of the pale shadows, until the only whiteness is on the outside of myself.

I hold my hand in front of my face, clenching and unclenching my fist. Ensuring the flesh, bone, and muscle respond exactly as I have come to expect. Next I concentrate on my heartbeat, the sound of my breathing, the blood flowing through my veins. All fine, in the ordinary sense. *Relax. The answers will come.*

Nearly dawn, and it's so cold. Colder than it should be, without his touch. I can't remember any dreams at all. But I've always been able to dream. Raven, I don't understand. Help me.

I fight to tear off the sheets. It's as though someone nailed me into a coffin rather than tucked me into bed. My feet land on the hard floor, and I creep across to the window. A hospital? Why should you bring me here?

I run my fingertips along the polished sill. Raindrops trickle down the outside of the glass, so tempting, so close. I press my forehead against their reflections, feeling a patch of cotton cushioning my brow. A dull ache drills into my brain, a memory...

Father.

I put my hands up to the glass and push away from the wall. This window has no latch. It's been designed never to be opened. A window with no soul. Just like my mother's window, the one that held her prisoner nearly four years, while she watched over me from above and within, before I could ever meet her.

Now the window is open inside me instead. Now I understand.

Once upon a time, I asked everyone I knew about the woman with my face who watched me from that attic window. My sister told me she was an evil witch, and if she ever escaped she would kill and then eat me. My father said I was lying, seeing what the devil wanted me to see. It was the maid who told me the truth.

She was the keeper of my soul. My guardian, my watchful angel. My flesh and blood. My—

"Mama." Even a whisper sounds horribly loud in this quiet space. I wrap my arms around my body, smiling at the memory of her embrace, after her window opened and we were finally allowed to meet.

"He kept me from you, *mon ange*. Oh, my sweet Jaime," she whispered, stroking my hair and face that were both so like to her own. I didn't understand many things she told me, not at first, but I understood her love. I understood the feeling of being...home. What she sacrificed to give me these feelings, I'll never truly know. I just know they all ended, with her life...

Until Raven. I was four years old, around the time I first met my mother. Damien is almost four, as well. And my father, who was not my father at all, is—

I close my eyes, focus on my own beloveds, draw them deep into the circle, like my mother drew me, for all that time we spent apart. Love goes beyond both physical pain and baser human needs. There are other ways.

I am learning them all.

Raven... Damien... I belong to you both. Just as you belong to me. If I had no dreams last night, then I'll dream you instead, become your own watchful angel, separated by no more than crumbling walls and temporary flesh, something I can't bring myself to hate and yet have always felt this urge to escape. But I was meant to wait, for both of you.

In my mind I see Raven, as we make love, and Damien, as he reaches out to touch my face. So like his father, so like me. Together, we can be complete. As a family...

In all of our dreams, in the here and now, we already are.

Through a sudden swirl of white, my knees give out beneath me. I grab hold of the sill, fighting to concentrate only on my breathing, struggling to steady the floor and myself. I need to be strong. He tried to kill me. But you saved me, Raven. Gave me my life, so that I might rescue you and your son, make us whole.

When everything stops spinning, I return to the bed. A small black box hanging by the mattress reveals a switch to another window that will not open, the television looming in the corner. I need to not be here, but simple distractions will kill time. So I flick on the set, immersing myself in the numbness of everyday life, reflections of a safer world where children are happy and easily placated by a series of colourful squiggles and grinning faces, most of which give me the creeps.

This could be for the last time. I know this, but I'm not afraid.

A certain calm accompanies the knowledge that there is no escaping fate.

The doctor who grants me my freedom is a little too reminiscent of those faceless faces on the screen, patting my leg and advising me to 'take it easy' for a couple of days. I'm about to tell him nothing is easy, but he's already vanished into the bowels of the hospital from whence he came. Is this it, then? Am I finally free to leave?

Once I've dressed myself, I amble down the corridor, suspicious of the walls to either side of me. I only pass a single nurse, who smiles and waves good-bye and says something nice about my hair. As I step into the elevator, I feel for the loose change that usually weighs down my pockets. There should be enough for at least one phone call.

Only two floors down to the ground, and I'm stepping out into the foyer. Outside, the rain falls in sheets and cars wash up little waves onto the few pedestrians who scuttle by, all of us anxious to be elsewhere.

Near the final exit, I spy a public phone. So close...

Before anyone else can beat me to it, I march to the stand, snatch up the receiver, deposit three coins, and dial.

Dammit. Wrong number. I hang up, and scrabble to retrieve the change. My fingers are shaking.

Behind me, someone sighs, none too subtly. I concentrate all the more on Monty's number and the keypad. I'm still double-checking the display, matching off each number with the corresponding one in my memory, even as the other end begins to ring. All clear.

The phone continues to ring. And ring.

Dammit, Raven, pick up already.

My heart's beating too fast. No, not here. Please, just wait until I'm home. Until all three of us are home. It won't be so long now.

The phone rings for the fourteenth time, and I slam down the receiver, again grabbing my change and glaring at it.

Raven... Are you okay? Could they—?

Another sigh, and the person behind me starts tapping a foot; their impatience has a beat, out of sync with my pulse.

No. I feel no pull of separation. Nothing bad is going to happen. Not yet.

I deposit the money one last time and dial the number in resignation, not bothering to check the display as I turn around and greet the restless woman with a pointed smile. She looks uncomfortable and pretends to hunt through her purse.

Five rings... Six...

Damn you.

Seven...

"Hello?" a sleepy voice answers.

My heart leaps into my throat, so for a moment I can't even speak.

"Hello?" He repeats the question in a louder voice, sounding no less disoriented.

"Are you drunk already?" I ask teasingly, though all I can imagine right now is hugging him and never letting go.

"Pegasus!" There's a pause, like he's collecting his thoughts. "I— Sorry, I was asleep. Then I heard the phone. I was dreaming... I had a dream."

I'm smiling like an idiot, just for hearing his voice. I know you had a dream. I sent one, all for you.

He clears his throat, before adding, "And no, I'm not fucking drunk. I'm not going to drink anymore."

I blink. He sounds so serious, and I can't think what to say.

"When are you coming home?"

I twirl the phone cord around my fingers, feeling foolish. "Well, I don't exactly know how to get home. Hence the phone call."

He manages a laugh. "Wait there. I'll come and get you."

"It's raining."

"I don't care. Just stay inside, okay? I'm leaving."

"Now?"

"No, next week. Jesus, Peg. I'll see you soon."

"Okay," I tell the engaged signal, and hang up.

The impatient woman has disappeared, and I'm all alone in the foyer. But I won't be free until I'm out of those doors. And I want to be outside. I don't mind the rain either, Raven. Rain can be my friend, until you come to my rescue.

Please don't take long. Rapunzel can be impatient, too.

I avoid both the cars and the stares of the pedestrians as I splash about in little puddles on the footpath and watch the rain drip from the end of my nose. I've been out here long enough for it to soak through to my skin; breathing in petrol fumes, feeling the wind cut right through me. The city air has never felt so cleansing.

I grab hold of the base of a no-parking sign, spiralling around it in homage to Gene Kelly until I make myself dizzy. Miniature rainbows tremble in patches of wet oil on the road, but looking at these only makes my headache arc up again, so instead I turn to the foamy streams that flow down through the gutters. From here, everything washes into the ocean. Just as I will, someday. I've heard life formed in the oceans of the world. It's only natural I should want my body returned there.

A tram glides by, driving a spray before it, and I glance up, just like I have for every single tram that's gone past since I stepped out the door. Only this time he really is trotting across the road, head lowered in a meek defence against the steady downpour. And he looks kind of cute with his blackened hair glistening and wet clothes sticking to his skin. Hands in his pockets, shrugging off the outside world. As he pulls up beside me, I wipe at my face, full of laughter, wild and free. He glances up, shakes his head in amused disbelief, then guides me to the nearest bit of shelter, beneath the hospital exit. All the while, I want to lick the rain off his skin so badly even the cold can't kill my body's natural response to him. My turn to stick my hands in my pockets, part of me hoping he doesn't notice. A larger part hoping he will.

Once we're under cover, he frowns and drags me in close. "You're all wet."

"So are you." That's all I can manage before his kiss, so longed for, melts away the last of the chill. I part my lips, allow him to force his tongue deeper into my mouth. His hardness and mine press against each other, as I pull my hands out of my pockets and reach up to his chest. *Is this how much you missed me? But it's almost okay. We're almost home. Can you see this new dawn as clearly as I can? Please...*

He hesitates. Maybe he feels it too, how we're getting too close here, how people are staring out of their windows, unknown quantities, evil thoughts that wish us harm. I could ignore them; I want to ignore them. But there's so much we need to do.

He takes off his long black coat and drapes it around my shoulders, then squeezes the rain out of my hair. "Sorry I took so long," he murmurs. "You should've waited inside."

"I didn't like being in there."

He nods, seeming to understand. I blink at him hopefully, then ask, "So...are we going to go rescue Damien?"

A shadow crosses his face, before he grabs my hand and walks me away from my former cell. "Not yet. It's too wet out here."

That is a reason, yes. But only one, and he's hiding so many.

I can wait, for you. But neither of us can afford to wait for too much longer.

I turn around to close the door. Both of us are drip-drip-dripping all over Monty and Noriko's plush carpet. Raven pushes against me, and I splay my hands over the wood, enjoying his warm kisses on my neck and his cold hands stripping me down to my skin. Such a familiar desperation, only now I feel so safe within its clutches. This, then, is the meaning of trust. And love.

He spins me around and drops reverently to his knees, nibbling at my belly, kissing his way up my thighs, hesitantly and gently taking my dick in his mouth, sucking me until the hardness returns. A new wetness and dizziness envelops me, spiralling all the way down into my soul.

Raven… I want you to want me too.

Am I allowed to want…this?

As if in answer, he gets to his feet, taking hold of my hand once more and dragging me into the bathroom. In a few moments, steam surrounds us, clogging up the mirror, and we distract one another with more delicate kisses as the tub fills.

He lowers himself in first, then pulls me down on top of him. The water, almost but not quite too hot, soaks into my skin. I snuggle up between his legs, and his arms go around me. It's enough, to allow myself to be held in this way. So warm, so safe.

The soap's an expensive brand smelling of lavender and something musky. He runs it over my chest, down my arms, and between my thighs. The water laps quietly around us, while his heavy breathing sends shivers down my neck. Outside, the rain scatters across the roof. Waves and sighs and raindrops, a dream of the ocean coming to find me; here, always here.

"I love you," he whispers in my ear.

We listen to the rain, and he massages my shoulders, and I

distract myself a moment longer by noticing such mundane things as the fact that my toenails need painting. Already, the water's going cold around us. Soon, it will be time to leave.

"Funny, I'd usually fall asleep, right about here," I murmur. "But now I feel wide awake."

A brief pause, and his hands fall from my shoulders. "You want to get out?"

As an answer I stand up awkwardly, and he follows close behind, plucking the towel off the rack just before my fingers can grab it. He dries me off himself, patting my skin delicately, and gently wringing out my hair. "I feel spoilt," I say.

He nibbles my earlobe, then says in all seriousness, "You deserve to be spoilt."

I stare at his chest. There's a new scar, this one shorter than most of the others, running below his nipple to about where his heart should be. I trace a finger over it; a little smear of blood comes off on my fingertip. Fresh, then. Probably from this morning, perhaps right before he made the journey to the hospital. "Is that one for me?" I ask.

He closes his eyes, nuzzles my cheek, and whispers in my ear, "Go get dressed."

I nod and pad down the hallway, finding the spare bedroom with ease. I'm still pondering a choice of clothing from the mismatched fragments inside the suitcase, when the door clicks shut behind me and strong hands push me onto the floor. He hovers above me, his tongue spiralling over my lips, my neck, my chest, as I hold my breath, desperate not to giggle when the kisses come too close to tickles. But he stops right over my belly, frowning like he wants to go further, if only...

I've just begun trailing a finger through his hair when he sits up abruptly, searching for something in my face and looking away too quickly to find it. Not fear, then. Shame?

"What?" I ask, watching him move over to sit on the bed,

rest his head in his hands. Staying on all fours, I scuttle across to him and pull his elbows off his knees, so there's no place for him to hide from me. Perhaps I'm being cruel, in a way, when I take each of his fingers in my mouth one by one and suck on them, lick them, nibble on them, suck them again, until his imagination kicks in too, and he laughs at me softly. With a smile, I drop his hand into his lap, and wait.

"It's not fair," he mumbles, "that I think of you...that I dream of you—" He rubs at his face.

"That you dream of me...?"

"That I dream of you...as his word for God. As his mama. Too much, to expect—"

He looks away, leaving the shadows to fall upon my heart again. "I'm not good enough, perhaps?"

"*What?* No, that's not it at—"

"There's a lot of things you don't think I'm good enough for." Too late, I bite my tongue. Where did that come from?

With a sigh of annoyance, he shoves me aside and starts fishing through the suitcase for some clothes of his own. "Fuck this. I'm going to get Damien."

I stop trying to unravel the strands of bitterness and paranoia all knotted up with my thoughts. *I'm going to get Damien.* Just you? By yourself? No, that isn't how it's supposed to—

"But it's raining," I tell him, distracted again as my mind at last reaches one end of the thread. *Make love to me, Raven.* So, it led me to a wish.

I swallow hard, quashing the words that I want—I need—to speak, holding my breath until my chest starts to hurt. Too deep a confession, not meant for this moment. I put his arms around me. And still, I don't say the words.

His head rests close to my heart, the heart across which these silent words carve so much pain. "I'm scared, too," is all I allow myself. Another truth. A truth that cuts, scars invisible to every eye but his.

"I'm sorry," he whispers.

"Don't." I disentangle myself from the hug. Already these barbed-wire thoughts begin to uncoil and fizz in the light. *Love goes beyond both physical pain and baser human needs. There are other ways...* I glance at him.

"What?" he asks, frowning suspiciously.

"You think of me...as Damien's mother?"

"And a child to my heart." He holds me tighter, as though I might try to escape. The rain continues to fall.

Many ways...

I am learning them all.

By the time the rain stops, he's almost asleep. I keep nudging him until he groans and sits up beside me. "Time to get dressed. The rains have passed us by."

Rubbing his eyes and mumbling something, he stretches and drifts off through the hallway. A moment later I hear the sounds of the kettle boiling in the kitchen, the chink of a spoon against a cup, and the buttons of a telephone dialling a number. This last sound guarantees my curiosity gets the better of me, and I wander out just in time to see him hang up the receiver, paler than usual as he leans over the counter, inhaling steam and the coffee's aroma.

"What's the matter?" I ask cautiously, taking the mug he passes me and sipping a little off the top.

He reaches for the pack of clove cigarettes lying conveniently within arm's reach and lights one up, evidently not caring that Noriko would go nuts if she came home and caught him smoking in here. Behind a lung full of smoke, he asks me, "What's the time?"

I glance over my shoulder at the Astro Boy clock on the wall. "One-fifteen."

He nods, expelling the smoke into the air. "We're gonna

need to be quick about this. No time for fucking around. I think Monty's due around seven, and Noriko's always home by six." He stares down at his cup, but makes no effort to drink from it. Above the counter, his hands are trembling so badly I don't think he could pick it up at the moment without spilling it.

"Raven," I start to say, but he quickly shakes his head, as though I've interrupted his train of thought.

"She's there."

At least that explains the phone call. "Should I go pack the rest of our things?"

"No, we'll leave the suitcase. We've gotta come back anyhow."

I don't ask why. Not really desiring caffeine, I push the cup towards the sink, knowing that if I stand here in this kitchen for too much longer, I'm going to end up with the shakes as well. Perhaps I already have, on the inside. Fear is contagious.

To keep up my momentum, I grab for his free hand, press the house keys into his palm, and close his fingers around them. "Come on." I nod at the cigarette. "You can smoke that on the way. You said it yourself, there is no time."

Still not meeting my eyes, he gulps down half the coffee. Then I catch hold of his sleeve, and pull him out the front door. With every step closer to Wendy's house, the greater my sense of destiny and doom.

It's only in this moment, huddled together beneath a tree on the opposite side of the street, that I understand how much he fears coming back here. Why he even killed to avoid doing so.

He stamps out the remains of the clove cigarette that's been dead for a good five minutes, and folds his arms across his tummy. His breath catches in his throat, threatening to choke him; when I hold him close, I can feel the pulse racing through his body.

I have to do something, and soon.

"Pegasus," he hisses, desperate to control the shivering that's ready to consume him from the inside out. "I'm so sorry, but...this house... I don't—I can't."

It's okay. This is my dream. My offering. One of the many ways of which I have spoken.

"Shh." I hug him even tighter, kissing his cheek, waiting for my own courage or something beyond courage to overtake me. I understand, Raven. I don't understand what she did to you to make you fear this place so much, but I can guess.

All places have auras. The one emanating from this house is so sickly yellow that it nearly makes me forget. Strange I never saw it like you do before today. But in those days I always assumed this was some place you'd chosen to be.

"I already had this nightmare," he tells me. "I can't go in there now, I'll never get out."

"Then I'll go," I say, determined.

His eyes fix on my face, wild and terrified like a fearful animal. "No. I can't let you—"

I press a finger to his lips. "Shh," I tell him again. "Just listen. Wait for me." I draw in a short breath. God only knows what state I could be in once we need to leave. "If I'm not back in twenty minutes, you'll just have to get over it and come right on in anyways." I try to sound light-hearted, but I doubt I'm close to pulling it off. "Okay?"

He opens his mouth, frowns in hesitation, and closes it again.

All right, then. If this is the way we have to play things. "Do you want us as a family, or forever incomplete?"

I regret these words, but by this stage they're all I have left. The familiar spark returns to his eyes, before he turns aside. I can tell he's more ashamed than angry, though. "Of course we'll be a family. That's all I ever fucking wished for." Softening somewhat, he adds, "I want you both."

I nod, just once. "Then give me the keys." The calm tone in my voice belies nothing in my heart. I won't show him that, though; won't show any of them.

This will be the last chance anyone in my so-called family ever has to hurt me. I can't say the words, but perhaps, after this, you'll see. Once and for all.

He surrenders the keys to this house of nightmares reluctantly. "Go wait around the corner," I tell him, and I linger until he disappears from view. You might not believe it, but you're much braver than I am.

So do you think he'll want you around his precious son, after this?

This is my only chance. The only choice, and the only way. This is what the dream showed me. This is all I can do.

I take a moment longer in a last attempt to cast these fears and doubts aside, before I bound across the street and onto Wendy's doorstep, pocketing the keys. *She's there.* That's what he told me. I don't need these, then. She must invite me in, of her own free will.

Staring intently at the door, I project my thoughts inside and onto her. A woman I no longer think of as my sister. Merely another obstacle.

This is the last choice you have, Wendy. Choose death, and pass on the souls of those you don't love to me.

Today, I become Death.

I ring the doorbell.

17 (RAVEN)

The Word For God

Rain's falling again, dripping off the branches, leaving teardrops on the cigarette. My third. And by the time this one's burned out, I'll have given you ten minutes more than you asked for. Will that be enough? Or too much?

Why are you doing this, Peg? Why did I let you? This is my nightmare, not yours. You shouldn't be facing it for me. That's not the way—not the way things were meant to be.

I brought you your son. Isn't that enough?

No, angel. It won't ever be enough.

Another fifteen minutes, gone in a heartbeat. My heart beats too slowly, for you.

I drop the butt into a puddle, cross the street, and come to stand again before that house.

I wait on the front step, gathering what's left of my courage, a useless defence against the cold. But it's all I've got. You're all I've got. Both of you.

The door stands slightly ajar. I put my hand on it, intending to barge right on in, play the triumphant hero who's come to the rescue, just like they do in the movies. But the second my skin makes contact with the wood, all those memories come back in a whirlwind. All these things I tried so hard to keep locked down in their graves: the nights of no escape, her constant lists of every possible reason I'd never be right and I'd never be enough, how all my beliefs were nothing but shadows, and I—

I let her poison in. I gave in so easy. Too easy. Her words... like my dad's words. And every time, I fell for it. I used to believe I could do so much. Ma told me—

But when it came down to it, I didn't believe her. I believed my dad, and you instead, Wendy. Your words were always so much easier. A simpler truth. Something I never once needed to question. The religion of my conscience, and the disease of my soul.

A memory of Damien's in my mind, his eyes red with tears while his mama hits him and makes sure he knows how this is all my fault—always my fault—for being such a failure. Transmitting the poison, spreading her disease, and I—I just watch. Why do I just watch? Why don't I do something? Anything.

Cos I no longer believed I could. I thought she was better than me, I thought she was right. And you, Pegasus— I never dared to believe you could love me. All I wished for was some kind of ending, a return to nothingness.

But nothing comes from nothing.

A last image flickers across my mind, light on shadow. This one stems from beyond the house, rooted in the depths of my insanity. The hospital ward, and a bed shrouded in white, and my hand peeling aside the veil...

Damien. Pegasus. All that I wished for.

I sneer at the house. I remember, all right. And because I remember, I'm not afraid of you.

I throw myself against the door, so hard it slams into the wall and the knob on the other side buries itself in the plaster. I want to hurt this house. I don't want anything left.

Daddy, a voice echoes from inside the crumbling plaster. *I had a bad dream.*

No, little angel, it can't hurt us anymore. She can't hurt us anymore. It's all going to be okay.

I stand in the deadened hallway. Somewhere beyond the walls, under the floorboards, inside the ceiling, I can hear a child crying. But what are you, really? Just another ghost, another nightmare? Are you still trying to fight me, house? Now I've seen the truth, do you think you can win?

I shake my head till the floor spins and the wailing fades. In its absence, I can hear my heart throbbing against my ribs. Guess I'm still afraid. But that's okay, too. Fear is anything you choose to make of it, and so it becomes my ally.

I walk on forward, defying the house to stop me with every step I take, even while I embrace its shadows as an extension of my scars.

I remember why I wanted to die. It's not the same anymore.

I find Pegasus in the bedroom, where the voices are loudest and the shadows most deep. He sits on the edge of the mattress, looking very small and holding my son—our son—while his whole body shakes.

Damien glances up as I enter; Pegasus doesn't. I shuffle into the one ray of light and stand before them, daring to hope. Enough light can drown a shadow, after all. And we're so close...we might even make it, now.

I spy a bloody trail, red on grey, winding across the hall towards the bathroom. The bathroom door is closed.

He doesn't want to look at me, and so I focus on my son. If I don't do that, if I forget again, we'll all be lost. Can't let that happen, no matter what.

I kneel at their feet, doing my best to ignore the blood on Peg's clothing, and his beautiful, spidery fingers, and his silken hair. *Better it staining the carpet than my soul...* I risk a glance at his face, but his eyes close, shutting me out.

"Pegasus." His name escapes my throat like coughing up a razor. I reach out, wanting to absorb all the pain. It belongs in me, after all.

He lets go of Damien, who falls into my lap with a whimper. Kittling, tiny angel boy. How much did you see?

He's warm in my arms, so solid and real. I think I might've dreamed this moment; I can't tell if I'm dreaming now. But outside the theatre, that's where the heroes fade. That doesn't mean I can't save you both. I've got to.

I force myself to my feet. "Can you do something for me, Day? Go get all your best clothes and favourite things, and put them in your trains bag. And when you're done, go wait out back, okay?"

He blinks once, then nods slowly. "Can I come with you now, Daddy?"

I smile at him. "Real soon, yeah. We're going on a holiday. Far away from here."

Together, we glance at Pegasus. I look away first. I can't let my heart break just yet.

"Peggy-sis is coming too?" It's more a demand than a question. Your son, too, Pegasus.

"Course he is. We're a family." I only hope, wherever you are, you can hear that. "Go get your things."

Nodding enthusiastically, he transforms into 'plane mode'. Spreading his arms wide, he zooms and zigzags out of the room. Still a little boy, not quite lost. One of my fears allayed, at least.

I fall onto the bed, ignoring the way Pegasus cringes as I shuffle in closer. Partly as a distraction, I fish out the pack of cloves, open it up, and shake it so a couple poke out the top. "Want one?" I ask, only half-joking.

Not even a flicker. But I don't believe this is the ending you saw, either.

With a sigh, I decide against another, too. Closing the pack,

I let my fingers go limp. It lands on the floor, more dull red. What am I meant to do here? What can I say?

I reach for him again, but he grabs my wrist and pushes me off. I've only got the truth. Your faith. My faith. "I believe you love me, now."

If he does hear me, he doesn't respond.

I keep trying. "You saved me from hell...from myself—"

A light of hatred flares in those grey eyes. Not hatred for me, though; I could deal with that. "Perhaps I don't love you at all." His voice rasps in his throat, from screaming and wanting to choke back the tears. Yeah, I know how that goes.

I glance at the cigarette pack on the floor. Maybe I should reconsider that smoke.

"Weren't you the one who said I never tell you? Why would I *want* to save you? Anyway, now we're even. You can walk away, run away—whatever you wish. We don't owe each other anything."

He draws in a ragged breath. I wait.

"You killed my father, so I killed her. That means the circle's complete, yes?"

I close my eyes. Auras of grey and red only intensify behind my lids. *The circle's complete.* Is that the truth? Your truth?

You killed my father. Then you knew. You figured it out. But I don't believe you. I can't believe you. I don't know what to believe.

I sigh. He's still not looking at me; somehow, that makes it easier. Maybe it doesn't matter what I think. Doesn't mean I can't have...faith. "Not our circle."

Again he tries to pull away from my embrace, but this time I'm not letting go and I'm not giving in. While he claws and screeches and slaps at me, I hold on tight, I let him hurt me, I relish this pain, because it's his gift to me. Even as he fights me off, a new calm lays my mind bare. I see myself, and I see you, freeing me forever from the bars of the cage.

Just like the night we made love.

He shudders and goes limp as a rag doll in my arms, his breath rasping in his chest. It's not over, angel. It's never going to be over. *Till death do us part?* Anyone who truly loved would know it goes so much deeper. And would never settle for saying those words.

"She's dead, then?" I hear myself asking.

Very slowly, he shakes his head. "I couldn't finish it...for you."

His tears trickle down my wrists, lighter than blood, and cleaner. "Hush," I whisper, kissing the top of his head, willing all my strength into him. "Go wash your hands, then get Damien to Monty's. Out the back, up the lane, and straight onto the tram. Yeah?"

He comes to life in my arms, pawing at me and swallowing hard. "Raven—I—I can't do this by myself, I can't—"

I grab hold of him till he falls silent again. "We're going home," I tell him. In that instant, all the auras of madness fade. And me? I don't ever want to look away. Yes, Pegasus. This is the truth, right here.

With some difficulty, I help us both into the kitchen. He leans against me, clasping my hand. *It's okay. I know this house. I can protect you from it. I can keep my promise, to guard your soul.*

At the filthy sink, I wash off all the blood while he gapes at his shaking fingers. "So much anger," he whispers. I put my hand to his throat, feeling for his heartbeat. *Soon, the cage will break open, and together we'll fly out.*

I think—I think now I can see how it ends as well...

Damien bursts in, clutching a bag full of toys and books. I spin around to face him. "You grab some clothes, too?"

He nods eagerly. "In my room. I couldn't carry, all by myself."

I smile at him, my arm tightening around Peg's waist so

there's no escape. "Peggy's going to take you to Uncy Monty's for a bit, okay?"

This doesn't go down well. Damien promptly dumps the bag and sticks out his lower lip. Oh, Day. Why do you think I'm always so ready to leave you? "I don't want you to go away again, Daddy," he says, with a loud sniffle.

I'm across the floor in an instant, sweeping him into my arms and kissing his nose. "I'm not going anywhere," I assure him, doing up the zipper on his little jacket. "Not without you. Daddy's just gotta take care of some stuff first. Okay?"

He bites his lip, then nods. I give his shoulder a rub and a squeeze, then glance behind me. Pegasus stares around the walls, though his gaze snaps back to my face as I place my son in his arms. Making a detour into Damien's bedroom, I fix up the clothes in the other bag, before I hand both it and the toys over to Pegasus. The minute they leave, we're a step closer. The minute I put an end to all this, we can go home.

"How much money have you got?" I ask.

He blinks in surprise. "What? Maybe— I don't know. Seven thousand dollars? From my mother, when she—" He trails off, with a frown.

"Can you get to it?"

"What do you think we've been living off since Lenny gave me the sack?"

Again the echoes of my brilliant failures, rising to the fore. Time for self-pity later, maybe. "Then I need you to go and withdraw the whole lot."

He looks at me like I've gone mad. "You're serious?"

"What do you reckon?" My eyes flicker over my son. He's snuggled against Peg's shoulder, contented. "Go. I'll meet you there in an hour, okay?"

I'm not waiting around for him to agree. I give them both a kiss, then turn away, dismissing them. A moment later I hear the back door slam, and I'm alone in this house once again.

A mother to my child. I hold myself, shrugging off the visions that threatened to overwhelm me when I first stepped inside. But I've got visions of my own, house. So I won't be needing any of yours.

I make my way up the hall. Spotting the blood on the carpet that leads right up to the bathroom door is easy now.

It's already over. Only one last thing left to do, before I save myself—once and for all—from hell.

The tiles are smeared with blood. A yellow haze blurs every corner, and unreality clings to the air. By now the aura of death's become all too familiar. Over in the corner, a red stain spreads across the bath mat, and Wendy slouches against the tub, broken and torn, staring at me soulless. A battered cabinet lies near her thighs, ripped from the wall, its mirror smashed in a hundred-hundred pieces. Shards of its glass float among the blood, debris on a red seashore, glittering diamonds in the light that flickers through the window. So morbidly pretty.

Anyway, she's breathing.

I perch nearby on the edge of the tub, then get around to lighting that clove at last. I don't bother offering.

Of course, she's watching me. I don't care. Don't feel anything, no hatred, no pity, no remorse. I exhale smoke. I won't feel any regret, either.

She's still watching, the hatred weakened but not entirely diminished, as I regard the flecks in the filter with new-found interest. "Guess I should call you an ambulance," I say.

She laughs at me, or tries to, till a choking cough overwhelms her. For a moment I can't help staring, mildly curious about the blood spilling down one corner of her mouth. The transformation's happening already, her slow return to nothing, all the poison seeping out from her veins. In the end, this is my freedom, not hers. Somehow I managed to sneak up and steal it from her.

"So. What did you do?" I ask.

She smiles, wiping clumsily at her bruised lips, able to find strength enough for hate. She hawks a gob of blood at my feet. "I told him the truth."

"Ah. *The truth.* Tell me. Please. About your truth."

"I told him...that he's just like his precious mama. Both of them, nothing but whores. Daddy told me everything. What she was, how she died. Why she abandoned us, all for some bullshit ideal about going off to be with her lover. *His* father. I thought it was only right that *he* knew how her own son meant nothing. How he could never win, just like her. Because you—you belong to me. And as long as I've got *your* precious son, you always will."

A small clump of ash falls into the little red sea. There it floats, like an island. Maybe he almost believed you, Wendy. But not for long. He's better than that. And by now he knows it.

I put on a smile. "Your truth, then. But that's not *The Truth*, is it? Does such a thing even exist, you reckon? And you know what I don't understand? Why do you *want* me to stay? I've got nothing to give, not to you." Not even malice, your most treasured gift to both me and my son.

She sneers at me. "Revenge." The blood's started dribbling down her chin.

"Indeed." I nod, and one of my knees cracks when I stand up. "Well, here it is—your revenge—all around us. It's staining the floor and spilling out your mouth. Even in death, you don't see. Hatred blinds you, Wendy, like it always did. Funny...once upon a time, I thought you were better than me. But now I know you're not the truth. You're going to die by your own poison, alone with your hate."

I make it as far as the door before her voice reaches my

ears. "Aren't you going to kill me, Raven?"

Is she begging me? "Weren't you listening? I've got nothing to give you." No life, no death. I got what I came for.

I've just stepped out into the hall, leaving dull brown footsteps on the carpet, when she calls my name again. Already, her voice sounds so distant. So, then she tells me, "I love you."

Those three little words nearly make me change my mind altogether, make me want to go right back in and wrap my hands around her throat and squeeze it tight while every last ounce of life and lust and vomit poured out over my skin.

But that would be a gift. Not for her. *Alone with your hate...* "Good-bye, Wendy."

I close the door on the maniacal laugh, locking off that part of the house forever.

Another step closer to freedom.

Back in the bedroom, I pull everything out from her side of the wardrobe. Anything that's old enough not to carry her smell or trigger her memory; that'll do, for starters.

I've got together maybe a couple of outfits when I come upon a small wooden chest, buried beneath a stack of old ballet shoes and a tutu. Frowning, I pull it out onto my lap. Roses and waves are carved around its edges, and it smells like the kind of smoke that brings on dreams that are hard to wake from. I can't see any obvious way to get the thing open.

I turn it over and over maybe a dozen times, before finally discovering a tiny latch on the bottom left corner. One pinch of that and the lid springs right open, spilling the contents onto the floor. Photographs, mostly, and a few envelopes. I go for the pictures first, folding my legs underneath me as I flick through each one. All of this one woman, this face that I recognise...

"Juliette," I whisper. But why are these here? Wendy must've stolen them. Her mama, too.

I turn over the next photo. Here she is again—the fey Juliette—sitting on a beach, holding the hand of a tiny androgynous creature who leans into her shoulder. Even here, his hair's long enough for a braid, his body draped in white lace, an echo of her sad smile on his lips. I brush aside a tear and wipe my hands on my jeans before I dare to trace the lines of his face. You were such a beautiful child. How anyone could have taken so much pleasure in your torment...

I slide the picture into my coat pocket. Who took all these photos, anyway?

And then I notice something else. How'd I miss it, before now?

After going through each and every photo all over again, I fumble with the clasp on the velvet choker, and lay it on the carpet beside the pile of portraits.

No doubting it. The pattern on the cross, spirals etched in silver, even the shape—they're identical. My eighteenth birthday present. All along, I had no fucking clue. This was his mama's necklace.

I pick it up, my throat constricting, my vision blurred. Cold metal brushes my lips as I kiss the cross, then fasten it around my neck once more. Forgive me, Pegasus. I never guessed how true your faith always was.

Next, I turn my attention to the envelopes. All of them sent from France, addressed via a post office to *Mlle Juliette Belmont*. Not her married name...

They've already been opened, so I pick one at random and unfold the notepaper. Holding it up to the light, I strain to read the faded ink. Not that it makes much difference. I can make out just enough to decipher that it's French, a class I failed miserably in school.

With a sigh of resignation, I pack the whole lot away, then

do up the latch and wipe my eyes, laughing at myself despite everything.

I pick up the dresses and the box, stuff them both into a plastic bag I found in the wardrobe, and return everything else to its place. Time to leave.

On my way out, I linger in front of the hallway telephone, then snatch up the receiver and dial those three zeroes. Seems to ring for ages before the other end picks up, and I'm asked which service I need: fire, police, or ambulance. I give them the address and a brief description of the scenario, but hang up the moment the operator asks my name.

It's over now. I can go.

I close the door to Damien's room, and leave the front door open a crack, same as I found it, before I at last turn my back on this house and its empty husk for good.

An hour later I arrive at Monty's, just like I promised. When the door finally opens, Damien bursts out, trying to crawl up my leg. I kiss the tears off Peg's cheeks, but he's distracted by the plastic bags, his raised brow asking the question for him.

Like I can't tell you've been sitting here crying all this time.

I stroke his cheek with my thumb. "Go wait in the bathroom." When he frowns at me, not understanding, I give him a nudge of encouragement. "We're in a hurry, remember?"

He glares at me, as if to say, 'I know that', but disappears obediently up the hall. I leave the bags where they are, lift Damien up at last, and carry him into the kitchen, resting him against my hip as I hunt through the phonebook. There it is. I dial the number.

"Who ya calling, Daddy?" he yells in my ear, right as someone picks up on the other end. I quickly hush him.

Turns out five-thirty is the soonest—and only—coach service up the high country this evening. So I go ahead and book three seats to drop us off as close to Monty's holiday house as we can get.

"What name?" the operator asks.

I squint at the receiver, cursing my lack of forethought. My own name I can give, simply cos I don't care anymore. It'll make things easier, later. But Pegasus— "Raven," I say, when the operator repeats the question as though I'm thirty years behind the rest of the world. "Raven and…Juliette. Belmont."

What the fuck are you doing? A little stone curdles inside my chest. Damien giggles and starts playing with the cross at my throat. The voice on the other end of the phone tells me I need to be at the terminus half an hour early to pick up the tickets, quotes me somewhere in the region of a hundred dollars, then hangs up. Service with a smile.

I put down the receiver and let him slide to the floor, though I need to manually extract each of his fingers from the choker before I can stand upright. "You hungry, kittling?"

He shakes his head, so I settle him in front of the telly with a cuddle and a favourite children's show, and go grab the bags out of the hall. Then I make my way into the bathroom. This is where things get interesting.

Pegasus jumps off the tub as I enter. "What's going on?" he asks, not taking his eyes off the bags.

"We're leaving soon, that's what. But first—" I pull out two boxes of dye. "What colour do you prefer? Brunette, or blond?"

He grabs his hair with both hands and pulls it behind his ears, out of my reach, backing away till he runs into the tub and nearly falls over. "No. Absolutely no. Please, not my hair."

I shrug, placing the boxes on the sink, like I'm ready to

give in so easy. "That's fine. But you know they'll be looking for us, soon enough." I frown. That point hardly needs belabouring. "It's either that, or I cut it."

With a whimper, he lets go of his hair altogether, wide-eyed and wild enough to fight me off if needs be. As if I could ever do that to you. I already told you—I already showed you—I'm not like them.

I pull him into a kiss, then turn him around, sit him down, and get to work on brushing the knots out. Next I grab a towel and arrange it over his shoulders.

"You're not doing this to yourself," he mutters, full of resentment.

"That's cos I don't care," is all I say, trying hard to avoid my own reflection in the mirror.

"What do you mean?"

I grimace. "Let's just say I'm starting to see...how it ends, as well."

I watch him dab at a stray tear. Then he sighs and points to the brown. Guess I don't need to ask why.

Reassuring him one last time before we get started that Ma went grey early so I've got plenty of practice, I don the plastic gloves and mix up the dye, which smells even worse than I remember. Apart from that, I enjoy fussing over him. Towards the end, he finally starts to relax, though by now both our eyes are watering from the stench of all the toxins that go into this stuff.

"Want a coffee?" I ask, disposing of the mess then rubbing at my nose. It's started to itch like crazy.

He nods, and goes on staring warily at his reflection. I give him a quick peck on the cheek, then sneeze my way out of the room.

Once in the kitchen, I turn on the kettle, blow my nose, and go check on my son. Much to my relief, I find him where I left him, staring intently at some commercial. "Daddy?" he says, as I enter.

"Yeah, kittling?"

"Why can't I be like him?"

He points at the TV. The usual mock imagery of the perfect nuclear family flashes subversively across the screen. Loving mama, daddy, and son, united in their love for the latest innovation in worming tablets. I make sure to unclench my fists before I crouch beside him on the carpet. "What do you mean?"

"My mama doesn't love me," he murmurs, turning from the set and looking down at his spotty-socked feet.

I sigh, then pull him onto my knee. "But you *are* loved. *I* love you." I squeeze him tight so he knows how much I mean it. "And Peggy loves you, too."

In the kitchen, a loud click announces that the kettle's done boiling. Giving him a final kiss, I head towards it. I'm halfway across the floor when he asks, "Can Peggy-sis be my mama instead?"

I stop in my tracks, then turn to face those three-year-old eyes, filled with hope and innocence and such capacity to see deep into the heart of the matter. Something even Wendy couldn't destroy, not for want of trying. "Why don't you ask him that?" I say, with a nervous glance to the hallway. And maybe then, Pegasus, you'll understand—

That my faith is every bit as true.

I find Noriko's copy of *The Velveteen Rabbit* stashed away in a bookcase, so Damien and I snuggle up on the sofa to read it. I'm trying real hard to ignore the clock, but time's always moving, whether I'm around to see it or not. The hiss of the shower from down the hall seems to drone on forever. Hurry up, Pegasus.

At last, with the squeak of a tap, the sound of running water stops. I've just finished the story when he calls my name.

I wander out to meet him. He's standing behind the bathroom door, torso and hair both covered with a towel. Glancing down the hall for my son and not finding him, he beckons me forward, then moves my head so I'm looking at the other plastic bag. The one I filled with Wendy's old dresses. His voice is cold as he asks, "What do you want from me, Raven?"

I hesitate, remembering the photo in my pocket, the gown folded at the bottom of the wardrobe, his childhood flashback to that bastard cutting his hair. "I want you to have a choice."

He glares at me. "You want me to *make* a choice, you mean." I open my mouth, but he's there ahead of me. "Is it because of what my father said?"

"What?"

"Don't *'what'*. Because he said I dressed like Mother. Is that why?"

Oh, that. I put my hands on my hips. "Well, to start with, he's hardly your father, is he? And you think I ever listened to a word that came out of the mouth of that c—" I check myself quickly, making sure to lower my voice. I've just caught sight of Damien lurking around the living room doorway. "I never listened to a goddamn word he ever said. Besides all of which, he's *dead*, isn't he? So think about that. Really."

In answer, he slams the door in my face. I drown a "Fuck!" in my palms, and then turn back to my son.

Ten minutes pass in front of an ad-free station on the TV. At a quarter-to-four, I lose my patience and call out into the hall, "Come on, Peg. We've gotta leave soon."

Five minutes after, I stride out of the room and nearly run right over him. He's huddled just a few paces back from the door, arms folded across his chest, leaning against the wall. I pull up, taking in the long lace-up boots, thick black tights, little corduroy dress and white skivvy. And the chocolate-coloured fringe falling over his face, turning sad silver eyes a smoky grey. "You're the prettiest girl I ever saw," I say, before I can help myself.

His eyes narrow. "Do you really think that's how it works?" Fingers start twirling a long brown wisp of hair, as he glances around the doorway, looking in on my son a moment. "Is this how you see me?" he asks, more softly. "Me taking her place on the throne, wearing her clothes?"

I shove my hands in my pockets. "It's not meant to deceive me." He twitches as I step forward and take both his hands in mine, and shivers as I start slowly kissing his fingertips. "I see beyond everything. I love *you*, no matter 'who' you are. But as some kind of replacement for *her*, after everything? Is that how you see *yourself*?"

His lower lip's just starting to quiver when Damien dashes out from the living room again, and we let go each other's hands reluctantly. As for my son, it takes him only a moment of gazing at Pegasus before he declares, in quite the serious voice, "You look very lovely, Peggy-sis."

"We can't leave the house together," I say, as we gather together our things, one of them being that wooden chest. Pegasus frowns at it, then lets me hand it over. "You'll take that," I tell him, "and the bags, and Damien. I'll go first; gotta get there early to pick up the tickets. Once I'm gone, you wait—give it fifteen minutes—and then call a taxi from the phone box round the corner. You got all that?"

I put my palm against his cheek, burying my fingers behind his ear, in among that strange new hair. I'm leaving him with *you*, Peg. This is how much *I trust you*.

I give them each a kiss—not a final kiss, just a kiss—and walk quickly from the house. I don't look back.

Don't be late. This is our only window of opportunity.

This is my only chance.

I pace up and down the terminus, clutching our tickets in one hand and a clove cigarette in the other, not concealing my impatience too well as I watch the driver load up suitcase after suitcase into the luggage compartment. We're scheduled to leave in fifteen minutes.

I take another drag, hugging myself against the onslaught of a cold wind that wants to undress me from the inside out. Trying so hard to stay calm.

But he was meant to be here more than half-an-hour ago.

The driver joins me, a round-bellied, balding, dwarfish creature, lighting up a cigarette of his own. The stale stench of burnt tobacco fills my nostrils as I get a face full of smoke. In a gruff voice, he mutters, "Women, eh? They're always late."

I grunt, which seems to be enough. My own fault, then, for making the one I love play this charade, for ever getting him involved at all. But—

I love you, Pegasus. What else was I meant to do? You should've told me, right from the start, if all this was so wrong. I can't lose everything so close to the edge. I just... can't.

I finish the last of the cigarette and throw the butt on the ground, grinding it out with my heel. Now there's only the cold. And her last words, ringing in my ears. Words I want to forget. Words I can only forget, if you—

"Daddy!" a voice screams out, and I whirl around despite myself. *Some other dad, some other son.* And then Damien's in my arms, and I'm holding him tighter than ever, and it feels like I wasn't even breathing before. I don't want to let him go. Now, I don't need to.

I watch Pegasus slide out of the taxi, a small but stupid smile glued to my face. Time returns to its former meaningless state, and I forget I was ever impatient or cold, as he draws near, clutching the wooden chest under one arm.

"You're late," I tell him.

"What can I say?" he murmurs, gazing shyly into my face. "Being a girl sucks. I should have remembered."

I blink, pondering, but it doesn't matter. I'm only for kissing him here. He brushes my lips, turning to eye the faces aboard the coach. But after this, he kisses me back, and we don't stop till the driver interrupts with a dry, "Better hope we stop by a hotel, cos you two really need to get a room," and Peg falls out of my embrace, unsteady on his feet.

We take a seat near the back, he and Damien snuggling together by the window. Damien bounces up and down, pointing out the obvious in a manner only toddlers can get away with. "We're on a bus!" And, "There's another bus!" And, "Our bus is bigger!" And, "What if this bus turned into a *plane*!"

I glance at Pegasus, but he's staring out the window, distance veiling his reflection. It strikes me that I've got no real idea what he feels about any of this. He's barely said a word to me, since—

With a sad, tired smile, he turns in my direction, not quite meeting my eyes as he squeezes my hand. "Sunset...," he murmurs. "Like the whole sky's bleeding to death." As he looks to the horizon, I feel a little spark of electricity pass through his fingertips. "So much blood. No matter where I look." He nods at the box that lies between us. "Maybe that's why. I couldn't open it. Not yet."

I put my arm around him, inhaling the remnants of the dye in his hair, an old, familiar scent. "It doesn't matter. It's going to be okay. Remember? We're going home."

But Pegasus, my angel—one of my angels, and the saviour of my soul—is already fast asleep. Twilight fades as the coach glides through suburbia, and I'm left with my own words, my son, and his warm breath on my neck for comfort.

It's okay. We're going home.

(PEGASUS) *18*

Illumination (The Bottom of Pandora's Box)

So much anger. So much blood. Red like the sunset, staining my soul.

I pretend to sleep, in the comfort of his arms. The only safety, the only reality I have left. I don't know where we're headed, but he tells me it's home, and so I believe. But I wonder…

I wonder if he really understands yet. If it's really had a chance to sink in. That this is *all* only temporary. That our real home is—

No, not yet. Don't think. Let me go.

But my mind is not the problem. The wounds go so much deeper than that, so much deeper, you see.

I want him to see, even as I fake sleep. And I want to sleep too, it's just…my body won't allow me to succumb to the nightmares that lie in wait to claim me. Not yet.

He wraps his arms around me, while Damien snuggles closer. My hand brushes against the wooden chest. I can't bring myself to look inside it. In the other stories, Pandora's box closes before it's too late. But not in my story. In my version, even with the shadows of death touching my heart, breaking it open to reveal both hope and despair, it's all for you, Raven.

I dig my nails into his hand, not wanting to hurt him so much as wanting him to feel my own pain. Although, in their way, they're one and the same. It's why you are...what you are. Why you've treated me the way you do, why we both remain.

My mind keeps crumbling at the edges, seeking escape, a refuge in dreams. But the only sanctuary is where it always has been, right here in his arms.

I don't want to remember. She made me remember, Raven. *Help me.*

Little blood-red clouds dissolve into foam as I look on, and I'm standing upon the beach.

No...

I'm nine years old, and watching from the window. She's so far off, I can barely see her.

No.

But at the very last moment, before her wings spread free, she turns to look at me.

Mother...

She sees me. She's...smiling at me.

No!

I open my eyes, gasping for air, as Raven strokes my hair, shushing me. I close my eyes again, remember to breathe.

How dare you, Wendy. How dare you try to take that from me, again. The way she looked that day, so smug, so smug knowing I'd lost and she'd won, that I had nobody left to love and protect me. No guiding light. No nothing.

Mother smiled at me. Mother loved me. How dare you attempt to cheapen that, to remind me of the ways in which I failed, so many times, in the years since her death. The many, long years.

So much anger. If I had my time again, I'd still do what I did—unleash this anger, rid myself of this poison, try to cleanse my soul. Only I would finish it for you, Raven. Just like I promised you. Just like I should have.

I am nobody's whore. That's not what you see, when you

look at me.

Is it?

No. *We're a family now*, that's what he said to me. The only promise that might keep it all at bay, until—

I wonder how long, before we reach this place he calls home.

I think I'm going to be sick.

"Wake up, angel."

A whisper caresses my cheek, and I open my eyes reluctantly. Raven stands over me, cuddling a very sleepy Damien to his chest. I struggle to rise from the seat and nearly sprain my left ankle as it gives way beneath my weight. Right before I fall, he steadies me, propping me against his shoulder for support. I need it, but not because of the prickling in my foot.

"Is this the last stop?" I glance out the window, seeing nothing but a few lights from a mostly deserted street. It's pitch black outside already. Everybody else seems to be getting off, a tired procession of yawning mouths and creaking bones.

"Nope. Halfway, I think. They stop here for refreshments." He stares deep into my face, as though trying to will me away from the other pain, before adding, "But this is where we get off." He leans in closer, kissing my forehead, resting the tip of his nose against mine. "We're almost home, angel."

Hearing those words, I allow him to usher me off the coach. The minute I'm outside, the cold night air stings my cheeks, working its way into my bones, shocking me awake. I take hold of the child, snuggling into him for warmth as he murmurs something and tries to go back to sleep, and Raven retrieves the suitcase from the driver.

He turns around to see me shivering, and frowns. "Go on. Inside. Get yourself something to eat. Something for this one, too."

I hesitate, then gape at the source of the lights. A service station that doubles as a restaurant and a general store. Nothing to enlighten me as to where we are, but I guess I'm on a first name basis with the owners, assuming that's who 'Rosemary and Jack', whose names adorn the front window in fading chipped paint, are. Everything's so quiet; the only sounds and signs of life come from behind the glass. The coach obscures most of my view, though beyond that, in either direction, distant lights twinkle along the highway it must have travelled. A long and winding road, indeed.

"Oi!" Raven snaps his fingers in front of my face, rousing me from my rambling thoughts and Damien from his sleep. "Inside, I said."

"What about you?" I ask, patting down my hair and dress as I catch a glimpse of my strange reflection in the glass. For the first time, I kind of wish I'd gone for the blond. *And you said this was only to deceive the others. But you were wrong, my sweet.*

He laughs, fishing through the pockets of his coat for a cigarette. "Are you kidding? We've been on that thing for nearly four hours. I'm dying for a smoke." A kiss on the cheek, too chaste for my wishes, before he lights up and wanders out into the black void. With no other option, I take in a deep breath and push my way through the door.

After being outside, it's deafening in here; thirty odd people crowded about tables, relieving themselves of the self-imposed silence of travel. Perhaps I do know where this is. It feels like the ends of the earth.

Damien's head lolls against my chest, and I decide, rather than to risk waking him, that my best plan of attack is to take a seat in the darkest corner, farthest from the door, and wait for Raven. My nausea hasn't worn off. Somehow, I doubt it ever will.

I pull up a chair and settle in, gazing around the timber

walls. At the other end of the room, a fire crackles beneath all the voices, a constant. I avoid catching the eye of the flame. I'm scared of what I might see, lurking within. Another reflection of myself, in hell.

A tear rolls down my cheek as Damien wriggles in my arms, moving into a comfier sleeping position. He feels warmer than the flames, in any case. Safer.

Now I understand.

We're a family.

Oh, God.

No, it can't. Not here. Please wait until they leave. Until everyone leaves, and I'm all alone.

But the sleeping child in my arms is a comforting reminder that I'll never be alone. I press my face against his hair, hiding my sorrow and elation from the world as my body at last allows me to break.

I don't know when Raven comes in. I don't hear the ringing of the bell that announced my own entrance. But here he is, holding me in his arms, staring at me, so full of concern, so full of—

You're free now. Your eyes tell me so. All you need are the wings on your back, an ocean full of mermaid's tears and starlight. My mother's eyes were exactly the same, in those final days.

"It's okay," he whispers. Tonight, he feels so strong, perhaps because I'm so weak.

Using a thumb, he wipes a trail of mascara off my cheek. "I'm going to get you something to eat. And you," he adds, ruffling the hair of the child in my arms, who's wide awake and staring into my face.

I start to protest, only to have him cut me off with a glare. "No. I told you, we're almost there. But we've got a long walk ahead of us, with all this." He nods at the suitcase and the ominous box. "I can't carry them, Damien, and you." Softening somewhat, he touches a thumb to my lip. "Soon as we're home, I'll run you a bath. Sit you down by the fire. Kiss away your fears."

He turns from me a little too quickly and saunters towards the counter. I watch him make small talk with the old man—Jack, I assume, and not Rosemary—before he pays for our meals and returns to the table.

Your feelings embarrass you, Raven. You're scared to share them with me, in case I use them against you like she did. We both wear her scars. But now, we're both—

"I'm hungry, Daddy," Damien whines, as his father takes a seat between us, fidgeting with the glass ashtray, the table's only centrepiece.

"I know, kittling." He goes on spinning the glass between his fingertips, creating a hypnotic effect. Damien opens his mouth and turns his attention to a stray lock of my hair, twisting it up into a little ball and sucking on it. All three of us are silent until our meals arrive, and then we eat. Slowly, the other passengers drift away, and the dull growl of the engine outside announces their departure. Raven stares into a black well of coffee, his third cup since we came in, and Damien chews on a straw. I watch them both, a guardian angel, out of practice, but with the instincts still remaining.

Finally, he leans back and slides the cup across to the far side of the table. "Time to go?" I ask.

With a sigh and a stretch, he nods. "I should fetch some supplies while we're here. Doubt there'll be much in the way of food up there, and we'll need breakfast for the morning."

"If there is a morning," I mutter, before I can stop myself.

As we stand, he turns on me. "There's always a morning, Pegasus. You taught me that."

He takes care of the shopping, which I carry, along with Damien, out the door. That leaves him with the suitcase, and the box. As we step outside, the cold hits me full-force.

The coach is gone, so there's no more windbreak, and I can actually see what there is of this town. No wonder it's so dark. A huge mountain range towers over us, ominous and omniscient, blacker than the sky.

He lights another cigarette, blowing a stream of smoke and frost into the air. I smell the crispness of the cloves, the freshness of the night, eucalyptus and snow, maybe. We're a long way from the ocean. This is what you wanted, isn't it.

This is what I want, too.

For now.

The night seems as endless as the winding dirt road we follow off the highway, heading deeper into a forest. So many stars, reminding me of that night at his mother's house. Every so often, when we stop to rest, I ask him about them again, allowing the simplest of touches and his voice to keep me whole. Damien seems content to dream in my arms. Such precious life I carry. So this is what it means.

Not a single car overtakes us for the entire journey. If there are any houses out here, they're far enough from the road to remain hidden.

Just as my arms and legs are about to give out, he pulls off the road onto a hidden track that weaves its way uphill. In the distance, maybe a few hundred metres, I can make out a log cabin snug among the trees, moonlight reflecting off the windows.

The most tender of kisses falls upon my lips. "Welcome home," he tells me, frozen tears glittering on his cheeks.

We turn on all the lights one by one, illuminating a trail for Damien to explore the entire house. He discovers a new burst of energy, and small footsteps thump up and down the hall, as Raven collapses into a chair in the living room and I wander off in search of the bathroom.

Welcome home.

In a tiny room at the end of the house, I stand in front of the mirror, gazing numbly at my reflection. A wild-eyed, too pale, brown-haired girl stares out at me, one brow raised defiantly as if asking me why I'm so afraid. So afraid of myself and how like my mother I actually am.

Then I make the mistake of looking down at my hands. The visions of the blood, the familiar nightmares, come rolling back in one greeny-red wave of disgust. I empty my tummy of the toasted cheese and tomato sandwich and the salad and the hot chocolate that comprised my only meal for the day in a neat little pile in the sink. As I run the tap, tears flood my vision, and the idea strikes me that perhaps I can cleanse myself by simpler means, that the stains only run skin deep.

I scrub at my hands under the steaming hot water, wanting to burn away the flesh, scrape it off, rid myself of everything.

Until Raven's touch on my shoulder jerks me awake, I don't realise the liquid's scalding my skin. Cursing a little too loudly since Damien's right here in his arms, I spring back from the basin, nursing my hands and hiding my tears, pretending I can't feel only because I can't face the truth. I can't ask him, even though I want to—

Why not? You already know...

What? What do I already know? That I'm nothing but a whore?

Laughter. Wendy's laughter. My mind's up to its old tricks. The voice is my sister's, but the sentiment belongs to—

"Pegasus," Raven whispers, turning off the tap and forcing me to meet his gaze. "You okay?"

Looking at me from his father's arms with his father's eyes, Damien tugs on my hair. "Read me story, Peggy-sis!"

I start to shake. I don't know if it's spread to the outside yet, but I can feel it, building up within. Raven, please make it stop, please help me...

"I can't." I almost choke on the whisper, clutching my arms tight against my chest and backing away until I'm huddled in a corner, with no place left to go.

"It's okay." He's reaching out to me like I'm some frightened animal, trying to gain my trust. Trying to take what's already been given, over and over again. "Why don't you read him something? Take your mind off things."

It's like I'm watching myself from some other plane, watching this pretty girl fly at him with grief and claws, snatching back and destroying those gifts I expended so much energy in setting free. Watching on as her words and the tone of her voice make the little boy cry; the look on Raven's face. Hurt, and something much worse. Disappointment.

Clutching his son close, he turns his back on his other creation. "I'm going to go tuck him in," he mutters, and leaves the bathroom, switching off the light.

The darkness draws me into my body and pulls down the shutters. Now I feel her pain, her regret, these tears that belong to this pretty girl. Why did you do that to him? This isn't how it's meant to be.

Is that how you see yourself?

You think he wants you like he wanted Wendy, and so, you play her role.

Feeling nauseous all over again, I struggle out of the room and pad down the hall. Most of the lights are off now. Only one sliver filters through a crack in a partly opened door. I creep towards it, seeking shelter, forgiveness, warmth.

From inside, I can hear Damien's voice. Between the gap, I watch Raven tuck him in, denying him a story, wiping away the tears. Damien. Crying. Because of me.

No amount of scrubbing or burning will work. Wendy, you poisoned me down to my soul.

"I don't like it when you fight, Daddy."

Raven hangs his head. "We weren't fighting, kittling. Go to sleep, okay?"

But he doesn't fool me and he doesn't fool his son. "You were so fighting. Like with Mama. Why did Peggy-sis yell at me, Daddy?"

"He didn't yell at you, Day. He yelled at me."

I back away from the door, so I can't see how the light and shadow play across his face when he turns from the little angel.

"Why?"

He sighs, and fragments of my soul crumble into dust. "Cos I'm an arsehole, apparently. Get some sleep. It'll all be better in the morning."

Will it? The door jerks open and we're suddenly face to face. A shiver trips across my heart as he grabs hold of my arm and drags me by the wrist, all the way down the hall. Once we're outside, he throws me against the verandah railing, knocking the air out of my lungs. *If you hurt me, Raven, that will help me. Only don't come too close. Don't want you infected, too.*

He whirls me around to face him again. But he's not going to hurt me; I can see that in his eyes. For a moment the world spins, my mind the axis. "Never," he snarls, "in front of my son. Do you understand me?"

I look at the space between us, the shadows slowly settling on the wooden palings. Now my whole body shakes with laughter, where there should be tears.

I don't want to take her place. *No, you promised me.* "*My son.*" I spit the words in his face. "What happened to '*We're a family*'?" My shoulders slump, as the short-lived hysterics die out. "She won, didn't she. After all this..." Now the tears come, when I want them the least.

"Pegasus." He whispers my name and lays his palms against my cheeks. You confuse me, Raven.

No. I confuse myself.

"It's over," he murmurs, drawing me so close I can feel him shaking, too. "She's not here anymore. Not in you, not in me...not in our son. Come to bed. It's been such a long day, for all of us."

He lifts me in his arms, cradling me like a second child. Without another word, he carries me inside.

We enter the room right next to Damien's. A four-poster bed takes up most of the floor, in front of an open fireplace. He lays me down upon the mattress, though as he lights the kindling I keep watching him. Just him. This is all I need. All I want. Feelings and truths, always growing beneath the poison, the hurt, the blood.

We're home.

Make love to me, Raven.

He steps back with a shy smile, seeing me staring at him so intently. Once he realises, though, he comes to sit beside me. He runs his fingers gently through my hair, then takes off my boots and stockings. I listen to his heart, beating steadily, his warm breath on my neck, while the ice slowly melts around us. I'm no longer afraid to look into the flames.

This is neither hell, nor the ends of the earth. It's only the beginning. And hell, my hell, exists within. Only you can end it.

I sigh, falling onto the bed, staring up at the shadows that dance to the music of the fire. He lies cautiously beside me, his thumb tracing spirals over my forehead. Whatever he sees in me now, he doesn't look afraid. Or disappointed.

"I'm sorry," I whisper, reaching up to stroke his cheek, but he shakes his head, refuting my apology. Taking my hand in his, he turns over my palm and kisses it. *Raven...*

You still make me shiver with such a touch.

"I love you," he tells me, words that make me shiver, too.

I push myself off the bed and stand over him, waiting for

bravery or foolishness to allow me to speak the words. *Waiting for faith.*

No. That's always been here. I can see myself, just as the dream shows me, floating in the ocean, all the blood washed away by the tears of the sea. Your kisses, making me—

Making me clean. Raven...

"What?" he asks, trying not to look worried as I don't say anything.

"Show me," I whisper.

Briefly, he frowns, not understanding. Slowly, I allow myself to smile.

Now he understands. As do I.

It's not too late.

He pulls me down onto the carpet in front of the fire, watching me tear open the button of his jeans and struggle with his zip. I don't feel sick anymore. More of the poison's being expelled with every breath I take.

"Pegasus..."

I strip off my underwear, willing my body to follow my mind where it will. "Yes?"

He laughs nervously as I sit above him, playing with his silken skin, the softness of his belly, the hardness of his—

"You don't need to do this," he tells me. "Any of it. Before, it was different. Wanting to be close, but afraid of—afraid of everything."

"Before, it was different for me, too," I remind him, leaning forward to give him a kiss, brown tresses falling over midnight blue. "And it's still different. You're not like the others. I know this now. I think I've known forever. You can touch me, if you want. I belong to you."

He raises a brow, and I sense his disbelief. "Selling your soul to me?"

I pluck the little knife out of my heart. It's the best you can do? It's always been too late for *selling*. "Giving it to you. This way it's worth so much more, don't you think?"

He looks at me long and hard, and I can see the internal struggle to trust my words as the truth. What did she do to you? I can take all of that away. This is my ocean, my heart, my song.

"Surrendering yourself, then?"

I smile at him. Foolish boy, always trying to run. But I won't ever let you. Where would you go? "That's right," I whisper, trailing a pattern of little kisses across his neck, up his chin, both leading and being drawn by him into a deeper kiss. Slowly, his tongue creeps over my lips, into my mouth, tasting me, touching me, his fingers working at the straps on my dress and pulling it down towards my tummy, pushing up the skivvy as he runs his palms over my bare skin, teasing my nipples. Raven...

It's been so long. I want—

I want you. And I'm not afraid. There are so many worse things to be afraid of than this.

We break apart from the kiss, so he can strip off the last of his clothing, revealing the scars to me again. I lean down and lick at them, tracing each one lovingly, memorising its pattern, texture and taste beneath my tongue. Memorising him. His hands run over the curves of my arse, and a little moan escapes his lips as he finds the hole and gently presses against it, testing me, teasing me, before sliding a finger all the way in.

I kiss the tears off his cheeks, not needing to ask why he's crying.

"Tell me you want me," he begs, and I smile. My mind wants to fly free. Only you have that key.

"I want you," I whisper, even as he rolls us over so I'm lying underneath him. I wish my desire could swallow you whole. I wish you could come all the way inside, dive in and escape with me.

"I'm a little afraid," he confesses, pouring out the clear liquid from an exotically shaped blue bottle we found on the mantelpiece, moistening his palm, and his penis.

I lick at a drop of blood that trickles down his neck, and recall Mother's words from my dream, from every dream. "No need to be afraid. You already surrendered your soul to me too, remember?"

"No, not that way. I'm scared...of hurting you again. Like I always do."

Oh, Raven. "This isn't it. You can't hurt me. The only ones who can do that—they're gone. The circle is complete."

He nods slowly. Yes, we're safe from them here.

"Please..." In my mind I'm already willing him not to stop me, as I reach down and gently take hold of him, helping to ease him inside. Then I return to watching his face, forcing my entire body to relax. *He's not going to hurt you.* He wouldn't.

He can't.

I gasp at the sensation of him being inside me, spreading a shiver across my heart. His own body reflects this, his face buried in my neck, his breath coming in ragged sobs, his arms shaking as he holds me close. I run my hands over his skin, drawing my nails across his flesh, my fingers slipping as his blood stains them wet.

I close my eyes; inside my mind, the ocean's crashing into the sunset. Both sky and wave disintegrate, reforming into one great spiral of grey and red. It sucks me down beneath its depths, and I don't fight it. Do I dare to drown, this time?

Further down, into the indigo void, the moon is a warped echo, little more. Its silver craters shiver into fragments as I swim right on through its reflection. All the way along a dimly lit tunnel, these moon-shards glow brighter than starlight, stuck to my skin, cradled within my ribcage in place of a heart. And here, just ahead of me, a silhouette lurks, taking on a new form even as I look. Black wings flare and spread to absorb all light, and all possibility. Raven...

Welcome home...

My eyes snap open. I can hear myself panting, crying, moaning. His wet palm is still cupped around my now limp dick, as he sobs helplessly against me. My heart... I have no strength for words. All I can do is hold him close, returning to my body gradually. Where have I been, where did I go? Inside your mind, your dreams, your soul?

He looks into my face, tears and blood staining his cheeks and chin. Sometimes real, sometimes imagined; I can't tell anymore. My beautiful angel.

He voices the words one more time, and this time they remain, as the curtain closes. "This is forever, Pegasus."

We lie awake on the silken sheets for what seems an eternity, and still this night refuses to end. He cuddles me protectively, as though fearful of sleep. I don't blame him. We two are the same.

So I listen to the sound of his breathing in the dark, and the whispers of the trees at the windows, and I watch the shadows play across the walls while I inhale the sweet smell of his sweat and feel our fluids intermingling, tickling my flesh.

This is forever.

I know. Strange how it all feels so fragile, these walls that define humanity and reality, now that I know. Now that I know I am right.

He sighs and rolls over, pulling me into a snug fit against his body, nuzzling against my ear. The fire died out not long ago, leaving us half-naked above the sheets, revealing ourselves to the moonlight. So pretty, the shadows it paints upon our skin. Who would have thought?

Will you miss this, too? When the time comes, will you refuse to lead, or refuse to follow?

This is forever.

This is forever. I smile. Behind me, he clears his throat, but then I feel him hesitate.

"What?" I venture, my voice sounding so loud in the long dark.

"You need to see...what's in that box."

I pull him even closer, refusing to allow our red thread to snap. Not tonight. Not yet. But soon. "I'll look. Tomorrow, I promise. After the new dawn..."

"I wish you knew—what it means— It's you who saved me from hell, Peg. I'm so sorry, that everything..." He trails off.

"Then save me back," I tell him, before I can stop myself.

With a heartfelt sigh, he says, "Angel, if I can't save you, there's no point to anything."

It's not enough yet, though. "Promise me," I whisper, as he kisses my neck.

A branch outside scrapes the side of the house, and the room falls into complete shadow as a cloud sweeps over the moon. It's still dark, when at last the words come.

"I promise you."

Little blood-red clouds dissolve into foam as I look on...
"Jaime!"
I'm standing upon the beach.
"Jaime?"
I'm nine years old.
"Jaime!"
She's so far off, I can barely see her.
"Jaime!"

But at the very last moment, before her wings spread free, she turns to look at me.

"Jaime."

Mother...

She haunts my dreams until dawn, her face in my mind much too clear to be that of a still-frame memory.

"Jaime."

She sees me. She's...

Smiling at me.

19 (RAVEN)

Nonsolitaire (Pandora II)

Three little things drag me out of sleep and throw me headfirst into the hazy dawn. A chorus of birds squawking and flapping right outside the window. The fact that the bed's empty, but for me. And the sound of screams and panicked cries coming from the room next door.

Damien...

Shit.

I fall off the mattress and stagger along the hall, nearly tripping over my own feet as I race to the side of his bed and put my palm against his cheek. He's dreaming—more likely trapped in some nightmare of the past, tossing and turning and crying out, "Peggy-sis!" and, "Please, don't kill me!" and, "Don't, Mama. That hurts!"

Barely awake myself, and not sure what else to do, I unwrap the sheets and pull him into my arms. "Hush, angel. It's Daddy—your daddy. You're here with me, you're safe, Peggy saved us both, remember? It's okay, I swear on my life, you're safe."

He starts up a low keening, shuddering against my chest. Jesus Christ, Peg, where the hell are you? You'd be so much better at dealing with this. But there's only me.

I rock him from side to side, murmuring a dozen variations on those words of comfort. It takes a long time before I feel him start to relax, and for the wailing and shaking to subside. Then he sits up in my lap and puts a warm hand to my cheek, an echo of my action from before. "Hey," I choke out. Whatever my lips are doing, I hope it manages to come out as something resembling a smile.

"Hi, Daddy." He sniffs and wipes his nose across his sleeve.

"You okay now, kittling?"

"Yeah. I had a nightmare."

No shit. I take a deep breath; at least my pulse is running somewhere closer to normal again. "You want to talk about it?"

He grabs at the cross, distracting himself for a good long moment, a frown of deep concentration on his face. Just as I open my mouth again, he says, "I dreamed you and Peggy-sis got wings. And you grew into angels. Then you both flew away and left me all alone. I was meant to get wings too, but Mama cut them off and locked me in the bathroom. She was mean to me."

I suck at my lip. His dreams are always so vivid. Same as mine were, before I found a way to deaden them with pot and alcohol. "Your mama can't hurt you ever again, Day. Besides, Peggy is your mama now, remember?"

He stares into my face, seeing past every layer, every lie and every truth. "Where *is* Peggy-sis, Daddy?"

I rub my eyes, vague memories of the empty bed floating into my head. "Gone for a walk, I reckon. How about we get you some breakfast?"

He watches me a moment longer before telling me, "Yes, please, Daddy", and I carry him off to the kitchen.

I fix his staple favourite of cornflakes and bananas, and leave the kettle to boil while I go through the contents of the fridge, freezer, and cupboards. All three seem reasonably well-stocked. Then again, winter isn't over yet. Monty and Noriko would've been up here not so long ago, during the peak of the ski season. Shame about that; Damien's never seen snow. Tomorrow's the first day of spring, and in a week he'll be four years old. And after then, I'll be twenty-one. Not that it counts for much. Wonder if I'll make it to my twenty-first birthday, all things considered. Now there's a happy thought.

I crouch in front of the refrigerator, staring absent-minded at the barely touched bottle of Bundy rum tucked inside the door right next to the milk. I'm about to reach for it when I realise he's standing nearby, gazing at me. I want to look away, but something else prevents me, something more important. The expression on his face...too old and too knowing. Wonder if I had that expression when I was his age?

Probably not. Without any doubt, mine would've been much colder. Nothing changes over time. Just gets stronger, like a disease, or weaker, like a candle dying out.

"Daddy, why are you crying?"

"I'm not crying," I tell him, but when I blink I feel tears sting my cheeks. Goddamn.

He smiles at me, a soft, reassuring smile that reminds me too much of Pegasus, and says, "I can always tell." Wiggling his way onto my lap, he traces his fingertips over my face till all the wetness is gone.

I can't bear it anymore. I lift him off the floor, clutching his soft body tight against mine. "It's okay, Daddy," he whispers in my ear, words that sound so much more believable coming from him. If I open my mouth, these emotions will choke me. So I grab for the bottle instead, then kick the fridge door closed. A sweeter poison, to go with my coffee. Why the hell not?

We head outside, and I take a seat on a wicker chair on the verandah with my cup and a cigarette, while my son rushes down into the garden—a strange arrangement of fairies and mushrooms and other grotesque little statues—immediately lost in one of his inscrutable games. Wet eucalyptus teases my nostrils along with the clove smoke as I light up. Towards the rear of the yard, above the foggy tips of a line of gum trees, the sky's all lit up in soft violet and gold. It's been so long since I sat and watched the dawn.

There's always a new dawn.

That's what you said to me. And I promised I'd save you from hell. But that would mean saving you from myself last of all, wouldn't it?

I glance at Damien. He's collecting wildflowers for the fairies, by the looks of it. But my smile fades when I glance down at the cup. I promised no more drinking, as well. And if I started again, would I ever stop? What am I looking for? Why is there always something lost?

I finish off the cigarette and then empty the tainted coffee onto the grass. I promised. And last of all, I promised you forever, Pegasus. I always keep my promises to you, one way or another.

I do a quick scan of the trees surrounding the house before I sit down again, but the forest is way too dense, and the property itself way too big; he could be near or far and I wouldn't have a chance in hell of seeing him from here. Eventually I close my eyes, leaning back in the chair. Numbness drifts in, overcoming my body, overriding that feeling of needing to sleep, and I hate—I hate not being able to feel anything, not even fear. So tired, and that's always when the paranoia kicks in…

But what if they come for me? No. It's all only a matter of time. So *when* will they come for me? And what do I do to stop it all, to protect my loves from what happens then?

I had a nightmare.

Too many abstractions, too many thoughts, too many emotions buried beneath cotton wool. It's like watching the ocean from behind frosted glass, watching the waves always return to the shoreline, washing me up, returning me to nothingness instead of you.

Peg. Where are you? I don't want this numbness anymore, don't want to be alone. I just want to feel, babe, like I did last night, I need—

Need clarity.

Need you here.

Need to feel...

I push myself to my feet. Glancing at my son to confirm he's engrossed within his game, I drift off towards the bathroom, all awash at sea.

I stand in front of the mirror, squinting in the morning sun that streams down from the skylight as I pull off my long-sleeved t-shirt and toss it carelessly on the tiles. Funny how I can only look at myself, my body, my cage, when I've got the desire to hurt it.

It takes several minutes of poking and picking at an old pink shaver to finally dismantle the thing and pry the blade free. At least my mind gets something to do, something to focus on other than my own spiralling mess of thoughts and weaknesses. Both my index fingers and thumbs are bleeding before I've got it ready, but I don't notice any pain. Not yet, but soon. The closest thing to being with Pegasus I can replicate, when I'm alone. Beats what some people do, when they're alone.

At least this way I'm not left feeling dirty afterwards. Just cleansed. But still alone...

The closest I can get to being with you.

The blade catches a glint from the sun. It strikes my face and triggers a flash of déjà vu. Just like a gag reflex, up comes the memory of a night I tried to force from my mind forever.

It was the night of my biggest mistake, and my greatest

blessing. The night Damien was conceived, the night Wendy first got her claws into me. I wasn't expecting to see her at that bar off Inkerman Street; as best as I knew it, she didn't drink. But it was raining hard, a steamy summer night, and Pegasus couldn't make it. So I was alone, more than I am here. She perched beside me on a bar stool, moving ever closer, sipping her one glass of champagne to my three shots of scotch—always her shout—and rinse, repeat, till we both lost count. In those days, of course, I wasn't anywhere near being in control. I was too young. She was too young. I'm not sure how we got in under the staff radar, but I guess it was their will, and my fate.

I sigh, turning the blade over in my fingers, testing for the sharpest edge.

She took me home to one of her family's houses, the very same one that would later become my tomb. Taught my body to betray me, even as my mind wished for anything but what we were doing, what she was tricking me into. I remember thinking of Pegasus, longing for Pegasus, wondering why he hadn't been able to come.

The few glasses of champagne, along with what she made me do to her, were enough to send her into a deep sleep shortly afterwards. That left me to sit on the edge of the bed, shaking and whispering his name, willing the dawn to come, willing it to all be over, willing myself to wake up in my own bed. Wishing I hadn't been so goddamn weak.

I made myself sick, pining for the dawn. After throwing up in the toilet, I found her daddy's razor—an old-fashioned one, the type they use in barber's shops. If I hadn't been so fucking drunk, I could've ended it right there and then. But my mind wasn't far gone enough yet. I kept weeping for Pegasus and shedding tears for myself. And the razor smiled in the moonlight, a colder, purer glow, as I slid it over the inside of my forearm, cutting skin like velvet, blood drip-drip-dripping onto the floor, cleansing myself of her poison.

Even then I could sense it, mutating my cells. Given that, it felt right to hurt the cage.

The blade clanged against the tiles, so loud in the cold, echoing, empty space of my mind that for a moment I feared it might wake her. But it never did. Instead I just sat and stared, watching my essence spill across my skin. Asking myself, over and over, *Is this what you want, Raven? Do you want to die like this?*

Do I want to die?

But it wasn't my voice, asking the question. It was his. And I remembered his gentle touch, the distant knowledge of truth as he'd kissed my scars and made me see we were the same. *Where are you, Pegasus?* I begged the endless void of night. *Was all that just a trick of the light, or do you* really *care?*

I traced a finger through the pool of blood, spelling out each letter of his name, lovingly rendered within my own pain. Kissing my fingertips, I passed this love down to my own creation. Right about then, I knew I was lost completely. So I spent the dregs of that night drifting in and out of a fitful sleep, waking to wash away my artistry upon the arrival of a miserable dawn. She should've found it then, my cry for help, and it should've been over, once and for all. But she never did.

After that, I learned there was only one way to cleanse myself. And a few weeks later, I found out about Damien, and how that was what she wanted—all she'd wanted—all along.

No one ever cared that I wanted him, too. Except for Pegasus.

Pegasus...

A cold draft sweeps in from down the hall. And the razor, despite its small size, is penetrating my skin. Cutting along that old scar, a well-travelled path, more deeply than I ever intended. No. I don't want to die. Not like this. Not just yet...

Something hard and made of wood clonks to the floor behind me. In another moment, the blade's knocked out of my hand and clatters into the sink, spots of red staining the perfect white porcelain, just like his skin. It's no surprise.

He stands right here between me and the mirror, slightly out of breath, his eyes burning diamond fire, his fingers gripping my wrists. "Don't."

I blink in surprise; the word cuts through me more sharply than metal. As my body comes online again, my flesh starts to sting, especially round the cut, and more drops of blood fall on his pretty grey dress.

But don't you remember? Last time you kissed me. Last time, you cut me as well. "Why's it so different?" I ask hoarsely. "Why stop me today?"

Tears form on the edge of his lashes, more enchanting in the sunlight than any tiny trinkets crafted by man, as he lets go my hands. "Because today I can see the look in your eyes." He sniffs, then glances behind me. I follow his gaze; the wooden chest lies on the floor, its contents spilled out across the hallway.

Now when I look at his face, there's only resentful bitterness. "What?" he snaps, not waiting for me to speak. "Did you think I was never coming back?"

I swallow, mostly to choke down the need to tell him *I love you. I rescued you, and you rescued me. But only for a little while, isn't that how it is? Tell me how it ends, then, so I can fight this fog tearing down the corners of my mind. Please.*

"One day, you won't," is all I can bring myself to say.

"No, Raven. I'll be—" He clears his throat, annoyed by the effort. "I'll be waiting for you. Haven't you figured it out?"

When he puts it that way, seems like it must be so damn obvious. But—

I shiver, looking away. "You should know I haven't got any power for answers."

Shaking his head, he leans in, with his words kissing my ears. "How it ends..."

How? Tell me how, Pegasus.

I slump forward into his embrace, focusing on a spot of blood in the sink behind him. Red rose petals, white rose petals, everything a blur of then and now and when. He finds me a bandage from the first-aid kit in the medicine cabinet. Then, after washing off my arm, he winds the cloth round and round it and tells me, "You forget too quickly." Once the ends are fastened, he takes my face in his hands. He's smiling at me. He's here. He won't let me go. "It's not numbness you feel at all."

He sounds so sure of this, as he lets one hand slide down to grasp mine, and leads me into the bedroom. I stare into the ashes, black in the fireplace, and I remember again. I promised him. *Forever*.

Then that's how it ends.

I'm forever afraid of how I feel, but this is something different again. Lust, love, and sorrow all intertwining, like tangles of thorns cutting into my skin. I'm not going to hurt you, Pegasus. I just want you.

Need you.

Love you.

I pull off the dress, tear down his leggings, and prop him up against the open window. Parting his legs, I open him up, for me.

The first was for love. This is for completion. My promise. My vow. *Forever*.

He wraps himself around me, caressing my shoulders with his nails and my neck with his teeth, as I cover my dick with the scented oil and slowly make my way inside him. This is like—this feels like—

Being home.

So warm within that I can feel the thorns breaking off, white roses blooming in their stead. White, not red, just like his wings. I can fly, when you're here with me. I can be anything, feel anything, because this is all for you.

Arching his spine, he leans back to let me enter as deep as I can go, his throat now exposed to my own teeth and tongue. My name escapes his lips in a series of little moans and sighs, before our mouths press together. The kisses start off life as delicate butterfly things, then grow ever more bat-like, violent and desperate.

You're right. I'm not the same as them. If any of them ever felt this, they could've saved you, could've made you feel love. I'm only late. But not too late.

I lap at his body lovingly, memorising his taste, his scent of musk and roses, biting his neck, caressing his nipples, gently taking hold of his dick, stroking velvet.

So much more cleansing than anything I could hope to achieve by myself.

He surrenders to everything, his breathing in my ear alone threatening to drive me over the edge. But I don't want that, yet. Living my dream, lost so deep, I want to make him feel this too. I want him to know, want him to tell me so. Need to hear the words...

Slowing my rhythm, taming my intensity—just a little—I press my forehead against his glowing cheek for a moment, my breath still ragged in my ears. "Why do you let me do this to you?"

"Do what to me?" he asks, raising an eyebrow, faking innocence. When he aims a lick at my neck, little goosebumps bubble up and down my skin, but more than skin deep. All things with you run true, just like this. You make me feel, too much.

"Make love to you," I answer.

"Hmm." He smiles at me, a playful gleam mixed with seduction. "That's why." Digging his nails into my shoulders, he moves even closer, squeezing my dick so I can't escape.

There's no such thing as too much. I gasp and close my eyes; I'm starting to lose control. Yes...let me lose myself in you, and me-and-you-and-me-and-you.

I'm making love to an angel, all crystal-seafoam feathers and alabaster skin. And the shards break off and return to the waves, but he holds on tight. You give up your wings, Pegasus? Why? For me?

No. For completion.

I push him against the window, keep on falling into his soul, dooming myself, a death so unlike that understood by too many men and their coward hearts.

With one last shudder spent between us, he swallows my moan with a deeper kiss. I am the ocean, returning to the shoreline, and everything of me exists within him. "I won't hurt myself anymore," I whisper in his ear, but he just puts a finger to my lips and kisses my cheek.

All my strength's gone, and I can't hold him up any longer. Reluctantly, we pull apart. I whimper as my knees give out beneath me, while he makes a little show of pulling up his leggings and slipping back into the woollen dress, a languid grin on his face. I wonder if he knows how much power he's got, to make me feel anything. Everything. Just enough.

He grabs for my hands, kissing my fingers, pulling me along till we stand in the doorway. "Come, Raven," he whispers. "It's a new day. And our son is waiting."

I pull my sleeve down over my bandaged wrist, making sure to hide the evidence. What did you find in your Pandora's box? And will our son continue to wait, like you did?

Smiling sadly, he keeps tugging on my other arm, and I let him lead me where he will.

Whatever the answers now, I trust him.

(PEGASUS) 20

Reality Vs. Dream

I'm running.

Neither away from nor towards anything, simply running, as children are wont to do. For I am a child, so small I'm almost nothing. I could disappear, but for now I've chosen to run instead. The breeze in my hair, the warm sand under my toes, the ocean spray leaping up to nip at my legs and fingertips when I dare to come too close. There's no sun, yet it's so bright, and so…

Warm. I remember this warmth, somehow. I remember this place. My mind struggles, but trapped within the dreams of a child, I'm seeing all these things, each for the first time. There are no memories, not yet. They remain to be created.

And so, I have no way of knowing how close or how far from home I really am. Perhaps this is why I'm running.

It seems I must have come a very long way before something black flickers into being in front of me: a shadow crouching on the rocks. Gradually I slow my pace, slower, slower, the clock winding down, time coming to a standstill, eternity to nothingness, until I stop completely, as static as the figure before me, the outline of a man who seems to exist outside of existence.

He's been looking out to sea, at the waves I've been trying to avoid even while teasing them. I still can't see his face in any detail. We are strangers, he and I, here in this place, though some greater part of me knows this is not the truth at all.

"Do you know my name?" he asks me, his voice little more than a whisper, another shadow, shadows within shadows, in this bright warm land that has no sun, no illumination of truth. I've been hoping to catch some glimpse of the reality behind the mask—a smile, some recognition, anything.

Again, nothing. And so I just stare up at him, unable to speak.

"No," he says, "I didn't think so."

I can't help but wonder if he sees things so much differently than I, or whether I, too, am no more than a shadow to him. This thought frightens me, and I see the warmth is a lie.

"I'm waiting here for the only person in the entire world who knows my true name and my face," he continues on. "You don't know where this place is, so I shall tell you. It's after the very end of the world, little one. Take a look around, and your own senses shall confirm my words truth."

I do as he asks, glancing behind me, away from the ocean and the rocks and the beach. And what I see next makes me want to scream, only I can't make any sound. Lights, many colours blurring to a sludge of browny-grey, and translucent hands clawing at a transparent wall, like nails scratching against a membrane of life. Skyscrapers and factories, forests and mountains, empty bodies, all of them contained behind this wall, dying to be reborn, living and dying again, with every breath I take. So much pain. I hear their dirge, I feel their tears within my heart, but they won't touch me, for I am no part of this. We are separate, they and I.

And then, there is this man. The man with no name and no face, but a being who feels more real to me than those cruel shadows taunting me from behind their barricade.

"Here she comes," he murmurs, and the tone in his voice gives me a reason to face the ocean, despite my fear of it. He was a poet, this man, when not cast down to a withered shadow. I can hear it in his voice, feel it like a smile that remains unseen. My sense of loneliness intensifies and I long to know his face, even as a rainbow unfolds from the sky and she—the She of his dreams—comes gliding towards us, her delicate footsteps painting a path across the infinite band of colours, down to the sand.

I feel a shiver cross my soul as she touches down right beside me. She's nothing but a shadow to my eyes as well. But the feelings…this knowledge…this yearning. Please, don't take only him and leave me all alone. What will I do? There's nothing else here for me.

The wailing of the vicious souls behind me cuts in and out on the breeze, a timely reminder. Please don't leave me to them.

Tears blind my sight as she stops to caress my cheek with her lips, whispering my name. "Jaime."

Jaime. Yes, that is my name. How can she say it so perfectly? As though she knows me, in my entirety, and sees I am more than nothing.

I blink away the tears, just in time to watch her repeat the process with my poor friend the shadow, listening very carefully as she reveals his name with the same sense of knowledge. "Nicholet."

Nicholet. The name circles my inner landscape, like a bird released within. This name has a meaning, same as my own does, but my heart is distant and I'm unable to find it here.

They're walking away from me now, as she takes his hand and leads him on towards the waves. The rainbow is gone. But they don't need it anymore. They're spreading their wings. They're leaving me behind.

The cruel voices howl at my back, driving the wind to whip around my ears and penetrate my body. And before I dare to understand what I'm doing, I'm running again, running after the two shadows, the only two who know me, the only two who care.

But the woman turns to me, her own form no longer so grey. She's smiling at me. It's the most beautiful thing I've ever seen. And yet so familiar to me, comforting. Why?

"Oh, no, you can't come with us," she says. Even in the midst of her rejection, that voice won't allow me to feel any pain. "Somebody else is waiting for you here."

I look about, hopeful and anxious, trusting her words, but I can't see anyone. I've come so far, I can't even make out the creatures behind the wall. Nor another shadow. I'm so terribly alone.

I'm so terribly alone.

She's still smiling at me, though. "You don't remember yet, but someday, you will."

This time she really is leaving me, leaving with the shadow—her shadow—leaving me behind. I start to run after them both again, hoping to convince them, but something else pulls me back. The source of the brightness, and the warmth...

Strong hands, holding me down, holding me close. *Loneliness.* What is loneliness? Only fleeting. You're here. I understand. Now I have the words.

"Your name... I know your name now," I say, my smile becoming warmth, my body becoming a shadow, as I let myself fall.

"Raven," I whisper, opening my eyes. His arms are around me, holding me close. Where was I just now? Alone?

No, not alone. Not forever. You were there, too. You're always there.

He's staring into my face, yearning for rest and my own release. Was I in pain? "What?" I whisper gently, reaching up to touch his cheek.

He frowns a moment, swallowing down his sorrow before

answering me. "You were screaming for your mama. In your sleep."

I stroke his face, wanting to memorise the touch of his skin, wanting to tell him they were leaving me behind all over again. But he ducks out of my caress, gazing instead at a spot on the wall over my head.

"Is she calling for you again?" he asks, his effort to be distant not hiding his pain. *You waited for me so long. Just as I waited for you. You always think I'm so ready to leave without you.*

I'm not. You'll discover this truth for yourself, as our time draws closer, and her voice—this light—within me grows stronger. "No. She was calling for my father." He glares at me, so I qualify this statement. "My real father. I had to wait for you. I chose to wait for you."

I sit up, taking his hand in my own and kissing his cheek, like my mother kissed me in the dream. "Your name... I know your name now, Raven."

Beside me, he softens, then gently pushes me onto the mattress and strokes my hair. I wish for him always to look at me this way. Such love, and such warmth. I've begun to remember, yes.

"It's too early." His hair tickles my nose, smelling of cloves and eucalyptus, as he tucks me in. "Go back to sleep."

I want to watch him forever, but even as he begins to massage my temples, my eyelids are growing heavier, my mind falling with them. Slowly, I allow myself to sink, but I so want to take him with me, just like it will be—

Just like it will be, when we go home.

"Yes." My voice emerges as only a dull murmur. I hope he can make sense of it all. "It's not here yet, but I can feel it... closer, always closer. I feel you. And I feel her. Both of you, inside me, beating stronger than my own heart. Can you love me...for eternity? It's a very long time, you know."

I'm not sure if I'm dreaming again yet, but his kisses are

falling upon my lips and his tears upon my cheeks. "I already promised you forever," he reminds me.

Yes. Forever. Eternity equals forever.

We're sitting side by side on the sand. My parents have left us, and his strong wings surround me, cuddling me close. I've never felt so safe.

Eternity. *Forever.* So close.

I stand up and smile at him, waiting for him to shyly reciprocate before I offer my hand. Inside my heart, I can feel it already. I don't need to turn and look. It's all for you, my love. "Come with me."

And the rainbow appears before us once again.

Reality.

What is reality? Is it merely that which exists the moment I open my eyes, and ceases to exist the moment my conscious mind falls away?

No, it's more than that. Both more and less than the sum of its parts. For I am whole. I am almost whole. Almost complete. I await my own reality, which lies existent within the dream, my dreams, my world.

I always thought of reality as such a cold entity. Harsh light, cruel words, things delivered to hurt. But that was before I knew the truth.

Before I could remember.

Before I knew your name.

Before I gave myself to you.

I wake from the dream, always so alone. One day I will rescue you. Free us both from our solitary confinement, just as it is when we make love. Just as it will be, when we go home.

I brush aside the tears, then reach under the bed. Out comes Pandora's box. I sit up to pry it open, leaf through its contents, recreate my own reality, once again. The letters... But I've already read them. Letters from Nicholet. Letters from my father. The shadow of my dream.

I find quickly that which I am seeking, my entire being tense with the knowledge. Time. What is time?

I already promised you forever.

Time is nothing, when one has something that outlasts it.

I still believed in time in this photo, as Mother held me, and I feared even then it would not be forever. I always knew they'd try to separate us. For they always tried. Only to fail. They've failed so miserably, haven't they, Mama?

It's no longer me who is the failure. Raven, you rescued me from that. My salvation. My white rose...

I sigh softly, trying to remember, like I tried within the dream. I have this photo memorised—my mother's face—so even if in dreams she appears to me in shadow, I can at least touch her in the reality of my conscious mind. And it won't be so long to wait. Won't be so long to remember.

For I know, without trying—and even though I do try- that I don't remember. I don't remember the weather, or what season it was, my mother's perfume, or the man behind the camera. It all eludes me. Each intricate element remains a shadow, dying in a place without light, before she ever promised me he would come.

All of it. I can't remember.

I put the photo away again. It has to be soon.

Raven, I can't feel you...

But now, from somewhere without, I do.

Echoes from down the hallway flow into my heart. Someone else is crying. Someone else feels this loneliness and loss. Someone else...

I wipe at my face, and throw on a stray pullover. Then I leave the room and pad down the hall, to where I can feel it the strongest, outside Damien's door. Cautiously nudging it open, I peer inside. Raven's sitting on the bed, holding his son, who's in tears.

My tears.

Without turning around, he says in a tight voice, "It was the same dream again."

My dream...

As our eyes meet, Damien wiggles out of his father's arms and comes running towards me. As he stares up at me, I swear he's reaching into my soul. "Please don't leave me, Peggy-sis!"

Avoiding Raven's accusatory glare, I lean down and pick up this tiny creature, holding him close and wishing all my warmth—our love—into him. He sees everything.

Then is reality something two or more people share? Something that can be verified?

"Let's find you something to eat, hmm? And then, I'll tell you a story."

In the kitchen, I blow his nose, and prepare some toast, before switching on the kettle to make Raven and I a coffee. His curiosity piqued by the space-age toaster, he seems content enough, childlike and happy, though I know too truly how appearances deceive.

Childlike. He understands too much, to be as a child.

He smiles at me as I touch his cheek. I kiss his nose, then make my way back to the bedroom. It's not enough for Pandora to have her box and have opened it. No. Now she must share. In such a way, do these things become reality.

I linger outside the door a moment. Down the hall, the shower's running. I smile to think of Raven inside, remembering how he held me so, in the bath. How he holds me...

I retrieve the box and dash to the kitchen in time to snatch up the two pieces of toast and turn off the shrieking kettle. But it can wait, the coffee, until he emerges from the shower in a little while, water plastering his hair to his face, little droplets beading his pale, broken skin.

Never again will I forget. Not a single thing.

After spreading some butter and jam on the toast, I take a seat beside Damien at the table, smiling as he forgets all about the food the moment I present him with the box and show him how to undo the latch at the bottom. Not questioning me once, simply watching and paying attention, he masters it on the second attempt; tiny, pudgy fingers being no hindrance. One day they'll be beautiful, graceful creatures. Just like Raven's.

I show him all the pictures, watch him trace the lines of Mother's face, laughing shyly and nodding when he recognises me among the images. But when I start to explain about his grandmother, he only shakes his head. "I know who she is."

I blink. *You're so like your father. And he knows it. He knows that's why my sister hurt you so much.* "How do you know Juliette?"

"She's in my dream," he tells me. "She takes you and Daddy away."

Mother...

"Does she say anything?" I ask.

A little frown flickers over his brow. "She says I can't go with you. But I try not to be sad, cos you go someplace no one can hurt you like Mama's friend hurt me."

"Oh, angel," I whisper, resting against him. *Someplace no one can hurt you.* You know. How can you know? You...recognise me?

"It's okay," he says. "Peggy-sis is my mama now." I feel myself blush, and he giggles. Underneath the table, I plant my feet firmly on the floor. It still doesn't feel like reality. This is how I can tell that it is.

Outside my own mind he keeps talking, and I remember my vow, making sure I save every single word.

"In my dream, you get big white wings and you fly, whoosh!" He throws his arms into the air, mimicking a bird taking off. "Daddy's got black wings, but he doesn't fly till you show him how. Will you show me too, Peggy-sis?"

I'm about to respond—or try to—when I feel a strange chill coming from the hall. Raven's standing in the doorway, watching. I want to hold him, but he's pushing me away before I've even left my chair.

"It was only a dream, kittling. Peggy doesn't really fly."

My eyes drift from his face down to the latch on the box. I don't?

Peggy doesn't really fly.

I can, for you.

"Yes he does!" Damien insists. "His mama taught him." Throwing his arms around my neck, he adds, "And he's going to teach you, and you've gotta teach me!"

Raven becoming Damien's Juliette. There's the thing about a circle. Once it's complete, it has no ending.

But Raven shoots us both a warning glare. "Enough." His son trembles and pouts, and folds his arms across his chest. I wait, neither blinking nor looking away. It won't be me who backs down first.

You can tell us to be quiet all you like, but you can never deny it.

He shuffles across to the refrigerator, ignoring the kettle and coffee altogether and fixing himself a glass of rum and coke instead. Who are you seeking to escape here, my love? You know that's not the way. I am your escape. Come with me.

Noticing how tired he looks, I ask him, "When did you last sleep?"

Moving away to stand over the sink, he offers nothing more than a shrug and a muttered, "Dunno," before he downs the contents of the glass in a single shot. After he slams it down on the counter, there's a moment's silence. But he won't fetch another; he promised me. And if he tries, then I'll stop him.

Never in front of my son...

No. Never in front of *our* son.

"Daddy's crying." The sudden whisper tickles my ear and makes me jump.

Raven? I glance at him, but as he regards us both suspiciously, his eyes are dry.

I see that, yes, but reality lies beyond those senses.

"In here," Damien continues, pointing to my chest. Wrong side, but otherwise right about the spot my heart would be. "Where no one sees, only me."

I smile, accepting the challenge. "I do, too." Not shy in the least, I sidle up to Raven, grabbing hold of both his hands as he begins to shake. Please don't be afraid. Aren't you so tired, of that?

He tries to pull away, but I won't let any part of him go. Not his hands, not his gaze, and not his soul. I'm yours. That means you can't cast me aside. Touch me.

Look at me.

Love me...

He gasps in surprise, but just as I wish, he's unable to break my hold. "Your eyes. They look the same way they did, the day—"

Breaking off mid-sentence, he frowns and looks at his feet.

"The day I realised there was a new dawn," I finish for him. "The day I realised how I felt...for you."

Kissing the scars, telling him the truth. There's nothing I wouldn't have done for you. Still nothing I wouldn't do.

Now I draw him gently towards me, and lead him into the bedroom.

No one can tell me what I'm feeling is wrong. This is the

true nature of reality.

I push him onto the bed, and order him to sleep. He manages a laugh, but I recognise it for what it is, an attempt to throw me off the scent. I don't believe the laughter. I believe what I can feel.

"You have to rest, Raven. How long has it been, hmm?"

He shakes his head, running his hands through his hair. "I can't. I can't sleep, Pegasus."

"You're afraid of the dreams, aren't you." I brush a few stray strands of blue off his face. "But it's okay, this dream. Dream of me, and you'll find me. Everywhere." Cautiously I lean down, planting a kiss on his lips, and he wraps his arms around me. Sitting up, pressing against me, he returns the kiss with a hunger all his own. He wants to be reassured. He needs me. The intensity sets my mind whirling dangerously. Consciousness becomes buried. All else disappears.

But he's already pushing me aside, hugging himself in an effort to tame the uncontrollable shaking. I reach out for him, asking, "What's wrong?", but the shivering only grows stronger as he shakes his head again. Finally, he takes hold of my hand, brings it to his lips, and bestows a gentle kiss on my knuckles. It takes another moment before he's able to speak.

"It's— This isn't what I want it to be about anymore."

My heart skips a beat, and another. *The intensity...the hunger... him pressing against me...*

Sex? It's never been about sex. You told me as much. Don't you even remember?

"It's not," I murmur, unthreading my fingertips from his and moving in to stroke his hair again.

He snatches at my hand and holds it at bay, but his hatred isn't for me. He remembers, all right. He just doesn't understand. "But I make it that way," he insists, dropping my wrist and trailing his fingers along my thigh instead. "Please don't wear the dress again. Not just for me."

I clench my fists involuntarily. Oh, not just for you. Do you *really* think—?

I open my mouth, but another glance is enough to keep me silent, for now.

"I don't want things to be about sex. I love you, Pegasus... and sometimes it's the only way I can show you, so it's not the same—not the same as it was with her—but when I think of this...this cage...I hate its desires. I hate it."

There it is. These reasons I knew already. Did you ever try to tell her such things? I can imagine how she would have reacted. No wonder you're afraid I'll reject you. No one understands you. But I do.

Tell me.

"Well, what *do* you want, then?" I ask gently.

"To...go home, I think," he whispers, one last little shudder consuming him, before he falls silent, hanging his head. Expecting me to give up on him too, like so many others.

But they don't matter. I'm here for you. Just as Mother promised. I chose this. I chose to wait, for you.

It's my turn to take hold of his hand and kiss it. "I'll grant you anything you wish for. We can go home, if that's what you want." Taking a deep breath, I reveal my own truths to him, those the dreams have shown me. "This is who I am, what I am. I exist only within you. The outside world... their reality— None of them see. To them, I no longer exist. Maybe I never did. Only now, I don't care."

He's frowning at me, not daring to believe. You will soon enough, my love. Your dreams are my truth, just as your truth is my dream. I wish I could say the words, the ones that would reassure him the most. But I can't, not yet. I'm saving them for the final moment, when no more doubts exist. When she crosses the rainbow, for us—

"What do you mean?" he asks, and I struggle to recall what I actually said, separating the inner visions from those without.

"I'm your dream. I'm never going to let you go. So please, don't be afraid." He sniffs loudly, but I'm not done yet. "It's all right. You're my dream, too. We go home."

"Promise me."

"Shh." I start rocking him gently, side to side. "Of course I promise. I'll take you there, free you from the cage, from all your pain. Teach you how to fly. It's destiny. We go home."

One little sob, and then the room returns to silence. But not complete silence. I sense... I feel...

I frown, glancing over my shoulder. I should have known. How long has he been standing here—Raven's child, our son—watching on? How much has he heard? How much does he not already know?

His eyes...his eyes tell me everything. There's not a thing that escapes his knowledge. His dreams, they must be mirror images of mine.

Those beautiful eyes close as he leaves the room, shutting the door quietly behind him. Trying to become a shadow. But that's not what you are. If I could take you with us—

But no. You must find your own reasons. Your own ability, to love.

Someone else must show you how to fly.

"We'll wait for you," I whisper after him, cradling the sleeping Raven in my arms, arranging the pillow and blankets around him. And so I remain, his guardian angel, for a few minutes more.

Until all sunlight fades within him, and I follow Damien out of the room.

(RAVEN) *21*

Chosen Whispers

Nightmare...
Daddy, I had a nightmare...
Daddy!
I open my eyes, fighting for consciousness and air. Blood stains and black clouds meld into striped pillowcases and wisps of auburn, and the face of a sleeping angel comes slowly into focus. Damien's curled up between us, snoring peacefully against my stomach. A family...

My head feels like it slammed into a brick wall. I sit up and stretch, hear the bones crackle all down my spine—but no wings to shake out, not here. Some part of me's still caught up in dreams of smashing my body against a metal cage, hung in a room of all-consuming darkness, awaiting my sentence. One arm stuck out beyond the bars, and my scarred fingers, encrusted with the gored remains of shadows that got too close, straining to reach some last grain of light that shines in the distance like a lonely star.

Only a nightmare. That's all. But one star is never lonely.

Very carefully, I swing my legs off the mattress and stare down at my loves. Yes, that was only a nightmare. But this. This is a dream.

I'm your dream...

The thought of our separation seems so real in the cracks between waking and memories of holding death in my hands.

But all these things I did—for you, Pegasus, and you, Damien—real or imagined, they're only symbols of protection. *Smashing my body against a metal cage, hung in a room of all-consuming darkness, awaiting my sentence.* Better it be me who stands in shackles beneath their judgements than you; I couldn't stand it.

Both of you my angels, shining in the distance. That's the way it is. You'll stay perfect, you'll remain free. As for me...I'm not afraid to die. I'd sacrifice anything. Your faith runs deeper through my heart than my own blood. Only one thing I've got left to ask of you. Not for you to say the words. Not for you to desire this cage. And you already promised...to take me home.

Both of you so perfect in the sanctuary of your sleep, visions to break through the black veil, gentle dreams to kiss away my own pain and every last trace of the terrible scars. Mama and child. So perfect.

"Teach me to fly," I whisper, and tiptoe from the room.

I nurse a cup of coffee out on the verandah, ignoring the older desires and habits that won't die quietly. I'm not giving in to a coward's heart this time. And anyway, I refuse to go back to a clarity that isn't truth.

Pandora's box, the stolen present, lies open on the table beside me. Every now and then I stop myself from reaching out to flick through its contents again. What more do I expect to see? What more do I *need* to see? She left these things for you, Pegasus. Eternal memories, wisps of a dream no one could ever kill. Fragments of devotion. A reminder.

I rub at my face, then gulp down the rest of the coffee and start prowling the floorboards. I haven't got any such fragments. Or reminders.

Is that what it comes down to, in the end? I've got nothing left for Damien. The only traces of my existence are part of

Pegasus, and my son himself.

No. I don't want that to be the only truth. I don't want there to be doubts, lingering questions born of doubt, no sense at all of anything or anyone in the void where I should've been. I frown, scratching at my hair. That can't be the truth I leave.

Filled with new determination, I stalk back inside the house and spend the next five minutes hunting through each room. I know what I'm looking for. Some sort of container for any tiny shards that might be left—if not as elaborate as the box of Pandora, then at least something of beauty; another reminder.

I unearth this sought-after thing—fittingly—in the room that now belongs to him. It's a music box, no doubt one of many from another of Noriko's eccentric collections. Black and smooth, it catches my eye in the hazy afternoon sunlight. I pick it up and examine the carved image on its lid: a Japanese maiden, her body floating Ophelia-like amid a river of blue and white roses. When I open it, no music plays, but I find the key on the shelf nearby and wind it slowly, till a haunting melody falls like teardrops and lost childhood afternoons and rain.

She's got dozens of these things; she won't mind if I take it, probably. She left it here, after all, in a flash of synchronicity. And this is too important. She'll understand, after everything.

I close the lid reluctantly. There must be something left.

Next I find the suitcase and start fishing through its driftwood assortment of my life—our life, together. In the end, what's in here is all the world will see. That and an approximation of the story, told by ones who never made the words to begin with. Illusions and material possessions. Neither of them the truth.

I lay aside all the things that should belong. The tape Juliette made, before she died. Her photograph, for so long the only remaining link to her in Peggy's life. The high school pictures of him and I. The photo I stole from the original box, of mama and child. My hand pauses as I touch the wrapping of the white silk lace dress, but this—just this—isn't for sharing, not by me. Last of all a CD. The Cardinal Vanity demo we recorded together, maybe a year ago?

Time flies so quickly...

Now the suitcase is empty and the music box nowhere near full. These are the only things I've got. I've lived my life as a ghost, on the outskirts of everyone else's reality. What am I? Who am I? What remains to give him?

Outside, it's started raining. The sound draws me back out onto the verandah, where I salvage the wooden box and retrieve my coffee cup. Above the ridge that walls us in, the sky's become an artist's canvas of melancholia. Vague swirls of purple-grey cloud the sunset's red glare, and a bitter mist rolls in over the hilltops and down into the forest. A wild wind blows straight through my heart, strips me down to my soul.

And oh, I remember this feeling. Like an affirmation. I remember being a child and *knowing* this freedom, an essence bound to my very existence. That was before I got so afraid, and let the bars shrink tight around me. After that, instead of freedom and nights spent howling up at the moon, all I could do was shiver under its cold light, its air just another blade against my skin.

These things, Damien. My chosen whispers. I want *you* to remember them, too. Need you to remember me.

All I've got, is all I'm taking from you.

I'm still wiping the wind's sting out of my eyes as two arms encircle me, fingers splaying over my chest.

Pegasus. Help me...

He doesn't say anything. Just holds on and waits, watching alongside me, till I summon up the courage to speak the first truth that hits my mind. "Living a whole life in darkness, how could I expect...to leave anything more than lies and shadows?"

"Shh," he tells me. "That's not what you really believe. Just a false image they forced upon you." He turns me around, and I stand before him. I'll let myself be judged, same as in the nightmare. But he only smiles at me. "When the final days are upon us, that's when you fly, black-winged angel. When you set free all the poetry in your soul. Don't despair, not for this."

Every time I look at you, I so want to kiss you, hold you inside me, let you guide me to the shores of truth. I don't need to ask who I am, when you're here with me.

"My father told my mother this, too, before he died. Before she died...before she wrote my song. You can leave it for Damien." Another secretive smile. "I don't mind."

For a moment all I can do is stand here, circling his hands with my thumbs, trying to establish which of my wants are right, which of my feelings are truth, and which of my truths are eternal. Then, something flickers among the dregs of my mind, and I ask him, "How did your real dad die?"

I'm not sure why this, of all questions. Straight away, though, his smile fades, and somewhere within, I get that sickening glow of triumph, like I proved my point, whatever point it was I was trying to make.

"Did Wendy not tell you so much?" he answers, squeezing my fingers together hard on purpose. "My—*her*—father knew, ever since I was born, that Mother belonged to someone else. It just took a lot of patience for him to prove it, and more to kill it, that's all. Years and years of spying her out, of selling his soul in so many dark places, before he—" He bites his lip. "They go on for eleven years, the letters in the box. Since before I was even conceived. Then, about ten years ago, they stop. Every one of them was opened, but the way they're written... I can't tell if Mother ever read them. And still, for all that time, my father waited for her. His name was Nicholet."

"But you don't remember anything about him, do you?"

With a sad little sigh, he glances away. I'm sorry. But now you know how it is for me. And for my son.

A last flash of golden light blazes through a fracture in the clouds. Out of the corner of my eye, I can see him watching it too, gathering its strength to him. Your body might wish to return to its home—the ocean, the source of all life—but your soul, your true self, your true home? Well, they lie somewhere else entirely. A place even birds could never fly. But your wings, they might be strong enough.

"I never could, before," he says now, his words floating down through layers of my reverie. "But lately I've been dreaming of him, a lot. Hearing his voice, talking with him, even if I can't see his face. He feels so much closer."

So much closer. But not close enough, not yet, right, Pegasus?

"I've got to leave something for Damien," I insist, quiet but firm.

His gaze flickers over me, piercing deeper than shadow, like maybe he hasn't quite forgiven me for reminding him of Wendy and her old man's treachery. "They, too, are close. But the final days are not yet here."

We drift towards each other, our lips brushing roughly together...but one kiss is always lonely. I surrender myself, forgetting my cage and dreams of that other cage, as the kisses grow more passionate, echoing intensity.

Why is it always so easy with you, not to give up, but to give in? How can you undress my mind of all its storms, make everything okay?

We go home, Raven.

My heart beats faster, a different sense of urgency overtaking me, as he pulls off my sweater, pushing me up against the railings, biting my lips, nibbling and licking my tongue. Laughing at me, a mysterious music. Rain trickles over the scars on my back, teaching me how to fly. Everything falls away.

I grab hold of him, one hand on his hair, the other around his neck. He freezes a moment, but I don't want to hurt him, just desire him...close. Closer than the cage, even taken to my extremes, would ever let me come. Need—a wish—to truly be free, to never be separate, to be complete beyond completion. By now, even the breeze is dead. Only our hearts, beating as one wild thing. Can you hear?

"So quiet," I whisper. "So alone."

Pegasus takes in the smallest breath. "Loneliness...that comes from outside," he tells me. "External influences, tastes, memories, skin. Self broken apart from its natural state. It doesn't last forever. When you exist within me, you need never feel loneliness, ever again."

I take his words as a promise, accept them as a gift, my body pressing against his, inhaling his musky floral scent. *Tastes, memories, skin.* Tastes. I've never...tasted you. I could lose myself in you. It's all I want to do.

But a small voice calls to me from the doorway. "Daddy, I'm lonely."

Another angel. The other half of my soul. My reason. With three simple words, he's got complete power over breaking my heart.

On my way past, Pegasus touches my arm. "Hey," he tells me, staring deep. "It doesn't matter what you leave. It matters what you give. This is how we teach one another to fly."

He moves forward, sweeping my son into a hug and dabbing kisses all over his cheeks. "Like father like son, hmm? Why so sad? Soon we celebrate the day an angel was born."

Yeah. Three days. It's gotta last at least that long. For me to protect them, if it's all I can do—

"Who?" Damien demands, wriggling in Peggy's arms.

He responds with a little squeeze, but his eyes remain fixed on me as he answers, "You."

Me. Fifteen days. Too much to ask for, probably.

The final days are not yet here...

I force myself to remember this, as he hands over Damien and announces he's going to take a bath. I catch the tiny hand in mine, stop it tracing one of my scars, and then whisper in my son's ear, "Peggy does know how to fly."

Damien smiles up at me, as though pleased I've finally accepted this as fact. "I know," he says proudly.

Oh, kittling. What will you do without me?

And the real question, the one whose answer lurks beyond every shadow...

What will I do, without you?

"Come with me," I whispered in his ear shortly after, and now we're traipsing through the forest, wet silver bark and leaves squishing beneath our feet.

"Where are we going, Daddy?" he asks, trotting along cheerfully behind me.

"No idea," I answer, grinning. "How about we just see where we end up?" We've long since lost sight of the house, so I hope I remember how to get us home.

Side by side, hand in hand, we climb through a gully and over a ridge onto flat ground. The trees are spaced further apart here, but thick ferns cluster around their trunks. Damien zooms ahead of me, running hard, never tiring. As I pick out a path, my mind keeps churning the last vestiges of this morning's nightmare back to the surface. I'm still thinking about bars and bloodied fingers and wings, when a distant voice cries, "Daddy!"

Fuck. I've gotten so wrapped up in my own thoughts I haven't been keeping an eye out for him. I stop in my tracks, listening hard over my thumping heartbeat, till it comes again. "Daddy, quick!"

I urge myself forward, his position fixed in my mind. A quick turn to the left, swatting fronds aside and tripping over tree roots, before I come to a halt in front of a barbed wire fence, strung up between a series of moss-covered posts. Only a few feet ahead, the ground drops out of sight, leaving us with an uninterrupted view of the mountains, and a vast lake, hundreds of metres away below the horizon. Mist races across its glassy surface. In the dull light, the water shimmers.

"Pretty," my son coos, and reaches for my hand. Lifting him up, I tentatively climb over the wire. Together we take a seat on a patch of grass, as far from the edge as I can get.

He squirms in my lap, stretching forward, but I pull him closer, fingers tingling when I stroke his hair. "You stay with me, okay? Damien can't fly just yet."

With a giggle, he sprawls in my arms. I close my eyes, rest my chin on his head. Only a little while ago, the forest behind us seemed so silent. Now it's come alive with bell miners and kookaburras, and the secret whispers of leaves, and limbs creaking in the wind. I hope, next time, I can bring Peggy here, too. Something about this endless sky makes me think it would bring him peace.

Next time...

"Why are you scared, Daddy?"

The question startles me out of my waking dream, but before I can attempt some kind of answer, he lays the softest of kisses upon my cheek. "I won't fly away and forget you."

I hold him tight, my protection against these feelings, this inner vision of myself, shattering and reforming anew. I want to say, "I love you", but the longest time passes before I can bring myself to speak. When I finally do, my words surprise me. "How about I tell you a story, kittling?"

He nods eagerly. For a moment I panic, not sure where I'm going with any of this, but from somewhere within, if I keep reaching past my fears, I'm able to drag myself through the void, out the other side of the nightmare. That's where it begins.

"Well," I say, my voice breaking, "you see... Once upon a time, there was an angel. With huge black wings. Blacker than night, blacker than the shadows that scare you in the dark, blacker than the spots between the stars where dreams are born. And just like stars, they shone in the darkness, these wings, and reflected every sorrow and fragment of poetry the angel had ever heard. But they were also his downfall. Because of them, because of their reflections, people didn't understand him. They feared him. He'd seen planets die and dreams wither, heard children laugh and mermaids sing. But everyone he came into contact with eventually turned away from him. Evil, they called him, and failure, monster, nightmare. They bound him up with thorns, and speared his body, and locked him in a great cage carved out of silver ice, and hung the cage from a hook sunk into infinity in a room of no walls and no light.

"So the angel fell into a dark gloom. He forgot what he knew, and grew to distrust his wings and all the things he'd seen. Hearing nothing, seeing nothing, and feeling only a dull emptiness, till...one day, the angel had a dream. It's kind of hard to describe the dream, except that it was like seeing something wonderful—like a star being born, or a wish coming true—right out of the corner of your eye. It was a dream of what it meant to be loved. And when the angel awoke, alone again, and still in the dark, but this time *remembering*, he started to cry, for the very first time. And each tear, as it fell, morphed into a white rose petal, till all these petals lined the floor of the cage. Then, once you could no longer even see the floor through so many petals, they began to hum, and to glow, and to glitter with the light of a rainbow, shining out through the void.

"At first, the angel was blinded, after living so long in darkness and despair, but as his eyes adjusted and he followed the line of the rainbow's path right to the very end, he caught sight of another very beautiful angel, right up close to the cage, white wings spun with grey feathers that reflected the same dream he'd just woken from. And this other angel was smiling down upon him."

"Peggy-sis!" Damien whispers in awe.

My trance state broken, I look down at him and raise a brow. In answer, he pokes at my chest and says, so matter-of-fact, "Peggy-sis always saves Daddy." He throws his arms around mine, so hard I fall against the fence post. "Please tell me that story again sometime."

I manage a laugh. "But I never got around to finishing—"

Never mind, then. He's already out of my arms, ducking through the wire, perilously close to the spikes, and running off in the direction we came from. Only stopping to make sure I'm ready to follow, he says, "It's okay. I know how it ends, Daddy. Let's go home."

I linger a moment, the shiver that traverses my spine rooting my feet to the earth. Then, as he keeps on running into the forest, I step over the fence and take up the chase, casting one last glance over my shoulder at the eerie-magical place we're leaving behind. *Next time, Pegasus.*

Memories of beauty, things to be shared, and therefore a chance for them to survive beyond a single life.

Tonight the air's crisp and clear. I let Pegasus lead me out onto the verandah; this time's my turn to hug him from behind. We gaze at the stars, mist lingering around our lips as we breathe in unison.

"Hard to believe he's four—or nearly so," he murmurs. "I remember, you know. The night he was born."

I close my eyes, nuzzling against his neck, as shame cuts into my heart. Yeah. Even if I was what most observers would've termed blind drunk, I can still call up vague flashes of that evening, too: Monty trying to drag me out of the bar, me making a fool of myself, the red-black lips and painted nails and eyelids of various whores—male or female, didn't matter—Pegasus laying his hand on mine, speaking the words, the words that would break the spell forever. *Your son is waiting. For you.*

After that, I spent the entire trip to the hospital crying in his lap.

I never did get blessed with that so-called gift of being able to drink and forget. Even after all these years, I remember. Every goddamn thing.

But all I say out loud is, "He knows too much."

Peg leans back, with a languorous sigh. His hair smells of honey and roses; he must've washed it while we were gone adventuring. "Then that's as it should be, don't you think?"

With a smile, he reaches out to the sky, framing the stars between his fingers. I move in closer, running a hand under his long-sleeve t-shirt, caressing his stomach, the bones of his hips. So warm in my arms, fragile yet strong.

"They're so close tonight," he says. "Like they're whispering her song to me. I've been hearing her voice, inside my soul, nearer than dreams."

They, too, are close. But the final days are not yet here.

You told me that mere hours ago. How fast is the second-hand moving? How close? How will I know when—?

Maybe I'm crying. His lips are wet. "Please don't be sad," he says. "One day you'll see how beautiful it is."

I won't fly away and forget you...

"One day soon," I mutter.

"Yes." His fingers encircle my wrists, and pull me against him. "But until then, please just hold me. From inside out and outside in. Until I can feel your heartbeat. Until it's your blood pulsing through my veins instead."

It's too hard to separate love from despair from hope from pain, in the fire that spreads across my chest. My tongue and teeth force their way into his mouth, licking, sucking, biting; ready to devour him. I drag us both down to our knees on the floorboards, and my fingers go to work on undoing the buttons of his velvet jeans. Once I'm there, my hand slides in beneath his underwear. I've never—never done this before; who knows if I can? But I've lost the ability to care for myself, buried beneath the need to care for him. "This isn't about sex," I whisper in his ear, stroking the soft skin beneath my palm, closing my fingertips around him, "and this isn't for the cage. This is all only for you, because...I love you."

His sigh is like a kind of permission. I duck my head and kiss the tip of his penis, then run my tongue down the stem. Above me, he gasps and caresses my hair. *It's all right, angel. I can't hurt you. You know, by now, that's never been my wish.*

I open my mouth to him, dry and sweet, wary of my teeth and going too fast. Now his fingers knot themselves up in the roots of my hair. I can tell he's trying so hard not to push me down for fear of gagging me. For a moment I withdraw, teasing him with my breath and tongue, laughing to hear him moan, before I swallow him again, trying to relax my throat muscles without choking, remembering to breathe as he moves against my lips.

"Raven!" Suddenly his hands are trying to pull me off. *No, no, angel, you don't get away so easy.*

I've never tasted you.

He gasps again as I start to suck on him, nibble and lick at his pulsating skin, my heartbeat, his breathing, speeding up together...

I let my mind fall away, my throat relaxing for one last throb, and he's washing over my tongue, down my throat, sobbing quietly, long tresses tickling my cheek and neck as he grips my hands, and I—I drink in all of him, waiting for every trace of his hardness to disappear before I release him.

He collapses into my arms, both of us trembling but unafraid, embers burning bright in defiance of the cold night air. At last, he places a kiss on my lips. Then he just shakes his head, unable to speak.

It doesn't matter, though. We've reached some state of mind and being, where words are no longer needed.

I tuck his dick carefully into his pants, and do up the buttons on his jeans. Then I lay my head in his lap, looking up at his face while he looks up at the stars. He's still panting softly as I reach out to stroke his cheek. "Thank you... for waiting for me."

He smiles down at me and it's my turn to gasp, as I catch a glimpse of the white-winged creature I described to Damien, in my story that came out of nowhere.

No, nothing comes from nothing. *My angel.* That's what it comes down to, in the end. These things, my chosen whispers.

All I've got, is all I'm giving to you.

(PEGASUS) 22

Angel Tears

Dreams.

Here, forever, is a dream. A fragment, a petal fallen from the rose, a feather from an angel's wing.

Dreaming, waking. How can I tell the difference? Perhaps I can't, and when I open my eyes, I'm only dreaming still. Does it matter?

I stare at myself in the bathroom mirror. Behind me, Damien talks incessantly about his own latest dream, and Raven runs us a bath. Who can say which calms me more: the words of flying and roses, or the sound of rushing water. I pull the angel boy into my arms, stealing his warmth like the morning sunlight. Is this how it was for my mother, too? I have no charms, no despair, which would allow me the power of such creation, and yet—

My child.

You always knew, Raven. You never said anything, but you always knew.

He turns off the tap, and the last of the rainbows fades from my sight. As he loops my hair up in a bun, I can tell he's been crying. But soon, my love, I will break your heart and scatter it to the waves and the wind, and there'll be no time left for tears.

I allow him to take my hand and guide us down into the tub. He snuggles in behind me, and I watch our child float languidly in a sea of bubbles, all the while he washes me reverently.

But with you, my love, I am already clean.

The bubbly water takes on such forms as the ocean's foam, tears of mermaids, tears of my mother, washing over my body to drown me. Do I dare go under?

I blink, and Damien's pulling me up, and I breathe. Time to get out, then.

Raven watches us from our bedroom door. The strangest of smiles plays over his lips—lips I could not kiss too often if I spent the remainder of our final days together doing nothing else—as Damien helps me pick out something pretty from the small collection stashed in the closet.

"This one!" He yanks it off a hanger and holds it out: some short, white angora thing. I pull it on over my stockings and stuffed bra, sitting on the edge of the bed. He grabs the brush, and runs it gently through my hair. I can see his frowns of concentration in the mirror. He's being so careful not to hurt me. We could be here all day, but I wouldn't mind. I have no real wish to face the world most deem to be reality so soon. I could remain, safe within this dream, forever.

If only so.

I glance at Raven and pat the mattress, inviting him to sit. After a moment's hesitation, he wanders in, lost and wary. I watch his face in the mirror, lonely, his fingers stroking mine. *I love you.*

Love...

He takes the brush from Damien and ties my hair in a white ribbon, then dabs at my lashes with mascara. I look away from the pretty girl in the mirror as he falls to his knees, kissing each of my fingertips in turn, then buries his head in my lap. "Hold me," I whisper.

Obediently, he pulls me up with him into embrace, then places one finger over my lips. "I've got something for you."

Saying only this, he leads me outside. Icy leaves and moss crunch beneath our feet as we follow the overgrown garden around the side of the house. Just beneath what might be our window—or Damien's—he halts, and beckons me forward. And here, among the ferny weeds and wildflowers, hides a miniature rosebush, each of its white petals dusted with crystalline tears.

Confused, I turn to face him. The morning mist swirls around us like wisps of silk. *How? How did you know to find this? Or is this your own creation, made real within my dream?* The cold air nips at my skin as I take in a breath and shiver. *Don't ever let me go, whatever the answer is.*

But even as I make my wish, a small frown crosses his face, and he draws away. "Come on. It's bloody freezing out here. The journey will keep us warm."

No, that's the coldest part. I'd tell him so, but he's only referring to our journey into civilisation, risking contact to gather what we need for the birthday tomorrow. *You'll protect us there, won't you?*

I allow our fingers to drift apart, intending to follow him inside. *But not yet.*

I glance at the rosebush, hesitating. Remembering—

Jaime.

Mother.

I remember watching from her bed, and how her lacy skirts swirled about her ankles as she danced before me, and how her silken gown was the perfect compliment to a trio of white roses she held at her heart. Presents from my father, from Nicholet?

Sweeping me into her arms, she handed me a single stem, then danced me over to the window, to the end of love. Here we looked out across the ocean, a fearful creature: beautiful, changing, but ever true. "I am as Rapunzel in her tower," she told me, "but when the sky opens for us and the rainbow appears, he'll come to save me. Until then, this is all for us.

"And afterwards, it will be all for you."

I stare down at the rosebush. Faith, and you found these, or dreamed them into existence. All for me. Eternity.

"I haven't forgotten, Mother," I tell the roses quietly, before returning inside.

The walk into town is longer than I remember it being. This time we take turns giving Damien a piggyback, or leave him to toddle along between us. And when one of us isn't carrying our child, Raven takes hold of my hand, or smokes. Despite our exertions, the cold never does let up. I focus on my frozen toes and my every next step; I'm not allowing myself to think about my own exhaustion or what might happen once we get there.

On the edge of town, Damien stares at all the children playing in a schoolyard. His fingers curl around the chain link fence, sad incomprehension too plain for his father or I to miss. But Raven hides his face from me.

By the time we fall into a chair at the local café, we're each ready for an early lunch. The little town doesn't seem as deserted as I remember it, either. Housewives, farmers, and a steady procession of bored teenagers drift along the main street, and that mountain, ancient and ominous, casts its shadow over all of us. I gaze at it, feeling cowed and trapped, until Raven returns from placing our order. After neatly extracting the salt and pepper shakers from a curious Damien, he allows his fingertips to brush mine, smiling at me briefly, his eyes darting from stranger to stranger as though they all might be able to see the blood on our hands.

I reach up and touch his face. Being in here is a little death. Even as my mirror self, my heart is not free to love you as I wish, wild and unrestrained. They all remind me, in their ways.

Still. *I love you, Raven.*

Food arrives, and Damien makes short work of two whole sandwiches and a donut, while Raven and I pick over our meals with too much apathy. He's the first to give in, abandoning his plate and indicating his son with a nod. "So, how do we go about this? I kind of wanted it to be a surprise."

The birthday present. I brush a scrap of lettuce off my dress, before pushing aside my own plate and taking a sip of my coffee instead.

Leaning forward, he sniffs in amusement. "Mind you, with the size of this place, if we find him anything, I guess we're doing well."

I arch a brow. "This coming from someone who found me a rosebush in a winter garden overrun by weeds?"

My taunting rewards me with a rare laugh, before he wanders up to the counter to pay our bill. Damien's watching me, his lips covered in sugar, his nose dotted with jam. Then he disappears under the table and resurfaces on my lap. I wipe his face, and whisper little nothings and everythings in his ear, while we wait for his father to come back.

"Your stories are so pretty, Peggy-sis," he murmurs, snuggling into me. I stroke his hair, and wish I could curl up this same way against his father. Am I so tired, or is it simply the dream, trying to reel me in, to reassemble all my broken fragments in some weak attempt to quell this dread of separation?

I'm startled out of my half-sleep, he and I both, by the sudden appearance of an old lady, right up in our faces. Mindless of our reverie, or the way Damien shrinks back from her, she coos at him and tells him what a handsome young man he is, what an angelic face, and finally, the killing blow with a wrinkled smile, "He looks just like his mother."

She ambles out the door, leaving me to face the sight of Raven, standing before us with his hands in his pockets. He's grinning.

Peggy-sis is my mama now.

Taking hold of my hand, he ushers us out of the café. It's only when he winks at me that I realise she wasn't talking about Wendy.

Mother to an angel, and the circle does not end...

He wasn't wrong. Nothing in this street seems fashioned with the world of a child's imagination in mind. A bank, an outlet for farming machinery, the single hotel, the café, the corner store and service station. Everything seems so concerned with the mundane cycles necessary to maintain human existence, but not to nourish it. I'm more amused by the looks some of the younger women are treating me to...jealous, jealous, why are you showing me such jealousy? If you had any idea... And then there's the way Raven makes a habit of finding my hand or my waist to grab hold of anytime another man wanders by, only to let go of me a few paces later.

This time, when it happens again, I'm ready for him. I pull up and dig my nails into his skin, forcing him to turn and look at me. Even now his beautiful eyes narrow, their gaze wishing death upon some flannel-shirt yokel as it pushes him aside and glances back over its shoulder. Not seeing *me*, though. Only through a cracked lens of the most base desires, focused on a mindless slavery to putrescent meat and primal reactions and bodily fluids. I know how these things work far better than you do, Raven. Is this why you'd keep me so close?

"What?" he snaps, after the latest presumed danger has passed us by.

"You think I'd prefer to be with them, yes?" Not letting go of his hand, I skip a little closer. Damien's the only thing that comes between us, and, as it stands, his only protection. "Do you think I'd allow one of them to just carry me off?" I nuzzle against his neck, pressing in as close as I can with a child on my hip. "Or do you think maybe I'd leave you here, all by yourself?" And force his hand down to brush between his legs. "Taking your love, your child, your soul—leave you to face the consequences of what you did for us all—this is what you think?"

My words are cruel, but necessary, if he's ever going to see. Let them stare. Let them judge. I would make love to you right here, in exactly this spot. They stare anyway, and they forever presume to know. Your androgynous whore, this is me. Only for you, the meaning is different.

Already he's growing hard beneath his jeans, and my own reaction is making me uncomfortable, tucked away inside my stockings. His breathing ragged, he's giving in. Then he snatches his hand from mine, betrayal and jealousy and all the things he fears the most forming a barrier around him. "Fuck you, Pegasus," he whispers, and runs his hands through his hair.

I move in again, kinder to him now. "I want *you*, Raven. You, and only you. I want to take you home. You're the only one with the blood on his hands, and the roses, and the child, and the wings."

With a frown, he shakes his head. But when I embrace him, there's nowhere left for him to go. "Pegasus..."

"I am no longer their whore." I speak the words in a low voice, pressing my face against his.

"I'm sorry."

"No. It's all for you. Tell me you know. Tell me."

He meets my gaze halfway. Admitting what he could mean to me terrifies him. That's okay. This is something of him I want inside me, too.

"You wish for all of me. Only me." The statement lingers in the air, with the uncertainty of a question. I nod, encouraging him, bringing him too far. "You give up your wings for me, every time we make love. White feathers and rose petals. You on the other side of my cage, breaking through. Everything you are, my salvation."

Damien seems to be watching him very carefully. I ask, "Don't you know you're these things to me, too?"

He sneers, but it's only self-preservation instincts that warn him not to believe me. "I want *them* to know that."

"But do you?"

"Yes," he hisses.

"Good." I let go of a wiggling Damien, who bounces to the ground and runs a little way ahead. "Because they have no right at all to *'know'*. I don't belong to them."

And so they keep staring as we continue on, all the way down the end of the street. The mountain still shadows us, and all the shops remain uninspired and uninspiring. Raven sighs and puts his hands on his hips, just as Damien disappears into the final store. Stopping to exchange a single glance, we claw a way through the beaded curtain and follow him in.

Inside, the shop floor is dimly lit, not enough to hide the wallpaper, its colour scheme straight out of a 70s nightmare. My nose twitches; the stench of mothballs and cheap perfume is soaked into everything. Ahead of me, separated by aisles of gaudy clothes and antique furniture, an elderly lady, her hat stuck with peacock feathers, turns up her nose at us over a cash register. We step forward hesitantly, still holding hands.

Our son is easily found, at least, over by a hatstand, playing among a pile of soft toys. I try not to look at them; the idea of such trinkets will forever make me sad. Father had all of mine removed before I left, except for the rabbit Wendy already stole only days after my mother's death. Unloved toys are a symbol for man's disassociation from childhood. Forced disassociation.

Raven squeezes my hand, and we kneel on either side of Damien as he points to the toy of choice. A white velveteen horse with satiny silver wings, blue eyes more suited to a porcelain doll than some stuffed creature of myth. "Look, Daddy. It's a Peggy-sis!"

From the startled look on the old lady's face, it's obvious Raven's willingness to pay the first price she names is something of a rarity around here. He even wishes her a good day, much to her chagrin, and leads us out of the shop. Damien sports a contented smile as he clings to his newest prized possession.

We cross to the quieter side of the street, past a fruit and vegetable stall and a dog grooming shop, and we're standing on the corner, right outside the hotel. Raven's slowed to a pause, eying the front window, desiring that which he has no control over. So it is with all things in your life, and no more than with me. But you have the power to control all your demons. I have watched you. "Do you want to go in?"

He hesitates, glancing down at Damien who stands between us, oblivious to everything but the toy. I lay my hand on his. No longer for destruction of the self. And if not for this, then what for? "It's no longer the same. You love me too much. You have no power to hurt me. And you never had any power to hurt him."

Closing his eyes, he brushes his lips against my neck. I nip at his earlobe, feeling that same need to be free, to express desire, to fly without wings. This is why. This is what for.

"Music!" Damien squeals, as the door opens and an erstwhile patron slouches into the street. I catch a glimpse inside the foyer, before the door swings shut again. More than enough time to recognise the shape of a piano at the far end of the bar.

A little hand grabs hold of my index finger. Damien still, using all his strength to pull me closer. "Want to watch you play music!" he adds, in case this wasn't already obvious.

Music. Another means of expression. Oh, but I haven't played for so long. Not since Lenny took that from me. Only fear stays my will. The oldest fear, reminders of how such an opening of the soul always led to such destruction, rape, blood, torment. Except with you, Raven. You were always the only one, and even then I—

But now, I want— Could I allow myself, to want...?

"I don't think they'd say yes," I hear myself say, part of me relieved to hear a snort behind me.

"That's bullshit and you know it," he says.

"Really." I give him a look, just to confirm we're playing the same game here. My fingers are already tingling.

"So prove me wrong."

"Fine," I say, feigning stubbornness. "I will."

I pull on the door, and he saunters straight up to the bar. It's as though, the minute he steps inside, something of the old confidence returns, revelling in the knowledge that what destroyed his father will surely destroy him, every bit as slowly, so to hell with everything. He needed as much of an excuse as I did, that's all.

Or maybe the ordering of the familiar scotch and coke is merely uncontrollable habit. Either way, you're beautiful.

The bartender grunts at me suspiciously. Raven must be asking permission. I suppose I don't meet anyone's preconceptions of a concert-grade pianist. "Well, s'pose it'll be all right," he grunts. "But if any of these bastards complain, you're done."

Glancing around the front foyer and into the back bar, I spy three elderly gentleman at a table in the farthest corner, smoking cigarettes and discussing the race section of a local paper over half-finished pots of beer. The rest of the place is deserted.

Raven takes the deal. He even smirks as he places our drinks on a nearby table, then leads me to the piano. I shudder at the sight of the grinning keys. If I ever actually wanted to pass out, right now would do just fine, thank you. Instead, my body gifts me a sudden flash of adrenaline and clarity. Raven lifts Damien and the soft toy onto the piano top, and pushes me onto the stool. I glance at him helplessly, but he only teases free my hair and whispers, "Play for us, angel."

I close my eyes, place my hands over the keyboard, let the memories fall from my fingertips, hesitantly at first, then gathering in intensity, a slow summer storm of deep chords and legato melancholy. Some of the keys are sticky, some are slightly out of tune, but not so most listeners would notice. Also in music, often enough, ignorance is bliss.

But perfection. I'm unsure of achieving perfection. My mother was the most wonderful pianist I ever heard, drawing me in beneath her wings whenever her fingers graced a keyboard, and she taught me...she taught me everything, and she told me— Told me I was wonderful. That I'd inherited her passion, her perception of beauty. The only contact we were first allowed was through her music, those haunting melodies that crept down from her room during my sleeping and waking hours. She played with the fragile strength of a woman who knew that although she had lost her soul, she would one day take it all back, one great wave to sweep everything away. Death without despair. Feathers from angel's wings. Waiting for signs from rainbows.

And here I am, aware of all these things, as though for the first time, as though for the last time, washing over me, drawing me down into the waves, falling through the world, up into the sky, soaring through all our hearts. For sorrow, for joy, for freedom. Taking on her form, inside and out. Right now, this is as much of myself as I have, and it has always been enough.

It has always been enough.

I can see them now, waiting for me. Raven holding his son, being held by my mother, thorns and feathers and roses.

Angel. He stretches out his black wings, and reaches for my hand. Something shines inside the wings, some dream we've yet to share. As our fingers touch, a greeny-silver sludge bleeds out of my fingertips. But this poison never did belong to me. And once there's nothing left of it, my heart will be pure, for you. For sorrow, for joy, for freedom.

"Teach me how to fly," his voice whispers, the words right against my ear, and I sit up, choking on my own breath, opening my eyes. Damien's gazing at me in adoration, and the song—music I recall feeling but never hearing—is over.

Over...

Trembling, I turn to face Raven, who sits only a few feet away. The elderly patrons are cheering me on. *What more could I give thee? Blood?*

Not here. "I want to go." I grip his hand, watching his smile disappear as the first tears form on my lashes.

"What's wrong?"

But I can't, don't you see? You don't already know? Not here not here not here, dammit. I shake my head, feeling the tears trickling down my cheeks, biting my lip to prevent them swelling to sobs.

"Okay," he whispers, and with this final granting of permission, I slide off the piano stool and dash outside, ignoring the bartender's crude compliments on my way through the foyer.

"That was beautiful!" Damien cries, pushing open the door not a moment later, staring up at me expectantly.

"Thank you," is all I can bring myself to say, trying to pull myself together. *Why did I run?*

Perhaps it's not what you're running from, but where you're running to.

This voice in my mind, it's too much a mix of Raven's and my mother's to pull apart undamaged.

"I'm sorry," he murmurs, and I fall against him, weak at the knees. *Oh, my love, please don't...*

Damien tugs on my fingers again, this time pulling me in the opposite direction. "We go home now, Peggy-sis," he says. Nodding in agreement, Raven puts an arm around my waist and leads me away without asking. Having no need, when one knows such answers, when one hears such music, when one kisses away such angel tears.

I lie in the bath while the candles burn low, and ever stranger distortions of myself flicker over the walls. I'm alone; Raven's off somewhere else, playing with Damien before bed, before the big day tomorrow. I think he wants to ask me, about today. About many things, yes, but especially today.

I hold one hand in front of my face, then wave my fingertips over the nearest candle, wishing for butterflies of paradise, other creations that are too beautiful to survive for long in this place. I wonder about the rosebush, if that was not a dream, if this is not a dream.

It doesn't matter, remember? So I create my own butterflies on the shadowed tiles instead, paradise beckoning to me from the flames.

It's every bit as beautiful as I promised you, yes? Mother says to me, dropping rose petals upon the water, cradling me close as we lie naked together on the shores of the sea. Her hair shines like silver silk, her skin softer than the petals, her scent just like I remember it, my own scent of musk and roses, but something else as well, something feminine I can't understand, though I want to. I reach out to her, my hand on her heart, while the dying rays of sunset dance over our bodies.

"I always believed you, Mother," I tell her, closing my eyes as she wraps her arms around me, and so we go under. Even as we disappear beneath the waves, I can hear her singing to me. I don't need to see, to know that she is smiling...

I'm nearly asleep when the piercing ring of the phone from the kitchen jerks me awake. Confused and dazed, I splash about in the dark tub, until the feeling flows back into my limbs. Damn, it's cold in here.

Maybe Raven will answer it. I glance over at the towel rack, out of my reach. How quickly can I make it there before I freeze half to death?

The phone continues to ring. Perhaps Raven isn't around to answer it, after all. With a sigh of resignation, I get up, though I lose my balance and almost fall back in before I manage to hop out of the bath. Two quick steps across the floor is all it costs me, and I hastily wrap one towel around my body and another around my wet hair, then dash down the hall, towards the kitchen.

My fingers are almost touching the receiver when a hot pain shoots down my arm, and a warm body pushes against me. It's Raven, physically restraining me. I watch the phone helplessly as it continues to ring, wishing it would shut up, while he rubs my arm in the spot where it burns. "Our wake-up call," he murmurs in my ear, and I feel my heart stop beating. Two more rings, before the house returns to silence and I can breathe again. But he still doesn't let me go. "We don't need to talk to him, not yet. We already knew what was coming."

Him? I frown, while my mind runs through the limited possibilities. "Monty?"

Raven kisses my neck, crafting a pattern of goosebumps to follow his touch across my belly and chest. "Yeah."

"Where's Damien?"

"In bed. You were in that bath for a lifetime."

I turn in his arms. *We already knew what was coming.* So many repressed emotions, but once again I pick the easiest selection. "She's dead, no?" But I already know the answer. I knew today, with visions of the poison dripping from my fingertips while I played.

He shudders. *Our wake-up call.* I'm not surprised he's terrified they could take it all away, even before tomorrow.

"We could be anywhere," I try to assure him, reaching up to touch his face. With a shrug, he turns his back on me, shoulders shaking.

So, now we truly are a family.

"Raven," I call softly, "look at me."

And as he raises his head, I let the towels fall from my hair and body, and here I am now, standing naked in the moonlight. I allow him his moment of adoration, before I open out my arms, and he comes to me, ever drawn and ever faithful, falling into my embrace. We move slowly, softly, against one another, across the centre of the floor, and I begin to understand that element—that third scent—of my mother.

This is enough. Almost enough. But soon, remembering, I feel her inside me, too. I peel off his shirt, pull down his jeans, trace spirals over his torso with my tongue.

I wish for abandonment, for loss, to be broken and reformed, for both of us. Love me, as I love you. So very perfectly.

After nestling against his balls and dick, and licking the moisture off the tip of his penis, I get up, too warm to think clearly. He shivers as my hand drifts down between his thighs and forces them apart. You're scared, only because you plan to sacrifice yourself for us, my love. It's always been clear to me, even hidden beneath the denial of my sickness, that day I last saw my sister.

But she's dead now, the Wendy-bird. I don't need to deny anything. Fear doesn't matter. Even loss doesn't matter. Only one thing has permanence.

"Come with me," I tell him, leading him to the bedroom, where I open the curtains and windows. He huddles behind me, breathing in shivers. It must be so cold outside; already the glass is frosted over, ice biting my fingertips as I lean over and spread my arms wide, leaving myself open to everything. "Tonight is the last time we'll look at the stars from this side, together."

"Pegasus, please..." His hands splay across my chest, pulling me closer, need, helplessness, and love, all confused with desire. "You feel so warm. How can you feel so warm?"

I turn to face him, smiling, laughing, adoring the broken expressions crossing his face. Balling one of his hands into a fist, I lick teasingly at his fingers, inviting him down between my legs, whispering these things, once fears, always desires, forever dreams. "I'm not afraid to make love to you, Raven... to allow you to make love to me. Break me open, apart, free my soul, my dreams, my heart. We can fly, we can cry, tears of blood. I'm not scared, so why should you be, my darling?"

"I'm afraid to hurt you," he confesses to my kiss.

"Then hurt me," I say, my voice rasping in my throat, "and you need never feel afraid. I want this. Please."

One of my fingers burrows up inside him, making him cry out. Does this hurt you too, my love?

But he's parting his legs further, making room for more, biting down on the flesh of my shoulder, asking again how it is that I feel so warm.

I kiss him hard and deep, wishing for my wings, pleading with him. "It must be tonight. Tomorrow, we celebrate the birth of an angel. And then—?"

"And then we'll call Monty." He's trembling, ready to break. Oh, Raven, this will be so perfect. Both of us, so willing. Both of us.

I fall into his needy embrace, laughing as he moans when I withdraw my fingers, my own dick throbbing against his tummy, the heat ever rising, mist and dreams to cloud my visions.

"And then we go home," I finish for him. "The final days are upon us."

Falling like music over my heart.

As he buries his face in my neck, I feel a tear crawl down my chest. So it begins, for there simply is no end.

23 (RAVEN)

Glass Embrace

Roses are white.

Moonlight on petals, stars on snow. All so white. So perfect. So cold.

I'm kneeling before you, and you're a vision, a dream. You couldn't be anything more and yet…you're everything.

Everything.

And I, nothing but the mirror that absorbs and reflects.

I feel your pain, your sorrow, your joy, all crazy-tangled up in my own. Standing beneath the moonlight, barefoot on the snow, holding a single white rose, and gazing at the sky. Down here I await your final freedom, and your sign. With the flesh ripped away, I long for such a touch. It's not—no longer the physical perception, but more of what lies within. What me and my son loved forever. The reason I'm still waiting.

This truth. This truth no one else can know or touch, this truth that remains an absolute.

How can you feel so warm?

My fingers tremble, tingling with the ghosts of sensation. He chooses this moment to turn to me, and I see my own contrast, reflected and absorbed, blood staining the white snow, and I see—

He turns to me, and he's smiling. And the rose…is bound to one wrist, thorns breaking the skin, and I can see, through

the light spilling out of him...
I know the way home.

Running, I'm slipping, I'm fading, I'm my own heart beating and breaking inside my chest. I fall so many times, but in the end I keep running, choking, breathing, searching. And yet I can't find—

Pegasus, why did you let it come to this? Why did I ask? *Teach me to fly...*

No.

I tumble through the snow, rolling a ways before coming to a stop, staring up at the stars, the moon, the puffs of mist. This is how it was that night. The night I handed over the blade. The night I told him I loved him.

When my heartbeat's died down, I expect to hear nothing. But nothing comes from nothing. This place is alive, inside and out. Even while shadows dance among the trees, and the night wind bites down hard on my veins, I'm so lost and unafraid. I found you before. I waited for you. I'll always wait for you.

Now I hear a voice, wraith-song flowing over me, tempting me back. I roll over in the snow, inching forward, slowly at first, till I rebuild enough of a concept of self—no, not self, merely the cage, that old hatred rebirthing—to stand, to walk, to run again. But I can't hate it anymore. For it and I are no longer one, a line more clearly defined than mere alienation, self-mutilation. Tonight you held the thorn at my heart and made me watch.

One day, the angel had a dream. It was a dream of what it meant to be loved.

This light, that blurred vision, maybe it's only a tear. Yet as I stagger out of the clearing and fall to my knees, driven by reverence rather than clumsiness, I blink, and I can see...

My girl on a swing, my angel-winged thing. He sits here, naked, perched on an old board hung between two vines, swaying to and fro, the rose around his wrist. And he smiles at me, and the song swells about us, surrounding us in a ring of white fire.

I watch him, possessed but cautious, two images shifting, three, maybe more. Juliette, Damien, me... Everything exists within you, Pegasus, and you—

I exist only within you...

His words, I remember. I remember...

I look down. Blood stains the snow: my blood. Warm arms lift me up, lips burning my skin as he kisses away the tears, skin burning my lips as I kiss away the blood that smears the thorns, a more delicate aura of ethereal perfection visited upon the rose. I take hold of his wrists, so wishing to sink beneath his skin, into a place of sanctuary no one else can reach.

But knowing *not yet*, I gaze into his eyes instead, broken reflections of my soul right here, if I dare to look close enough. And anyway I can't ever be lost if I know exactly where it is I both need and desire to be. "Please hold me," I tell him. "I'm like glass, and wish to break."

My fingertips brush the rose's petals, and he sighs and trembles. "Then what's inside the glass may be released. No one understands your path but me." He stares down at the rose, and murmurs, "I lied to you, Raven. There are things I don't remember, about us. But we'll remember, when we make it there."

"Home?"

"Come," he says, so self-assured, drawing me up into the fold of his wings, closer to the light of the moon. "Now we walk within my dream. Together."

"For the last time."

"No." He smiles, glowing with defiance and hope. "Forever. We're free."

I wake in a cold sweat, wrenched into my body. Fog and smoke burn in my head. With a wry smile, I stare down at my wrists. You don't want to let me go so easy, cage. But you know—

You know...

Come. Walk within my dream.

Pegasus holds me tight in my longed-for glass embrace, and some part of me struggles to remember, even as another part struggles to forget. And Damien, sitting in my lap—a twin reminder of why that wish for nothingness could never come true—lays a kiss right on top of my ear and tells me, "Don't cry, Daddy, it's my birthday!" He shoves something into my arms, then jumps off the bed, and a moment later he's already thumping up and down the hall.

I glance at what he's left me with. His birthday present, the soft toy we bought yesterday. Pegasus laughs at my frown of confusion as I turn it over in my hands. I put a palm to his glowing cheek. Oh, babe, you can't be well, not with a temperature like this. And soon, I won't be around to look after you.

Smiling sadly, he presses his lips to my skin, then gets to his feet and pulls me off the bed. "Come with me," he says. "This time, I have something to show *you*."

Déjà vu shadows my footsteps as I follow him into the living room. So sure of what happens next, like it's already been dreamed for me, by him. He draws aside the curtains, and holds my son to the window. All three of us look out over a world shrouded in white. Snow. It's snowing...on the sixth day of spring.

Squeaking in delight, Damien wriggles out of Peggy's arms and makes a dash for it. I catch him right in the doorway. "Not without a coat, you don't."

After the protests stop, I set him down so he can grab his

jacket off a kitchen chair. He keeps from fidgeting just long enough to let me do up the zip, before he races outside. Excited giggles and shrieks echo across the yard. Today, however, I can only associate this snow with inevitable death, not the purity of last night.

"I'm going out, too," Peg says, squeezing my fingertips. I start to tell him he should put on a coat as well, over the black sweater and white shorts that are his only protection against the cold. Though with how hot he feels right now, the snow might all simply melt the minute he lands a toe on it.

Somehow I find myself a cup of coffee and a cigarette, barely conscious of movement or existence as I take a seat on the ramp at the verandah's edge. I watch him teach Damien how to roll and throw snowballs. Another sip of my coffee, another drag of my cigarette. If only time could freeze around us, like this frigid air.

The final days are upon us.

Even as ghosts to the world, we're still a family. But if this were my dream, my ultimate truth...

I'd come home, through that gate right there. I'd be the antithesis of my old man, just daring to smile, with a toy under one arm, and a flower in my hand. My son—our son—would come running, leap into my arms like I was somebody to be proud of, somebody of worth, somebody... And I'd hold him close, never forgetting the long hours we were parted, never ever taking for granted how warm and alive he feels in my arms, how innocent, despite the pain she branded him with. Even so, I wouldn't think of losing him, only of love.

And after that, I'd move on, out into the garden, towards the swing, where Pegasus would be waiting, showered with roses, his crystalline wings hiding his nakedness from all eyes but mine. And I'd fall into his scented lap, kiss the blood off the thorns, grant him the same power of healing over me. I'd shed the cage and exist within, black feathers on white, glittering and warm and safe in the sunset.

I look up with a start. The cigarette's burned itself out between my fingers. And my coffee's gone cold. They've moved further away, leaving me so alone. Why do I sit here, so alone and drowning in what-could've-beens, when this right-now is all there is, and not the least of anything?

Launching myself towards them, I nearly end up arse over teakettle as I skid down the icy ramp, stopping only to gather up enough ammunition to fling a snowball straight at Pegasus. Damien lets out a holler and declares this an act of war. Laughing hard, I take off again, making a mad dash for the garden where I found the rosebush. I used to run this fast when I was young, enjoying the knowledge that no one could catch me, not ever. Strength from solitude. My only strength, in those days.

Somehow we end up back where we started, near the front gate. They lie on top of me, Damien pounding me with snowballs, and Peggy pinning my arms over my head, till coughing and spluttering I beg for surrender. Damien lets out another roar, then bounces onto my stomach, knocking all the air out of me. I blink away tears of exertion while they ponder their captive's fate.

"Ah," says Pegasus conspiratorially, "so now, he's all ours. What should we do with him, hmm?"

They both stare down at me, Damien's frown of concentration belying how seriously he's considering the question. I'm even starting to get worried, when his face lights up. "I know! Peggy-sis, you have to kiss Daddy!" He falls off me in a fit of giggles. Pegasus arches a brow and leans forward, smelling of roses and with that light in his eyes, and last night's intensity is never far away.

"In that case, I definitely surrender," I say.

"Only because you're everything," he whispers, and our lips meet. So warm, I could melt, and drown, and then—

The piercing ring of the telephone sounds an alarm from

inside the house. I break out of the kiss, looking to him for help, but he's already moving aside. Fuck. Of course, he's right. This time, we've got no choice.

I trudge back up the ramp, and into the house. Inside the kitchen, the caller ID reveals it's Noriko's mobile. *No choice.*

I stare at the phone, another season passing with every breath I take. Trying to dodge this moment, desperate to figure out some other way.

Yeah, there's another way. You let them find you here, one way or another, haul your arses off in front of your son. That's something to remember you by, all right.

Or you keep running like foxes, and next time, you don't get any warning, no wake-up call at all.

Fuck fuck fuck. I snatch up the receiver, pin it close to my ear, squeezing my eyes shut as I struggle to compose my thoughts.

"Raven!" Her voice is barely a whisper, but strange emotions stir through my body like goosebumps on the inside to hear it again. Impossible reminders, of both past and future.

You looked after me as best you could, Noriko, when there was no one else. And I know... I know you looked after Pegasus, too. After—afterwards, would you, could you, look after—?

"Raven? Please say something. They're looking for you."

Finally, I force out the words. The only words that matter in this moment. "Tonight, I promise. Please, somehow, just till tonight. Look for me in town. Around midnight."

Terrified by the sound of my own desperation echoing inside the receiver and inside my head, I slam down the phone again. Peg's arms are around me already, his voice hushing my shock, keeping me whole. But once I've stopped shaking he nudges me aside and says, "Why don't you two go play, huh? Your chef wants to commandeer the kitchen for a while."

Works for me. I need to be out of this house, as far from

the phone as I can get. After this, it takes me all of an hour to relax, to assure myself she isn't going to call again and tell me it's too late, that they've already found us, that we aren't worth the risk, that we aren't—

I'm pushing Damien on Peggy's swing when he breaks off from the song he's been improvising and asks me, "You won't forget me, will you, Daddy?"

I grab hold of the vines and chains, forcing the swing to a stop, and kneel in front of him. When I reach out to touch his face, he grabs my hand, nuzzling against my palm and kissing it. I take in a deep breath. "Is that what your dreams tell you?"

He scuffs a foot against the ground. "Will I have to go live with her again? Will they hurt me?"

I slump to my hands and knees in front of him, staring at my fingers buried in the snow, willing my body to sink down to where my heart's already fallen. No legal hearing in the world would listen to my reasons as reason. But this is the only reason they've got, for what they're about to do to us.

"Peggy saved you too, kittling. You don't need to go back there. You don't ever need to go back there."

"But I want to come," he murmurs, a tiny frown twisting his features into something with the power to destroy me.

"You can't..."

"Then who'll teach me to fly?"

I go to cover my eyes with one hand, but he tugs my fingers away from my face. Pegasus...you'd tell him better than this, he'd believe you.

He needs to hear it from you, Raven.

Do I even want for this? Do I want my son growing up with such knowledge? What's the alternative? Nothing to keep him whole when they try and tear him to shreds? And they *will* try, if he's got anything of myself or Pegasus inside him. It's started already. That's how we got here to begin with.

It doesn't matter what you leave. It matters what you give. That's how we teach one another to fly.

I draw in a deep breath. "When you're old enough, you'll understand this." I falter. I've got the gift of his undivided attention. He already believes, he already knows. He just needs to hear it. *Just like you, with your need for words of love.* "I'll never forget you, kittling. And I've tried to leave as much as I can, so you don't forget me. But—" Enough. That thread doesn't guide either of us down the right path. "We belong to you, Peggy and me. When you look at the stars, the clouds, a rainbow...you'll find us there." I try not to choke on my own words, rubbing at my nose. "But most of all, we live, in you. Always. Like the angel in the story, trapped in his cage, a butterfly in glass. And if you break the glass—" I fall into a sitting position atop a mound of snow, burying my face in my hands. The swing creaks, preparing me for his embrace.

"Then the butterfly flies away," he says, stroking my hair. *He's so much of your son, Pegasus.*

"Are you okay, Daddy?"

I manage a tentative nod, and he smiles, all the fears and doubts dissolving. "Good. It's my birthday. You can't cry on my birthday."

He takes off in the direction of the house. Looking back, I see Pegasus waiting in the doorway.

Then the butterfly flies away...
If you break the glass.

Damien sits at the head of the table, wiggling and bouncing up and down in his chair, excited by all the food and the blinding array of decorations, most of them scavenged from a box of Christmas trinkets. Once Peg joins us with two glasses of wine and a red cordial, I light the candles, and we sing 'Happy Birthday', and shower him with kisses and streamers. Then we all take a seat, and the feast begins.

So this is how it should be, always. Mama, daddy, son, defined by love over all other things. This...this is all I wanted, all along?

Pegasus reaches out and squeezes my hand, then drapes a blue streamer across my hair and gives me a look, a silent order to eat. After lunch is over and done with, Damien sits between his new toy and the old faithful Mr. Rabbit, while we take turns reading him stories, and when we run out of books, we make them up, dreaming new worlds and old into being. Love, death, salvation, roses, cages, shadows, angels... After a while, all our stories meld into one great dream.

Only once the words begin to fade do I make a move for the phone.

I pause in front of it, cracking my knuckles. Almost in slow-motion, I pick up the receiver and dial the number—not hers, never again hers, even if it's the one my mind keeps regurgitating at me—distracting myself with the sounds of my son and my beloved tidying up around me.

After seven rings, an old man's voice answers, sounding half asleep. I book two tickets on the bus that leaves for the city at six tonight. Same as last time, I give a false name to cover Pegasus, and everything's sorted.

Hang up the phone. Another nail works itself loose from my heart. Two tickets. One for him. One for Damien. Simpler, that way.

He's begun stacking dishes in the machine, and I find myself talking over the top of him. As if it's no big deal at all, I tell him what name to claim the seats under, and a dozen other mundane plans for later. It's already obvious that I don't need to mention how Damien won't need to sit on his knee for this trip.

Not quite meeting my gaze, he crouches in front of the dishwasher, slams the door closed, and stabs at the switch. Hot water hisses down the pipe, and he straightens up. "Damien said you have something to show me."

I blink, slow on the uptake, so he adds, "He said, where you told him the 'Peggy-sis' story."

"Oh." I swallow. "Yeah, all right... Peg, please—"

"It's okay." He places a hand on my shoulder, caresses it all too briefly. "There's only now anymore. So this is enough. Right in this moment, *this* is enough. You see?"

I don't know.

With a flick of the wrist, he passes over my coat. "Let's go."

Somehow, even in this glittering light and all the snow, Damien manages to find the way. I keep hold of Peggy's hand while we're in the forest, enjoying—preserving—the this-is-how-it-always-should-be feeling of him walking beside me, the sight of his breath rising in puffs of mist, the sound of his voice as he randomly sings or whispers next to my ear.

We reach the barbed-wire fence, and here all three of us gaze out over the valley, down at the smoky trails swirling across the glassy lake.

"How long have you known about this place?" he asks me.

I shrug. "Not long. We found it a few days ago, by accident. Or instinct. It seemed the sort of place you should be..."

Motioning for me to help him get over the fence, he stoops down and bundles Damien into his arms, murmuring encouragements in his ear. I push down on the barbed-wire, then climb over to join them.

Only Pegasus keeps marching forward, till he's just a step from the edge. I swallow, hard, and he whirls around to face me, all on fire with defiance, loss, and love. My son nestles on his hip. "What will you do, Raven, if I take one more step?"

I open my mouth, close it again right away. Depending on how I answer this, Damien might get his wish. And tonight would never matter. And I could go with them. And everything...everything would be so exact. But—

Kittling... Angel... My place in your story will be done with, soon enough. It's not mine, anymore, to break the circle.

My body's already trembling as I take a step forward, and another, and another, trying to keep myself under control. I creep closer, focusing on my heartbeat, never looking up from the ground, not till I'm standing right in front of them, holding my breath in case even that's enough to blow them both over the edge. I don't want to fall too soon. Or the ground to crumble beneath my feet, or the wind to knock me off balance, and goddamn this sickness in my stomach.

I force myself to look at Pegasus. Cold, cruel angel, awaiting my answer. I want to touch him, but I can't tell if he trusts me. If he thinks I'm fighting him, he'll simply walk off the—

I fold my arms tight across my chest, trying my best to find clarity while a shiver crawls up and down my spine. And he waits, and he waits.

Break me open, apart, free my soul, my dreams, my heart. We can fly, we can cry, tears of blood.

We did all that, you and me, last night.

When you break the glass...

I can feel this scar on my chest, and the nausea's fading. I think I understand. I trust you. Completely. "Wherever you lead," I tell him like a vow, "I'll always follow."

He smiles at me, glowing as he hands over Damien. I can't help a sigh of relief. Then, still smiling, he turns, facing the clouds, above and below. Now I'm not looking into his eyes, I know he's going to—

I open my mouth, but nothing comes. Instead it's my son's voice calling out, "You can't fly yet, Peggy-sis. I don't see your wings."

He glances at us over his shoulder. He knows I'm afraid, afraid to lose him. There's something more, but all my thoughts are still wrapped in cotton wool. He sighs, stretching out one arm and then the other, examining each in turn, as though to confirm there really are no wings in sight. "Ah, so you're right. Just as well one of us noticed. Your father was ready to follow me blindfolded."

He winks at me sadly, then takes hold of my arm and guides me back from the edge, over to the sanctuary of the fence. At least here, I can think. Though at this point in time, maybe cognitive thought processes are the last thing I should be wishing for. I stare down at my fingernails, but they won't come into focus, so I gnaw at my fingertips instead.

Finally, he puts an arm around my waist, and points to a dark patch of cloud hanging low on the mountainside. Just as he lowers his hand, a rainbow slowly shimmers over the ridge. Then the wind changes, and those dark clouds come rolling straight towards us, bringing their storms, and their premonitions of storms.

Wishing for rainbows, and now chased by the wind. We dash through the forest, following our tracks back through the snow. I laugh till I run out of breath for laughter, keeping enough for a final whoop. So, this is us. So this is what it feels like, having wings.

Let's just see you try and catch me.

We fall upon the towels in the bathroom, sweating and soaked. By the time we get dry, Damien's worn out and stumbles straight into bed. I lean over the mattress and stroke his forehead. Fast asleep before I can even tuck him in. My own exhaustion's starting to sink in, just watching him.

"Come," Pegasus whispers in my ear. He sits beside me and pulls me down into his lap, long spidery fingers threading through my hair and massaging the knots out of my left shoulder.

I'm almost dreaming altogether when he says, "You never told me. How you felt, when she died."

I open my eyes. Seems like it's only a question, not an accusation. "That he was safe, no matter what happens to us."

"What happens to us," he echoes after me, then lays a kiss on his fingers and touches them to my cheek.

"Hush. Just hold me."

So we're lying in the freeze-frame, staring into each other till the lines between self and love burn away. He breaks the spell first, letting my head slide off his lap before he goes wandering up the hall. Sounds like he gets as far as the kitchen. Then his footsteps come scampering back, and now he's standing over the bed. "When does the coach leave?" he asks, grabbing my hands as I try and pull him down next to me.

"Six. Ish."

"It's five o'clock. It's too close, Raven."

I blink, and sit up, and blink again. The adrenaline's already surging through my veins, same as when we ran from the storm. Same as we're always running. "I'll call a taxi."

As I stand up, he draws me into a deep kiss. Time enough to melt, desiring more, and then he leads me to the phone. During the conversation with the local taxi company, I've gotta look up where we are on a map taped to the fridge to give out directions to the property. After this, facing him fills my stomach with lead.

"You're not coming with us," he says flatly. "Are you."

"I'll come in the taxi. Into town."

He grits his teeth, then says, "I meant after that."

I touch his cheek. "It's my destiny…to wait for my Pegasus."

"Please don't wait too long." He takes me in his arms, and we hold one another in stillness and peace, for the last time…

on this side.

It's ten minutes before six, and the sky's bleeding out over the dark mountains, when we step out of the car. I haul the suitcase out of the boot. They'll be taking it back with them. I left everything for Pegasus: Damien, the music box, and most of the money.

I stare down at my son, fast asleep in his arms, as the cold bores through the invisible holes in my forehead. His hair whips around his rosy cheeks, just as it did in the forest, perched on the edge of reality and dream. "I don't know how to do this," I tell him.

He takes my hand in his. "It's not forever. *We* are."

I throw my arms around him, kissing away the stains of my tears, sins upon the immaculate powdered skin. I've got so much to tell you, but I can't say the words, I can't speak, I can't—

He already knows.

He already knows.

Still asleep, Damien murmurs something, cocooned between us. "Don't be scared," Peggy whispers in my ear. He nuzzles against my cheek, and gazes longingly into my face. "You know exactly what to do. This is your dream."

A little laugh escapes me. I want to say something to the contrary, but end up throwing one hand in the air. So cold.

"We go home."

All around us, people have begun to appear, more and more of them shuffling past to get onboard the coach. Standing here, we've become a rock in the stream. The driver takes the liberty of stowing away the suitcase; already our fingertips slip one another's grasp—me, and Peggy and my sleeping son.

Then he lifts his hand to my chin, raising my face, pressing his lips to mine. I open my mouth, tasting him, letting him taste me. Taste, touch, caress, a teardrop, a...

Dream.

And now he's moving away from me, the last passenger up the steps. Leaving me so small, so empty. Nobody sees. They never did. You're the only ones.

I fold my arms over my chest, holding in the whirlwind, as the engine starts and he edges up to a window seat, pressing his hand to the glass, cradling Damien on his knee. I can already feel myself coming apart at the seams, like all those knots on the inside are untangling, snapping one by one, spilling forth sorrow, devotion, and despair. And love.

I give him all these things, for sake-keeping, as I blow him a kiss, touch the cross, and the coach rumbles out onto the highway.

I stare after it, till that pair of angels disappear from view, and all light within me shuts down and dies.

So, onwards, to the pub. Onwards to get as wasted as Ravenly possible with the money he left in my jacket pocket. I don't need to care what happens to me anymore.

I never have to care again.

And right now this faith, even more beautiful for being so twisted and broken, is all I've got. Yes, drink. Not for escapism, and not for clarity, but fuck-it-all just cos.

I push open the doors. First duty is to call Noriko, keeping that promise; second is to caress the edges of oblivion, make-believe that a state of mind—a non-state—could be a blade against my neck.

Gotta keep moving, closer to the end.

Outside, it's still snowing.

Five hours later, give or take what feels like a year, I stagger out of the pub, courting a particularly violent shade of nausea. The doors slam shut behind me, locking me out with the night. Maybe I overstayed my welcome.

I stare down the road, trying to focus—mind and vision—only vaguely able to recall the finer details of my last conversation: a lengthy discussion with some local high-school teacher, on the principles and possibilities of quantum physics, and godonlyknows how many drinks between. His wife...she was only young; she died last summer. But all those impressive words, and impenetrable arguments, clutching at straws with precision instruments, notions of faith, elevated above the noise-floor of words by mathematical rules, threads of science as proof...*as proof...*

Except now I'm just a ghost again, seeking solitude when solitude's already suffocating me, wandering homesick beneath the stars.

We're made out of stars. When we die, perhaps that's where we'll return.

That was me, wasn't it? Telling him...

Laughter, a soft strange sound, carrying echoes of truth and insanity and sorrow.

I find the solitude I seek where else but the local graveyard, a few blocks off the main road. Gum trees sway with a lonely knowledge, leaves rustle like waves. Bathed in this ethereal glow from moonlight on snow, I pass through the gates and down the main avenue, playing the vampire seeking redemption, all the way to the end, to the statue of an angel. I get a feeling like it's been waiting for me. Waiting to judge, waiting to set me free, waiting to cage me.

No, that's too close...too close to sobriety. Hold me, Pegasus. Come back, wings or no. There must be another way, something I didn't see before, where it doesn't hurt like this hurts, where it isn't so cold that even time's frozen over.

Just like glass, I wish to break...

But that's the only way.

Noriko, where are you? Why don't you come? Or you, Monty, or you, Ma, Dad, Damien...Pegasus?

Raven.

I jerk upright, my heartbeat thudding. Under my palms, ripples of consciousness make a pulse within the angel's marble skin. Long silver tresses fall beneath its thorny crown, brushing over my wrists, then sinking into my veins. It's coming to life, beneath my hand.

"Pegasus." I reach out for him—stone effigy, pale apparition—speaking his name like an enchantment. *My Pegasus.*

But I asked you to leave. I gave you such perfect instruction in how to set up and deliver my doom. I could never let you suffer—for my sins, my mistakes, what she did to our son...

Except the form's shifting, altering subtly, the lips softening, edges taking on a distinct female flow. I don't even need to ask, don't need to look, can't bear to see. I hang my head in shame, and kneel before her. Oh, I know who you are, sure as if I belonged to you myself.

Juliette.

What's inside the glass may be released.

Her voice is siren and wraith and Lilith and Eve, this voice that sings to me. This is the source, of all nightmare and knowledge, faith and dream, rose and thorn, life itself. And I've got no words to give her.

I don't need any. She reaches down, and our fingertips brush together just long enough for me to feel all the pain, the dirt, the treachery, the poison, and the fear, leaking out of me, leaving me drained, clean, free. She presses a rose into my palm. And then she hardens into night and stone, just a statue again.

I open my eyes and look down at the flower. But all that's left is the stem of bitter-sharp thorns, twined around my fingers. I hold it against my wrist, to the light of the moon, illuminated by memory...*bound to one wrist, thorns breaking the skin...*

All I can do is burst out laughing. Surrender myself to my own form of consumption.

Insanity equals salvation.

I wake, not remembering having slept, in a warm and unfamiliar place. But the moment the ceiling comes into focus and the dancing shadows leave my mind and join the others, I realise exactly where I am. Noriko leans over me, her skin worn by too many tears and no dreams. By some premonition, she's changed her hair colour again, the red of congealed blood. I admire it from a distance while she strokes my forehead, telling me, "Monty found you, Raven. You passed out."

She backs away as I sit up slowly, trying to sense... "Are Peg and Damien okay?" My voice rasps in my throat, and my tongue's all hairy and heavy. Guess I really did drink too much.

A new shadow flickers in the doorway, and Monty's stomping towards me. I watch him, slowly and vaguely making sense of his 'What the hell have you done?' tirade. So many words.

What good are words? All I've got is the truth. There simply isn't anything else.

Noriko hushes him, seeing something I don't. I let her take my hand, help me out of bed, and guide me across the hall to the door of the spare room. I take a few steps inside, but no more; an invisible indivisible wall separates me from my loves, a barrier that will not break on this side. There in the bed we once shared so long ago, Peggy and Damien sleep, curled up ouroboros-like together.

I blow them a kiss, sighing in contentment as Damien smiles and Peggy snuggles instinctively closer to him. I whisper, "I love you," one last time, before closing the door behind me, leaving the bedroom for good.

I remember. I'll always remember. I'm no longer afraid, no longer hurting. Everything melts away, and soon I'll be able to spread my wings.

Noriko's still waiting, out in the hall. Behind her, in their bedroom, Monty slouches on the bed, shoulders shaking. Are you crying, cousin? Why? There's no need for tears anymore.

She tries to tell me something about Peggy having a terrible fever, but I drift past her, staring down at Monty, more guardian and friend to me than my own dad ever was. Yeah, you too. You'll take such good care of my son. Filling the hole in your own heart. You were so broken when Noriko lost her baby. You think I don't remember, so safe in the cotton wool of self-absorbed teenage angst. You've got no idea. But I remember everything.

"It's time," I tell him. "You know."

Time to confess my sins. And bury my love down deep under lock and key, till the final rainbow comes. I'll wait for you, Pegasus. Just like you waited for me.

Monty nods, resigned to our fate. I watch him kiss her goodbye, before he leads me away. Now my tears are all dried up, I can't feel a thing. They won't fall again.

In the silence of the car I stare at the scars on my wrists, all the way to the police station. Resigned to my fate, a cage within a cage.

It doesn't matter. All this is just a trick of the light. This isn't where it ends. This is just a temporary step, between tomorrow...

And forever.

Then the butterfly flies away...

24 (PEGASUS)

Juliette Smiling/Final Dawn

Light.

A light, shining through the window, landing on the soft white keys, over white fingers, down upon me. Where does it come from, this light?

I'm in the same room—the very same place—where you first told me you loved me. Tonight, you're not here to hear, but I'll play for you all the same. I want you to listen. It's so...

Crystal. Empty glass, on top of the piano. The light plays over it, melting rose petals, flickering in and out of the hourglass, spiralling round and round. I fall into the music. As tears follow the light, I fall...

I can't bring myself to say your name anymore. The time for words long passed, now there's only this light. I gaze at the curtain, through the window, beyond the curtain, out across the night sky. This place she offered me: sanctuary, a place you once called home. Were you happy here? I know about your parents, about your past. But beyond that, were you happy?

This place, it's only a dream. And when the dream is over, then...

Then we come to find ourselves at the end of the rainbow, and...

Please hold me. I'm like glass, and wish to break.

I've been so asleep. Soon, it will be dawn. Already the light grows sharper. I'm remembering all these things...

"Come with me," I tell him, leading him to the bedroom, where I open the curtains and windows. He huddles behind me, breathing in shivers. It must be so cold outside; already the glass is frosted over, ice biting my fingertips as I lean over and spread my arms wide, leaving myself open to everything. "Tonight is the last time we'll look at the stars from this side, together."

"Pegasus, please..." His hands splay across my chest, pulling me closer, need, helplessness, and love, all confused with desire. "You feel so warm. How can you feel so warm?"

I turn to face him, smiling, laughing, adoring the broken expressions crossing his face. Balling one of his hands into a fist, I lick teasingly at his fingers, inviting him down between my legs, whispering these things, once fears, always desires, forever dreams. "I'm not afraid to make love to you, Raven... to allow you to make love to me. Break me open, apart, free my soul, my dreams, my heart. We can fly, we can cry, tears of blood. I'm not scared, so why should you be, my darling?"

"I'm afraid to hurt you," he confesses to my kiss.

"Then hurt me," I say, my voice rasping in my throat, "and you need never feel afraid. I want this. Please."

One of my fingers burrows up inside him, making him cry out. Does this hurt you too, my love?

But he's parting his legs further, making room for more, biting down on the flesh of my shoulder, asking again how it is that I feel so warm.

I kiss him hard and deep, wishing for my wings, pleading with him. "It must be tonight. Tomorrow, we celebrate the birth of an angel. And then—?"

"And then we'll call Monty." He's trembling, ready to break.

Oh, Raven, this will be so perfect. Both of us, so willing. Both of us.

I fall into his needy embrace, laughing as he moans when I withdraw my fingers, my own dick throbbing against his tummy, the heat ever rising, mist and dreams to cloud my visions.

"And then we go home," I finish for him. "The final days are upon us."

Falling like music over my heart.

As he buries his face in my neck, I feel a tear crawl down my chest. So it begins, for there simply is no end.

Echoing whispers chase down the silence. Here in my heart, a barbed-wire glow uncoils, spreading along my spine and twisting inside my tummy. White blood trickles in sticky droplets down my thighs. This is how I can feel so warm.

I crouch between his legs, forked tongue and serpent's charms playing over his flesh, never giving him enough, daring him to take.

Then hurt me, and you need never feel afraid.

You and I, burning, disintegrating, no need for words, the silent wish.

With a whimper, he spins me round and shoves me against the wall. He's playing to hurt, but I only smile, as I throw my arms out wide. Take this as a sign, then, of my willing sacrifice. I would die for you.

His fingers encircle my throat, catching my gasp, while his other hand turns to teasing my dick. Now each hand tightens to a stranglehold, both of us flirting with darkness. "Pegasus. Please…"

Raven, are you crying?

"Don't make me do this to you. Make it stop."

"I have to show you," I whisper, turning around as he lets me go—and oh, how his eyes are so hypnotic in their fear, and their surrendering to fear. Easier if he thinks I have such control. Otherwise, he might never forgive himself. "And this is the only way through. Please help me. Please, let me—"

Knowing the rest, he falls to his knees in resignation, holding me tight as he takes my balls into his mouth, and nibbles and bites at me. Flames of pain flicker between my legs, and through red and white sparks I gaze upon him, all sharpened teeth and tears. Then, clawing at my wrists, he pulls me down, turns me over, and knots his fingers up inside me.

These aren't his tears anymore. I know, from these moans that burn my throat as the perfect harmony to his love, his pain, his thorns. And through all this, somehow, I'm still reaching out to the light.

So beautiful. We can make it...

There.

My fingers have me under a spell, dancing over the keys. But inside this shell, somewhere, I can taste the sounds and breathe their music.

Please listen.

Please.

Ideals of love, perfection, devotion, falling across my skin. I smile; we enter the light, me adorned in torn lace and feathers, him so beautiful in the cold fires of his regret. He's hurt me enough, for this.

Once we're on the inside, everything seems so warm, so safe. I stroke his face, making a wish for the dream to begin and end. "It's okay", I tell him, though my lips move only to kiss him. *It's okay.*

He falls into me, and I spread my wings, lifting us into the sky. You know it, too, my love. We're closer, ever closer, and the rainbow's bleeding through the chinks in my heart. If we go much further, we need never worry about finding a way back. Is this how—?

No, the clouds are blackening, thickening around our bodies into two separate shells, tearing us apart again. "Raven!"

I wake to our names, screamed together in a heartbeat, cold sweat already frozen on our skin. I'm leading him towards the bathroom, where the little souvenir from last time lingers, safe in an envelope in the medicine cabinet. He doesn't know I kept it. At first, I couldn't name what reason I'd ever give for keeping it. But here we are, him whispering, "Angel", and me tracing my hand under his chin, forcing his gaze to meet its mirror self. Then I press the envelope into his palm.

I hold him against me while I open the fold and slip the razor blade out.

"Please, don't make me watch," he begs. Already hopeless when arousal blossoms like a fever between us. We both follow the blade's path, slicing the flesh over his heart. So the blood quenches the white rose. It's okay...

Except that it isn't. The razor bounces into the basin. I'm still staring at its bloody edge on the white porcelain, when a punch to the mirror sends a shower of glass raining down over the sink and the floor. Raven leans against the emptied frame, one hand over his face, gasping for air. Why should the storm follow us here? Is it me who did this to you? Or all those nights of wanting me, and being chained by her?

But I wasn't too late, my darkling angel. I'm here, now, bound to you, seeking you, waiting for you still. I'll wait again, over and over. I'll wait forever.

I see how it is, though. You hate the cage, yet you're a willing prisoner. This here, this now, is this all there's supposed to be? That's what they told you, isn't it? Only I don't understand—never understood—for a moment why you'd believe. This is my dream, for you. In a dream you can have anything you want. Be anything you wish. Do—feel—everything.

Mother. You promised, in the bathtub tonight. In the waves. In your arms.

I look down. Blood stains my feet, the tiles, and my love. I didn't give you this—this everything—to chain yourself with my sister's falsehoods. Why hold on to such things?

So this is how it is. I drained her poison, but you never did. And that means there's no protection against me becoming infected again.

I have to— I can't— This isn't—

When his eyes meet mine and I see that blood reflected there, somehow all I can do is run.

This love you speak of. This is the protection. Find me, Raven, and love me again.

You'll understand, when you make it back to me.

Find me, Raven. And love me again.

Rain falls harder as I trace these words into the melody, and the light fades. Was it ever really here?

Please, I don't want...to forget. I'm so tired. I've always been here, waiting...

I'm so tired.

Snow shrouds the world. Rising mist and shadows that flicker beneath the moonlight invite me to come play in the grounds of my madness. And it's so hot on the inside, anyhow.

I step out to embrace the night. But I'm not alone. Even as I start to run, the laughter of old familiar ghosts chases me down.

pain—knowing—faith—whore—darkness—light—Mother—Nicholet—

Wendy. Yes, it's her laughter here the loudest. Now she's sidling up to me, stepping out of the empty spaces between the stars and trees. Creature once called my sister, wilful end product of my mother's long destruction, child of rape.

Blood-encrusted tendrils crawl over her scalp and squirm at her throat. Her eyes dart from side to side, black as burnt wood, gaping out of a face pockmarked with putrid lesions and bruises. Her decaying body still attempts to mock me with its distorted images of immaculate womanhood. She's even touching herself while she speaks, spitting out bile and blood—such crude words to describe her so-called charms. She parades before me, her every move accompanied by a loud squelching and the faint waft of meat left out to rot. I hold myself, hold in the light that simmers inside, flared and fed by a single thought. *Sometimes I wish for the dream to be over...*

I stare at her hard as she repeats the words, tells me how her father had Mother bring her into the world. Always it comes down to those same fateful words: *rape*, the effect, and *whore*, the cause. Only this time, Wendy, I have something for you. Raven wanted you to have it. He passed it on to me. And now, it's come home to you.

The light inside me erupts. Black-rainbow fragments of self rush outwards—some shards reforming to make something new, too many dispersing, lost forever. Now it's my turn to become the mirror.

You tricked me, *soeur*, used me, abused me, scarred me, made me into nothing, sucked dry any strength—any self-worth—like a leech, and you hurt... And you poisoned everything.

I fall on her, wrenching her lips apart so I can drive my tongue deep enough to snuff her spark for good. "I love you," I tell her, the killing words, and I hold on tight, until the scream fades and her thrashing dies away. I don't dare look at this new thing the shards made me become, but at least

I can feel him here in my heart again.

Raven…

I open my eyes, and breathe. I'm alone, with Mother. She's singing to me, pushing me on a swing, white petals drifting from her hair and landing on me. Breathe…I'm only a child, and she's here. We're so happy together, you and I alone.

But not happy for you, no? He hurt Nicholet, didn't he, Mother? He…hurt my father. That was your sorrow, the roses, the lies. So many lies, all for the sake of the truth. I know how it is. He tried to do that to me, too. Except I was lucky. Raven saved me.

Was Nicholet a Raven of your own? Did he ever not believe you, like Raven often doubts me? Did he not believe in the truth of dreams? In himself? He should have rescued his princess, carried her over the ocean, across the rainbow…

I scrape my feet against the ground to stop the swing.

Yet this is how it happened. Leaning forward, she croons the words in my ear. *I believed, in the truth of dreams. I chose the wrong path, and the wrong path chose me, for but a little while. It doesn't matter, in the end. Faith: as long as it exists, it can carry anyone you love. We are the same, Jaime. Happiest when dreamed into existence by the most beautiful of dreamers. They never realise this, of course.*

I rest against her thighs, trying to unknot all the meanings in her words. One of my palms presses between her legs and comes away stained with blood. I wish I could heal what was done to her.

She hums another two lines of her nursery rhyme, then puts her hand on my shoulder. She's not looking my way as she says, *I know you've been very tired. Soon,* mon ange, *you can come home.*

The words of her song and the movement of the swing lull me to sleep, as the warmth claims me.

I'm singing these words on my own tonight, nothing but white keys on black to serve as witness and accomplice. Shame your mother gave up on this, Raven, allowed that man—your father—to beat her down till nothing in her life could be enough to save her. You are not like your mother, and you are not like your father.

Raven. I've missed saying your name. Even if you aren't in my arms, I know you can hear me. Mother told me, that night, that she needed to give you something. And here I have this rose stem tied around my wrist. I don't remember tying it myself.

Mother, it's almost dawn. Like a nightingale I sing, waiting for that final call, the beckoning to flight. You'll hear it also, Raven. You are listening, aren't you?

My voice isn't as beautiful as that of my mother, but I'll sing it for you all the same.

This bed, so safe for being so familiar. I've shared this bed before. Tasted blood, despair, love, and now—

A murmur beneath the doona, and I haul him up onto my pillow, so we're facing the morning together. I sigh, and I look at him, and he looks at me, and we hold one another, our only defence left against the encroaching emptiness. Just lie quietly beneath the covers, try to stay warm. Damien.

I start to cry, and his little hand reaches up to brush away the tears. Monty's house, Noriko's house. I came here—we came here—I don't quite remember how. But we left Raven behind, left him to his sacrifice. Even now, my mind's replaying the well-rehearsed testimonial he drilled into me; phrases to doom him, excuses to keep me—

Free to fly ahead, find the rainbow.

Yes. Yes, I'm already there, really. I just need to—

Close my eyes, shut out this grey world, seal in the tears,

keep what little warmth I have left safe for our son. And so when that same little hand next brushes my face, I pull it gently to my lips and kiss it, over and over.

Damien...

I'm sorry.

I have lived so many lives
I have lived them all for you
I have nowhere left to run
I have nothing left to hide
I am spreading forth my wings
I am taking off my skin
Now I open up my arms
and let you in...

I understand how you felt, but why you had to, anyway.

So I'll continue to wait. I am trying to be patient, Mother, truly I am. But the dawn's almost here. And the music... it's pouring out of my soul. Soon, there won't be anything left at all.

Is this my transformation...to butterfly?

All I ask of Noriko is that she dye my hair. Another part of Raven's plan, but also my wish. To be as I was meant to be. Whatever that is.

Two hours later, blond-haired Jaime Belmont emerges from the bathroom, and submits to the startled gaze of Noriko and Raven's mother. *Nadja de Winter.* She must have arrived while I stared at my reflection. Maybe I'd been trying to gaze a hole right through. Hoping to find my own mother there, like I did once before.

Damien crawls onto my knee, stroking my tresses, and

murmuring questions about his father. Nadja watches me, guarded but not surprised. She doesn't grieve for her son. That doubt eats at her, more than ever, that he might have enough of his father in him, enough for all of this.

Noriko stalks towards me, then presses a palm to my forehead. She announces, as she did the last eight times we did this, that I have a fever. Yes. I know I'm sick. It's a gift from my mother, this ice and fire and panicked flesh. A reminder that I don't need to see out the other side of mirrors to know the truth.

But Mother's voice is hushed here, so I sing to our child, rocking him side to side in my arms as her lullaby falls from my lips. And we almost forget...but that's before the woman comes to take him away. Only I can't seem to let go, and he starts to cry, and the lullaby breaks, but she's bigger than me, Raven, so faceless and righteous, and she's only going to hurt us all more if I don't...

I stare at my hands, my palms, try to dissect the lifeline, focus on the part of me that's on fire, while Damien screams. My name, his father's name, the word 'No', repeated in random patterns, and how it's important—he's waiting for his daddy. It doesn't stop, the screaming, until that unfamiliar engine starts, and the strange white car pulls out of the driveway, and the fire burns low.

They're gone. You left me to this, Raven. Damien—our child, our angel, our son. I feel— I can't think of anything I could possibly do, beyond lie down right here right now and will my heart to stop beating. Even so, the more I try, the faster it pounds, blood pulsing through my ears, driving the fever higher and higher.

A touch on my hand sends me leaping to my feet, arms folded tightly over my chest to prevent the yell escaping, knees shaking as I fight against falling. No one to help us. It's all up to me.

Damien, Damien, Damien...

Mother! I don't know how to leave a little boy crying and broken and alone. It reminds me, too much—

Rain trickles over the glass in front of my nose. I've been standing here all this time, staring out the window. Too many frames of déjà vu: window in a hospital, window like my mother's, window that would not open. Yes. Window open within my soul instead. Concentrate.

Damien...I love you so.

I shove against the pane, propelling myself straight into the arms of the hovering Noriko. *I love you.* But I never told—

The unspoken words leave a bitter taste at the back of my mouth. "I feel as though I'm a guest of honour at my own funeral." My cold laugh somehow convinces her that she should hold me, and me that I should push her away.

Anyway, my turn will come. The hour of interrogation draws near. I find myself trapped between her and Nadja, as we leave the house behind. This place where I met you, where it all began. And in all this time, I never once said, never told you—

If I survive their examinations, then I will confide in you, I swear. When that hour comes, I won't have anything left to lose.

*That place where I met you...*on that day Noriko brought me home. Her boyfriend and his cousin were starting a band, she said—*hint hint*—once I'd confessed to playing piano. A sign of how far I'd fallen into her trust, and how deeply she'd burrowed into my head. And why not, when it was me she'd picked? So many of them, those boys in that house of torment, fantasising and pleading for her sessions, as though she was some exotic dancer instead of a mind-spinner, a psychologist. Yes, I remember their jealousy at the selection of the bird-boned, blond-haired weirdo, who carried around a teddy bear in his purple backpack and looked more like a girl.

Anyway, there I was, perched on a footstool in her living room, drinking green tea from a large yellow cup, overwhelmed by the garish displays of colour all around us: paisley curtains and carpets of red and pink and orange, blue paper fans stencilled with butterflies, and last of all the magazines spread over the coffee table, Japanese boys gracing every cover, photographed in sexual ambiguity and clad in androgyny.

She flopped on the sofa in front of me and draped her green boot-clad calves across the table. Dozens of metal bracelets jingled when she tossed her hair about. Then she looked at me, and I looked at her, and she smiled. "Maybe you can relax for now? Ages before those two get home. Especially Raven."

I sipped at my tea. "Raven? Is that your boyfriend?"

"Are you kidding?" She raised a brow, grinning, then cleared her throat. "No, it's Monty's cousin. Or 'He of the Eternal Detention Sentence'."

Crossing my legs, I started picturing what he might be like, this Raven boy she obviously wanted me to be friends with. I knew enough of detention rooms at those other places, places that never kept me caged very long. All filled with boys who hated themselves, and hated me even more.

"You know what?" she said then. "I had this idea for a long time. Maybe it's crazy. You trust me, right?" Though the question set my nerves on edge, I didn't fight against her dragging me off the footstool and into the bathroom.

So it was that I was gazing in suspicious admiration at this strange lilac-haired creature, when the front door slammed and two sets of feet came shuffling down the hall. Monty, wearing a suit and bow-tie, stooped to sweep Noriko up and spin her round, before releasing her with a kiss. She nudged him in the ribs and pointed at me; with a cheeky grin, he waved 'hi'. And Raven, kicking his school bag across the floor with breathtaking contempt—he never noticed me at all—as he made a beeline for the fridge.

I found myself most wanting to touch the long blue-black tufts that obscured a good third of his face. Instead I folded my arms across my chest and prayed quietly for oblivion, no matter what form it took. Stupid that I could have felt this way, any way, so soon. *Dangerous* stupid. Why should anyone care for me, once they knew what I was?

Idle streams of self-loathing, and daring and not daring to believe, flowed through my mind as I watched him flick the top off a beer bottle with a lighter and take a long swig. From the angry words that came out of Monty's mouth, I could tell this was a regular part in some homecoming routine. "Raven," Noriko called, not batting a lash, "we have a guest. You're so rude; say hello."

He glanced from Monty, to Noriko, to me, one hand pushing his fringe off his forehead so we could actually see each other. I'll remember that moment always. The first glimpse of the most beautiful, tortured eyes I'd ever seen. Shades of impossible blue, like his hair, and…he was smiling at me.

I think—I think I even smiled back. And I didn't look away. That's how I first came to notice the scar.

This is how it was, I first loved you.

These, and thoughts like these, are all I have left for comfort and company, while I sit apart from Noriko and Nadja, then Monty and several police officers—watching the detectives—in a cold, cold room. The brash lighting and the smell of vinyl furnishings makes my head hurt, but I am a good boy, and I give them everything Raven wanted them to hear, everything they really want to hear, and to hell with all of us.

I want to be sick. I'm going to be sick. I'm going to be so sick there'll be nothing left, only blood and entrails spilling out across the nice white bathroom tiles.

But nothing comes, and I remain trapped in my own perfect prison. Raven, are you here?

A hundred metres outside the police station, Monty slams me into a fence, demanding to know what I'm playing at.

Are you anywhere, anymore? A distant heart, safe in your shell, floating out there somewhere, away with the clouds?

Why is Monty so angry at me?

"Do you have *any* idea of what you just did? You weren't even listening to me! How the hell could you be so fucking brain dead?"

"Monty," Noriko growls.

Oh. I see. He thinks those lies were all of my choosing, my construction, my self-defence. I might ask you the same thing, cousin-after-a-fashion.

"No," he says, and he turns on her, and runs his hands through his hair. "You shut up with your libertarian excuses, and your goddamn social work amateur psychology *'everything will be just fine'* bullshit."

I blink at her, but her face remains blank. Perhaps they've done this before.

"This is my *cousin*, Noriko. And I'm not letting him turn out like Andrej." From the way he lowers his voice and glances at Nadja as he speaks that name, I know he's talking about Raven's father.

I look to the ground. No. Raven won't end up anything like his father. He's mine. And Mother and I, we'll keep him, so safe.

But Monty renews his attack on me, mistaking my smile of faith for mockery. "This—*this* is what you wanted? You—" He snarls, stabbing a finger at my face, hatred masking such intense sorrow. "I curse the day you came into my life. You're nothing but a—"

I watch his mouth moving in slow motion, waiting for him

to say it. Noriko's starting to protest, when another voice stuns us all into silence. "Enough!"

Warily, I glance across at Nadja, who leans on Noriko's arm, fierce in her frailty, shaking with the effort as she gazes back at me, unflinching. What does she see?

She turns now to Monty. "I have one thing to tell you, about your cousin, Montgomery. Do you know what that is? You took him in, but did you ever really know how he protected me from your demon uncle? If you ever dared admit it to yourself, you'd know it already. I didn't understand any of it either, not in those days. Now, I think I do."

My vision's so blurred with tears that Monty almost disappears as he hangs his head. I don't want to be here, not for this. They all love you, *so much*, Raven. And you really have no idea. How can I take you, if—?

It's too late, for this.

"My son always knows what he's doing," she says, folding her hands over her purse. "And I'll tell you one more thing. I met that *suka*, and her father, just one time. One time was enough. She conspired to keep me from my own grandson. And she almost destroyed him. Both of them. And every day, you knew the truth, as well as I do. You took care of him, yes, but where were you for so many years, with all these confessions of cousinly love?"

Shrunken and spent, she lets Noriko guide her to the car. They both climb in. A tram glides past. Monty glances at me, waiting to catch my eye before looking away. "We should go get a drink, or something."

But when he opens his mouth, that unfinished sentence, it's all I can hear. *You're nothing but a—*

"What am I, Monty?"

With an angst-filled groan, he starts searching through his pockets for nothing in particular. "Just—forget it, forget I said anything, will you? Please."

Forget, forget, yes, soon I will forget. But that time, it's not here yet, Monty. You should tell me what you think of me, while you have the chance.

I creep towards him, staring into his face. "I am nothing but a whore. Isn't that it? How the rest of the song goes?"

"It's—" He tries to speak, stammers a moment going nowhere, then breaks off in ragged frustration.

"W. H. O. R. E."

"No, Peg, I—" A last sigh. "I'm sorry."

With a sad smile, I close my eyes, and stand on tiptoe to kiss his cheek. I keep a tight hold on his arm, even as he shudders and tries to extricate himself. Yes, Monty, I know. Boys don't kiss other boys. Even boys who look like girls, and sometimes are. Boys who look like their mothers.

"I won't be a whore for very much longer." I squeeze his hand and step backwards, making it a promise.

Beneath the empty sky—grey, an endless expanse of grey—I feel the shell start to crack. At last.

I try my best to remember those shades of impossible blue, as I follow him away.

The shell starts to crack. At last. Yes...

I sigh, and rest the side of my face against the closed piano lid. Now there's no more music. The tape stopped recording a short time after my tears. Soon, I should label it.

I've got to leave something for Damien. Yes...

My lashes flutter, flicker-flutter closed. No clocks, no light. Time...stops.

I've given up waiting, I think.

The dark, lonely streets keep calling me. Unable to focus, or sleep, I wander through the fog, under the white lamps.

It's been raining on and off; by the time I make it to the top of the hill, I'm already soaked. Staring down into a leafy, dead-end street, I catch the echoes of a child's sobs. A chance apparition, perhaps, of Damien, or me. Up in the fishbowl sky, some of the clouds are starting to clear, enough to see a scattering of stars. When we die, that's what we become. They don't look real, not here.

I sit in the gutter, inviting numbness. The phantom cries have stopped. Dawn crawls in, bringing no hope, just as it did the first morning I realised I would never again play for my mother's smile. But there'll always be a new dawn.

Won't there?

I trudge all the way back to Monty and Noriko's, but this place is strange to me now.

You're not a whore, Pegasus. You're a beautiful young man, and I promise you, as long as I'm here, you'll be safe.

Noriko. But those words were given to me long ago. We all know I'm not welcome anymore. I stand on the doormat, frowning at my bare feet. Once again, I've managed to forget such fundamental things as shoes and socks. Whatever. Anyway, the bathroom window is still open, so I crawl inside, sneak down the hall, and curl up on my makeshift bed on the sofa, pulling the doona over my face. I don't need to see this side anymore.

And then there's tomorrow. They told me I could visit you, Raven. What will I say?

That your carefully laid plans all worked, of course. Just as you knew they would. That they stole away our son. Just as you knew they would. And—

And…

I snuggle deeper into the covers, but make no plans to sleep.

What good the dreams, when the artist of my soul is in chains?

You remember the night he was born?

I remember. Holding him, for the first time, and wishing... Remembering. Understanding. The meaning of the word for God. *Mother.*

You're my mama now, Peggy-sis.

Our child waits, so far, on the other side of the woods. That path is not for you and I to take, not anymore.

Circles, ashes, and stars. I love you.

Love you.

Love...

We're late, since I manage to throw up all down one side of the taxi, much to the driver's loud disgust. Nadja holds me for the rest of the journey, stroking my hair, now and then whispering that it will be okay in-between berating the driver. I help her play pretend.

She should have her time with him first. So while I wait, to keep the razor-wielding shadows in my mind at bay, I tear out a strand of my hair, wrap it round a finger...another strand, another finger. By the time she emerges, a small blond tumbleweed coils by my feet.

"Go to him," she tells me, and I stand up so fast, shivering, that pinpricks of starlight appear everywhere I look. My heart's stopping-starting-stopping. *It will be okay.* I can still pretend.

A heavy-set door slams behind me, and I'm following a stumpy uniformed being down a fluorescent corridor, into a room carved in two by a perspex screen. I thought there'd be tables and chairs and grieving wives and ashtrays and knitting, but I guess this is something more high security. Chairs on either side, partitions, phones. Is it safe to laugh yet? Such synchronicity. Angels and their cages, you know.

The guard leads me over to the far end, where Raven sits, blue and grey. I fall against the screen, our hands and faces both pressing against it, like creatures trapped inside a warped mirror. But he won't cry, so I won't either. They wouldn't allow him to keep those emotions here.

Still, I thought I prepared myself better than this, when I notice the cross I gave him is—

Don't be stupid. They wouldn't allow him to keep that either.

Forgetting he can't hear me, I speak his name, and he slides into the chair, watching me distantly. Curious, perhaps, to see if I break. I follow the mirror's logic and sit in front of him. We each take hold of a receiver, our fingers spread against the glass again. I'm on the wrong side of the mirror. The wrong side of the dream.

"You look like your mama," is the first thing he says to me, grief and elation choking his voice.

I sniff. I can't reach you, and I can't touch you, and I want to scream.

"Did you...?" He glances in the direction of the guard over his right shoulder, and lowers his voice. "Did everything work out okay?"

I clench the phone. Of course he'd ask. Didn't I tell myself already? "Did I doom you, you mean?"

He shrugs, not breaking my gaze. "If you like."

"Yes." It's me who looks away from these duelling reflections; two sets of tortured eyes making me dizzy, nausea returning. I don't have anything left to be rid of.

I didn't the first time.

"Thank you," he whispers, bowing his head too, and we fall silent. Finally, he adds, "I'm sorry...I just...like listening to you breathe. It reminds me. Of when I could keep you safe."

His turn to sniff, and the chill renews its attack on my nerve endings with a vengeance, and all of a sudden I'm telling him about how they took Damien, how Monty told me that word, that word that I hate, how his mother defended us, about the ghost child crying in the rain—all these things, until there's only three words left to say and I become magically mute, deafened by the pulse pounding against my forehead.

"Pegasus."

His voice, it's…enough. Raven, I—

"I asked Ma," he tells me, winding the phone cord around his fingers, "if you could go stay with her for a while." He manages a laugh, but he seems confused, focused on my hand, as though wondering why the mirror stopped working.

With a hesitant smile, I start twisting the cord around my fingers, too. Relieved, he adds, "I won't be there, this time, to stop you. But I promise—"

"I won't have to wait so long…"

"Yeah." He nods. "I promise."

I lean against the glass, and he does too, and I pretend we're touching. "Close your eyes."

A tear trickles down my cheek, but I brush it away, desiring concentration. One brief glance up, to make sure he's listening. Yes, his eyes are closed, all his hurt contained, in me. So I close mine as well, tracing patterns between us. "Stroking your cheek… We're lying on the sand, and I'm kissing you, Raven. I can hear the waves, already. So warm, so safe, when you're with me. Can you feel it?"

"Yes," he hisses. For the first time, I'm aware of him breathing, how our hearts beat in perfect sync.

"The rainbow hasn't come to us yet, but this is where we have to wait for it."

"Just like the dream…"

"The dream will be over soon. And then, that's reality, on the other side of the rainbow. Just like I showed you, that night."

I move back, watching him nod, his shoulders slumped

in defeat.

"Raven, look at me."

He does as I ask, and I reach up and touch his face, and the mirror dissolves, liquid glass, but this time I won't allow it to choke me.

"I love you," I tell him, and hang up the phone. His gasp of surprise and that look of shocked regret burn in my mind, only it's time already. The guard on his side takes the receiver out of his hand and jostles him out of the room.

So what of the reflection, when its creator leaves the mirror? I am the answer. I am all that's left.

Nadja waits at the other end of the fluorescent tunnel, too pale in her black floral dress and crocheted shawl. "We can go home now," I whisper, and she nods, signing a cross over my forehead like she knows what these words really mean. Taking her hand, I guide her away, frail woman, broken child, rainbows bleeding out from both our cracked shells.

I have a notion, in these fading moments, to write you a letter. So many words, the stories of our heart, inadequately told, but when one already knows—*love*—that's okay. Words for each of you. Raven. Damien. Nadja. Noriko.

I sign each one with a single word, the name my mother gave me, almost nineteen years ago.

Jaime.

A meaning of love. All I have left, to carry me home.

After a last supper barely touched, Nadja and I retire to our rooms. I sleep fitfully in Raven's bed, whispering his name like a charm whenever the convulsions take fast hold.

I make sure to keep the window open, all the better to hear the siren song of the sea. And the stars look real again from here. This is all that matters. If I can be close to the ocean, I won't miss my calling.

Sometime during the dead of night, I feel myself drawn out from the covers. Padding downstairs in bare feet, I stop to touch a hallway mirror. "Juliette." The looking-glass image smiles before vanishing, and I'm left with only me, a wide-eyed porcelain doll thing, clad in Mother's white dress, silk flowing over my skin, preparing me for the water. I untie each ribbon to free my hair, which drifts over my shoulders, all the way to my hips.

After knotting a ribbon around either wrist, I spread my arms before the glass, invoking my ritual. The air's so cold, and there's so little moonlight, and I'm beginning to hear...

The music of our souls, entwining around me, drawing me to it, begging me.

The music of a piano, my mother's song.

I step into the living room, hovering by the keys, watching on as the ghost of a blue-haired boy with beautiful, tortured eyes tells me that he loves me. It's his first time, and he's terrified of it.

This time round, I reach up to touch his face, whispering the words that will set us free. "I love you too, Raven."

And the beautiful boy, fragile and ferocious, falls through my embrace and into my heart, where I can keep him safe forever and always.

It's now.

I'm waiting in front of the door, not surprised when it swings open at my barest touch, and he stands before me, no longer a shadow.

"Father?"

A single long finger beckons me forward. "You know where we are going, little one?"

Oh, yes. I know. Into his arms—through his arms—I float out this doorway that's flooded with light, and down and down, towards the ocean.

The song is calling. I can hear my mother's voice, so clear in this hour.

And the dawn is come, and I keep walking—not down to where Raven and I washed ashore—but ever climbing, alongside the coast. The sea grows more distant, far beneath my feet, and by the time I'm at the top of the cliff, her voice has stopped singing.

I fall to my knees, surrendering everything, the wild winds catching my breath as strands of hair lash my face. Across the horizon, the cloudy sky's already transforming from grey to lilac, so inviting out there on the waves. She may have stopped singing, yet she's calling to me still.

We can fly, Jaime. In a dream, we can do anything we want to... anything at all.

These tears that sting my eyes...they're different, Raven. I want you to have these precious things, last truths for lining the floor of your cage, same as in all your stories.

Getting to my feet, I roll my shoulders, testing my wings. Shedding my ribbons on the breeze, along with the dirt, along with my fear. If I fall, she will catch me.

Clear my mind. Take a last breath.

Mother, I'm ready.

Nothing left.

One step off the edge, no turning back, heartbeat nearly giving out, mind giddy with nausea and laughter, terror and ecstasy. No rainbows, though, and no wings. Not really.

But Raven is watching me. I knew he would be. This is how we fly, my love.

Such a beautiful dreamer you are. I blow him a kiss, and turn away.

Pegasus screams and begs forgiveness, but I'm only smiling, as the waves take on the form of my mother, rising out of the ocean, up, up...

To catch me in her—

"Mama, when will we be there?"

"But we're here already. All you need to do, is open your eyes, *mon ange.*"

Light shifting, colours tinkling, laughter like a distant wind chime. Children playing at being mermaids and seahorses, down in the garden where it smells of spring.

"You see?" *She squeezes my hand.* "You know this place, don't you?"

"Of course I do, Mama.

"We're home."

Home...

(RAVEN) *25*

Now, The Last Thorn

You see... Once upon a time, there was an angel. With huge black wings. Blacker than night, blacker than the shadows that scare you in the dark, blacker than the spots between the stars where dreams are born. And just like stars, they shone in the darkness, these wings, and reflected every sorrow and fragment of poetry the angel had ever heard. But they were also his downfall. Because of them, because of their reflections, people didn't understand him. They feared him. He'd seen planets die and dreams wither, heard children laugh and mermaids sing. But everyone he came into contact with eventually turned away from him. Evil, they called him, and failure, monster, nightmare. They bound him up with thorns, and speared his body, and locked him in a great cage carved out of silver ice, and hung the cage from a hook sunk into infinity in a room of no walls and no light.

So the angel fell into a dark gloom. He forgot what he knew, and grew to distrust his wings and all the things he'd seen. Hearing nothing, seeing nothing, and feeling only a dull emptiness, till...one day, the angel had a dream. It's kind of hard to describe the dream, except that it was like seeing something wonderful—like a star being born, or a wish coming true—right out of the corner of your eye. It was a dream of what it meant to be loved. And when the angel awoke, alone again, and still in the dark, but this time remembering, *he started to cry, for the very first time. And each tear, as it fell, morphed into a white rose petal, till all these petals lined the floor of the cage. Then, once you could no longer even see the floor through so many petals, they began to hum, and to glow, and to glitter with the light of a rainbow, shining out through the void.*

At first, the angel was blinded, after living so long in darkness and despair, but as his eyes adjusted and he followed the line of the rainbow's path right to the very end, he caught sight of another very beautiful angel, right up close to the cage, white wings spun with grey feathers that reflected the same dream he'd just woken from. And this other angel was smiling down upon him.

And all of this so long ago, in a time and space that doesn't exist anymore.

My beautiful Pegasus, lost to a dream. I must wait for you once more, believing life begins again. Only now I know better.

As the shadows dance and die a thousand times, I wait. *My beautiful Pegasus.* My beautiful…

Jaime.

It's a dark night. No moon, and no stars. I remember it for this, the slamming of the front door, and her warmth departing as she leaves me to surrender herself to him. A night the same as any other.

But beneath the surface, the darkness gets into everything, seeps into my heart, fills my mind with blood and shadow. I remember it so well. I'm seven years old…again…

He throws her onto the mattress, ignoring my presence for the secondary mistake I already know myself to be. The one time we spend together as father and son is when I'm forced to listen to Ma's screams, her pain…her pleasure. Always the same, this transformation, from victim to accomplice. She always gives in, her mind so weak, her flesh too willing.

I remember the betrayal as though it's the first time, every time. *It isn't rape if you tell him not to stop, Ma.*

I'm shaking, this night, by the time he's done with her and

gets around to noticing me. Hands become more familiar shapes once they're made into fists. Hatred is the easiest mask to cover up my true feelings, and I hate them both, but I hate myself best of all. And no less than on this night, when he passes on his sickness, the night he hurts me too much.

He takes hold of my hands, both of us stained in the bloody darkness, both of us reeking of the one poison. He tells me we're the same.

This is the night I make up my mind, that neither of us deserves to be safe from death.

Ma's voice, screaming my name, haunts my dreams for more than a year after he's gone. Figure our dreams must be the same, once the strangers come to take her away too, leaving me behind. I'm finally alone.

This is what you wanted, isn't it, Raven?

No.

Is it not?

No.

Then what? Tell me.

I want the same damn thing I always wanted, all those years ago, formed as a child, broken as a creature doomed never to be man or child. I'm not worthy of salvation. That's why they took her, not me.

Don't you see it? Look in the mirror, that hatred is all you are.

They could never love...

Love. Does love even exist?

Yes.

If love is real, it's something you'll never feel. You failed, Raven. You failed by fulfilling that prophecy you feared and hated the most.

No. There never was anything as simple as choice.

This has no meaning or value. You are your father's son.

No...

The other half of your promise remains incomplete. Or had you forgotten?

No, I—

The knife looks so beautiful in the morning light. Can't you feel that beauty?

I don't want to look, but this voice in my mind's got such a hold on me I can't bring myself to move. No, I've got to—

What? The voice keeps up the taunts, as I move closer to the glowing object, to caress the blade. I'm looking at myself outside the mirror, outside my body. *The cage door is open. They've been too careless. So why is it you can't fly free?*

I've got no wings.

Even in the final moments you shield yourself with your unworthiness.

No, I've got to wait.

For what?

I don't know.

Understanding?

Maybe.

Love?

...Yeah.

But love is for those with warm hearts and beautiful dreams. What's in your heart? What do you dream of, Raven?

I don't know.

Yes, you do. Her voice, screaming—is it your name, Raven, is she screaming for you to stop?

No.

Would she prefer the betrayal over the salvation you offered?

No!

She's crying, why don't you see? Tears more delicate and flawed and real than the throbbing in your hands you can't make stop after hitting him so hard. Look at yourself and tell me you're worthy of love.

I stare at my wrists instead, till the voice fades to nothingness, and I'm alone, again.

The knife falls to the floor without making a sound. Beyond the reach of any pain, the soft stains appear, surprisingly delicate.

I crawl to the bedroom, watching the petals drip drip drip onto the carpet, down into the abyss I've become, swallowed up by the nothingness. Why must I always be alone? I wanted—

God, I don't know what I wanted, but I know it was different, before that night. A long time before.

What am I seeing, here in my heart? The words elude me, the onlookers who aren't real don't care. I—

Arms to hold me when I begin to cry. Stupid of me to cry, when nothing can be changed. I think I whisper her name as the world fades to grey, that girl my cousin plans to have children with...

Perhaps next time I can be worthy. The one I might love could find me then, unstained by blood or tears, uncomplicated like the world in a way I'm not, now.

A mistake...

I wake in the room of white light with no windows, and they've cleaned off all my blood. I didn't dream her voice screaming my name. From this moment on, I never dream. Or, at least, I manage to convince myself and the others of this.

But I still look for a white feather on my pillow every morning, though never expecting to find it.

I resign myself to fate.

All alone, so all alone, roaming the blackest eternity. I can't feel myself. Can't cry either, not even for those things

I used to love.

Watching the blood, drip drip drip, sensing otherwise blind through the endless darkness. Feeling my mind, turning over with my stomach. Fuck you. How dare all of you leave me alone like this?

I was so, so close. Was that really happiness?

Don't say those words to me, those words that always turn out to be a lie. How the fuck could I be worthy of those words?

Your eyes tear through me so much deeper than the knife ever could.

All alone, so all alone, I whisper the name of the one I love. The name I never knew before. Eternally too late, my most beautiful irony. My love too worthless for you to wait around any longer. Isn't that the truth?

Even so, I can't hate you, I can't hate any of you. I can only hate myself. And when there's nothing else left, I can see I'm the poison that flows through these veins.

Poison...

Leaving fingerprints on the walls, I stare through my emptiness, out to the other side. Truth taunts me, as cold as the surface beneath my flesh. I'm the angel who could never fly.

I want to be so much better, next time.

I know, the moment he enters the cell, that everything's over. Everything's finally come undone.

I sit and watch the thread of my life untangle itself into a flat-line emulation, as he passes over the envelope, a single word upon its face, written in that perfect script, wasted on that word. My name.

I've got neither name nor form as I take the letter from Monty—Monty, not Pegasus—and I read the final good-bye.

Beautiful white-winged angel tells me to wait for him, to come with him, to come home...*one day*.

Sad yet perfect silver eyes tells me he loves me, and signs it with his own name, the name I never knew. Je taime. J'aime. Jaime. A word for love.

I grasp hold of this tiny sphere of light, though I'm scared to even touch it, and more scared to let it go. Love's always been a trap to taunt me with its promises of unendings and almost enoughs—*wait, be patient, and salvation will come*.

Endless laughter, and I can't make it stop. It's my laughter. I'm laughing cos this is the only response I've got.

I think I always thought we'd go together, somehow. Holding hands like kids, and you'd teach me how to fly; you'd show me the light I've been so afraid of, let it shatter the cage and shine on my disintegration. But this tiny sphere is all there is. I cradle it beside me, in the cold shadows of my solitary confinement. Even while I let every one of those faceless animals do anything they want to me, till anger—which is only soothing for being something stark against all the other nothings—takes control and I need to be beaten into submission again.

Reality. Have I ever been there? I thought, maybe once, but now my only reality lies safe within this tiny sphere.

You took everything, Pegasus. You took everything away and left nothing for me. Same as your sister, for her part. And I killed you both. Is it any wonder?

No, different with you. You were the first, last, and only... I wanted to give those things to you. And I engineered my own self-destruction so artfully I never noticed, not till it had me in its stranglehold, too late to escape or cry out for help.

Besides, who would listen? Who could ever have understood?

At night, I whisper to the tiny sphere, the sad secret of

this truth: the only one who understands or can help me now is myself.

But I hate myself.

I gave you the power of destruction thinking only I could trigger it. Stupidity.

At night, when I'm alone with my cage, I let it cry, and I let it break, unable to finish the job on the outside that's already begun within. If I ever get hold of a knife again, it will become my paintbrush. I will make myself the perfect canvas, the perfect reflection. Then all the world might be able to look in and see what they've done to me...

What I've done to my self...

No more barriers. Would they understand, finally? Or would they simply paint over the bleeding cracks in the ice, sew me back together like a poor child's doll, pet me on the head and toss me into the cage again? Would anyone even notice the difference?

Monty murmurs something about a funeral. Shadows dance in front of my face, taunting me, disappearing when I focus on them, reforming as thorns around the outskirts of my sight. When I can find the words, I tell him at last that they shouldn't put my beautiful angel in a box, they should scatter him over the waves and leave him to become eternal seafoam, just as he wished. My voice is barely a whisper, parched and foreign-sounding within the splintering walls of my cage. I look up, wondering if he can hear me. But he's gone, and there's nobody here.

Nobody.

It's a dark night. No moon, and no stars. I remember it for this, the slamming of the door behind me, all warmth departing as I return to hell. A night the same as any other, stained forever with that same darkness. I remember it so well. I'm eighteen years old, and too drunk to care.

Her eyes and hands are everywhere, wanting to maul the cage, keeping me so trapped through proof of my unworthiness that I can't even think to pray for salvation.

I want to imagine his face in her place, but everything is wrong.

You should be with the person who makes you happy, Raven.

No. Me, just me. I'm not allowed to feel. And besides, the person I love doesn't want me around. He would've come, that night. He'd come any night, to save me from this.

Now I can't get away, and I don't want to get away. Maybe she can be the one to destroy me. It's the best I can hope for.

When I came to her I was fucked up, but somewhere inside I think I still had some inkling of self-worth...

She rips it into shreds with her perfect claws, dancing over my skin, dresses me in thorns like the ultimate prize. I lose myself because she's *always* watching me, wanting to be there inside my head all the time, and I can never break free.

I dream of being alone when I'm optimistic enough to think I might survive such a thing. I dream these things during the day, when we're out walking, me and my tiny son, my second angel. And I dream such a thing when we end our visits with the one I love and he turns away, dismissing me. That's not the path, then.

Nights are forever bitterly cold, and I seek refuge in the same things that destroyed my dad. I become that person, stretching the mould to fit like a straight-jacket, in the belief it will kill me more easily.

I'm so tragically wrong that after she's done with me and lying deep within her empty sleep, I laugh at myself in this darkness, till the tears wear me down, and I stagger to the bathroom, puking up our twin poisons, and I turn to the blade and set about freeing myself again.

This sequence, this snapshot, becomes my life. Once she's gotten inside my head, there's nothing I can do to stop her.

Feelings become weaknesses, truths the object of ridicule and scorn. I give up on every childhood dream, my last shrinking refuges stowed away in razors and music and my son. So much easier to lie here and do nothing. So much easier to believe what she tells me about myself.

Resigning myself to my own cowardice that doesn't let me cut myself deep enough to put an end to all this, I lie in the dark and pray to a god I never had faith in. Please let it all end soon. There's no point to this. I will believe in you, if only you'll destroy me.

I touch a photo of Pegasus in the darkness, the only one of us I could keep. Please kill me more quickly than this.

In the morning I always wake to her interrogations, poking about inside my skull, her words demanding more pieces of me—she can never, ever get enough. Or is it that I can't *be* enough? Either way…

Soon I give up on praying to God who, even if He does exist, seems to enjoy mocking me all the more by ignoring my pleas. I ponder His alternative, except all I'm seeking by this time is to escape hell, not spend eternity there.

When she finds the photo of Pegasus and I, she rips it into shreds, and turns to face me once again.

This is an infinite loop. I accept this, too easily.

Not easily enough.

Bail hearings, doors and keys and money changing hands for my safe-keeping, and here I am, stepping out into the dim light of the world, standing beside Monty. Free of one cage, still trapped firmly within the first.

Did you expect it to be any different? Really?

Yeah. Yeah, I really did, damn you all to hell.

I grow tired of all the voices, this chorus to rouse my fleeting anger. Anger is something, and I can't be something anymore. I must be nothing.

So there's only emptiness. This way, the voice I've been waiting for will get a chance to be heard.

People, others, here...familiar faces, familiar place. I was born nearby, child who somehow escaped death with a blunt object before ever getting a chance at life, unlike the first. Maybe you've gone to meet him in my stead, Pegasus. I always was the poorest substitute.

No one can look at me, so I'm not afraid of trying to stare right through every one of them. At least they didn't bring our son. He should believe in his heart that his angel really flew away, not be distracted by the empty cage rotting in the box they lower into the ground. It's all I can do to trap my tears as the coffin disappears from view, and a scream pierces my heart. To sidetrack myself from having any feelings of my own, I go back to concentrating on the others. Another cowardly attempt to save myself, heart bound shut with barbed wire and dozens of thorns.

Monty stands, one hand in his pocket, the other over his heart, eyes closed. By his mud-encrusted feet, Noriko sits cross-legged, face turned up to the heavens, index fingers touching her thumbs, arms outstretched over her knees. I watch the rise and fall of her chest, so hypnotic, so constant. She doesn't blink. Things she knows that I could never understand. Did you escape all this; did you make it to where Pegasus is? Tell me...

And last of all, Ma. Do you blame yourself for everything? You should. You did everything you could to protect me while I lay half dormant within you, and you were enough, for that. You told me I could do anything I wanted, never stopping to think what would happen when I eventually and inevitably found out that I couldn't. And you let me live, so I might destroy everything I ever cared about. Yes, Ma, you are so to blame.

Each one of you who cared enough to keep me alive, only so it could all come to this. Maybe that's why none of you can look me in the eye. Or maybe it's cos I no longer exist.

With every one of the sermon's passing words, I can feel myself disappear. Dissolving into the earth as they fill the box over, inscribing its resting place with white roses, and the name I knew too late.

I become the worms that eat into decomposing flesh.

I become the flesh itself, dripping off the bones, the stench, and last of all, the lifeless emptiness.

Three spears of light rip the sky apart, and it begins to rain. I watch she whom no one else can see turn her back on me and walk into the ocean, steps in time to a melody only half-remembered. When I look down, I realise she's left another thorn for me, glistening at my feet. Her last gift.

I love you, Raven.

"Pegasus," I whisper, clutching at the cross around my neck, another gift that when kept from me kept me from myself.

Overhead, the clouds are parting. It's already over. Soon, the rainbow will come. I can finish it, like this. I can finally be that strong.

The sun shines down on me alone, a halo of illumination just for me, and somewhere beyond, my son. If I can find my way through the clouds and ice, I know I can make it home to you. Now I see how it ends, beautiful angel. I've been such a fool.

I smile.

I think...this is the first time since that night I've seen my face in a mirror. Lit only by the full moon, I erase the shapes. I could be brave enough, just in this moment, not to hate myself.

Pegasus. I've been waiting for you. Please touch me. Please hold my hand. It made me so happy, when you did that. I always wondered if you ever saw.

Strands of silver drape over my wet skin, reflected in the light like a knife, as he kneels to kiss the scars on my wrists, the delicate thorns left for me as a sign by his mama. The kisses sting, but they won't heal to become scars, not this time.

It's okay...

He smiles at me, blood staining his lips, his whole body shining through the shadow as he beckons to me. Our feet pad across the staining tiles, and we return to the bed where we once lay together, each of us saving the other from our hurts. *Protection.*

It can be this way again. Even if he's the one whispering, *Sleep, my beautiful angel,* in my ears, and teasing free my wings. He plucks out a single black feather, placing it carefully upon the pillow by my face, then one of his own, black and white merging into soft grey as I feel my tiredness, my self, all draining away.

Yes. I accept this. This is all I can do.

Is it enough, Pegasus?

You are enough, Raven. Truly.

Through the clouds, I'm finding my way. It seems so easy to fly, I wonder how I could've been so afraid before.

Leaving only our son, to remember us as real.

When I find you again, Pegasus, I will lay you down on the soft sand by our ocean and cover your soul with my wings and kisses.

Kisses are feathers. My wings are very strong.

And, following the truth in my heart, when I make it home to you, I'll finally give you what I was never brave enough to give you before.

*Everything, of my self. You might love me again.
I fly higher...the world beneath us regrets and forgets.
Soon, it will be dawn.*

(EPILOGUE) 26

At the End of the Rainbow

Every birthday from the time I turned nine, Nori and I, and sometimes Monty or Grandma, would come to this place, each of us bearing a white and blue rose. We'd kiss the flowers, speak our thoughts as some kind of prayer in her native tongue, then toss the petals out over the ocean.

The blue roses were very rare and hard to come by, but she grew them for me, since that was my wish. The way she tended her garden with such quiet love, while I hid in the shadows and watched on behind the thorns, taught me how love could exist so simply, for anything.

Today I'm twenty-one years old. That's the same age you were, Father, and since Nori's gone away from us this spring, I've come to you all by myself. Hitched the long road down from the high country, all the way to the south-west coast. This is why I'm so late, why the sun's already sinking into the ocean, staining the waters like a blob of paint. Guess it doesn't matter. By now, the waves must know me by name.

The first stars are waking up on the opposite horizon. The sign... I open my satchel, pull out the book of words I already prepared, and gather the flowers. A blue rose for the beautiful, tortured Raven. A white rose for the wistful, dreaming Pegasus.

Everyone goes away from me eventually. But that's okay, how it is.

I climb to the edge of the cliff, and gaze out over the end

of the world. Spread my arms wide, a stem in either hand. Pegasus—Jaime—is this how it felt? Smiling, I close my eyes to the yearning light, and then I release the roses into the air, set them sailing off over the ocean, these fragments of myself. The pain's short-lived, even if the force that drives it is eternal. But if I keep the cage door open, I can connect with anyone. You'll never be lost to me, not ever.

I climb down from the cliff, back to the graves. Here between them, I make my bed. Lying on my back, I hold tight to the silver cross, and read and re-read your letters and try to scribble some sense out of my thoughts, till the light fails. Then I move on to the memories in my heart.

I know I'll see you again, someday.

Someday, at the end of the rainbow.

LaVergne, TN USA
31 March 2011
222387LV00001B/128/P